## ACE BOOKS BY ILONA ANDREWS

# MAGIC
# BINDS

Ilona Andrews

ACE
New York

ACE
Published by Berkley
An imprint of Penguin Random House LLC
375 Hudson Street, New York, New York 10014

ISBN: 9780425270707

Ace hardcover edition / September 2016
Ace mass-market edition / May 2017

Printed in the United States of America
1  3  5  7  9  10  8  6  4  2

Cover art by Juliana Kolesova

*To Uncle Gene. We miss you.*

# ACKNOWLEDGMENTS

We would like to thank our agent, Nancy Yost, and the wonderful crew at NYLA for their dedication, professional expertise, and friendships. We appreciate you very much.

We are deeply grateful to our editor, Anne Sowards, for steering us through this project and once again taking a mess and through careful guidance turning it into a book. Our work is so much stronger because of you.

Thank you to all of the wonderful people who worked to bring the manuscript to publication: the production editor, Michelle Kasper; the assistant production editor, Jennifer Myers; the art director, Judith Lagerman; and Juliana Kolesova, the artist responsible for the image on the cover.

Thank you to Stephanie Mowery, Shannon Daigle, Sandra Bullock, and Kristi DeCourcy for early feedback.

The following people generously donated their time and effort to read the book early: Robin Snyder, Valerie Hockens, Ronnie Buck, Kathryn Holland, Susan Hester, Jennifer Whaley, Ying Dallimore, Julie Krick, Carrie Harlan, Paroma

Chakravarty, Lisa Louk, Jill Woodley, Jessica Haluska, Beatrix Kaser, William Stonier, Omar Jimenez, and AMW. Special thanks to Becky Slemons for coming up with a title for this book.

## ≡ CHAPTER ≡

# 1

THE SKULL GLARED at me out of empty eye sockets. Odd runes marked its forehead, carved into the yellowed bone and filled with black ink. Its thick bottom jaw supported a row of conical fangs, long and sharp like the teeth of a crocodile. The skull sat on top of an old stop sign. Someone had painted the surface of the octagon white and written KEEP OUT across it in large jagged letters. A reddish-brown splatter stained the bottom edge, looking suspiciously like dried blood. I leaned closer. Yep, blood. Some hair, too. Human hair.

Curran frowned at the sign. "Do you think he's trying to tell us something?"

"I don't know. He's being so subtle about it."

I looked past the sign. About a hundred yards back, a large two-story house waited. It was clearly built post-Shift, out of solid timber and brown stone laid by hand to ensure it would survive the magic waves. But instead of the usual simple square or rectangular box of most post-Shift buildings, this house had all the pre-Shift bells and whistles of a modern prairie home: rows of big windows, sweeping horizontal lines, and a spacious layout. Except prairie-style homes usually had long flat roofs and little ornamentation, while this place sported pitched roofs with elaborate carved gables, beautiful bargeboards, and ornate wooden windows.

"It's like someone took a Russian log cabin and a pre-Shift contemporary house, stuck them into a blender, and dumped it over there."

Curran frowned. "It's his . . . What do you call it? Terem."

"A terem is where Russian princesses lived."

"Exactly."

Between us and the house lay a field of black dirt. It looked soft and powdery, like potting soil or a freshly plowed field. A path of rickety old boards, half rotten and splitting, curved across the field to the front door. I didn't have a good feeling about that dirt.

We'd tried to circle the house and ran into a thick, thorn-studded natural fence formed by wild rosebushes, black-berry brambles, and trees. The fence was twelve feet tall and when Curran tried to jump high enough to see over it, the thorny vines snapped out like lassos and made a heroic effort to pull him in. After I helped him pick the needles out of his hands, we decided a frontal assault was the better option.

"No animal tracks on the dirt," I said.

"No animal scents either," Curran said. "There are scent trails all around us through the woods, but none here."

"That's why he has giant windows and no grates on them. Nothing can get close to the house."

"It's that, or he doesn't care. Why the hell doesn't he answer his phone?"

Who knew why the priest of the god of All Evil and Darkness did anything?

I picked up a small rock, tossed it into the dirt, and braced myself. Nothing. No toothy jaws exploded through the soil, no magic fire, no earth-shattering kaboom. The rock just sat there.

We could come back later, when the magic was down. That would be the sensible thing to do. However, we had driven ten miles through lousy traffic in the punishing heat of Georgia's summer and then hiked another mile through the woods to get here, and our deadline was fast approaching. One way or another, I was getting into that house.

I put my foot onto the first board. It sank a little under my weight, but held. Step. Another step. Still holding.

I tiptoed across the boards, Curran right behind me. *Think sneaky thoughts.*

The dark soil shivered.

Two more steps.

A mound formed to the right of us, the dirt shifting like waves of some jet-black sea.

Uh-oh.

"To the right," I murmured.

"I see it."

Long serpentine bone spines pierced the mound and slid through the soil toward us, like fins of a sea serpent gliding under the surface of a midnight-black, powdery ocean.

We sprinted to the door.

Out of the corner of my eye, I saw a cloud of loose soil burst to the left. A black scorpion the size of a pony shot out and scrambled after us.

If we killed his pet scorpion, we'd never hear the end of it.

I ran up the porch and pounded on the door. "Roman!"

Behind me the bone spines whipped out of the soil. What I'd thought were fins turned into a cluster of tentacles, each consisting of bone segments held together by remnants of cartilage and dried, ropy connective tissue. The tentacles snapped, grabbing Curran. He locked his hands on the bones and strained, pulling them apart. Bone crunched, connective tissue tore, and the left tentacle flailed, half of it on the ground.

"Roman!" Damn it all to hell.

A bone tentacle grabbed me and yanked me back and up, dangling me six feet off the ground. The scorpion dashed forward, its barb poised for the kill.

The door swung open, revealing Roman. He wore a

T-shirt and plaid pajama bottoms, and his dark hair, shaved on the sides into a long horselike mane, stuck out on the left side of his head. He looked like he'd been sleeping.

"What's all this?"

Everything stopped.

Roman squinted at me. "What are you guys doing here?"

"We had to come here because you don't answer your damn phone." Curran's voice had that icy quality that said his patience was at an end.

"I didn't answer it because I unplugged it."

Roman waved his hand. The scorpion retreated. The tentacles gently set me down and slithered back into the ground.

"You would unplug yours too if you were related to my family. My parents are fighting again and they're trying to make me choose sides. I told them they could talk to me when they start acting like responsible adults."

Fat chance of that. Roman's father, Grigorii, was the head black volhv in the city. His mother, Evdokia, was one-third of the Witch Oracle. When they had fights, things didn't boil over, they exploded. Literally.

"So far I've avoided both of them, so I'm enjoying the peace and quiet. Come in."

He held the door open. I walked past him into a large living room. Golden wooden floors, huge fireplace, thirty-foot ceilings, and soft furniture. Bookshelves lined the far wall, crammed to the brink. The place looked downright cozy.

Curran walked in behind me and took in the living room. His thick eyebrows rose.

"What?" Roman asked.

"No altar?" Curran asked. "No bloody knives and frightened virgins?"

"No sacrificial pit ringed with skulls?" I asked.

"Ha. Ha." Roman rolled his eyes. "Never heard that one before. I keep the virgins chained up in the basement. Do you want some coffee?"

I shook my head.

"Yes," Curran said.

"Black?"

"No, put cream in it."

"Good man. Only two kinds of people drink their coffee black: cops and serial killers. Sit, sit."

I sat on the sofa and almost sank into it. I'd need help getting up. Curran sprawled next to me.

"This is nice," he said.

"Mm-hm."

"We should get one for the living room."

"We'd get blood on it."

Curran shrugged. "So?"

Roman appeared with two mugs, one pitch-black and the other clearly half-filled with cream. He gave the lighter mug to Curran.

"Drinking yours black, I see," I told him.

He shrugged and sat on the couch. "Eh . . . goes with the job. So what can I do for you?"

"We're getting married," I said.

"I know. Congratulations. On Ivan Kupala night. I don't know if that's good or bad, but it's brave."

Ivan Kupala night was the time of wild magic in Slavic folklore. The ancient Russians believed that on that date the boundaries between the worlds blurred. In our case, it meant a really strong magic wave. Odd things happened on Ivan Kupala night. Given a choice, I would've picked a different day, but Curran had set the date. To him it was the last day of werewolf summer, a shapeshifter holiday and a perfect day for our wedding. I told him I would marry him, and if he wanted to get married on Ivan Kupala night, then we'd get married on Ivan Kupala night. After moving the date a dozen times, that was the least I could do.

"So did you come to invite me?" Roman asked.

"Yes," Curran said. "We'd like you to officiate."

"I'm sorry?"

"We'd like you to marry us," I said.

Roman's eyes went wide. He pointed to himself. "Me?"

"Yes," Curran said.

"Marry you?"

"Yes."

"You do know what I do, right?"

"Yes," I said. "You're Chernobog's priest."

"Chernobog" literally meant Black God, who was also known by other fun names like Black Serpent, Lord of Darkness, God of freezing cold, destruction, evil, and death. Some ancient Slavs divided their pantheon into opposing forces of light and dark. These forces existed in a balance, and according to that view, Chernobog was a necessary evil. Somebody had to be his priest, and Roman had ended up with the job. According to him, it was the family business.

Roman leaned forward, his dark eyes intense. "You sure about this?"

"Yes," Curran said.

"Not going to change your mind?"

What was it with the twenty questions? "Will you do it or not?"

"Of course I'll do it." Roman jumped off the couch. "Ha! Nobody ever asks me to marry them. They always go to Nikolai, my cousin—Vasiliy's oldest son."

Roman had a vast family tree, but I remembered Vasiliy, his uncle. Vasiliy was a priest of Belobog, Chernobog's brother and exact opposite. He was also very proud of his children, especially Nikolai, and bragged about them every chance he got.

Roman ducked behind the couch and emerged with a phone.

"When some supernatural filth tries to carry off the children, call Roman so he can wade through blood and sewage to rescue them, but when it's something nice like a wedding or a naming, oh no, we can't have Chernobog's volhv involved. It's bad luck. Get Nikolai. When he finds out who I'm going to marry, he'll have an aneurysm. His head will explode. It's good that he's a doctor, maybe he can treat himself."

He plugged the phone into the outlet.

It rang.

Roman stared at it as if it were a viper.

The phone rang again.

He unplugged it. "There."

"It can't be that bad," I told him.

"Oh, it's bad." Roman nodded. "My dad refused to help my second sister buy a house, because he doesn't like her boyfriend. My mother called him and it went badly. She cursed him. Every time he urinates, the stream arches up and over."

Oh.

Curran winced.

"You hungry? Do you want something to eat?" Roman wagged his eyebrows. "I have smoked brisket."

My fiancé leaned forward, suddenly interested. "Moist or dry?"

"Moist. What am I, a heathen?"

Technically, he was a heathen.

"We can't," I told him. "We have to leave. We have Conclave tonight."

"I didn't know you still go to that," Roman said.

"Ghastek outed her," Curran said.

The Conclave began as a monthly meeting between the People and the Pack. As the two largest supernatural factions in the city, they often came into conflict, and at some point it was decided that talking and resolving small problems was preferable to being on the brink of a bloodbath every five minutes. Over the years, the Conclave evolved into a meeting where the powerful of Atlanta came together to discuss business. We had attended plenty of Conclaves when Curran was Beast Lord, but once he retired, I thought our tortures were over. Yeah, not so fast.

"Back in March, Roland's crews started harassing the teamsters," I said.

"In the city?" Roman raised his eyebrows.

"No." I had claimed the city of Atlanta to save it from my father, assuming responsibility for it. My father and I existed in a state of uneasy peace, and so far he hadn't openly breached it. "They would do it five, six miles outside of the land I claimed. The teamsters would be driving their wagons or trucks, and suddenly there would be twenty armed people blocking the road and asking them where they were going and why. It made the union nervous, so a teamster rep came to the Conclave and asked what anyone would be doing about that."

"Why not go to the Order?" Roman said. "That's what they do."

"The Order and the union couldn't come to an agreement," Curran said.

The Order of Knights of Merciful Aid offered that aid under some conditions, not the least of which was that once they took a job, they finished it on their terms, and their clients didn't always like the outcome.

"So the teamster rep asked the People point-blank to stop harassing their convoys," Curran said, "and Ghastek told him that Kate was the only person capable of making it happen."

"Did you?"

"I did," I said. "And now I have to go to the Conclave meetings."

"I'm there as a supportive spouse-to-be." Curran grinned, flashing his teeth.

"So why did your father mess with the convoys?" Roman asked.

"No reason. He does it to aggravate me. He's an immortal wizard with a megalomaniac complex. He doesn't understand words like 'no' and 'boundaries.' It bugs him that I have this land. He can't let it go, so he sits on my border and pokes it. He tried to build a tower on the edge of Atlanta. I made him move it, so now he's building himself 'a small residence' about five miles out."

"How small?" Roman asked.

"About thirty thousand square feet," Curran said.

Roman whistled, then knocked on the wooden table and spat over his shoulder three times.

Curran looked at me.

"Whistling in the house is bad luck," I explained.

"You'll whistle all your money away," Roman said. "Thirty thousand square feet, huh?"

"Give or take. He keeps screwing with her," Curran said.

"His construction crews obstruct the Pack hunting grounds outside Atlanta. His soldiers nag the small settlements outside the claimed area, trying to get people to sell their land to him."

My father was slowly driving me insane. He'd cross into my territory when the magic was up, so I would feel his presence, then leave before I could get there to bust him. The first few times he had done it, I rode out, dreading a war, but there was never anyone to fight. Sometimes I woke up in the middle of the night because I'd feel him enter my land, and then I'd lie there gritting my teeth and fighting with myself to keep from grabbing my sword and running out of the house to hunt him down.

"Don't forget the monsters," I said. "They keep spawning outside the boundary and then raid Atlanta."

"Most of the time we can't tie it back to him," Curran said. "When we can, she calls him on it. He apologizes and makes generous reparations."

"And then we all somehow end up eating in some seafood joint, where he orders the whole menu and the waiters serve us glassy-eyed," I said.

Curran finished his coffee in one gulp. "Last week a flock of harpies attacked Druid Hills. It took the Guild six hours to put them down. One merc ended up in the hospital with some kind of acute magical rabies."

"Well, at least it's rabies," Roman said. "They carry leprosy, too."

"I called Roland about it," I said. "He said, 'Who knows why harpies do anything, Blossom?' And then he told me he had two tickets to see Aivisha sing and one of them had my name on it."

"Parents." Roman heaved a sigh. "Can't live with them. Can't get away from them. When you try to move, they buy a house in your new neighborhood."

"That's one thing about having both of your parents murdered," Curran said. "I don't have parent problems."

Roman and I looked at him.

"We really do have to go," I said.

"Thanks for the coffee." Curran put his empty mug on the table.

"No trouble," Roman said. "I'll get started on this wedding thing."

"We really appreciate it," I said.

"Oh no, no. My pleasure."

We got up, walked to the door, and I swung it open. A black raven flew past me and landed on the back of the couch.

Roman slapped his hand over his face.

"There you are," the raven said in Evdokia's voice. "Ungrateful son."

"Here we go . . ." Roman muttered.

"Eighteen hours in labor and this is what I get. He can't even pick up the phone to talk to his own mother."

"Mother, can't you see I have people here?"

"I bet if their mothers called them, they would pick up."

That would be a neat trick for both of us. Sadly, dead mothers didn't come back to life, even in post-Shift Atlanta.

"Nice to see you, Roman." I grabbed Curran by the hand.

The bird swiveled toward me. "Katya!"

Oh no.

"Don't you leave. I need to talk to you."

"Got to go, bye!"

I jumped out of the house. Curran was only half a second behind me, and he pushed the door closed. I sped down the wooden path before Evdokia decided to track me down.

"Are you actually running away from Evdokia?"

"Yes, I am." The witches weren't exactly pleased with me. They had trusted me to protect Atlanta and its covens, and I had claimed the city instead.

"Maybe we could skip the Conclave tonight," Curran said.

"We can't."

"Why?"

"Because it's Mahon's turn to attend."

The Kodiak of Atlanta was brave and powerful and the closest thing to a father Curran had. He also had an uncanny ability to alienate everyone in the room and then have to defend himself when a brawl broke out. He took self-defense seriously. Sometimes there was no building left standing when he was done.

"Jim will be there," Curran said.

"Nope." The Pack rotated Conclave duty between the alphas, so if something happened at the Conclave, the leadership of the Pack as a whole wouldn't be wiped out. "Jim was at the last one. You would know this if you hadn't skipped it to go fight that thing in the sewers. It will be Raphael and Andrea, Desandra, and your father. Unsupervised."

Curran swore. "What the hell is Jim thinking with that lineup?"

"Serves you right for pretending you don't have parent problems."

He growled something under his breath.

Mahon and I didn't always see eye to eye. He'd thought I wouldn't make a good mate for Curran and that I was the reason Curran left the Pack, and he'd told me so, but now he'd come to terms with it. We both loved Curran, so we had to deal with each other and we made the best of it. Although lately Mahon had been unusually nice to me. It was probably a trap.

"We make it through the Conclave and then we can go home, drink coffee, and eat the apple pie I made last night," I said. "It will be glorious."

He put his arm around me. "The Conclave is only a dinner."

"Don't say it."

"How . . ."

I glared at him. "I mean it! I want a nice quiet night."

". . . bad could it be?"

"Now you ruined it. If a burning giant busts through a window while we're at the Conclave and tries to squish people, I will so punch you in the arm."

He laughed and we jogged down the winding forest path to our car.

. . .

BERNARD'S WAS ALWAYS full but never crowded. Housed in a massive English-style mansion in an affluent northern neighborhood, Bernard's restaurant was one of those places where you had to make a reservation two weeks in advance, minimum. The food was beautiful and expensive, the portions tiny—and the patrons were the real draw. Men in thousand-dollar suits and women in glittering dresses with shiny rocks on their necks and wrists mingled and had polite conversation in hushed voices while sipping wine and expensive liquor.

Curran and I walked into Bernard's in our work clothes: worn jeans, T-shirts, and boots. I would've preferred my sword too, but Bernard's had a strict no-weapons policy, so Sarrat had to wait in the car.

People stared as we walked to the conference room. People always stared. Whispers floated.

"Is that her?"

"She doesn't look like . . ."

Ugh.

Curran turned toward the sound, his eyes iced over, his expression flat. The whispers died.

We entered the conference room, where a single long table had been set. The Pack was already there. Mahon sat in the center seat facing the door, Raphael on his right, Desandra three seats down on his left. Mahon saw us and grinned, stroking his beard, which used to be black but now was shot through with silver. When you saw the Kodiak of Atlanta, one word immediately sprang to mind: "big." Tall, with massive shoulders, barrel-chested and broad but not fat, Mahon telegraphed strength and raw physical power. While Curran held the coiled promise of explosive violence, Mahon looked like if the roof suddenly caved in, he would catch it, grunt, and hold it up.

Next to him, Raphael couldn't be more different. Lean, tall, and dark, with piercing blue eyes, the alpha of the bouda clan wasn't traditionally handsome, but there was something about his face that made women obsess. They looked at him and thought of sex. Then they looked at his better half and decided that he wasn't worth dying over. Especially lately, because Andrea was nine months pregnant and communicating mostly in snarls. And she wasn't at the table.

Desandra, beautiful, blond, and built like a female prizefighter, poked at some painstaking arrangement of flowers and sliced meats on her plate that was probably supposed to be some sort of gourmet dish. She saluted us with a fork and went back to poking.

Curran sat next to Mahon. I took the chair between him and Desandra and leaned forward, so I could see Raphael. "Where is Andrea?"

"In the Keep," he said. "Doolittle wants to keep an eye on her."

"Is everything okay?" She was due any day.

"It's fine," Raphael said. "Doolittle is just hovering."

And the Pack's medmage was probably the only one who could force Andrea to comply.

"Boy." Mahon clapped his hand on Curran's shoulder. His whole face was glowing. Curran grinned back. It almost made the Conclave worth it.

"Old man," Curran said.

"You're looking thinner. Trimming down for the wedding? Or she not feeding you enough?"

"He eats what he kills," I said. "I can't help it that he's a lousy hunter."

Mahon chuckled.

"I've been busy," Curran said. "The Guild takes a lot of work. Outside the Keep, it's not all feasts and honey muffins. You should try it sometime. You're getting a gut and winter isn't coming for six months."

"Oh." Mahon turned, rummaged in the bag he'd hung on the chair, and pulled out a large rectangular Tupperware container. "Martha sent these for you since you never come to the house."

Curran popped the lid off. Six perfect golden muffins. The aroma of honey and vanilla floated around the table. Desandra came to life like a winter wolf who heard a bunny nearby.

Curran took one muffin, passed it to me, and bit into a second one. "We came to your house last week."

"I was out on clan business. That doesn't count."

I bit into the muffin and, for the five seconds it took me to chew, went to heaven.

The People filed into the room. Ghastek was in the lead: tall, painfully thin, and made even thinner by the dark suit he wore. Rowena walked a step behind him, shockingly stunning as always. Today she wore a whiskey-colored cocktail dress that hugged her generous breasts and hips, while accentuating her narrow waist. Her waterfall of red hair was plaited into a very wide braid and twisted into a knot on the side. I wouldn't even know how to start that hairdo.

I missed my long hair. It was barely past my shoulders now and there wasn't much I could do with it, besides letting it loose or pulling it back into a ponytail.

Curran leaned toward me, his voice barely above a whisper. "Why didn't those two ever get together?"

"I have no idea. Why would they?"

"Because all the other Masters of the Dead are in relationships. These two are unattached and always together."

Shapeshifters gossiped worse than old ladies. "Maybe they did get together and we don't know?"

Curran shook his head slightly. "No, I had them under surveillance for years. He never came out of her house and she never came out of his."

The People took the seats across from us.

"Any pressing business?" Ghastek asked.

Mahon pulled out a piece of lined paper.

Half an hour later both the People and the Pack ran out of things to discuss. Nothing major had happened, and the budding dispute over a real estate office on the border between the Pack and the People was quickly resolved.

Wine was served, followed by elaborate desserts that had absolutely nothing on Martha's honey muffins. It was actually kind of nice, sitting there, sipping the sweet wine. I never thought I would miss the Pack, but I did, a little. I missed the big meals and the closeness.

"Congratulations on the upcoming wedding," Ghastek said.

"Thank you," I said.

Technically, Ghastek and the entire Atlanta office of the People belonged to my father, who had been quietly reinforcing them. Two new Masters of the Dead had been assigned to Ghastek, bringing the total count of the Masters of the Dead to eight. Several new journeymen had joined the Casino as well. I made it a habit to drive by it once in a while and every time I did, I felt more vampires within the white textured walls of the palace than I had before. Ghastek was a dagger poised at my back. So far that dagger remained sheathed and perfectly cordial, but I never forgot where his allegiance lay.

"Ghastek, why haven't you married?" I asked.

He gave me a thin-lipped smile. "Because if I were to get married, I would want to have a family. To me, marriage means children."

"So what's the problem? Shooting blanks?" Desandra asked.

*Kill me.*

"No," Ghastek told her. "In case you haven't noticed, this city is under siege. It would be irresponsible to bring a child into the world when you can't keep him or her safe."

"So move," Desandra said.

"There is no place on this planet that is safe from her father," Rowena said. "As long as he lives . . ."

Ghastek put his long fingers on her hand. Rowena caught herself. ". . . as long as he lives, we serve at his pleasure. Our lives are not our own."

Nick Feldman walked through the door. The Order of Merciful Aid typically didn't attend the Conclave. Not good. Not good at all.

"Here comes the knight-protector," Raphael warned quietly.

Everyone looked at Nick. He stopped by the table. When I first met Nick, he'd looked like a filthy bum who cleaned up well when the occasion demanded it. When I saw him again, he was working undercover for Hugh d'Ambray, my father's Warlord, and he'd looked like one of Hugh's inner circle: hard, fast, without any weakness, like a weapon honed to unbreakable toughness. Now he was somewhere in between. Still no weaknesses, short brown hair, leaden eyes, and a kind of quiet menace that set me on edge.

Nick hated me. My mother was the reason for Nick's unhappy childhood. I suspected it wasn't the main reason he hated me, but it definitely helped. Nick detested me because he got close and personal with my father. He'd seen with his own eyes how Roland operated, and he thought I would turn out the same way. I was happy to disappoint him.

"Enjoying dinner like one big happy family?" he said.

"The knight-protector honors us with his presence," Rowena said.

"Hey, handsome." Desandra winked at him. "Remember me?"

They had gotten into it before and nearly killed each other. Nick didn't look at her, but a small muscle in the corner of his left eye jerked. He remembered, alright.

"What can we do for you?" Curran asked.

"For me, nothing." Nick was looking at me.

"Just spit it out," I told him.

He tossed a handful of pieces of paper on the table. They spread out as they fell. Photographs. My father's stone "residence." Soldiers in black dragging a large body between them toward the gates, nude from the waist up, purple and red bruises covering the snow-white skin. A black bag hid the head. Another shot, showing the person's legs, the feet mangled like hamburger meat. Whoever it was, he or she was too large to be a normal human.

Raphael picked up a photograph next to him, got up, and carefully placed it in front of me.

The hood was off. A scraggly mane of bluish hair hung down around the prisoner's shoulders. His face was raw, but I still recognized it. Saiman in his natural form.

My father had kidnapped Saiman.

Rage boiled inside me, instant and scalding hot.

I had tolerated all of my father's bullshit, but kidnapping my people, this was going too far.

"When did this happen?" Curran asked, his voice calm.

"Yesterday evening."

Saiman used to be my go-to expert for all things weird and magical, but the last time I tried to hire him, he told me that sooner or later my father would murder me, and he wasn't stupid enough to play for the losing team. I knew Saiman was the center of his own universe, but it had still surprised me. I had saved him more than once. I didn't expect friendship—that was beyond him—but I had expected some loyalty. One thing I knew for sure: Saiman would not work with my father. Roland terrified him. One hint of interest from him, and Saiman would run and never look back.

I wished I could reach across the distance and drop a burning space rock on my father's house.

Nick was looking at me. Some part of him must've enjoyed this. He wasn't smiling, but I saw it in his eyes.

I forced my voice to sound even. "Is the Order taking the case?"

"No. The Order must be petitioned, and no petition has been filed."

"Shouldn't this fall under the citizen-in-danger provision?" I asked. "An agent of the Order took these pictures. They saw that Saiman was in immediate danger, yet they did nothing."

"We are doing something," Nick said. "I'm notifying you."

"Your compassion is staggering," Ghastek said.

Nick turned his lead gaze to the Master of the Dead. "Considering the involved citizen's origins and his long and creative criminal record, his rescue is a low priority. In fact, the city is safer without him in it."

"Then why tell me at all?" I asked.

"Because I enjoy watching you and your father rip into each other like two feral cats thrown into the same bag. If one of you kills the other, the world will be better off." Nick smiled. "Give him hell, Sharrim."

Mahon pounded his fist on the table. The wood thudded like a drum. "You will keep a civil tongue in your mouth when you speak to my daughter-in-law!"

"Your daughter-in-law is an abomination," Nick told him.

Mahon surged up. Raphael grabbed his right arm. Curran grabbed his left.

"That's right, hold back the rabid bear," Nick said. "This is why the world treats you like animals."

I jumped onto the table, ran over to Mahon, and put myself between him and Nick. "It's okay. He runs his mouth because he can't do anything else."

Nick turned around and walked out of the room.

Curran strained, flexing. "Sit down, old man. Sit down."

Finally, Mahon dropped back into his seat. "That fucking prick."

Raphael collapsed into his chair.

I sat on the table between the plates. Bernard's manager would have a cow, but I didn't care. Holding Mahon back took everything I had.

Ghastek and Rowena stared at me.

"Did you know?" I asked.

Ghastek shook his head. "They don't notify us of what he does."

"What are you going to do?" Desandra asked.

"We'll have to go and get him," I said. I'd rather eat broken glass.

"That degenerate?" Raphael asked. "Why not leave him there?"

"Because Roland can't take people out of the city whenever he wants to," Curran said. His face was dark. "And that asshole knew that when he brought the pictures."

"You should've let me twist his head off," Mahon said. "You can't let people insult your wife, Curran. One day you'll have to choose diplomacy or your spouse. I'm telling you now, it's got to be your wife. Diplomacy doesn't care if you live or die. Your wife does."

====== CHAPTER ======
2

THE BATTERED CORPSE of I-85 stretched in front of me, winding into the distance, flanked by trees. Brilliant blue sky rose high above it, suffused with sunshine. It was barely six and already the temperatures threatened to slide into the nineties. It would be one hell of a hot day.

I glanced behind me at the ten mercenaries parked by Curran. They came in all shapes and sizes. Eduardo towered over everyone except Douglas King, who was enormous, six five, with shoulders that wouldn't fit through the door and legs like tree trunks. Douglas shaved his head, because he felt he wasn't communicating his badassness well enough, and he painted what he claimed to be magic runes on his scalp and the side of his face in black camo paint. The runes were bullshit. I had told him that before. He didn't care.

Next to him, the five-foot-tall Ella seemed even smaller. Perfectly ordinary, with brown hair about an inch longer than her shoulders and a pretty, pleasant face, which was usually free of makeup, she would've been at home in a sandwich shop or a vet's office. People tended to underestimate her.

Petite and wicked fast, Ella liked the wakizashi and she cut things to ribbons with it.

The rest of the mercs fell between these two extremes: lean and bulky, tall and short, some carrying blades, others carrying bows. They were Curran's elite team, the nucleus around which he was building the new Guild.

He'd formed this team when he took a job everyone in the city turned down. Even the Red Guard had bowed out. The Four Horsemen, the Guild's best team, straightout called it suicide. Curran and I took the gig, Eduardo threw in his lot with us, and somehow the Guild coughed up nine people crazy enough to join us and good enough to live through it. We got the job done, the Guild's gigs doubled overnight, and the ten of them got a certain reputation. They were the Guild's best of the best and after that job, they would die for Curran.

Neither of us had a good feeling about the upcoming conversation with Roland. Curran would stay behind. First, it would make the negotiations easier. Things would get heated, and given that my father and my fiancé got into pissing matches over which way the wind was blowing, it would be better to handle this one by myself. And second, if something happened to me, Curran was the only one who could hold the city and possibly get me back out.

He would try. If things did go sour, he would sprout fangs and claws and march his team of hard cases brandishing savage weapons into Lawrenceville to try to pry me loose from my father's grasp. I had to make sure it didn't come to that, because it wouldn't end well for everyone involved.

I leaned over to Curran and kissed him. His arms closed around me and he squeezed me to him for one bone-crunching second.

"I'm off."

"I'll be right here," he said.

"Have fun with your A-team. Sharpen some knives. Clean some guns. Don't kill anybody while I'm gone."

"I can't make any promises."

I climbed into Cuddles's saddle. The black and white mammoth donkey twitched her ears.

"I'll tell dear old Dad you're sorry you missed him."

Behind Curran, Eduardo snorted.

Curran bared his teeth. "Not as sorry as he'll be if I have to come and see him."

"Hey, Daniels," Ella called out. "Bring us back some cookies."

"What makes you think there will be cookies?"

"When I go home to see my parents, there are always cookies."

If Roland did have cookies, they'd probably make me spit fire. "I'll see what I can do."

I started down the road. In its glory days I-85 was a giant of an interstate road, six regular lanes and two express lanes on each side. The magic had fed the tree growth. The pavement crumbled at the edges under the relentless onslaught of magic waves, making it easier for the roots to raise the asphalt, and the once mighty highway turned into a forest road. The huge hickories, maples, and white ashes flanked it, warring for space with colossal live oaks tinseled with Spanish moss. The heat was brutal, the sun pounding the road like a hammer. It would take me about twenty minutes to get to Lawrenceville, and by the time I made it, I'd arrive well-done with a crispy crust. I stuck to the tree shadows.

What the hell could Roland possibly want with Saiman?

Thinking about it made me clench my teeth. He came into my territory. He took one of my people out. No matter how I felt about him, Saiman was an inhabitant of Atlanta. If I had hackles, they would be standing up.

You'd think he would stop screwing with me fourteen days before my wedding. As a common courtesy.

I still hadn't bought the dress. I'd gone shopping for it three times and come back empty-handed because I didn't see anything I wanted.

Ahead Derek stepped out from behind a thick ash, moving with the easy gliding grace of a shapeshifter. In his early twenties, with broad shoulders, and a face hardened by life's grinder, he looked at me with dark eyes. With some shapeshifters the nature of their beast was more obvious. Even in his human body, Derek looked like a wolf. A predatory, solitary, smart wolf.

"I was beginning to wonder where you were."

The former boy wonder shrugged his shoulders. "I scouted ahead." His voice matched his looks: low, threatening, and rough.

"Anything?"

"No patrols between us and Lawrenceville."

I wasn't sure if that was good—because I wouldn't have to intimidate and possibly kill anyone—or bad, because my father apparently worried so little about me presenting a threat that he neglected to defend his base.

"You look like you want to murder somebody," Derek said.

"Don't I normally look that way?"

"Not like this."

"It's probably because I have one nerve left and my father keeps jumping up and down on it."

I kept riding. Derek trotted next to me.

"Curran told me about the Conclave," he said.

"Mm-hm."

"Why does Nick hate you?" he asked.

"You know the story about Voron and me? How after Roland killed my mother, Voron raised me?"

Derek nodded.

"Whenever we came through the Atlanta area, Greg Feldman would visit us. When I was older, I thought it was odd, because Greg was a knight-diviner and Voron steered clear of the Order whenever he could. I asked him about it once, and he told me that he, my mother, Greg, and Greg's ex-wife, Anna, used to be friends. Then after Voron died, Greg became my guardian. Occasionally he would take me to Anna's house. She didn't like me at first, but eventually she helped me. She is a precog. I used to wonder why I haven't heard from her for a while, but it makes sense now."

"Okay," Derek said. "How does Nick fit into it?"

"You remember when Hugh killed the knights in the Atlanta chapter of the Order, and Nick dropped his cover?

Maxine called him Nick Feldman. When we got back to the Keep, I asked Jim to look into it. He did. Nick Feldman is Greg Feldman's son."

Derek frowned. "You didn't know he had a son?"

"No. Greg took care of me for about ten years. Neither he nor Anna ever mentioned a child. There were no pictures and nobody ever said his name. So after Jim told me, I called Anna."

It had taken four phone calls and a promise to come find her in her country home in North Carolina before she finally called back.

"I had always thought that Greg and Voron had been friends. I have a picture of the four of them, Greg and Anna and Voron and my mother, standing together. Apparently, all of that is bullshit. They knew each other, but they weren't friends. My mother had worked for the Order for a short time before marrying Roland. She met Greg, and Greg fell in love with her. He told Anna, but Nick was two years old and they decided to stay together for his sake. My mother and Greg reconnected again when she and Voron were running from Roland. At the time, I was a baby. Greg left Anna the day he found out my mother died. Nick was six."

"I don't get it," Derek said. "Why leave when the other woman is dead?"

"I don't know. I have no idea what went on in Greg's head. Maybe he thought he was betraying my mother's memory somehow by staying with Anna."

Thinking about it put all those meetings between Voron and Greg in a new light. They weren't two friends catching up. They were two men mourning the death of the same woman.

"He and Anna shared custody, but when Nick was twelve, he applied to Squire's Rest. It's the Order's preparatory boarding school, the place you go before the Academy makes you into a knight. Nick got in and they never saw him again. According to Anna, Nick hated both her and Greg. When he became part of the Crusader program, Greg was told to remove all traces of Nick, photos, documents, everything, for Nick's safety and the safety of his family. Eventually Nick went undercover with Hugh for over two years. So my mother broke up his parents' marriage and my father was the reason he had to do despicable shit for two years. I'm not his favorite person."

"I get being mad at his parents and at your mother, but you were a baby."

I sighed. "Maybe if I were the daughter of the other woman his father loved, or the child his dad took in instead of him, or Roland's daughter, he could deal with it. But I'm all of those things. He will get over it or he won't, Derek. I don't really care."

I did a little bit. Nick was Greg's older child, and Greg was my guardian and looked over me the way a father would, which meant that in my head Nick hovered perilously close to the "older brother" category. If he ever found out about it, he would probably choke on whatever he was drinking at the time.

The trees pulled away from the road like two hands opening, giving way to a clear grassy plain, with the old highway rolling across it all the way to a short blocky tower. It looked like it was designed to be a good deal taller. A fortress was beginning to take shape around it, its walls three-quarters finished. Damn it.

"I thought you said he agreed to stop building on our border," Derek said.

"He agreed to stop building the tower. We agreed that he's allowed a residence."

"That's not a residence. That's a castle."

"I can see that," I growled.

And it had gone up fast, too. Three months ago, there was nothing except a foundation. Now there was a mostly finished wall, and the main building and smaller structures inside that wall, and long blood-red pennants streaming in the breeze from the parapets. Made himself comfortable, did he?

A rider shot out of the copse of trees on our left, pushing hard at a full gallop and carrying a long sky-blue standard on a tall flagpole. I would've recognized that horse anywhere.

Built like a small draft horse, black dappled with light gray, she pounded the road with her white-feathered hoofs. Her mane, long, white, and wavy, flared in the wind. Her rider, slender, blond hair tied back in a ponytail, sat like she was born on that horse. Julie and Peanut, heading straight for Roland's castle.

I'd told her where I was going this morning and told her to stay at Cutting Edge. Instead she came here and waited until she saw me so she could dramatically ride for the castle ahead of me. Why me? Why?

"I'm going to kill her."

"She's your Herald," Derek said. "That's your color. Blue for humanity."

My what?

He made a big show of moving a few feet to the side.

I looked at him.

"In case your head explodes," he said helpfully.

"Not another word."

He chuckled under his breath, the rough lupine laugh of an amused wolf. *Laugh it up, why don't you?*

My father had had two warlords in the modern age. The first, Voron, left his service to save me, because my mother's magic convinced him he hopelessly loved her. Hugh d'Ambray was the second, and during his training under Voron, Hugh served as Roland's Herald. According to Voron, that was the way my father had done things thousands of years ago, before the magic disappeared from the world and his wizard empire collapsed. First, you became Herald, then you became Warlord. Now Julie had decided that she was my Herald. I never told her any of this. She must still be talking to Roland. I didn't know how, and when I had asked her about it a few weeks ago, she denied it.

Apparently, she'd lied.

I gritted my teeth.

Nothing good would come from Julie talking to Roland. He was poison. I had busted up one of their conversations before, and I did my best to keep more from happening.

Logic, explanations, sincere requests, threats, groundings—
none of it made any difference. Nothing short of a direct
order would do, and I wasn't ready to burn that bridge yet.
Not only that, but that direct order would have to be worded
in such a way as to prevent any loopholes. I would have to
hire Barabas just to write it out.

Julie was talking to my father and I was powerless to stop
it. My father kept coming into my territory, taunting me,
and I couldn't stop that either. And now Julie was riding into
his castle to announce me.

I raised my head and sat up straighter. Cuddles picked
up on my mood and broke into a canter. Derek shifted into
a run, keeping up. Julie and I would have a long talk when
we got home. I didn't want a Herald, but I wouldn't leave
her without backup either. I would ride into that damn castle like I had a Herald announce every moment of my day,
complete with fanfare and banner waving.

Four guards in leather armor stood by the entrance of
the castle, two men and two women, all trim, grim, and
looking like someone had found some attack dogs, turned
them into human shape, and groomed them into paragons
of military perfection. They bowed their heads in unison.
Four voices chorused, "Sharrim."

Great. This would be a wonderful visit; I just knew it.

I rode into the courtyard and dismounted next to Julie,
who stood at parade rest holding the stupid banner. A small
stand waited next to her. They brought her a stand for her
flag.

A man approached and knelt on one knee. I had seen him
before. He was in his fifties, with a head of graying hair,
and he looked like he had spent all of his years fighting for
one thing or another. Having people kneel in front of me
ranked somewhere between getting a root canal and cleaning out a sewer on the list of things I hated.

"You honor us, Sharrim. I have informed Sharrum of
your arrival. He is overjoyed."

*I bet he is.* "Thank you for the warm welcome."

"Do you require anything of me?"

"Not at this time."

He rose, his head still bowed, and backed away to stand a few dozen feet to the left.

Around us, the soldiers manning the walls tried not to gawk. A woman exited one of the side buildings, saw us, turned around, and went back inside.

"You're grounded," I said under my breath.

"I don't have a social life anyway," Julie murmured. "Barabas called the house before I left. He says not to burn any bridges."

That was Barabas's standing legal advice when it came to my father. If I burned this bridge, it would mean war.

"Where is he?"

"He's at home," Julie said. "Christopher had a nervous breakdown and burned a book."

That made no sense. Christopher loved books. They were his escape and treasure.

"Which book was it?"

*"Bullfinch's Mythology."*

What could possibly have set him off about poor Bullfinch?

To the right a man and a woman walked out on the wall from a small side tower. The man wore a trench coat despite the heat. Sewn and patched with everything from leather cording to bits of fur, it looked like every time it had been cut or torn, he'd slapped whatever fabric or leather he had handy over the rip. There was a particular patch on the left side that I didn't like.

His face was too smooth for a human, the lines perfect, the dark eyes tilted down at the inside corners. His hair was cut short and tousled as if he'd slept on it and hadn't bothered brushing it for a couple of days, but it was a deep glossy black and looked soft. He was clean-shaven, without so much as a shadow of stubble on his jaw, but somehow managed to look unkempt. The color of his face was odd too, an even olive hue. When most people described skin as olive, they meant a golden-brown color with a slight green undertone. His olive wasn't darker, but stronger somehow, more saturated with green. The hilt of a sword protruded over his shoulder, wrapped with a purple cord. The same purple showed beneath his coat.

The woman towered next to him. Easily over six feet, dark skinned, with broad shoulders, she wore chain mail over a black tactical outfit and carried a large hammer. The body beneath the chain mail was lean: small bust, hard waist, narrow hips. She was corded with muscle. Her hair, in short dreadlocks, was pulled back from her face. Shades hid her eyes. Her features were large and handsome, and fully human, although she looked like she could punch through a solid wall. A purple scarf, gossamer light, hung from her waist.

"On the wall, the pair to the right," I said quietly.

Both Derek and Julie kept looking straight ahead, but I knew they saw them.

"That's human skin on the left side of his coat."

If things went sour, those two would prove to be a problem.

Forty feet above us, the door of the tower opened and my father stepped out onto the stone landing. Magic clung to him like a tattered cloak. He was reeling it in as fast as he could, but I still felt it. We'd interrupted something.

"Blossom!"

"Father." There. I said it and didn't choke on it.

"So good to see you."

He started down the stairs. My father looked like every orphan's dream. He'd let himself age, for my benefit, into a man who could reasonably have a twenty-eight-year-old daughter. His hair was salt-and-pepper, and he'd let some wrinkles gather at the corners of his eyes and mouth, enough to suggest experience, but he moved like a young man in his athletic prime. His body, clad in jeans and a gray tunic with rolled-up sleeves, could've belonged to a merc who would've fit right into Curran's team.

His face was that of a prophet. Kindness and wisdom shone from his eyes. They promised knowledge and power, and right now they glowed with fatherly joy. Any child look-ing at him would know instinctively that he would be a great father; that he would be nurturing, patient, attentive, stern when the occasion required (but only because he wanted the best for his children), and above all, proud of your every achievement. If I had met him at fifteen, when Voron died and my world shattered, I wouldn't have been able to resist, despite all of Voron's conditioning and training to kill Roland. I had been so alone then and desperate for any hint of human warmth.

Julie was an orphan. She had me and Curran, but we were her second family.

I stared at that fatherly facade and wished I could pry her away from him. If wishes had power, mine would've brought down this castle in an avalanche of stone and dust.

"Have you eaten? I can have lunch served. I found the most amazing red curry recipe."

Yes, come, have some magically delicious curry in the house of a legendary wizard hell-bent on grinding the world under his boot. What could go wrong? "No, thank you. I'm not hungry."

"Come, walk with me. I want to show you something."

I glanced at Derek and shook my head slightly. *Stay put.* He nodded.

I motioned to Julie. She thrust her flag into the stand and followed me, keeping about four feet of distance. I was about to rub my father's nose in the mess he'd made. He would show his ugly side. I'd seen it before once or twice and it wasn't something one forgot. It was high time Julie saw it, too.

My father and I strolled across the yard, up the stairs, and onto the wall. A complex network of ditches crossed the ground on the left side and stretched out to hug the castle in a rough crescent. Hills of sand and smooth pebbles in a dozen colors and sizes rose on the sides. I tried to picture the lines of the trenches in my head as they would look from above, but they didn't look like anything. If this was the layout of a spell, it would be hellishly complicated.

What kind of spell would require sand and stone? Was he building a stone golem? That would be a really big golem. Judging by the amount of materials, it would have to be a colossus. But why use pebbles; why not carve him out of rock?

Maybe it was a summoning. What was he summoning, that he would need a space the size of twenty football fields . . .

"I've decided to build a water garden."

Oh.

"I told you of the water gardens in my childhood palace. I want my grandchildren to make their own treasured memories."

The recollection hit me like a sudden punch in the gut: my father on a grassy hill, taking away my son as I screamed. I had seen the vision in the mind of a djinn. Djinn weren't the most trustworthy creatures, but the witches had confirmed it. If . . . no, *when*. When Curran and I had a son, my father would try to take him. I held on to that thought and forced it down before it had a chance to surface on my face.

"We are diverting the river. The weather is mild enough and with a bit of magical prompting, I will turn this place into a small paradise. What do you think?"

*Open your mouth and say something. Say something.*
"Sounds like it will be beautiful."

"It will."

"Do you think Grandmother would like to see it?" *Stab, stab, stab.*

"Your grandmother is best left undisturbed."

"She is suffering. Alone, imprisoned in a stone box."

He sighed. "Some things cannot be helped."

"Aren't you afraid that someone will free her?" Someone like me.

"If someone were to try to enter Mishmar, I would know and I would come looking for them. They would never leave."

*Thanks for the warning, Dad.*

"She isn't alive, Blossom. She is a wild force, a tempest without ego. One can only speculate what damage she would cause if unleashed."

*Aha. Of course, you buried her away from everything she loves because she is too dangerous.*

We resumed our strolling along the walls, slowly circling the tower.

"How go the preparations for the wedding?"

"Very well. How goes the world domination?"

"It has its moments."

We strolled down the wall. That was probably enough small talk. If I let him run the conversation, I'd never get Saiman back.

"A resident of Atlanta was brought here. I'm here to take him home."

"Ah." Roland nodded.

We turned the corner and I caught a glimpse of Julie's face as she walked behind us. She was looking at the empty field beyond the eastern wall. Her eyes widened, her face sharpened, and her skin went two shades whiter. I glanced at the field. Beautiful emerald-green grass. Julie stared at it with freaked-out eyes. She definitely saw something.

We kept moving.

*Don't burn bridges. Stay civil.* "You kidnapped Saiman."

"I invited him to be my guest."

I pulled a photograph of Saiman's brutalized body out of my pocket and passed it to him.

Roland glanced at it. "Perhaps 'guest' was a bit of an overstatement."

"You can't snatch Atlanta citizens any time you feel like it."

"Technically I can. I choose not to, because you and I have made a certain agreement, but it is definitely within my power."

I opened my mouth and snapped it shut. We'd stopped at a square widening in the wall that would probably become the basis for a flanking tower. In the field, on the right, a man hung on a cross. Bloody, his clothes torn, his face a mess, he sagged off the boards. I would've guessed he was dead, except he was staring straight at Roland, his eyes defiant.

"Father!"

"Yes?"

"A man is being crucified."

He glanced in that direction and a shadow flickered through his face. "So he is."

It was the same look Julie gave me when she thought she had gotten away with stealing beer out of the keg but forgot about the empty mug on her desk. He had forgotten about the man he was slowly killing.

Julie glanced behind her, at the empty field. *Okay, that's about enough of that.* I had to get her as close to the exit as I could now.

"I require privacy," I told her. "Go back and wait with Derek, please."

She bowed, turned, and walked away.

"You give her too little credit," Roland said.

"I give her all the credit. I also never forget that she's sixteen years old."

"A wonderful age. Full of possibilities."

*Possibilities that you have no business contemplating.* "What did he do?"

Roland sighed.

"What was so bad that you decided to torture him?"

Roland looked after Julie. "The problem with warlords is that the position is fundamentally flawed by its very nature. A general who is unable to lead is useless, but to lead, he must inspire loyalty. When the troops rush the field, knowing they may lay down their lives, they look to their general, not to the king behind him. Sooner or later, their loyalties become divided. They abandon their king and look instead to the one who bled and suffered with them."

He looked at the human wreck on the cross.

"Is that one of Hugh's men?"

"Yes."

"What did he do?"

"He refused my orders. I told him to do something and he told me that he was a soldier, not a butcher. The great hypocrisy of this pseudo-moral stance lies in the fact that if Hugh had given him the same order, he probably would've obeyed. I merely reminded him that he draws his breath at my discretion."

And he'd ordered him tied to the cross. So the death would take longer. "That's barbaric."

Roland turned to me with a small smile. "No. Barbarism usually produces swift death. Cruelty is the mark of a civilized human. I still have a hundred Iron Dogs in this location. He's an excellent visual aid."

And that was it right there in a nutshell. Nothing was off-limits as long as it let him accomplish his goal.

"How long has he been up there?"

"Five days. He should've been dead by now, but he's using magic to keep himself alive despite the pain. The will to live is a truly remarkable thing."

I wanted to march down there and take Hugh's man off of it. I wasn't kind. I could be cruel. I had used my sword to punish before, but at my absolute worst, the punishment I delivered lasted minutes. The man on the cross had been there for days. The Iron Dog might have belonged to Hugh, but there was a line between good and evil, and that kind of torture crossed it. This was bigger than Hugh and me. This was about right and wrong.

"And if Hugh returns?"

"He won't. I purged him."

"You what?"

"That which is freely given can also be taken away. I've severed the link between us. He still has the benefit of our blood with all its power—that, unfortunately, I cannot strip without taking his life—but we aren't bound. The light of his gift is no longer precious to me."

The small hairs on the back of my neck rose. My father no longer cared if Hugh lived or died. "You made him mortal."

"Yes. Even with his healing ability I expect he won't last the next century."

"Does he know?"

"Yes."

Hugh had been my father's wrecking ball. Roland would

point at a target, and Hugh would smash it, until only blood and ash remained. Then my father would sweep in to rein in his cruel violent Warlord, and Hugh's victims would rejoice, because anything was better than Hugh. Roland was Hugh's reason for living. And now his god had rejected and abandoned him.

I hated Hugh for a list of things a mile long. His people murdered Aunt B. He used magic to throw me into my father's prison and slowly starved me to death, trying to break my will. He murdered one of my friends in front of me. But I understood Hugh. He was an instrument of my father's will, as much as I had been an instrument of Voron's. Voron pointed and I killed, without question and, worse, without doubt. It took his death and years on my own before I broke free. I knew exactly how much that rejection from the man who raised you like a father could hurt. I had thought Voron cared for me. When I found out that he'd been training me so he could watch the pain on my father's face as Roland killed me, it nearly broke me, and by then Voron had been dead for a decade.

"You were everything to him. He committed all those atrocities for you, and you've stripped him of your love, the thing he cared most about."

"Hugh outlived his usefulness. His life had been a series of uncomplicated tasks and eventually he became his work."

And whose fault was that? "You plucked him from the street. He was raised exactly the way you wanted him to be."

"He had potential," Roland said, his voice wistful. "So much magic. He was like a fallen star, a glowing meteor. I melted it down and forged it into a sword. You are right, it's not truly his fault, but the fact remains—the world is becoming more complex, not less. Some swords are meant to be forged only once. It's better to start fresh."

Julie. Julie was a glowing meteor too, young and malleable, easy to melt down and reforge. *You fucking asshole. You cannot have Julie. Hell would sprout roses first.* I unclenched my teeth and forced my voice to sound even. "It would've been kinder to kill him."

Roland's smile never faltered, but for a moment, the warmth in his eyes cooled and I glimpsed the icy steel beneath. "I am not kind, my daughter. I am fair."

I had to get out of here before I did something I would regret. But I also had to spring Saiman free and avoid a war with Roland.

"Return Saiman to me."

"The frost giant left the borders of your city voluntarily. My people didn't trespass."

So they lay in wait and nabbed him while he was traveling. Damn it. "It doesn't matter. His residence is in Atlanta. His business interests are in Atlanta. He owns property, he employs people, and he pays his taxes in Atlanta. He's mine."

Roland pondered it for a long moment. "No. I need him."

*Right. Obey the letter of the agreement but not the spirit.* "You're forcing me to act."

"You don't even like him." Roland's eyes narrowed. "What's the harm of me keeping the creature?"

"It's the principle. I would do the same thing if I had never met him before. Return my frost giant, Father."

"Or?"

"Or I'll have to retrieve him. I won't abandon my people."

"I hate when we fight." Roland tilted his head. "What if I offer you that life?" He nodded at the cross. "A consolation prize. It bothers you. I can see it in your eyes. You may take Hugh's second-in-command, daughter. Do with him as you will."

"Thank you. I *will* take him since you're giving him to me. But I still need my frost giant."

"Do not raise your hand against me, Kate. All you have to do is walk away."

All of his promises went right out the window as soon as there was something he wanted. The urge to scream in his face was getting to me. Screaming would accomplish nothing, except plunge us into a conflict we weren't ready for. "Not going to happen."

He sighed.

"You're not giving me a choice. If I follow your logic, then any of the people who leave the boundaries of my city are fair game. Since you're parked right outside the city border, Atlanta is under siege and a siege is an act of war. You're in breach, Father."

Roland laughed quietly.

"This is solved very simply. Give back what you've taken. You started this. I'm merely reacting."

"You're not ready to oppose me. Don't open this door. You don't have the ruthlessness to fight me."

I'd had enough. "Father, when was the last time you killed someone? I don't mean with magic, I mean with your hands, close enough that you could look into their eyes? I killed a woman a week ago to keep her from sacrificing her children to some forgotten god. I have killed so many, I don't remember all their faces. They blend. The door is already wide open and you were the one who opened it. Are you ready for me to walk through it?"

A shadow crossed his face. I felt the magic rise within him like a brilliant new star being born from the empty darkness.

*"My proud daughter, my sensitive, kind child, compassionate toward her enemy, you have saved one man from his fate. But what will you do about them?"*

Magic rolled from him. The empty field to the left of us shimmered. Crosses appeared, like a mirage in the desert manifesting in the wavering hot air. Men and women, young and old, hanging from the wood. Oh dear God . . . There had to be thirty crosses in that field. The bodies sagged, completely still. Nobody moved.

The odor reached me, the awful polluting stench of human flesh rotting. They were dead. All of them.

Ice rolled down my back. The horror of it was too much.

Roland looked at the lone survivor on the cross. The face of the Iron Dog contorted. His cross was facing the others.

"You made him watch." They died in agony, one by one, and the Iron Dog saw it all.

*"You have no idea of the things I'm capable of. You*

*cannot stand against me. When I ordered him to kill these people, it was a kindness. He disobeyed and would not give them swift death, so I showed him what his defiance cost."*

The ice reached the small of my back and exploded into an inferno. Roland was watching me now to make sure I got the message. *Oh no, Father. Don't worry. I've got it.*

*"But for his disobedience, this wouldn't have come to pass."*

My magic screamed and bucked inside me, trying to break free, leaking into my voice. *"No."*

Roland's eyes narrowed.

*"You speak as if it's some outside force that tortured and murdered these people. As if it's some disaster that was inevitable, and you, through your benevolence, tried to hold it off, but your subordinates failed you. But it's you. You decided to kill them. You decided to crucify them. You. You are the source of this evil. It's your fault, not his. You are the sick bastard who decided that he has the right to mass murder."*

Roland recoiled. His eyes blazed. His magic shot out in a furious torrent, boiling like a thundercloud around him.

Screw it. I let go. My power burst out of me, matching his. The castle wall shuddered under us.

I glared at him. *"You have no right. Have you ever wondered why you always have to burn and kill your way to power? Why nobody ever comes and says, 'Please, mighty Nimrod, lead us'? It's because your reign brings pain and suffering. Nobody wants you in charge."*

*"YOU WILL NOT SPEAK TO ME LIKE THIS."*

His magic splayed out, shooting up. Wind tore at me, raging out of nowhere. The stones under us rattled. Several stone blocks slid out, tumbling over the edge. In the courtyard, people cringed.

*"You're a usurper, Father. You keep doing horrible things for the greater good, but there is no greater good. There is only this."* I pointed at the crosses. *"This is what our family stands for. Not for peace, happiness, or progress. This is your legacy. You're a tyrant. The evil creature that people use to scare their children at night. On this entire*

*planet, you are the only person who thinks you are fit to rule."*

"SILENCE!"

The blast of magic hit me, nearly taking me off my feet. Oh no. He would not shut me up. I had things I needed to get off my chest. They'd been building for months.

My magic surged back. If it had a voice, it would've roared.

*"You can't handle any authority but your own. Even now, it gnaws at you that I have this city. You can't let it go. You scheme, and manipulate, and push me, and when I'm forced to retaliate, you'll placate your guilty conscience by telling yourself you gave me a choice. If only I would go along with your blatant disregard for your own word, none of it would happen. You'll pretend it's really my fault. It's yours, Father. Your own sister chose to die rather than live in the world you wanted to create."*

His hand shot out, but I saw it a mile away. He was a wizard, but I was a professional killer. The slap never landed. Roland stared at my hand blocking his.

*"I'm leaving now, Father. I'll come for Saiman. You took him from me, I* **will** *take him back, and then we'll be even and you'll have a choice to make."*

I turned and walked off the wall. There was nothing else to say. People fled from my path. The two fighters from the wall had disappeared. A storm spun above the castle, dark clouds churning. I couldn't have cared less.

Derek and Julie waited for me, standing still in the human chaos, as Roland's people tried to secure the castle against the rising wind. Julie's face was bloodless. She was holding the reins of her and my horses, trying to keep them in place as they eyed the storm with rising panic. Derek's expression said nothing, flat and impassive. His eyes shone yellow-green. He was on the edge of violence. I marched past them, out the gates, and to the cross. They followed me. My father was still where I had left him, watching.

I looked at Derek and pointed at the cross. He moved behind it.

I pictured my father's face in the wood, took a step, and hammered a side kick into the base of the cross. I sank all my strength and fury into it. The wood cracked. I kicked it again and again and again. The cross toppled down, with the man on it, and Derek caught it. I pulled a knife out of its sheath and sliced through the rope on the Iron Dog's ankles and wrists. Derek pulled him off the cross and slung him over Cuddles's back. I swung into the saddle and rode off, Derek and Julie following me.

Behind us, dark clouds boiled, hiding the sun.

≡ CHAPTER ≡

# 3

WHEN WE RODE to the meeting spot, Curran's group had gained two new members. Barabas, his spiky hair standing straight up, was playing cards with Evelyn, one of Jim's scouts.

Ella eyed the Iron Dog slung over my saddle. "That's not a cookie."

Curran saw my face. His expression hardened.

"How's the bridge?" Barabas called out.

"There is no bridge."

Barabas opened his mouth and closed it with a click.

"When is he coming?" Curran asked.

"I don't know."

Derek took the Iron Dog off the horse. Hugh's man looked dead.

Derek slapped his face lightly. "Hey."

The man's eyelashes flickered.

Derek looked up. "Water?"

One of the mercenaries passed him a canteen, and Derek held the flask to the man's mouth.

The prisoner came to life and gripped the canteen, drinking.

"Not too much," I said, dismounting. "He'll vomit."

"Who is this?" Curran asked.

"Hugh's second-in-command."

Curran stared at me for a long second.

"What was said, exactly?" Barabas asked.

"I told my father that he had to give Saiman back. He gave me this man as a consolation prize. Roland had ordered him to murder some people. The Iron Dog refused, so my father decided to torture and slowly kill him. Then my father condescended to explain to me that when people didn't play ball, things like that happened. I told him what I thought about that."

Barabas squeezed his eyes shut for a moment. "How did he take it?"

"Look behind me."

Barabas glanced at the storm raging in the east. "I knew I should've come with you. This is my own fault. Did he say anything about declaring war or coming for you?"

"No. He tried to slap me."

"He what?" Curran snarled. His eyes went gold.

"He tried to slap me. I blocked it and told him that I would get Saiman back, it would make us even, and then he would have to decide what he would do about it."

"Did he say anything else?" Barabas asked.

"No."

The Iron Dog retched and vomited water on the ground.

"So no declaration of war has been made. We can work with this." Barabas exhaled.

Yeah, right. "I don't want to work with it."

"I completely understand." The weremongoose nodded his red head. "That's why I would advise you to avoid speaking with your father while we untie this knot and hopefully prevent the city from being plunged into a horrible war with mass casualties."

"Yes, of course, this is all my fault."

"Yes, it is," Barabas said. "All you had to do was walk in there and have a simple conversation with your father."

Simple? "You know what I don't need, Barabas? I don't need you to criticize how *I speak to my father*."

The mercs took a step back in unison.

Curran put his hand on my shoulder.

"Be careful, Kate," Barabas said, his expression unreadable. "Your magic is showing."

"Do you know where I found him?" I pointed to the Iron Dog. "I took him off a cross. There were thirty more like it."

"Thirty-two," a hoarse voice said.

I turned. The Iron Dog sat up, his light gray eyes open.

"Thirty-two people," he repeated quietly. "It took them three days to die."

"Because he had refused to kill them, my father made him watch. This is what you're asking me to negotiate with, Barabas."

"This is exactly why we need you to negotiate."

"I'm getting sick of you ordering me around on my own land."

"Enough," Curran said.

Barabas took a step back. "We'll talk about this another time."

Curran crouched by the sitting man. "What happened?"

"There was a compound five miles to the south," the man said, his words ragged. "Some kind of religious group. Roland wanted the land. He didn't say why. He offered to buy it, but they wouldn't sell it to him. Something they told him must've pissed him off, because he ordered me to take my people and clear it out. He said he wanted them buried off the land, somewhere else. I told him I was a soldier. I wouldn't order my people to butcher unarmed civilians."

"And if Hugh told you to do it?" Curran asked.

The Iron Dog faced him, his eyes clear. "He wouldn't."

Yeah, right. "I find that hard to believe," I said.

"I'm a soldier," the Iron Dog said. "Not a Ripper. Soldiers fight other soldiers."

"He's telling the truth," Julie said behind me. "When Hugh needed a massacre, he'd use the Rippers. Most of them are dead now."

*Don't explode.* Nothing good ever came from exploding.

I turned to her.

"The Iron Dogs have six cohorts," Julie said. "The first five cohorts have four hundred and eighty soldiers per cohort, broken into six centuries of eighty soldiers each. The Sixth Cohort had two hundred and forty people and was known as the Rippers, the shock troops. Each cohort had a captain. Hibla was the captain of the Rippers. This man is Stoyan Iliev, captain of the First Cohort. He was the first captain Hugh recruited himself."

Great. I'd rescued Hugh's bestie.

Stoyan turned to me. "I was in the Swan Palace. I saw you kill Hibla. If you're going to kill me, give me a sword first."

"Settle down," Derek told him. "You can't hold a sword. You can't even keep water down. She didn't pull you off a cross so she could kill you."

"It doesn't matter anymore," the Iron Dog said. "If it weren't that, it would've been something else. Of the six cohorts, the Rippers are completely gone and the rest are at less than fifty percent of their capacity. Roland is purging the ranks. Anyone loyal to Hugh has been killed or run off, and the Legatus of the Golden Legion openly hunts people Roland exiles. If you're not going to kill me, what are you going to do with me?"

Curran looked at me. "He's yours. It's your call."

I sighed. "We'll take you to the Guild medic. The magic is up and our medmage is good. You have twenty-four hours to get on your feet. Don't be in the city when the sun rises tomorrow."

"I won't," he said.

"Good. Load him up." Curran rose and walked over to me. "Come talk to me."

I followed him down the road.

He dipped his head and looked at me. "What happened?"

"He crucified families, Curran. I could smell their rotting bodies. And then he had the audacity to tell me that this is what happens to people who disobey him. Disobey. Like I'm one of his flunkies who stare at him with adoration and throw themselves off a cliff because he frowned at them. I can't take it anymore. He sits there and taunts me. I have to protect my land."

"When did it become 'my land'?" he asked quietly. "It was 'the city' just a few months ago."

"It became my land when I claimed it. Nobody else wanted to step up and defend it from him."

"What about them?" He nodded slightly toward the mercs arranging Stoyan in a vehicle. "Did they not step up? Did I not step up?"

I wanted to hit him.

Full stop.

I took a deep breath and blew the air out.

Where did that come from? I loved him.

"Barabas is a friend," Curran said.

"And?"

"You seem to have forgotten that. I'm reminding you."

I didn't like the way he was looking at me. Like he was trying to figure out if there was something wrong with me.

"Roland's grooming Julie to become his next Warlord. She's still talking to him and there is nothing I can do to stop it."

"I'll speak to her," Curran said.

"It won't do any good. We both talked this into the ground. He's got his claws into her and I don't know how to pry her loose."

"We'll fight for her," he said. "To the very end. But she's her own person, Kate."

"She's a kid! He's thousands of years old!"

"She's sixteen and it's an old sixteen. She loves you and me. I'm not worried. He tried his shit on me, he tried it on you, and we're both still here. We didn't run off to join his crazy parade. Julie is our child. She bucks against authority. I don't think it's as bad as you think. But there will come a point when she'll make a decision you don't like and you'll be powerless to stop it."

But I wasn't powerless. I could order her and she wouldn't be able to refuse my command. And then I would become my father.

"I'm going to the office," I told him. I was done talking. I needed space and time to sort myself out.

"Okay," he said. "I'll drop by later, after I'm done at the Guild."

"If you want." Okay, I was being a total ass now. "I'd like to see you."

"As you wish," he said.

I DROVE TO the office in our Jeep, wishing I could punch something in the face to vent my frustration. Barabas was right. I'd lost my temper. Curran was right, too. Barabas was a friend and deserved better. The fact that they were right only made me madder.

Something happened there when Curran stood in front of me. Something that almost overrode my brakes. He challenged my authority, just like my father challenged my right to hold the land, and I had felt myself teetering on the precipice. The urge to enforce my will was so strong. Thinking about it made me uneasy.

This wasn't me. None of this was me.

I had a lot of energy I desperately needed to burn off. My whole body buzzed. I had packed a magical punch but never let it rip, and the unspent magic was driving me crazy.

I parked in front of Cutting Edge, walked to the office, and stuck my key into the lock. The key wouldn't turn. Being a trained detective, I deduced that the door was unlocked.

I didn't want to see anybody or talk to anybody. I wanted an hour by myself so I could have a lovely date with a heavy punching bag.

Standing here with the key in the lock was stupid, so I opened the door and walked in. Ascanio, our bouda intern, sat at his desk, holding cards. Roman occupied the chair across from him.

Oy.

The black volhv was wearing his trademark black robe with silver embroidery along the hem. His knotted six-foot-tall staff stood propped against the wall. The staff's top, carved into a monstrous bird head, remained wooden for now. I gave it the evil eye. It had the annoying habit of coming to life and trying to bite me.

"So three of a kind beats two pair?" Ascanio said.

"Yes."

"But that makes no sense. Two pair requires four cards, but three of a kind only requires three. That's harder to get."

"Statistically, the odds of getting two pair are higher than three cards of the same rank."

"You're wasting your time," I told him. "Ascanio has the worst poker face I've ever seen."

"I have a strategy," Ascanio announced.

"Aha."

"I'm going to play with women and distract them with my smolder." Ascanio unleashed a devastating smile. He was, without a doubt, the most beautiful seventeen-year-old kid I'd ever seen. He even beat out pre-injury Derek, although Derek always had a kind of boyish, disarming sincerity about him, while Ascanio knew exactly what he was doing. Which was why he needed to be taken down a notch.

"Let's see it."

"See what?" He blinked.

"The smolder."

Okay, I had to admit the smolder looked pretty good. "Needs improvement. Work more on seductive and less on constipated."

"I don't look constipated."

I glanced at Roman.

"Nah," the volhv said. "Constipated isn't your problem. You're too slick about it. Women sense when you're faking."

"What am I supposed to do about that?"

"Stop trying so hard." The black volhv pivoted to me. "I have questions."

"Can it wait?"

"No. Your wedding is in two weeks. Have you prepared your guest list?"

"Why do I need a list? I kind of figured that whoever wanted to show up would show up."

"You need a list so you know how many people you are feeding. Do you have a caterer?"

"No."

"But you did order the cake?"

"Umm . . ."

"Florist?"

"Florist?"

"The person who delivers expensive flowers and sets them up in pretty arrangements everyone ignores?"

"No."

Roman blinked. "I'm almost afraid to ask. Do you at least have the dress?"

"Yes."

"Is it white?"

"Yes."

He squinted at me. "Is it a wedding dress?"

"It's a white dress."

"Have you worn it before?"

"Maybe."

Ascanio snickered.

"The ring, Kate?"

Oh crap.

Roman heaved a sigh. "What do you think this is, a party where you get to show up, say 'I do,' and go home?"

"Yes?" That's kind of how it went in my head.

"You do realize most of the *Who's Who* in Atlanta are going to want an invite to this?"

"They can bite me. This wedding is for me and Curran, not for them."

Roman leaned his elbow on the table and rested his cheek on his hand, looking at me with a kind of amused hopelessness.

"What?"

"So I should tell my mother not to bother coming?"

Offending Evdokia and the Witch Covens of Atlanta wasn't on my agenda. I was on thin ice with them as it was.

"Your mother is invited."

"What about the Pack? The Beast Lord is Curran's best friend."

Grrr. "The Pack is invited, too."

"And Luther?"

"Luther?" What did Biohazard's self-appointed wizard at large have to do with it?

"I ran into him on the way here and happened to mention the wedding."

Aha. "You boasted that you would be officiating."

"Yes, I did, and I regret nothing. The entire Biohazard Department will be coming."

I squeezed my eyes shut and tried to count to ten in my head. Sometimes it helped. One . . . two . . .

"Also, your father."

My eyes snapped open. "What about my father?"

Roman blinked. "That was a bona fide snarl."

Ascanio nodded, his eyes wide. "Yes, she gets scary sometimes. She's very difficult to work for."

"I can imagine." Roman nodded at me. "Roland will be attending and he'll probably invite some people."

"By the time the wedding comes about, we may be at war. He won't be attending, take my word for it."

"Kate, you're a good person. But you're delusional. That's okay. You're getting married. You're supposed to be delusional, irrational, and crazy."

"Again, this wedding is for me and Curran. You're not turning it into a three-ring circus."

"No." Roman got up off his chair. "The wedding night is for you and Curran. The wedding is for everyone else and it's the price you pay so you can get to the wedding night. Don't worry. I'll take care of everything. Anyway, we have bigger problems. The Witch Oracle wants to see you."

"No." When the Witch Oracle had something to tell me, it was never anything good, like *You'll live long, grow fat, and be happy.* It was always, *The world is ending. Fix it!*

"My mother was very insistent." The good-natured

amusement slid off Roman's face, and his eyes turned grave. "Sienna foresaw something."

I bet she did. "I'm not going, Roman. I have my hands full here, and if something bad is about to happen, I don't want to know."

"It's about your son," he said.


"How far is this place?" I peered down the overgrown road. The Jeep roared and spat thunder, squeezing miles out of charged water. Usually when the Witch Oracle wanted to see me, I met them at Centennial Park, once the site of an Olympic Games celebration and now a dense but carefully managed wilderness in the center of Atlanta belonging to the Covens. Meeting them there also involved climbing into the mouth of a magical tortoise, which wasn't my favorite.

This time Roman said they were waiting for me at some place called Cochran Mill Park. According to Roman, it was less of a park and more of a forest now, and getting to it apparently required two hours of driving through hellish traffic and bad roads. We got stuck behind a camel for fifteen minutes because the damn thing came to a detour around a sinkhole and refused to walk on the wooden planks. Finally, the rider got off and pulled the reins, screaming and waving his arms, and the poor camel vomited all over the man's head. Served him right.

Now we drove on South Fulton Parkway, which had long ago given up all pretense of fighting off the encroachment of the magic woods. The maples, hickories, and poplars crowded the crumbling pavement, braiding their branches overhead, and driving down its length was like entering a tunnel of green, with the sun a hint of brighter green above.

"Why here?" I asked. "Why not at the tortoise?"

"The park is being watched," he said.

"By whom?"

Roman gave me a look.

Right. "Why would my father be interested in the Covens?"

"It's not the Covens. It's the Oracle. And especially you coming to see the Oracle. Turn off here."

I turned right onto a dirt road and the Jeep rolled and careened its way to a small parking lot. I parked and got out.

"We go on foot from here," Roman announced, and started down a narrow trail.

Around us the forest was filled with sound and light. Birds chirped, sang, and warbled, squirrels chittered, and foxes barked. A wolf howl soared to the sky, too distant to be a threat. A fat badger wobbled out into our path, looked at me with small eyes as if offended I dared to intrude into his domain, and took off, unhurried. This was a witch forest. It belonged to animals and those whose magic was attuned to nature. Normal humans didn't visit often and weren't welcome.

"Cheer up," Roman said. "The sun is shining and the air is clean. It's a nice day for a hike."

If only I could get my father and the crosses out of my head. I really hoped I didn't start a war this morning.

The trees parted, revealing a rocky basin of clear water, framed by huge boulders and cushioned with emerald-green trees. A sixty-foot wall of rock jutted above it. Atlanta didn't really have mountains, with the exception of Stone Mountain, which was basically a huge boulder that had somehow gone astray from its friends, the Appalachians. This place looked like it belonged in northwest Georgia.

I glanced at Roman.

"It used to be less impressive," he said. "During the next-to-last flare there was a magic explosion here. A mountain thrust out of the ground, and cracks traveled all the way up to Little Bear Creek, opening it up. Now it's Little Bear River." He pointed with his staff at the rocks. "We wait here."

We sat on the boulders. I watched the water. The pool was crystal clear and small waterfalls skipped down the rocks at its far end. So beautiful and serene. Roman was right. It was a good day for a hike.

Three women walked out of the woods to the right of us. Evdokia came first; plump, middle-aged, her brown hair reaching to her midback, she moved along the path to the water, her simple white tunic brushing at the leaves. Roman did resemble his mother. It didn't seem like it at first, with his mustache, beard, and the long horse mane of hair along his scalp, but there was a lot of Evdokia in him. It hid in the corners of his mouth when he smiled and shone from his eyes when he thought he said something funny. I'd met his father. He was a rail-thin, dour man. If Grigorii ever smiled, his face would crack and fall off his head.

Behind Evdokia, Sienna led Maria down the path. In the few years I'd known them, Maria had gone from a fierce ancient crone to simply ancient. She used to remind me of a raptor, gaunt, harsh, her claws poised for the kill. Now she emanated age the way very old trees did. The white tunic hung off her shoulders, the wide sleeves making her bony arms look fragile enough to snap with a squeeze of your fingers. Sienna, on the other hand, had changed for the better. No longer sickly, she moved smoothly now, her body lean but curved where it counted. Blond hair cascaded from her head in rich waves.

The three witches reached the water and I realized they were barefoot. They turned and followed the barely visible path toward the wall of rock.

"Come on." Roman rose.

We trailed the witches around the stone fall to a small fissure in the granite, barely wide enough for two people to pass through shoulder to shoulder. The witches went in one by one.

"After you." The volhv nodded at the opening.

Great. Come down to the witch forest, enter a deep dark cave. What could go wrong? Just once I would like to have an important meeting in a happy little meadow or an orchard.

I ducked through the opening and closed my eyes for a few moments to get them accustomed to the gloom. A small cave lay before me, almost perfectly round. A pool of water filled most of it, except for a narrow rim of dark boulders by the walls and a small wooden deck with some benches. Above us, the dome of the cave split and a waterfall cascaded into the pool, backlit by sunshine.

The older witches arranged themselves on the deck. I picked my way toward them, Roman behind me.

Sienna waded into the water. It came up to her hips and her white tunic floated around her.

She shivered and rubbed her arms. "Cold."

"You wanted to do this," Maria told her.

"I did." Sienna reached for a dark object floating in the water and pulled it to her. A wooden bucket. She dipped it into the water and poured it over her head. "Oh Goddess."

"Is the turtle sick?" I asked to needle them.

Maria gave me a look sharp enough to draw blood. "Hold your tongue, evil spawn."

*There's the old harpy I know. All is right with the world.*

"This is a sacred place now," Evdokia told me. "It's easier to summon the visions here."

"I've been looking into your future." Sienna moved toward the waterfall.

"I don't want to know." I didn't. Once you knew the visions, they chained you, forcing you down a predetermined path. It was best to make my own road.

"You do." Sienna turned to me, her back to the cascade.

I sighed.

"Tell her," Maria snapped.

"If you marry Curran Lennart, he will die."

Someone reached through my chest and stuck a long needle into my heart. Sienna was almost never wrong.

"Show me."

The young witch stepped backward into the waterfall. Magic moved around Sienna, like an engine turning over, and a light slowly appeared to the left of the waterfall, opening up like a fast-blooming flower. A battlefield. Bodies collided, some armored, some furry. Weapons clashed, arrows hit home with the shrill whistle of torn air, and magic boiled flesh. A din hung above the chaos, the kind of cacophony only a battlefield in the middle of a melee can produce: screams and wails, grunts, metal screeching against metal, shapeshifters snarling, inhuman shrieks, all blending into an overwhelming cry that was the voice of war. It hit me, visceral and raw, and suddenly I was there, in the heart of the chaos, gripping my sword and looking for a target. The air smelled of blood and smoke. Ashes swirled around the combatants.

Beyond it all a tower rose above a castle, the familiar half-finished structure I had seen this morning, now whole. A huge gray creature, half-man, half-beast, knocked vampire bodies aside as he charged toward it. Blood stained his fur. He didn't roar. He just ran, pushing his body to the limit.

Curran.

The tower loomed. My father stood atop it in a crimson robe, holding a spear made from his blood. My heart skipped a beat.

Curran leapt, channeling all of his speed into a powerful jump. He shot up, finally snarling, his fangs exposed, claws out.

My father thrust the spear. It was an expert thrust. It punched through Curran's chest.

Blood poured.

He didn't grip the spear. He didn't try to free himself. Why wasn't he trying to free himself? I'd seen him take wounds that almost cut him in half. Why wasn't he fighting?

Curran's body collapsed into human form but instead of its normal color, his skin turned the dull gray of duct tape.

Oh dear God. The Lyc-V saturating his body had died. All of it. At once.

My father gripped the spear and turned it. The perspective of the vision shifted and I was right there, standing next to Roland. Curran's face was slack, his eyes empty. The ground disappeared from under my feet and I fell down into a cold pit. I fell and fell and couldn't stop. Dead. He was *dead*.

My father grunted and hurled Curran's body back into the battle below. Past the field, the sunset was blood-red. Atlanta was burning, caught in the hot maw of an inferno. Black oily smoke boiled from the ruins of the city, melding into a funeral shroud above.

The vision ended, the other reality with the battle and Curran's corpse tearing like a thin paper screen, and I

landed in my own body back in the cave. My legs were wet.
I was standing in the middle of the pool, holding Sarrat in
my hand. Coils of pale vapor rose from the blade, reacting
to the echoes of my grief.

My face was burning. My mouth tasted bitter.

I returned my saber to its sheath on my back, dipped my
hands into the cold water, and let it cool my skin.

Nobody said a word.

I finally made my lips move. "Is it always a spear?"
Spears could be broken.

"Sometimes it's a sword," Sienna said. "Sometimes an
arrow. Roland is always the origin of it and Curran always
dies."

Damn it.

"What if I don't marry him?"

"It's worse," Sienna said.

"How do you know?"

"Because I've looked into your future over fifty times in
the last month. I think that sometimes you waver, because
you aren't sure if you should marry him. The vision changes
then. Do you want to see or do you want me to tell you?"

I braced myself. "Show me."

She stepped back into the waterfall. The battle splayed
out before me again, the blood and smoke, swirling around
me. I spun around. Behind me Atlanta burned.

A cry made me turn.

My father stood in the same spot atop the tower. In front
of him, on the wall, a creature knelt, swathed in rags. It held
a baby up with clawed hands.

*I had to get to the tower.*

I ran like I'd never run before in my whole life. The air
turned to fire in my lungs. Bodies bounced off me. My
magic flared behind me, glowing.

My father held out his hand, his face twisted with grief.
The older warrior who had knelt before me in the courtyard
this morning handed him the blood spear.

No!

I was almost to the tower.

My father gritted his teeth, his face supernaturally clear before me. Tears welled in his eyes. He plunged the spear down. A baby screamed, his cry severing my soul. My father pulled the weapon up, raising it like a flag.

My baby boy jerked, impaled on the spear. His pain cut me like a knife and kept cutting and cutting, carving pieces off my soul. He was crying for me, reaching with his little arms, and I could do nothing.

His little heart beat one last time and stopped.

Heat exploded in me. My heart burst.

Water. Cold soothing water. I dived this time, trying to dilute some of the heat emanating from my skin. I stayed under until all of the air in my lungs was gone. When I surfaced, the cave was silent.

I waded to the rocky shoulder and dragged myself out onto one of the large dark boulders. Sienna stepped out of the waterfall, her hair plastered to her head, her face pale; she made her way to the other side of the cave and collapsed on her back.

"Are you okay?" Roman asked.

"She watched her child die," Evdokia said. "Let her rest."

Rest was a luxury I couldn't afford. "Is there are any version of this that doesn't end with Atlanta burning and my son or Curran dying?"

"No," Sienna said. "I'm so sorry."

"How long have you been seeing this?"

"Over the past month."

"Why didn't you tell me?"

Sienna sighed. "I hoped I was wrong."

"Could you be wrong?" Roman asked. "These are only possibilities, not certainties."

"Predicting the future is like looking into the narrow end of a funnel," Sienna said. "The further in the future the events are, the more possibilities you see. The closer we get to the event itself, the clearer and more specific the most likely future becomes. These visions are too detailed. They are almost a certainty. As of now, one or the other will come to pass. The son or the father gives his life, Atlanta burns, and the rest of us suffer. I can't see any other possibilities. Believe me, I tried."

She turned her head and looked at me. "I tried, Kate. If Atlanta burns in that battle, I die."

"We all die," Evdokia said. "Everyone in this cave, except Kate."

"I can't see you in this battle," Sienna said. "It's hidden from me."

If she was seeing it in that much detail, these visions had to come from the very near future. "How long do we have?"

"A year at the longest if you don't marry Curran," Sienna said.

That meant sentencing our son to death. "And if I do?"

"Two weeks."

*Two weeks? What do I do? How do I fix this?*

"You're the wild card," Evdokia said. "She can't see you."

"It means one of two things," Sienna said. "Either you are irrelevant to what happens or you are the pin on which this future hinges. If it's the latter, then you have the power to alter it."

If only I knew how.

"This is just typical." Roman raised his eyes upward. "The one time I try to do something good, like join two people who are long overdue in holy matrimony. The one time! And it all goes to hell, doomsday prophecies and death. I've served you for ten years. Would it kill you to have my back one damn time?"

"Yes, of course, make it all about you." Evdokia sighed.

"Wait, you're marrying them?" Sienna asked.

Maria chortled. "He'll anoint them in blood. Should've asked Vasiliy."

Evdokia turned to her. "There is nothing wrong with my son marrying them. It will be the best wedding and he will be the best priest."

Maria opened her mouth.

"You better be careful what you say next," Evdokia said.

I raised my voice. "This isn't helping."

"You have to defeat him," Sienna said.

Nice how she avoided the word "kill."

An odd anxiety claimed me. I didn't want to kill my father.

It made no sense. He was a monster and a tyrant. If it was a choice between my life and his, he would take mine. I'd wanted to hurt him this morning. But he was my father. What the hell was wrong with me?

Thinking about it was too complicated so I shoved it aside. There would be time to puzzle over this later.

"Have you made any progress with the ifrit's box?" Evdokia asked. "You've been talking to Bahir and his people. Did you learn anything?"

"I can't figure out how it works. I talked to some very smart, educated people about it. They can't figure out how it works either. We don't have the box itself anymore, so we can't examine it. All we have are the incantations, which are a variant of a typical ward, infused with divine power. I don't know where to go from here."

"None of us have as much power over the future as you," Sienna said.

"She means you have to do something," Maria snapped.

"Do what?" I looked at her. She had been powerful for too long to flinch, but a hint of uncertainty showed in her eyes. "Well? I'm waiting for your wisdom."

"Do anything," the crone said. "We gave you this city—"

"No. I took the city. I took it by myself and I protected it from my father's claiming. You didn't help. You weren't there."

Maria's eyes blazed. "Remember who you're talking to!"

*"You should take your own advice."*

The cave fell completely silent. The witches stared at me. Sienna rubbed her throat, as if something was choking off her air.

The storm I'd had to contain this morning simmered under my skin. My father would kill Curran or our son. There was nothing I could do to stop him.

The magic inside me boiled. I had to vent or it would tear me apart. I looked up to the patch of light and sky above me and let it go.

The magic burst from me, surging upward, into the sky. The water of the basin rose in the air, stretching into a thousand glittering strands, revealing the rocky bottom of the pool. Power and fury poured out of me, flowing like a raging river.

The pressure eased. I shut off the current. The water crashed back into the basin.

"Oh, Katenka," Evdokia whispered.

Maria made a small choking noise. Sienna scrambled over to her. "Roman, help me. She needs some fresh air."

Together they lifted the old witch off her seat and led her outside.

"I saw my father this morning," I told Evdokia. The sky above me was so blue. If only I could sprout wings and fly far away from all my problems. "He kidnapped Saiman. He's refusing to release him and I can't ignore it. There will be war. I've signed my husband's and my child's death warrants."

Evdokia looked at me, her face at once sad and kind. "No. You didn't. We foresaw this days ago. One way or the other, it would've come to pass."

I came and sat by her. She reached out and stroked my hair. It felt so familiar. She must've done it when I was little, before Voron took me away.

"Help me." My voice came out quiet and ragged.

"Anything in my power," she promised. "All my magic is yours. I wish I knew what to do."

Sienna came back into the cave and sat by me.

"Why haven't the three of you left?" I asked.

"Because this is our city," Evdokia said. "Our home. We can't all leave, Katenka. The future will find us."

"Roman is right," Sienna said. "The future is fluid. But when it's this close and this certain, you have to do something really big to change it. Something that will alter everything. Something nobody would expect."

"I don't have any Rubicons to cross," I told her.

"Find one," Sienna said. "If anybody can do it, you can."

≡ CHAPTER ≡

# 4

THE MAGIC WAVE ended on our way back to the city and technology once again reasserted itself. When we got back to the office, it was early afternoon and nobody was there. Ascanio must have bailed early. My mammoth donkey was also MIA, probably back at our home, in the stables. I dropped Roman off, went into the office, and pulled a legal pad to me. I always thought better with a pen in hand.

I wrote *Choices* on the piece of paper and stared at it.

1. *Fight my father now, before he expects a direct assault.*
2. *Wait until my father attacks.*
3. *Play ball.*

Choice number one was right out. I still had no idea how to defeat my father. I'd felt his power this morning and, while I could hold my own, if he gave it his all, he would crush me. Also, I had no army. I could ask the Pack and the Witches for help, but they would expect some sort of strategy besides "let's all run at Roland's castle and get killed."

Choice number two wasn't much better. In theory, I was supposed to be able to protect Atlanta after claiming it. In practice, I had no idea how. When I reached for the magic of the land, it was like a placid ocean. Within its depths, life moved and shimmered. The waters were capable of storms, but I had no idea how to start one.

Choice number three was what my father wanted. That alone should've been enough to stop me. Except when I closed my eyes, I saw two lifeless bodies. If I went to him now, if I left Curran, he would survive. My father couldn't kill my child if the child didn't exist.

I loved them both. I loved my unborn future baby. I loved Curran, his eyes, his laugh, his smile. I woke up next to him, I ate breakfast with him, we went to work together, and we came home together. That was the core of who I was: Curran, Julie, Derek, even Grendel, the family I'd made. It was my life, the one I fought for, the one I built and wanted. We were together. That was how things were.

If I went to serve my father, I would save them, at least for a little while. But I was only good at one thing: killing. Sooner or later my father would use me in that capacity and then I would be taking someone else's Curran or Kate away from them. Because people would oppose my father, the kind of people who were bothered by crosses with human beings dying on them, and I would have to kill them.

I couldn't do it. I'd been Voron's attack dog for the first fifteen years of my life. I wouldn't be one again.

I crossed the list out and started over.

*New Plan*

1. *Get Awesome Cosmic Powers.*
2. *Nuke my dad.*
3. *Retire from the land-claiming business.*

I was so down with this plan. If only I had some way to implement it.

Maybe someone would bring me a magic scroll, an

incantation that would magically imprison my father in some cave. I would totally be willing to help old ladies carry wood, spin straw into gold, or go on a quest for that kind of scroll.

I stared at the door. *Come on, magic scroll.*

*Come on.*

Nope.

I needed to get out of the office and go home. I would feel better at home.

I would get home, work out, cook a big dinner because I felt like it, and figure out what I had to do about Saiman and my father.

WHEN I PULLED up to the house, Christopher was sitting in the driveway on the grass. That's right. The meditation.

Living under Barabas's care agreed with Christopher. Left to his own devices in the Keep, he often forgot about food and after a couple of weeks of self-imposed starvation, he'd look like a stiff wind would make him keel over, until Barabas or I would notice and make him eat. Now that he was staying in the house next to us, Barabas had assumed responsibility for Christopher's health, and the were-mongoose could be extremely single-minded.

I did my best to help. Between the two of us, Christopher ate on time, bathed every day, went with Barabas to the Guild, where he got regular exercise, and wore clean clothes. He was still thin, but his skin had a good color to it, and despite his pale, nearly colorless hair, he no longer looked like a ghost.

The only thing we couldn't heal was his mind. All the outside pressures were gone now. Christopher was safe, sheltered, fed, and among friends, but his mental health hadn't improved. We had taken him to Emory University School of Medicine, to Duke University, and even to Johns Hopkins, which was a trip I was doing my best to forget. We almost died, and while we were away, a local family we knew was murdered. Julie and Derek had handled it, but thinking about it still turned my stomach.

The doctors were in consensus: physically Christopher was fine. Psychologically he didn't match any specific disorder. Christopher always claimed that my father had shattered his mind. The people at Emory and Duke had agreed that someone had magically destroyed his psyche. The psychiatrist at Johns Hopkins was an exceptional empath, with the power to feel what others felt. After he spoke to Christopher, he said the trauma to his psyche was self-inflicted. Something bad had happened to Christopher. He refused to confront it, he didn't want to remember it, and so he deliberately remained as he was. Christopher offered no feedback. He sat quietly and smiled sadly through it all. He held the key to his own healing and there wasn't much any of us could do to get him to turn it.

I got out of the car. Christopher looked at me from his spot in the grass among the yellow dandelions and wild daisies. Since most of our annoying neighbors had moved away and taken the budding homeowners' association with them, Curran mowed the grass when he felt like it, and he didn't feel like killing the dandelions.

"Meditation?" Christopher asked.

"Not today," I told him. The last place I wanted to be was in my own head. "I'm sorry."

"That's okay."

To ask about the book or not to ask? If I asked him and he freaked out, I'd kick myself. Better talk to Barabas first.

"Where is Maggie?"

Christopher pulled out a canvas bag from behind him. A black furry head poked out and looked at me with the saddest brown eyes ever to belong to a dog. Maggie was an eight-pound creature that was probably part long-haired Chihuahua and part something very different. She was small and odd, and her black fur stuck out in wispy strands in strange places. She walked gingerly, always slightly awkward, and if she thought she was in trouble, she'd lift one of her paws and limp, pretending to be injured. Her greatest ambition in life was to lie on someone's lap, preferably under a blanket.

After Johns Hopkins, Barabas told me he wasn't giving up. I told him I wasn't either. I came up with daily meditation. Barabas came up with Maggie.

The little dog looked at me, turned, and crawled back into the bag. Right.

"Have you seen Curran or Julie?"

Christopher shook his head.

A Pack Jeep turned onto our street and slid to a stop in front of our house. The window rolled down and Andrea stuck her blond head out. "I'm free! Free!"

Oh boy. "Aren't you supposed to be in the Keep?" I could've sworn Raphael told me during the Conclave that Doolittle had confined her to the medward.

"Screw that. We're going to lunch."

"It's almost dinnertime."

"Then we're going to dinch. Or lunner. Or whatever the hell early-dinner-late-lunch stupid combo we can come up with."

"Now isn't . . ."

Andrea's eyes blazed. "Kate, I'm nine months pregnant and I'm hungry. Get in the damn car."

I got in the Jeep, and Andrea peeled out like a bat out of hell.

"We're going to Parthenon. We're going to have gyros." Her stomach was out so far, she must've moved the seat back, because she had to stretch to reach the wheel.

"The look of grim determination on your face is scary," I told her.

"I've been cooped up in the Keep's infirmary for the past two weeks," Andrea said.

"Why?"

She waved her hand. "Because Doolittle is a worrywart."

Crap. "Andrea, does Doolittle know where you are?"

"Yes."

"You sure about that?"

"Absolutely. I've let him know. Anyway, we are going to lunch!"

"Andr—"

"To lunch!" She flashed her teeth at me.

I shut up and let her drive.

Twenty minutes later she parked in front of Parthenon, and then I watched her try to get out of the Jeep. She scooted back into her seat as far as she could, then slowly edged out one leg, then half of her butt, then half her stomach. Andrea was short and the Jeep sat really high. Her foot was dangling down. I would offer to help, but she was armed at all times and could shoot the dots out of dominoes, and I didn't want to get murdered.

"Are you going to help me or not?" she growled.

I grabbed her arm and steadied her as she stepped out. "I thought you might shoot me."

"Ha-ha. Hilarious." She opened her eyes really wide. A ruby sheen rolled over her irises. "I smell food."

Uh-oh. "We are going to get food. Right now."

We burst through the doors of Parthenon like Greeks through the open gates of Troy. Five minutes later we were seated at our usual table in the garden section despite two flights of stairs, which Andrea insisted on climbing, and the heat of late afternoon. The owners had finally gotten rid of the chairs that were bolted to the floor, and I sat so I could watch the door and the two women on the right, who were the only other diners willing to brave the garden section in the heat. We ordered a heaping platter of meat, a pint of tzatziki sauce, and a bucket of fried okra, because Andrea really wanted it, and waited for our food.

She drank her iced tea and sighed.

"How's it going?"

She looked at me. "Is this a serious question? Are you really asking or just making conversation?"

"When have I ever just made conversation?"

"Okay." Andrea sipped some tea. "Well, I'm mean, too harsh, and I rule the clan like an iron-fisted bitch."

"Aha." I had no idea how anyone could lead the bouda clan. They were all nuts.

"Last Tuesday Lora, Karen, Thomas, and the new kid,

Kyle, were coming home from a bar where they tried to get drunk."

Getting drunk for a shapeshifter was a losing proposition. Their metabolism treated alcohol as poison, which it was, and purged it as fast as it entered the bloodstream. Curran had to guzzle an entire bottle of vodka to get a buzz for fifteen minutes, and since he hated the taste, he stuck to beer instead.

"So the way back took these four geniuses by the College of Mages."

Oh boy.

"The College of Mages happens to own a polar bear."

Better and better. "How did they get a polar bear?"

"Apparently it wandered out of the woods near Macon and it was glowing at the time, and some mages happened to be on a field trip, so they apprehended the polar bear and brought him back to the college to figure out what his deal is. They built him a very nice enclosure."

"Okay." Typical post-Shift thing.

"The ladies wanted to see the polar bear and the two guys didn't have the balls to say no, so they broke into the climate-controlled enclosure and then Lora decided to pet the bear, because it 'liked her.'"

Our gyros arrived. She picked up her first one, bit off a small piece, and chewed with obvious pleasure. "Where was I?"

"Adventurous bear petting."

"Yeah, well, the bear petted her back."

I laughed in spite of myself.

"I can't blame the bear." Andrea opened her eyes wide. "If some whiskey-soaked hyena-smelling human came toward me while I was trying to nap in my nice house, I'd pet it too. With my claws."

"Did the bear survive?"

"He survived. He was roughed up, the four of them bled all over the place trying to get the bear off Lora without hurting him, and of course, they got busted. They all got three weeks of Keep labor and that was too harsh and too mean. Never mind that I've got the College of Mages breathing down my neck about their bear being emotionally compromised and the Atlanta PAD wanting to file trespassing charges, but oh no, I was too harsh." She stopped eating for a second. "Do you know what one of them told me? He said that Aunt B would've never been that hard on them. Aunt B! Can you believe that shit?"

"She would've pulled their legs out." Aunt B hadn't played around.

"Who is this kinder, gentler Aunt B that they remember? I was her beta. I know exactly what kind of punishment that woman doled out. Other than that, I'm the size of a house, I can't even take a decent bite of my food or it will hurt, this kid is kicking me in the kidneys like a champ, and everyone else treats me like I'm made of glass." She looked at me for a moment. "And every waking moment I'm terrified that my baby will go loup at birth, and when I'm asleep, I have nightmares about it."

Both of Raphael's brothers went loup. "You've been taking the panacea."

"I know," she said.

"You're also beastkin. Your form is very steady. You aren't usually in danger of going loup even when you are badly hurt."

"I know." She sighed. "I know, I know, I know. I just want it all to be okay. I want to give birth to my healthy baby and be happy."

So did I.

"Your turn." Andrea pointed her second gyro at me. "How's it going? Not making conversation."

I opened my mouth. Nothing came out. There was so much.

Andrea stopped eating. "What is it?"

I struggled with it.

"Kate, is it the wedding? If you don't want to marry that jackass, you don't have to marry him. Say the word, and the clan will come and get you and Julie. He might be a lion, but I have the whole hyena clan."

"It's complicated."

She put her gyro down. "I'm listening."

Her tone told me there would be no getting out of it.

So I told her about my dad and the crosses, the slap, the urge to crush him, snapping at Barabas, the witches, and watching Curran and my son die.

Andrea sat still for a long moment. "Well, that fucking sucks."

"Yeah."

"Can you kill Roland?"

"I'm not sure I want to." And that came right out.

"Of course you don't want to. He's your father."

I stared at her. She rubbed her stomach and grimaced. "The kid won't settle down."

"How can I not want to kill him? He's evil, Andrea. He won't stop until he grinds everyone under his boot. A city, a state, a country won't be enough. He'll keep going until his empire spans the whole planet. He tortures people. He's been talking to Julie behind my back, trying to subvert her. Why am I having doubts? What is wrong with me?"

"He's your father. He made you, Kate. He's your link to your family, the only link you have. And he loves you in his own twisted way. I saw the way he looked at you when you claimed the city. He was practically bursting with pride. If you manage to stab him in the heart, he'll be proud of you with his dying breath. Of course, you're having doubts. You wouldn't be human if you weren't."

"You're not helping."

"Did you expect me to sugarcoat it? I'm your best friend. I'm in the business of telling it like it is. He's a horrible monster, but he loves you and he's trying to be a decent dad. It's just that normal people's decent and his decent aren't on the same planet. Can you even kill him? I mean, do you know how and are you able to physically do it?"

"No and probably not." Judging by the storm today, I had a long way to go. "I'm not even sure I can use power words against him. They are the best I've got, and the last time I used one against something with magic similar to Roland, my brain nearly exploded."

"Crap." She rubbed her stomach again. "Don't get frustrated. There is always a way. What about the ifrit's box? Can you trap or banish him with something similar?"

"Again, I don't know how. I tried to figure out how the box works, but it's too complicated and it operates on divine power. It took a lifetime of faith. Even Luther struck out with it. We don't understand enough about how it was made and we no longer have it."

"Okay, who can you ask besides Luther?"

"I've asked everybody." I threw my napkin onto the table. "There are no answers out there, Andrea. I've looked through all the books, I've done all the research, and I don't have any way to contain him."

"You're letting him get to you. You're like a walking mythological encyclopedia, Kate. You pull random mystical crap out of your head and figure out that a giant monster nobody has seen on the face of the planet for three thousand years is allergic to hedgehogs and then you find a cute hedgehog and stab the monster in the eye with it."

"Where do you even get this shit?"

"I'm giving you a theoretical example. There has to be something, some talisman, some spell, some creature, something that he has a weakness to."

"I'm his weakness. He hid those thirty crosses from me, because he wanted to be a good father and he didn't want me to get upset. He isn't killing me in the visions. He's killing my husband and my child!"

Two women at the far table glared at me. I looked back at them and they decided to glare somewhere else.

"The only person who was close enough and who could have known about his weakness is Erra, and I killed her. I'd ask my grandmother, but she's too far gone—she's an elemental presence, not a person. She doesn't answer questions. She . . . feels."

"Too bad you didn't ask your aunt more questions before you killed her . . ."

Andrea flinched and tensed.

"What is it?"

"We need to go to the Keep."

"Why?"

Panic shivered in her eyes. "The baby is coming."

"Now?"

"Yes, right now!"

Shit. I threw money on the table. "Can you make it down the stairs?"

She growled. "I'm a fucking former knight of the Order. Go get the car."

I sprinted out of the building to the car. The magic was down and the gasoline engine purred as soon as I turned the key. I roared out of the parking lot and screeched to a stop before the building. Andrea stumbled out. I jumped out, threw the back door open, and stuffed her into the backseat.

"I can get us to Memorial in twenty minutes. Hold on."

"No! We have to get back to the Keep. This is a high-risk pregnancy. Doolittle thinks I might die in labor."

Damn it all to hell and back. I ran around the car, landed in the driver's seat, buckled up, and floored it. "How is it that Doolittle let you out?"

"He didn't. I escaped."

"What? You told me he knew where you were."

"He did. I left him . . . a note . . . It's more like he knew where I wasn't . . . Argh, hurts like a sonovabitch."

"After you deliver this baby, I'm going to kill you. What the hell were you thinking?"

"I was thinking I'd been in the damn infirmary for two weeks and if I didn't get out, I'd bash my head against the wall. You don't understand. Physically I'm fine. It's only the labor that might be the problem. All I did was sit in there and think about my baby going loup. I had to get out."

"You hold on to that baby." I rocketed down the street like a bat out of hell, bouncing on every pimple in the pavement. "I don't know anything about delivering babies."

"I don't want you to deliver my baby. I want you to drive! Please drive."

She was breathing like a marathon runner. I glanced into the rearview mirror. Sweat drenched her face.

I drove like all the hounds of hell were chasing me.


THE KEEP WAS an hour away on a good day. I made it in forty minutes.

"Almost there."

"I can't hold on any longer." She was soaked in sweat. Her skin had gone sallow.

I barreled on down the narrow road, right past a Pack sentry. The gates to the courtyard stood wide open, showing the yard filled with shapeshifters, and I drove right into it. People dashed away from the speeding car, parting like waves . . . except one. Jim blocked my way. His eyes told me he wasn't moving.

I slammed on the brakes.

*Do not kill the Beast Lord, do not kill the Beast Lord . . .*

The car slid forward and stopped a mere foot from Jim. He yanked the driver's door open. "What the hell . . ."

"She's going into labor!"

He saw Andrea and roared, "Clear the way to the medward!"

Raphael shot out of the tower gates, scooped his wife out of the backseat, and ran into the tower.

"We've been looking for her for the last hour. Doolittle got so pissed off, he couldn't even talk. He just made animal noises. What were you thinking, taking a pregnant woman on bed rest out for a stroll?" Jim's eyes blazed.

*Typical. It's all my fault.* "She picked *me* up."

"Then you should've driven her right back to the Keep."

"Me and what army? I'd like to see you try to take the keys from her."

Ahead Andrea screamed.

I jumped out of the car and chased after Raphael.


WAITING WAS THE hardest part. They took Andrea into the medward, behind two sets of soundproof doors that muffled her screams. Raphael went in with her and when he'd carried her through the doors, I glimpsed Doolittle in his wheelchair and Nasrin, his second-in-command, attended by three nurses and a burly shapeshifter who looked like he could crush cement blocks into powder with his bare hands. I had to stay in the waiting area, a spacious room with an abundance of big pillows and soft couches.

A few minutes after I settled down, a man and a woman came in and took the spot by the door, opposite me. Pearce Bailey and Jezebel. The two renders, both from the bouda clan.

Pearce was compact, dark-skinned, with calculating eyes and a serious expression on his face. I didn't know much about him except for the fact that Aunt B had trusted him completely.

Jezebel, on other hand, I knew very well. A few weeks before I became Curran's Consort, Jezebel had challenged her sister Salome for her position in the bouda clan. According to Pack law, challenges were always to the death. Jezebel lost. She was clinically dead for several minutes, but somehow her body bounced back to life, and Salome couldn't bear to kill her again. This left Jezebel outside Clan Bouda's structure, so when I ended up in the Keep, alone, with Curran in a coma and facing challenger after challenger, Aunt B assigned Jezebel and Barabas to me to watch my back and help me navigate the murky waters of Pack politics. For almost two years Jezebel was my constant backup. As long as she was there, nobody would stab me in the back.

She was also about the only person Julie would listen to. Jezebel had watched over Julie for the duration of my time as Consort. I didn't know about every scrape Julie got into, but occasionally things would happen and Jezebel would handle it. My kid always came home alive and Jezebel always kept Julie's secrets.

After Curran and I separated from the Pack, I thought Jezebel would come with us, but she chose to remain with the Pack instead. She had been trained as a render before becoming my backup and Julie's guard, and she went back to it. Last I heard she had found a nice guy and adopted his little daughter.

"Hi, Jezebel."

"Hello, Alpha."

"Not an alpha anymore."

"You will always be my alpha. How's Julie?"

"She's doing well in school. She made friends. She had a sleepover the other night while the tech was up with two of her girlfriends. They watched a funny movie."

"Is she still struggling with math?"

"She got an A in geometry and a C in algebra. Apparently, algebra is boring."

"I'm glad she hasn't changed." Jezebel flashed her teeth in a quick smile.

"How are you?" I asked.

"I'm good. Can't complain. I'm glad to see you."

"I'm glad to see you too, Jezebel."

Jezebel's face settled back into a neutral expression. It was all business today and I was no longer in her direct chain of command.

The renders were the Pack's elite soldiers, as close to a biological weapon of mass destruction as you could get. They were strong, fast, and precise, and if Andrea or Raphael went nuts because their baby was born loup, the two renders would do whatever they had to do to neutralize them.

Both Pearce and Jezebel were watching me carefully. They assessed me as a potential threat. They weren't entirely wrong. If Andrea busted out of that door, carrying her child and trying to escape, I wasn't sure what I would do. I would probably help her. It would be wrong and would make things harder on everyone, but in that moment she would be my friend running for her life and I would do what I had to do to keep her safe. The renders would present a formidable obstacle: Pearce was bad news from what little I could remember of him, and Jezebel would prove a problem. I had seen her take people down, and once she got her hands on them, they didn't get back up.

I could see Jim's hand all over this. Julie owed Jezebel

her life for at least one incident. Jim handpicked Jezebel for this guard duty because he knew both Andrea and I would be reluctant to hurt her.

I would still fight them.

That was why I made a piss-poor Consort. Following the laws, even fair ones, was never my strongest suit.

Pearce rose and walked away. Jezebel and I kept eye contact, smiling at each other. The male render returned and sat back on the couch. Nobody said anything. I got up, took a paperback from a basket Doolittle kept by the door, and began reading.

We sat quietly for another half hour. Andrea would be fine. She would be completely fine. Her baby would be fine, too. I had gotten to the part where the diabolical serial killer had killed the heroine's dog and burned down her apartment when the two renders sat a little straighter in their seats. I glanced at the door. Curran came in, making no sound as he moved. He sat next to me, picked up my hand, and squeezed it.

"Are you okay?"

*No.* "Yes."

He kept his fingers wrapped around mine. Yeah, he wasn't buying it. That's the trouble with sharing your life with someone. They know when you bullshit.

The two renders relaxed.

"Called in the cavalry?" I asked them.

"Just being proactive," Pearce said.

Jezebel gave me an apologetic look.

"Andrea and Raphael are members of the Pack," Curran said. "The law is clear, and they know exactly what to do. You aren't a member of the Pack and you're the former Consort. It's confusing, and renders don't like confusing."

"No, my lord," Jezebel said. "We don't."

"Not your lord anymore." Curran smiled at her.

"How did it go at the Guild?" I asked.

"It went fine. Had some minor annoying things to take care of. Anyway, Ascanio said you went to see the witches."

My whole body tried to squeeze itself into a fist. "Later."

Curran studied me. "Okay. Later."

"Andrea's been taking panacea," I said.

"Yes."

"She will be fine."

He nodded. "Yes."

"Her baby won't go loup." I was talking to myself now.

"It will be okay, baby."

The double doors clanged open. The renders and I jumped to our feet. Curran wrapped his arms around me, pinning my back to his chest. Nasrin appeared in the doorway, her face tired.

I forgot how to breathe.

"Come on." Nasrin stepped aside, letting us through.

We followed her through the doors. My heart was beating too fast. Andrea half lay, half sat on the bed, propped up on pillows, her blond hair damp, looking like she'd sprinted all the way to Florida and back. Raphael stood next to her with his back to us. Doolittle slumped in his wheelchair, exhausted. The rest of the people must've left through the side door.

Where was the baby?

Raphael turned. A small bundle of blankets rested in his arms. He moved one of the folds aside, revealing a tiny red squished face and a shock of dark hair.

"Beatrice Kate Medrano," he said. "Named after her grandmother and you."

"Me?"

"You. If it weren't for you, we wouldn't have met," he said.

Andrea opened her eyes and smiled. "We're going to call her Baby B."

"No trace of loupism," Nasrin said behind us.

"Here." Raphael handed me the baby.

Aaa!

"It's okay." Andrea chuckled. "She isn't made of glass."

I very carefully took the baby. She was so tiny. So light. Her little hands were curled into fists. There was nothing and now there was a life. A little tiny helpless life.

I stood perfectly still and watched her breathe. She was full of light. It seemed to stream from her little plump cheeks and her dark eyelashes, suffusing her whole body. Her fingers were so tiny.

"Someone take my baby before Kate faints," Andrea said.

I realized I'd been holding my breath.

Curran gently took her out of my hands, held her for a long moment, and passed her to Raphael. Raphael sat on the bed next to Andrea and murmured something I couldn't quite catch. Andrea's eyes shone. Such a happy, content light. She looked completely at peace.

In four weeks Atlanta would burn.

Curran's hand rested on my shoulder.

Atlanta would burn, and Baby B's world would change. She wouldn't know it, because she was a tiny baby. But my father would reach out and strangle her future.

I didn't want her to die before she had a chance to grow up. I didn't want her to be enslaved. I didn't want her to go to sleep in our world and wake up in my father's and then grow up thinking that was the way things were supposed to be.

"Kate?" Curran said. "Baby?"

The magic seethed under my skin. "I need some air."

I turned and walked away, down the hallway. My legs carried me outside, onto the top of a short stone tower. Sunshine hit me. I inhaled, breathing deeply, feeling my lungs expand.

I had to stop this from coming. I had to.

"Hey." Curran blocked the daylight.

"Hey."

"Looking grim, ass kicker. Rough day?"

"I've had worse."

"Are you going to tell me what the witches said or do I have to ask our minister?"

He'd put two and two together.

"In about a month there will be a battle," I said. "Atlanta will burn. If we marry, you die. Roland kills you. I watched it happen."

I didn't want to tell him about our son. Not yet. When we talked about the future, he always talked about children. His father died protecting him, and Curran would do the same for our son. I had to shield him from knowing our baby might not have a chance. It was enough I knew. Telling him about it changed nothing at this point, except to pile more weight on him.

He shrugged. "I don't care. I'm not going to live my life according to someone else's vision. Your father can't dictate it. The witches can't dictate it. The only question that matters is do you want to marry me?"

"Yes."

"Then we get married. Fuck them." He put his arm around me and squeezed me to him. "If I'm going to die, I'd rather die married to you. But more important, what makes you think I'll roll over?"

"I didn't say you would. I have no plans to roll over. I want to win, but I don't know how."

I looked past the Keep's courtyard and the clear stretch of cut grass between the walls, to where the woods met the horizon. Somewhere out there my father was adding the tower to his castle. I had no doubt of it. The vision showed it complete. I would pull it down.

"We win the old-fashioned way," he said. "We outthink him and we fight. We'll do what we always do."

It wouldn't be enough, but if I said that, he'd tell me we wouldn't find out until we tried. That's what I would've said back to him.

"It could be worse," he said.

"How?"

"We could be fighting him and your aunt."

My memory served up Erra dying on the snow.

"She talked to me before she died."

"What did she say?"

"She said, 'Live long, child. Live long enough to see everyone you love die. Suffer the way I did.'"

In that moment on the snow, exhausted and bleeding, all

I cared about was killing her and making sure Curran and I survived. Now I finally got it.

"She didn't want to go through all this again." I glanced at the woods in front of us. "The land, my father's mind games, killing people . . . I think she decided she was done and the only way it would be over was if she died or he did. She let me kill her."

And I was a lot like my aunt. More than I cared to admit. Neither of us was well suited for diplomacy. The only reason I had lasted this long was because both Curran and Barabas pulled me back from the edge whenever I tried to charge it. My father had to have realized that left to my own devices, I'd snap and attack him.

"Your aunt fought plenty," Curran said. "Besides, Roland was the one who told you that. I don't trust his bullshit."

"Well, it bit him in the ass. I told him that even his own sister didn't want to live in the world he made."

Curran laughed.

"What?"

"You always know how to get under someone's skin."

"What's that supposed to mean?"

"It's your superpower. Trust me, I know."

He looked at me and laughed harder.

"What?"

"I love when you bare your teeth at me. All the shape-shifter living has been rubbing off on you. You'd make such a cute shapeshifter."

"I will fucking throw you off this tower."

"You and what army?" He spread his arms. "Give it all you've got, baby."

I thought about it and shook my head.

The smile vanished from his face. "Okay, now I am worried."

*Live long enough to see everyone you love die.*

She must've loved someone. She must've mourned him. She talked about her sons and having to kill them when they turned into homicidal psychopaths . . .

It hit me like a freight train. Wow.

This was a very stupid idea. An idiotic, stupid, suicidal idea.

*Find a Rubicon to cross. I'll show you a Rubicon.* This wasn't just crossing it, this was setting it on fire and blowing it up.

"Do you remember when we went to the Black Sea and you pretended to be infatuated with Lorelei?"

"Not that again." His face shut down.

"I'm going to do something very dangerous and stupid. I've done some idiotic things in my life, but this takes the cake."

"Tell me."

"No."

Gold rolled over his eyes. "What do you mean, no?"

"If I tell you, you will stop me from doing it."

"Now you have to tell me."

I shook my head. "I'm calling in the Lorelei favor. You have to let me run with this."

"Kate!"

"No." He would blow a gasket. If someone had told me my brilliant idea an hour ago, I'd have laughed and then bashed their face in.

"Tell me."

He was a cat and a control freak. It was killing him not to know.

"No. But I wanted to be up front and tell you that I have a plan and I'm going to have to leave the city for a few days." If I just disappeared, he would freak out and tear Atlanta apart to find me.

The beginning of a snarl rumbled in his throat. "You will tell me."

"Curran, please don't fight with me. Please. I'm at the end of my rope and I just saw the light at the end of the tunnel."

He snarled, frustration exploding out of him. "Fine. Am I allowed to help with your crazy scheme?"

"Can you rescue Saiman?"

"If I rescue Saiman, will you tell me?"

"If you rescue Saiman and things work out, it will all be in the open by the time I come back."

He circled me, stalking. "Or you could tell me now."

"My father thinks he has it all figured out. He's pushed us into a corner. He thinks we're trapped. But he doesn't get to win, Curran. He doesn't get to win. He won't destroy Baby B's world, he won't get to ruin our marriage, and he won't . . ."—*get his hands on our son*—". . . he won't win. I won't let him."

"That's better," he said, and his smile had a vicious edge to it. "That's my Kate."

He closed the distance between us fast and kissed me.

"I love you," I told him.

"I will bring you Saiman," he said. "I promise you, he'll be alive. And then you will tell me everything."

"Yes," I promised. "I will."

W E WENT DOWNSTAIRS and split up. Curran went to catch up with old friends, while I went to the guard station and asked to use their phone. They let me into an empty conference room and closed the door.

I dialed Sienna's number. She picked up on the first ring.

"Yes?"

"Look into my future."

Silence.

Sienna's ragged whisper filled the phone, distant. I couldn't make it out.

She gasped. "He's coming . . . Fly higher, horse. Higher! The bridge . . . Don't let go, Kate . . ."

The phone went silent. A flying horse. Was I riding a flying horse? I sure hoped not. Heights weren't my favorite. There was a bridge in Mishmar . . .

"What did you do?" she whispered.

"It's not what I did. It's what I decided to do. Does the city burn?"

"Kate, this is a path of sacrifice . . ."

"Sienna, does the city burn?"

"It may. But it may not. You've made the future murky."

I would take murky. Murky was great. "Good."

"Kate, wait. As I'm looking into your future, so is Roland. It makes no sense that he wouldn't. I don't know if he does it himself or if he has someone do it for him, but either way, your father will know very shortly that things have shifted and are uncertain."

*And he will likely do his best to knock me back on the course most convenient to him.* "So keep going and watch out for my father. Got it."

"In one of the flashes I caught, I saw you die tomorrow. The head may cause a problem. Be very careful."

The head? What head? I almost asked her and stopped myself. I'd gone down this twisted path a few times. Knowing too much about the future made things more complicated, not less.

"Thank you."

"You're welcome. Good luck, In-Shinar."

She hung up. I hung up too and stared at the phone. Shinar was the name of my father's old kingdom, the one that started it all. And I had zero clue what Sienna meant by that. Asking her would only lead to more trouble. Oracles never explained things. You asked them a question and they gave you an oddly shaped piece of a puzzle that didn't fit anywhere and explained nothing until it was too late.

I didn't have time to sit here and puzzle things out. I had to talk to Jim and convince him to go along with my plan. He would just love that talk.

DURING HIS TIME as Beast Lord, Curran never kept a formal office. He had a space nominally assigned to be his office, but he was never in it and avoided any attempt to enter it like the plague. When he had a backlog of paperwork to go through, he'd spread out at some table, preferably in close proximity to food. Jim kept an actual office at the end of the eighth floor. As I approached, I saw him through the wide open doors sitting at the desk, reading something from a manila folder.

A pair of guards were posted by the doors. I stopped and nodded at both of them. They used to be Curran's and my guards.

"Let her in," Jim called without looking up from his reading.

I walked past the guards into the office and sat in the chair in front of him. It was a nice office, spacious, with a plain wooden floor and its own private balcony. The sunlight streaming through the large windows made the severe stone feel airy. Shelves lined the walls, the books and files neatly arranged. Jim's massive desk was organized with military precision. Unlike most people, Jim clearly didn't have the compulsion to fill every horizontal surface with things he might one day need and papers he should throw away.

"Yes?" Jim asked.

"I need to have a private conversation."

He glanced up. "John, Ramona, go grab something to eat."

The two guards left without saying a word.

"Roland has Saiman."

Jim smiled, showing me sharp white teeth. Saiman was on Jim's *kill when not needed anymore* list. Saiman might have managed to secure Friend of the Pack status for himself, but the moment he did something to piss off the Pack, he'd feel Jim's claws around his spine and Jim's fangs on his throat.

"He's a resident of Atlanta, so Curran and I will retrieve him."

"You and Curran can do whatever you like. The Pack won't get involved. There is no benefit for us. If this is what you came to talk about, this will be a short conversation."

*Ass.* "No, I'm laying the groundwork. I went to see my father, as you know."

"You pissed him off." Jim studied me.

Yep, the scout had reported to him already.

"Yes. He refuses to return Saiman, which forces me to act. He can't handle the fact that I'm here and I have autonomy. He's unable to deal with another authority, especially because I'm his daughter."

"I'm still waiting to hear how any of this concerns me."

"The Witch Oracle has been looking into the future repeatedly over the past month. They predict a war. It will go one of two ways. One, my father kills Curran, the Pack is slaughtered, the city burns, the witches die."

His face betrayed no emotion.

"Two, my father kills my son. Impales him on a spear. The Pack is slaughtered, the city burns, the witches die. I saw the visions. Hell on Earth is coming." I leaned back. "We have four weeks before the first possibility might come to pass."

Silence lay between us, heavy like a brick.

"Do you have a plan?" he asked.

"Yes. I need my aunt's blood and bones."

"Why?"

"So I can take them to Mishmar."

He stared at me. A muscle jerked in his temple. *Oh no. I've given the Beast Lord apoplexy.* That seemed to be my calling in life.

"Are you okay?"

"I'm trying to decide if I really heard what you said or if somehow my brain quit on me and I hallucinated."

"Take your time."

"Mishmar. Your father's hellish prison he cobbled together from the remains of office buildings from Omaha, which he destroyed. The Mishmar that's stuffed to the brink with mutated vampires. That Mishmar."

"Yes."

"You barely got out alive from Mishmar the last time, and you had Curran, me, two alphas, one of the best fighters in the Pack, the best Master of the Dead in Atlanta, and Nasrin, the miracle-working medmage. You even had a guide. We still barely escaped."

"I'm not going in deep. Only to my grandmother's body."

"Okay, I'll bite. Why?"

"I'm going to bring my aunt's remains to my grandmother and beg for her help." Every convincing lie had some truth to it.

"You told us your grandmother is an entity beyond this world. She is filled with grief and rage and you want to take your aunt's bones there. Did you forget that you killed your aunt? You stabbed her in the eye. What is your grandmother going to say about that? Are you expecting a warm family reunion?"

"Jim, my aunt was the City Eater. She was larger than me, stronger than me, and a magical powerhouse. She wanted to die with honor and she let me take her life. It was her choice. I was a conveniently honed tool in the right place at the right time."

"And you think the insane thing that's your grandmother will understand all that?"

"Yes." No, but it didn't matter. If I told him my actual plan, he would think *I* was insane.

"Did you run any of this by Curran?"

"I told him I was about to do something idiotic and dangerous, and he told me to go ahead and let him know if he could help in any way."

"I don't understand your relationship."

"You don't have to. Jim, I'm desperate. I can't protect the city. I can't even protect the man I love or our child, if the visions are true. Today, right now, this is our chance to make sure Atlanta doesn't become another Omaha. Or we can move. Every time Roland gets near, we'll scoot a little farther west, until we end up in San Francisco."

Jim grimaced. When you're hitting home, keep going. I plowed on ahead.

"We both know that empires are built on trade routes and good logistics. Right now he's landlocked in the Midwest. He wants access to a port. He can't go west, because he'd have to clear mountains and a desert. He can't go down to Mississippi. Nobody wants to mess with Louisiana, because the native magic is too strong there and because his ships would have to clear the gulf, which is full of ship-eating things. That leaves him with the Eastern Seaboard. If he swings north, he will have to fight the federal government and he isn't ready for it. His only logical choice is Atlanta.

It's the key to the entire South. He can't have this city. He will drain it dry and I don't mean financially. I mean magically. If he claims it, he'll feed on it like a leech to boost his own power. You remember the Lighthouse Keepers. You know what happens when someone's magic is completely drained. Help me to keep this from happening."

He sighed. "What do you need?"

"The Pack has my aunt's body and blood. I'll need to pick it up so I can transport it to Mishmar."

"I couldn't keep you from taking it anyway," Jim said. "You're next of kin."

"I know." Georgia's legal code specifically stated that the bodies of all shapeshifters had to be returned to their families. The Pack had lobbied for this law to be passed. Curran had wanted it in place to make sure that no shapeshifter organs were sold on the black market. Because the law had originated from him, the Pack also codified and honored it, extending it to all Pack members rather than only shapeshifters. At the time I stabbed my aunt in the eye, I was a member of the Pack.

"I wanted you to know why."

Jim's face was grim. "And the Oracle thinks the battle is inevitable?"

"Yes."

His expression turned darker. I knew what he was thinking. To evacuate or not to evacuate. He'd have to make a decision regarding sending the children out of the Keep. He'd have to decide if he should pull in his forces to fight or scatter them to keep the casualties low. I've been in that precise spot before. The weight of every decision was enough to crush your spine.

"If I go to the Witch Oracle, will they show me the vision?" he asked.

"You can ask. There is no harm in it. All they can do is say no. Will you have the remains in some sort of portable form?"

"I'll look into it. Kate, don't think that it's you against him. That's how you talk about it, but it's not true. He's by himself, but you have all of us. We're in it together and we'll stand against him together. You have a lot of goodwill in this city."

"Thanks, Jim." That was unexpected.

"And if you ever turn into your father and feed on this city like a leech, I will kill you."

*Really? Not even in your wildest dreams.* "If I ever turn into my father, you will kneel and pledge yourself to me, Jim. And you will be happy doing it."

His expression turned flat.

I winked at him, got up, and left. That wasn't the smartest thing to say, but I was getting sick of people threatening me and he had no room to talk. Let him chew on that reality check.

OUR HOUSE WAS dark. No lights on except for a feylantern. I gave it the evil eye.

"Julie's avoiding me."

"Can you blame her?" Curran asked. "She knows she's in trouble. She's hoping you'll cool off."

"Avoiding me makes me more pissed off. Eventually, I'll go and find her, and she won't like it."

"No, you won't," he said. "You're too busy with—what was it again you were going to do?"

"Ha. Ha. Nice try."

"Tell me."

"No."

"Tell me."

"No."

The door in the house across from us opened. The place used to belong to my human nemesis, but she and her husband decided that we had poisoned their entire neighborhood and moved out. George and Eduardo snapped up their house. Curran had offered them one of the spare homes he had purchased, and initially they moved into the place next to Barabas. But once our neighbors put their house on the market, George and Eduardo walked through it and had to have it. I never asked where the money to buy it came from, but Mahon and Martha visited them often and Eduardo let it slip that they had no mortgage.

George stepped out onto the porch and waved at us. "Hey you, we have dinner!"

Curran's eyes lit up. "They have dinner."

I laughed and followed him out of the car to the house. The magic was so strong tonight. I could've stayed here on the street so I could feel it spread through my land and sense all the things within my borders soak it in.

The inside was bright and warm. The scent of roasted meat, fresh bread, and honey swirled around me. My mouth watered.

A big table had been set in the dining room, crammed to the brink with food. And Mahon and Martha sat at the table. Oy.

"Tam-tam-da-dam!" Natalie, George's younger sister, waved her arms. She looked a lot like George and her other older sister, Marion—same wild curly hair, same dusky skin, same bright big eyes. Natalie was seventeen and squeezing every last moment out of her childhood.

"Is that death march for me or for him?" I asked.

"For both."

"What are all of you doing here?" Curran settled into the seat next to Eduardo.

"Roof needs fixing," Eduardo said. "They came to help."

"And you didn't invite me?" Curran loaded his plate.

I sat next to him and George put a plate in front of me. "Eat."

I grabbed a big roll out of the basket, speared a chunk of roasted venison, and dug in. Mmm, food.

"There is plenty of work left for tomorrow," Mahon said. "Besides, you're busy with your Guild, aren't you?"

"I'm sure I can find an hour or two somewhere," Curran said.

"Has anyone seen Julie?" I asked.

"We've seen her," George said. "We're supposed to tell you that she's not dead, but she is staying over at the office tonight."

I'd growl, but I was too hungry.

For a few minutes nobody spoke. Shapeshifters worshipped food with a singular devotion and I was too starved to make conversation. We chewed, got more food, and chewed some more.

If I ate another bite, I would explode. I sighed, decided I did not need another roll, and drank some iced tea.

Martha was smiling at me across the table. Older, plump, with medium brown skin, she looked a lot like her daughters. She usually said little, at least to me, but I had watched her knit several sweaters and shawls during the Pack Council sessions.

She smiled brighter. "You're getting married."

Mahon grinned next to her. "Three out of four."

Reminding him that he was adamantly opposed to Curran and me getting married would ruin the mood.

"Now if only we could find a nice boy and marry that hellion off . . ." Mahon said.

The hellion stuck her tongue out. "Maybe I'll marry a girl."

"That will be fine," Mahon said. "As long as she loves you."

Natalie rolled her eyes.

"Are you thinking of children?" Martha asked.

"Mom!" George and Natalie said in the same voice.

"No," Curran said.

"Yes," I said at the same time.

He turned to look at me.

"Thinking," I said. *Please don't ask me anything else about children.*

Martha grinned even wider. If we turned off the lights, she and Mahon would probably glow.

"Are you thinking of children?" Mahon asked George.

Eduardo choked on a piece of bread and coughed quietly.

"Dad, keep your paws out of my marriage," George said.

Curran frowned. "I'll be right back."

He got up, brushed my shoulder with his hand in passing, and went outside.

"Someone's pulled up to your house," Eduardo told me.

Shapeshifters and their hearing.

"While he's gone," Martha said, "come with me."

I followed her into the back room. She took a small box from the night table and gave it to me.

"Something old."

Something old? Oh! The rhyme. Something old, something new, something I didn't remember and then there was blue in it somewhere . . . I opened the box. A dark chain lay inside.

"Go on," Martha said.

I picked it up. Heavy for its size. The chain kept going and suddenly a bright green gemstone emerged, about an inch and a half wide. I held it to the light. A bear, carved with painstaking precision, down to the fur.

"When Mahon and I met, there wasn't a lot of him left," Martha said. "Even when he was human, he was full of bear rage. But I knew there was a man in there somewhere, so I went and found him. Before we got married, he gave me a set of jewelry: a ring, earrings, bracelet, and a pendant. He said it was because I was the stronger bear." She smiled. "Back then we didn't have the fancy shapeshifter-safe alloys, so it's steel. But the stone is the real thing, peridot. I want you to have it."

Oh my God. "I can't."

"Yes, you can. I gave one to each of my girls when their weddings were coming up. Marion has the ring, George has the earrings, and Natalie is getting the bracelet. I want you to have the pendant. You don't want Curran to wear it instead of you, do you?"

"I can't."

"Why not?"

I opened my mouth.

"Yes?"

"Mahon doesn't even like me. He barely tolerates me."

"Of course he likes you. I like you, too. Now, he didn't always think you were a suitable wife for his special son, but he always liked you."

Could've fooled me. "What changed?"

"We saw you carry the djinn," Martha said. "We were both there and we saw you give it up and hand it to Curran and then we saw him give it back to you. What the two of you have is a rare thing. We don't love Curran *like* a son. He *is* our son, one of our children. Mahon may be an old stubborn bear, but he isn't blind or stupid. He knows Curran won't do better. We are lucky to have you for a daughter-in-law."

It was the stupidest thing, but I felt like crying.

She took the chain and put it into my hand. "You wear it. I want you to."

THE CHAIN FELT nice around my neck. I liked the weight of it. I helped with the dishes. Curran came back in at some point and helped me put the plates away. Then we said our good-byes and stepped outside.

If I could've hugged this evening, I would've, and I wasn't the huggy type.

"Who came to visit?" I asked as we crossed the road to our lawn.

"Jim."

I knew that tone of voice. That was his Beast Lord voice, neutral and calm right up to the point when it exploded into a roar.

"What did Jim say?"

"What did you say to him?"

Careful. Thin ice, proceed with caution. The last thing I needed to do was explain to him why I wanted to take Erra's bones out of storage or what I would be doing with them. "About what?"

He stopped in front of our house. "Don't play with me. What did you say to him about us getting married?"

"Nothing. We didn't discuss it."

"You said something, because he dropped everything and drove all this way to tell me not to marry you."

"What? Why?"

"Because he's concerned my feelings might not be my own."

*Jim, you jackass.* I knew he was paranoid, but this was completely crazy. "Whose feelings does he think you're having?"

"He thinks I'm being influenced by your magic."

"Oh. Good to know. The magic that I've never been able to use on anyone else to make my life infinitely easier? That magic?"

Gold rolled over his eyes. "What did you say?"

Oh, so the lights came on. Someone was fussy that his best friend came over all worried. "Such concern for Jim. So touching."

And we have a full-on alpha stare. Good to know where I stood on his ladder of important people.

I moved, circling Curran. My magic trailed me like a mantle in the night.

"He told me that he would kill me if I decided to use my power for my own gain. I told him the truth."

Curran moved with me. Anger flared in his eyes. He was still giving me the alpha stare. *So it's like that, huh? Alright. Let's play.*

"I told him that if I decided to use my power for myself, he would pledge his allegiance to me and he would like it. He would trip over his own feet to proclaim his devotion."

"Why the hell would you say that to him? He's the Beast Lord."

Oh noes. I paused. "Yes, how could I forget? What was I thinking? What do you suppose he will do?"

The magic waited, all around me. As if the entire ocean of life that was my land had taken a breath in anticipation.

"Do you think Jim might punish us? Or do you think I would kill him and laugh afterward?"

He raised his hand and motioned to me. "Okay. Come back to me from wherever you just went."

"I remember one time Jim and I did a job and he left me in the middle of a cage of live wire because the Pack needed him. I sat in there for eight hours, until the magic wave ended."

My own power was out now, fully on display. Curran shifted his weight on his feet. He felt it. He was ready to pounce.

"Oh, another thing I remember, when the rakshasas poured molten metal on Derek's face and Jim didn't know what to do, I stuck my neck out for him and he let his crew rip into me. And when I asked him how could he do this after he and I worked together for years, he told me I wasn't a shapeshifter. I would never be good enough."

"Jim has issues."

I smiled at Curran, my voice almost singsong. "Do you know why my father has problems with the shapeshifters? Because their magic is so old. It's primal. It predates even his. You have a special connection to the land. You are a native power."

He didn't answer, but he watched me like a hawk.

"But now I have a special connection with the land, too. I can feel the life within it. I can feel its heart beating. Like this."

I touched the surface of the ocean. It pulsed. Curran jumped backward a full fifteen feet.

Now that felt interesting. I touched it again. Another pulse.

"Every time I use my magic, everybody gets so concerned. I defend them, I bleed for them, and the moment the immediate danger passes, they let me know how much they disapprove. As if their fucking disapproval matters. As if I should ask their permission, like a servant, to do what is in my power."

"Kate," he said. "I know you're in there. Stop."

I brushed the ocean, giving it a hint of my power. The feylanterns flashed brighter on all the houses down the street.

"Have you ever wondered what would happen if I stopped listening to every pathetic creature who thought that they had a right to weigh in on my decisions? Wouldn't it be nice to not have to ask permission for something that's already yours? What's the point of having power if you never use it?"

I slapped it again and again, faster, picking up rhythm. *Thump, thump, thump.*

"I can crush all of them, but I won't. That would be wasteful and I'm not wasteful. I'll use my magic and turn them into willing happy slaves."

"No," Curran said. "You won't."

"Don't you love me, Curran? Don't you want me to bear your children? Can you imagine how powerful they will be?"

I pulled on my magic a tiny bit. It warmed me from within and I let it out. It felt like I was glowing, but I could see my arms and no glow seemed to be shining out.

Curran froze.

"Take my hand, Curran. You know you want to."

"No. This isn't you."

"Of course, it is. Jim told you so. Take my hand, baby. Be with me eternally. Rule with me. All you have to do is love me and I will give you all the power and immortality you could ever want."

The door of George's house swung open and Eduardo stepped out.

"Is everything okay?"

Aw. He ruined it. Well, it was fun while it lasted. I let go of the magic. "Everything is fine. Curran and I are having a married moment."

"Oh. Sorry." Eduardo turned and went back inside.

Curran looked like a flying magic fish had popped into existence in front of him and slapped his face with its tail.

"You should see your face!" I snickered.

He snarled. "Damn it, Kate!"

*That's right. You've been had.*

"Do you think this shit is funny?"

I kept laughing.

He swore.

"Woo-woo!" I waved my fingers at him in between bouts of laughter. "You and Jim are two idiots. Maybe you should marry each other. You can rule the Pack together."

"Why the hell would you do this to me?"

"Because you deserved it. Jim came to you with this nonsense and you got all concerned."

"I told Jim to go to hell. I also told him that if he ever

told me that my wife is a 'potential threat' again, I would become a real and immediate threat."

I laughed and opened my arms. "My hero."

"You're an asshole," he told me.

"You knew that before you asked me to marry you. What, no hug?"

"You know how paranoid Jim is. You know what he does to potential threats. He is proactive. Why did you have to screw with him?"

"Because he sat there, all self-important, and announced that he would kill me if I stepped out of his lines. Hey, I winked after I said it. It's not my fault he has no sense of humor."

He shook his head.

I dropped my arms. "Okay, why are you so freaked out?"

"Because you did that thing your father does."

"What thing?"

"The one where you smiled and it was like being blessed."

I opened my mouth. Nothing came out.

"I can handle your father, because I despise him." His gray eyes were hard. "But I love you. Don't do that to me again."

I was turning into my father.

I turned away from him before he saw my face. He moved behind me and then his arms closed around me. He'd seen it anyway.

"What did it feel like?" I asked, my voice quiet.

"It felt like a god noticed me," he said. "Warm and welcoming. Like the sun broke through the clouds."

The warmth of his arms shielded me. Curran would shield me from everything, except myself. That one was on me.

"I love you more than I've ever loved anyone," he said. "But I don't want a new sun or a goddess. I want you. A partner."

"I know." I pulled away from him and went to our house. He followed me.

I took off my shoes and went upstairs, to our bedroom. He followed me and said nothing. I took off Sarrat's harness and put the saber in its usual place on the night table by my side of the bed.

"Do you want to tell me about it?"

"There is nothing to tell. The magic is changing me, Curran, and I'm not always aware of it. You should bail while you can, before it all goes to hell."

"No."

"This might be your last chance to get out." I pulled off my pants and my shirt. I wanted to soak in the tub and wash the day off.

"I'm not going anywhere. Besides, hell is when you and I are at our best."

I stopped and looked at him.

"You know where my line is," he said.

I knew. We had both drawn them. If he ever pulled another stunt like he did at the Black Sea, pretending to be interested in another woman because he was trying to "keep me safe," I was done. And if I ever made another Julie by letting my blood burn away another person's will, he was done. He drew the line at slavery. That was a reasonable line.

I walked into the bathroom and started the water in the tub.

He stopped in the doorway, leaning against it, his arms crossed.

I tossed some Epsom salts into the bathtub. "I'm not sure if I will even be me at the end of it."

A warm hand rested on my back. He'd snuck up behind me.

I straightened. His arm caught my waist, pinning me to him.

"I'll be here," he said. "I'll fight for you. We'll beat this. We've beaten everything else."

Doolittle once told me that he wasn't afraid of me. He was afraid of what I might become in spite of myself. His fears were coming true.

"Power is a drug," Curran said. "Some people try it and can't wait to stop. Other people take it and want more and more, until nothing is left except getting more power."

"You know that's not me."

"I know. You're the least power-hungry person I've ever

met. You're also the most stubborn person I've ever met. Disrespectful. Mouthy."

"You mean independent and proactive in taking initiative."

"That, too. Also infuriating. And strong. You won't let anyone take your freedom, Kate."

He was right. I was damned if I would let magic dictate what I did or thought.

Curran had power. He had hundreds of people who waited with bated breath for him to tell them to do something, and he had walked away from it—for me. It could be done. He'd done it. I had to fight this one decision at a time.

It wouldn't change me. It wouldn't rule me. Not happening.

"Were you tempted, Your Furriness?" I asked.

"By your evil?" His voice was a hot, deep whisper near my ear.

"Yes."

"No. If you and I ruled forever, I would never have you all to myself. We tried that, remember?"

"So you're greedy?"

His voice raised the tiny hairs on the back of my neck. "You have no idea."

I was playing with fire. "How greedy are you?"

He spun me around, his eyes full of gold sparks and predatory excitement. "Let me show you."

We made it to the tub eventually. It took a lot longer than planned.

# ≡ CHAPTER ≡
## 6

I T WAS MORNING and I came downstairs because Barabas was at the front door and Curran was in the shower.

"Kate," he said. "Good morning."

"Good morning." I held the door open.

He walked in and followed me to the kitchen.

"Tea?" I asked. Peace offering.

"Yes, please."

"Earl Grey, mint, chamomile . . ."

"Chamomile."

I walked to the kitchen island, pulled a tin labeled TEN-SION TAMER off the shelf, and spooned some loose tea into a diffuser. Apparently his tension was in need of taming. This conversation would suck.

Silence stretched.

"Where is Christopher?" Kate Daniels, the ice breaker.

"Asleep in the hammock on the porch. He had a rough couple of days."

"Julie said he burned *Bullfinch's Mythology*."

Barabas sighed. "I bought a beautiful leather-bound edition for his birthday and hid it in the closet in the spare room.

He found it yesterday as I was about to leave. I went to say good-bye and found him burning it in the fire pit outside."

So not only had he burned a book, he'd burned the book Barabas bought him. Of all the people Christopher cared about, Barabas was the most important. I was a distant second.

"Did he say why he burned it?"

Barabas shook his head. "He stayed with it until it was ash, pacing back and forth around the fire pit. When it was gone, he got a blanket off the couch, lay in the hammock, and covered his head. He didn't even take Maggie with him. She was crying by his hammock until I put her with him. He got up in the afternoon to go meditate with you and then went back into the hammock. He's been withdrawn since then."

"I'm sorry," I told him.

"I can't figure it out. Was it something about the binding? He has other books bound in leather."

"Maybe he didn't like one of the myths."

Barabas sighed. "Sometimes I wish I could open his head and fiddle with his brain to put it back the way it needs to be."

I poured water into our teacups and pushed honey toward him.

Beating around the bush any longer would just waste his and my time. "I was rude to you yesterday. I'm sorry. I'm trying to stay myself, but it's been difficult lately."

"Apology accepted," he said quietly. "I'm sorry, too. I know you're under a lot of pressure. And you're right, I wasn't there."

Well, this wasn't awkward. Not at all. I stared into my tea.

"Do you know why I left the Pack?" Barabas asked.

"No." I never understood it. He had so much going for him there. Jezebel seemed absorbed in keeping track of Julie and guarding my back. She threw herself into it. Barabas, however, ended up running the Pack's legal department. He was viewed as the Beast Lord's personal lawyer. He didn't have the longest tenure or the most experience, but people deferred to him anyway.

"I went as far as I could go there," Barabas said. "I'll

never be an alpha. I don't want to be an alpha. I didn't even want to be the lead counsel. I like problem solving. I like taking a crisis, breaking it into manageable pieces, and finding a solution. I don't like the minutiae. I don't like paperwork."

"You like trials, though?" He always seemed really keyed up before the trials.

"The last trial I handled involved a custody dispute and the divorce of my mother's best friend's daughter and a human she married. The opposing counsel asked for copies of income tax returns for the last five years. We obliged and sent them to him. During the pretrial hearing, he couldn't figure out where they were, and then he found the tax returns for the first two years, but not the last three. He claimed we didn't provide them, which made no sense because he had the first two and they were all in the same packet. He speculated that they might have been lost in the mail, except we had hand-delivered them to his office. He's standing there shuffling his papers, and I wanted more than anything in the world to rip him open and chew on his insides."

I laughed into my cup.

"Standing still required such an effort of will, my hands actually shook." Barabas smiled. "One of my professors in law school referred to this as the glorious drudgery of the legal profession. I've had all the glory I can stand. Working for the Pack was just that, working for someone else. It was the thing I did, while waiting for something else to come along. I was a glorified servant."

"Barabas . . ."

He held up his hand. "I'm not implying that it was the result of something you or Curran did. It was simply the nature of the position. And there is honor in service to a greater cause. But I wanted something that was mine. Separating from the Pack would give me the chance to figure out what that something would be."

"Makes sense." Separating with us was about the only way a shapeshifter could leave the Pack and still reside in Atlanta.

"When I bought shares in the Guild, Curran and I became partners in an enterprise. 'Partners' being the key word here. We're equal. We're streamlining the Guild, hammering it into shape, and it's working. Our gig load has been steadily growing by five to ten percent each month."

He leaned forward, alert, his eyes bright and focused. "This is something that's mine."

I nodded.

"I like my work. I love the house I live in. I take care of Christopher. According to my mother, I've been a wild card in every relationship I've ever tried, always looking for someone to ground me, so being a caretaker is good for me. The point is, I finally enjoy my life, Kate. I don't want this to stop."

"Neither do I."

"When things happen that threaten it, I get alarmed. I'm sorry I overreacted. The Guild is my thing. I own it, I nurture it, I make it grow. So I understand, Kate. This city is your thing."

"I don't own it."

"And I'm relieved that you still hold to that. But the facts are as follows: You guard it, you protect it with your life, and you feel responsible for it. You want it to prosper and you don't want your father to lay claim to it. Setting aside legalities and moral scruples, you own it, Kate, and when your father stretches his hand toward it, you freak out."

"He has no right to it."

"It's important to remember that neither do you."

I felt an itch under my jaw, an uncomfortable need to clench my teeth.

He was watching me very closely. "Is it difficult to come to terms with that?"

"Yes." I should've lied.

"I think that's how your father must've started. I realize it's ancient history, eons ago, but he must've had a kingdom."

Oh, why not? It's not like I had to keep secrets anymore anyway.

"It was called the kingdom of Shinar. It started with the cities of Akkad, Erech, and Calneh. That entire region was a series of small kingdoms, all magically powerful and more or less equal, ruled by family dynasties. They were aware of other powers, as far north as France and as far south as the Congo, but they were content to stay in Mesopotamia. It was different back then. There were two more rivers, the climate was mild, and Mesopotamia was a beautiful garden."

"Like Eden." Barabas nodded.

"Not like. Eden's river had four tributaries—Pison, Gihon, Euphrates, and Hiddekel—that united into a single river before rushing into the sea. The Euphrates is still there. The Hiddekel is now called Tigris. The Pison was a river that flowed all the way through northern Arabia, a place known to the biblical Hebrews as Havilah. It has since dried up. The Gihon is the river Karum, which is now a lot smaller than it used to be. These four rivers joined together into a single enormous river that had flowed through the valley of Eden into the Persian Gulf until the plain of Eden drowned. The kingdoms were powerful but even they couldn't halt the Flandrian Transgression, when the glaciers melted and flooded the oceans."

Barabas stared at me like I had grown a second head. "Kate. Are you trying to tell me that your family comes from Eden?"

"From that general vicinity."

"So Roland, I mean Nimrod, is actually a grandson of Adam? Real Adam?"

I sighed. "Adam wasn't a person. Adam was a city."

He stared at me.

"In the language of the Ubaid, who were there first, Eden means 'fertile plain' and Adam means 'city of the plains.' There was a real Cain, but he didn't murder his biological brother. He favored agriculture and was forced out by the hunters and herders who saw his ways as having too great of an impact on their lands."

He didn't say anything.

"You asked how my father became what he is. I don't know all of the details, but at the start, he and my aunt were liberators. They brought freedom, civilization, and enlightenment, but they never stopped. They kept rolling, taking city after city and then snuffing out rebellions when their empire became too large."

"They were heroes," Barabas said softly.

"Until they became tyrants." And I understood exactly how it happened.

"Do you think people tried to stop them?"

"Probably. There must've been people who told them they were going too far, but I doubt they survived very long. My father doesn't like the word 'no.'"

"I'll be there to tell you 'no,'" he said.

"My family history isn't exactly inspiring. I may kill you one day, Barabas."

"I'll take that chance. I believe in you, Kate."

Curran walked down the stairs. He had to have heard that last bit. The man could hear the oven door opening all the way in the pasture, especially if he was waiting for a pie.

"Alright, then," Barabas said. "I've come to talk about Saiman. The problem, as I see it, is that Roland kidnapped Saiman, according to his own admission, when Saiman was outside your lands. Technically, he isn't in breach of the treaty the two of you signed."

"Yes, but if he sits by . . ."—*my*, no, wrong—"our land and grabs the citizens as they leave, then the city is under siege. A siege is an act of war, so he is in breach, which is what I told him. He didn't address it, so he knows he's in a gray area."

Barabas stopped for a moment. "Kate, sometimes you really surprise me. Yes, you're right. But it's still an indirect action. You and your father are in a state of cold war. If you respond directly by attempting to retrieve Saiman by force, the conflict heats up."

"She needs plausible deniability," Curran said. "We have to snatch the degenerate back, but she can't be directly involved."

"What are the chances that your father would retaliate directly if you weren't involved?" Barabas asked.

"Slim to none," I said.

Curran nodded. "Agreed. Roland maintains the outward appearance of being a man of his word. He means to rule. A ruler's word is binding."

"If he was displeased with something 'my people' had done, he would take it up with me."

"That was my assessment as well," Barabas said. "It's very clear from the photographic evidence that Saiman was taken against his will. It's unlikely he's having a pleasant visit. Given a chance, he would probably do almost anything to get out."

"Including hiring the Guild to rescue him," Curran said.

Barabas bared his teeth in a quick flash. "Indeed."

"For that to happen, we'd have to communicate with Saiman," I said.

"And that's where it all grinds to a screeching halt," Barabas said.

"But at least that's a specific problem we can work on," Curran said. "We need to go through the mercs and see if anyone has any talents that might let us communicate with Saiman inside Roland's compound."

"That's problem one. Problem two, Roland knows we'll be coming," Barabas said. "We have no element of surprise."

"I may be able to help with that," I said.

"How?" Curran asked.

To tell him or not to tell him? "Okay, remember the stupid reckless thing I can't tell you about?"

His eyes shone. Oh, yes, he remembered.

"It involves going back to Mishmar."

Barabas dropped his teacup and caught it an inch above the table. Shapeshifter reflexes for the win.

"Why?" Curran asked.

"I can't tell you."

A roar rumbled in Curran's throat. Barabas sat back a bit. I shuddered. "So scary. Still can't tell you."

He opened his mouth.

"Lorelei," I said.

Curran swore.

Barabas grinned.

"Don't," Curran warned him.

"My father told me that he has a warning system set up in Mishmar. The moment I walk in there, he'll drop everything and rush over there by some mysterious magical means. He didn't tell me how, but I think whatever method he'll be using will be damn fast."

"Why?" Barabas asked.

"Because he doesn't want me talking to my grandmother."

Barabas looked at Curran.

Curran shrugged. "It's a family thing. Sometimes your father puts your semidead grandmother into a really bad place and is ashamed of it."

"Yeah," Barabas said. "We've all been there."

"You two are a riot," I told them. "I don't think Dad will be teleporting, because teleporting carries risk. If a magic wave ends while he's in transit, he's dead, so his travel will take at least some time. If we time it right, I'll open Mishmar, he'll take off, and you'll get a shot at Saiman. You'll still have to go through my father's people."

"Not a problem," Curran said. "Something that is a problem: Mishmar is on your father's land. He's strongest there. If he's going to Mishmar, you need to get away before he gets there. How are you planning on doing that?"

"According to the Witch Oracle, on a flying horse." Also someone's head was involved and it was important. I wish I knew whose head.

"Kate," Curran said. "You're terrified of heights."

Heights or my son dying on my father's spear? Not even a choice. "Double excitement."

"Going to borrow Eduardo's father's horse?" Barabas asked.

"No, Amal won't let anyone but Bahir ride her. Julie talked about sightings of flying horses last week. I thought I'd tug on that and see what happens."

"You're not serious?" Curran frowned at me. "You don't even know if those flying horses are rideable."

"My father won't expect a flying horse. The Witch Oracle saw me on one, so the least I can do is cross it off my list. I don't have a lot of choices if I want to outrun my father. He can do many things, but last I checked he couldn't fly."

If Julie talked about it, she must have filed a report somewhere in the office. If there was one thing Julie was good at, it was keeping a record of everything odd she came across.

"So what will you do in Mishmar?" Curran asked casually.

I got up, kissed him, and went to get dressed.

WHEN I GOT to Cutting Edge, Peanut wasn't there. This was getting ridiculous.

Inside, Ascanio greeted me with a salute and a bright smile. "Good morning, Alpha Sharrim."

Why me? "Where is Julie?"

"Escaped half an hour ago."

Argh.

I went to the larger filing cabinet and rifled through the files. "Where is the Weird Crap folder?"

"Derek has it." Ascanio walked over to Derek's desk, grabbed the folder, and handed it to me.

I flipped through it, looking through paper notes and newspaper clippings. This was the folder where we stuffed everything that came across our desks that was too odd even for us or had no explanation. Let's see, tentacle monster in the sewer on Grimoire Street, ball of blue lightning, no, no, no . . . Here it was, a newspaper article with notes written in Julie's firm hand:

> Third report of a flying horse in the area. Horse is described as 15–17 hands tall and golden in color. Horse breeds of ancient Greece were mostly ponies: Skyros pony, 10 hands average, Thessalonian pony, 11 hands average. Weird.

I flipped the page back to the newspaper clipping.

*Milton County.*
    *Misdemeanors: Jeremiah B. Eakle and Chad L.*
*Eakle, charges of public indecency and disorderly*
*conduct while intoxicated.*

That was it. No additional text, no explanation of the article.
No notes. Were these the people who reported seeing the flying horse? How were they connected? I flipped through the
rest of the folder. The notes said this was the third report, so
where were the other two?

I looked at Ascanio. "Where's the rest?"

He shrugged his shoulders, his face a picture of perfect
innocence. "Julie was the one who filed it. I just work here.
I have no idea why the Blond Harpy does anything."

Argh.

I picked up the phone and called home. Maybe she went
back.

No answer.

There was a time when that would've freaked me the hell
out. Now I took it as a given. Julie, if she was home, wasn't
picking up. Now that I was calm and somewhat rational, I
didn't blame her. In her place, I wouldn't answer either. We
both knew an ugly conversation was coming. Sooner or later,
I would track her down. If I wasn't running out of time, I
would've done that already.

I dialed Beau Clayton's office.

No ringing, but lots of dry clicks. The magic must've
knocked out the phone lines somewhere on the way to Milton County.

"Stay here," I told Ascanio. "If Julie shows up, tell her that
she and I need to talk and to be home at a decent time tonight.
My decent, not hers. If Curran shows up, tell him I went to
see Beau Clayton. Everybody else can take a number, I'll deal
with it later. If my father shows up, don't talk to him."

Ascanio dropped the innocent act. His eyes turned
serious. "I want to come with you."

"Why?"

"Because I never get to and your father tried to slap you."

"And how do you know that?"

"You need backup."

He wasn't wrong. Given that he was seventeen now, six feet tall, and able to control his aggression enough to think during a fight, I could do worse.

I wrote *Went to see Beau* on a piece of paper and left it on my desk. "Let's go."

I swung the door open a moment before Derek walked through it.

"I heard the conversation. I'm coming," he said.

Ascanio rolled his eyes. "This will be fun."

Derek parked himself in the doorway. "You need backup."

"She has backup."

"Yes, but someone will have to carry the Prince of Hyenas if he accidentally stabs his pinkie toe, and she isn't a shapeshifter."

"Fine." I headed for my vehicle.

Behind me Ascanio snorted. "Idiot wolf."

"Spoiled bouda brat."

"Bigot."

"Crybaby."

"Shit for brains."

"Momma's boy."

*Universe, grant me patience.*

I WALKED INTO Beau's office carrying six bottles of root beer and a bucket of fried chicken. Beau raised his head from the paperwork he was reading behind his desk, sniffed the air, and sat up straighter.

Beau Clayton, the sheriff of Milton County, was a man who made his own legend. A few months ago Hugh d'Ambray had come to collect me and take me to meet my father. He went about it in a complicated way, and one of the Pack's members ended up murdering one of the People's Masters of the Dead. The People demanded that the Pack turn over the accused. We refused. They would've murdered her. She was entitled to a trial.

The People emptied the stables under the Casino and brought a vampire horde to attack the Keep. I was the Consort back then and most of our people were out of town. It was me and some regular Pack members, mostly parents with small children.

I had contacted the Atlanta PAD offering to surrender the guilty woman to their custody, but they didn't want to risk it. Nobody wanted to risk it, so as a last resort I called Beau Clayton, because one hundred twelve square yards of the Pack's land lay within Milton County. It had to be the flimsiest excuse ever used to establish jurisdiction.

The People besieged us, bringing hundreds of vampires. The field before the Keep was about to become a bloodbath. Beau Clayton chose that moment to ride between the two lines of fighters. He didn't bring an army. He brought two deputies, put himself between the Keep and the horde of undead, and told them that he had been lawfully elected sheriff by the people of Milton County. He was the law and he had arrived to take the suspect into his custody. And then he told them to disperse.

I didn't get to see the end of it all, but war didn't break out on that field. The People took their vampires and went home. Beau took his suspect into custody and proceeded unmolested to the Milton County jail. People started calling him Beau the Brave.

Looking at Beau, it was easy to see why he would inspire legends. Huge, six foot six, with massive shoulders and powerful arms, he made his big wooden desk look small, but it wasn't his size alone. There was something unflappable about Beau. A kind of measured steady calm. He knew exactly what his mission in life was: he was the voice of reason and when reason failed, he enforced the law.

"Is that fried chicken?"

"Yes."

"Virginia's fried chicken?"

Virginia made the best fried chicken in North Atlanta and never tried to pass rat meat off as chicken tenders. I managed to look offended. "Of course it is. Who do you take me for?"

Beau leaned back. "Might you be trying to bribe a law enforcement official, Ms. Daniels?"

"You bet."

Beau glanced at Derek. "Gaunt."

Derek nodded. "Sheriff."

Beau turned to Ascanio. "And who would you be?"

I almost opened my mouth to tell him he was our intern and stopped myself. He was willing to take adult risks, he would get an adult introduction. "He's Ascanio Ferara of Clan Bouda. He works with me."

Ascanio blinked.

Beau took a long look at Ascanio, probably committing the name and face combination to the extensive files in his sheriff memory. "So how's business?"

"Fair to middling. How's yours?"

"About the same. Things quieted down a bit in the last six months."

"It's because of your name recognition." I opened my root beer and took a swig. "'Beau the Brave' has a certain menacing ring to it."

Beau grunted.

"Imagine, in about three hundred years, they will tell legends about you," I said.

"They will," Derek added. "Beau the Brave, nine feet tall, able to behead ten vampires in a single swing."

"Never thought about it much," Beau said. "But if it keeps the ne'er-do-wells from causing mischief, I can live with it."

"Ne'er-do-wells?" Derek asked.

"I read." Beau looked slightly offended.

"Ancient literature?" Ascanio inquired. "Did it have words like 'dame' and 'stool pigeon' in it?"

"Do you make your deputies call you 'copper'?" Derek asked.

"Have you two ever thought of taking your show on the road?" Beau asked them.

If Beau's legend grew big enough and enough people believed in it, he would live for a long time and he might even grow taller. I didn't have the heart to tell him that. He didn't look comfortable with the whole thing as it was.

"So what can I do for you?" he asked.

I took out the scrap of the article and pushed it across the table toward him.

He glanced at the clipping. "What's your interest in the Eakle brothers?"

"I don't have any."

"Ahh. You're in the market for a gold winged horse."

Gold? Julie's notes said golden in color. "Something like that. Can you tell me more?"

Beau sipped his root beer. "Chad and Jeremy Eakle are Caleb and Mary Eakle's sons. Nice enough fellows, but not a lot of brains between the two of them. Never been in serious trouble. My deputies had a few run-ins with them some years back, when they were in high school. Nothing too bad, typical petty things bored kids do: throwing beer bottles at stop signs, making bonfires, mooning people off the Cassidy Bridge. The usual. Both have jobs and families now. Both go to church."

"Sound like good law-abiding citizens," I said. Making Beau spill the beans faster would require more magic than my father and I could put together.

"Pretty much. Last Saturday, they were drinking beer and fishing in the Blue River Forest. They'd been at it for a few hours, in which they went halfway through a small keg from Jekyll Brewery."

A small keg in post-Shift Atlanta held three gallons, which meant the two Eakle brothers had put away about a six-pack and change each.

"The day turned hot. Since nobody was around, they'd taken off their clothes to go swimming, when a 'big gold horse' with wings walked out of the woods on the opposite bank and started drinking. The two geniuses decided to try to catch it and made it partway across the river, when, according to them, 'a winged devil' landed on the horse and told them to run before he devoured their souls."

Well, that escalated quickly. Winged devil, huh. "And this devil rode the horse?"

"Supposedly."

So the winged horses were rideable.

"Apparently, the Eakle boys took him seriously, because they got the hell out of the river and ran naked and screaming through the woods right into a Girl Scout campground, where two rival troops of Girl Scouts were having an archery competition. The Girl Scouts joined forces to subdue the interlopers."

Ascanio snorted.

Beau's eyes shone. "When my deputies got there, they were trussed up like two hogs. Jeremiah Eakle sustained an arrow shot to his left buttock. It was determined not to be life-threatening, so the arrow was extracted, and we booked them for indecent exposure and intoxication in a public place. They've sobered up and were released on their own recognizance. They don't remember much, except for the soul-devouring bit."

Just my luck.

"However, I, being an experienced member of law enforcement, sent one of my deputies to check out their story and collect their clothes, and she recovered some evidence from the scene. Evidence that may be of interest to you."

Why did I get the sudden feeling that this would cost me? "May I see that evidence?"

"I need a favor," Beau said.

Of course. "Shoot."

"There is an elderly woman. Jene Boudreaux."

He pronounced "Jene" as *Zhe-nay*.

"She is in her eighties, lives alone, and her neighbors have been reporting odd things. Weird noises, disconcerting smells, and one of them swears he saw her pick up a dead pigeon his cat didn't finish off the lawn and take it into her house. So I had my people do a health and welfare check.

If she was starving and resorting to picking up dead pigeons, we have a moral obligation to do something about it. My deputy went out there. She was muttering under her breath and then out of nowhere she lunged at him and bit him on the shoulder hard enough to draw blood. He took her in after that."

"Did you check her teeth?" I asked. The teeth were one of the first parts to show signs of a human turning into something else.

"Yes. Normal human teeth. I had a chat with her. We didn't get anywhere. So we put her in a cell and called down to the psychiatric unit in the city to come and evaluate her. She was in that cell for about an hour. When Connie went to do her rounds, she found the cell door open and the old lady was gone."

Better and better. "Nobody saw her leave?"

Beau shook his head. "And the cameras weren't running, since the magic was up. A group of kids walking home from school saw her take off for the woods. We tried to follow her with bloodhounds, but the dogs refused to track. She's been gone about ten hours. Since you have not one but two members of the Pack at your disposal, here's the deal. You track down Jene Boudreaux, and I'll let you examine the evidence you need."

Even if the evidence was crap, I still owed Beau. "I'll take that deal, but I want to see her house. I'd like to know what I'm walking into."

"Fine by me." Beau raised his voice. "Robby!"

A lanky blond deputy materialized in the doorway.

"This is Robert Holland," Beau said. "Robert will go with you and provide assistance and legal authority."

"Folks." Holland nodded at us.

"Mrs. Boudreaux has been a part of our community for all of her life," Beau said. "Her husband drove my sons to school in his armored bus when he was alive. She is known to people. I want it to be understood that even if Mrs. Boudreaux isn't herself, Deputy Holland is the one who gives the all clear. If violence is inevitable, it must be authorized by one of us."

Fine by me.

JENE BOUDREAUX LIVED in a small older house typical of the pre-Shift Georgia suburbs: one story, about twelve hundred square feet, a wooden fence and an abundance of plants and hedges up front. The plants had seen better days and the hedges were blocking the windows.

Twenty feet from the house, Derek and Ascanio stopped in unison.

"Odd smell?" I guessed.

"Mm-hm." Derek inhaled and grimaced. "Smells like hot iron."

A few feet from the door I smelled it too, a thick, sharp odor. It didn't smell like anything in particular; it was its own ugly scent that cut across my senses like a knife. Something bad lived here.

Robert Holland put the key into the lock and opened the door. "We confiscated the keys when we arrested her."

"Did you get to see her at all during any of this?"

He shook his head. "Shannon made the arrest. I do know her. My mother used to run a crafting club, where the older ladies would gather together, socialize, and knit or quilt."

The knitting circle. More and more of those were springing up, as machine-knit clothes became harder to come by.

"Old ladies come in two flavors: sweet or mean. She was the mean kind. But my momma always tried to include her, until she flat-out refused to come about three years ago."

The inside of the house was dark. Thick curtains blocked the light. I pulled them aside, letting the day in through the glass patio door. No bars on the frame. Odd. Apparently Jene wasn't afraid of whatever the magic-fueled night could spawn.

A layer of dust coated the old furniture. Derek tried it with his fingers. "Sticky."

Not dust, grime. The kind of grime that accumulated after years of willful neglect.

"When did she go weird?" Ascanio asked.

"She was always an odd bird," Holland said. "She had a real glare on her. I checked the log. We'd been called out before about a year ago. Some kids were playing on the street and being loud. They said she came out of the house and clicked her teeth at them. Scared them half to death. Parents filed a complaint. There were probably incidents before that, but most folks here live and let live, so it's hard to say."

Great. Kate Daniels, tracker of old ladies with a biting fetish. And me without my armor.

Derek pulled the glass door open and stepped out into the yard.

No pictures on the walls. No dishes in the sink. Dust on the sink's edges. Not cleaning is one thing, but when you ran water, inevitably some splashed on the counter. No splash marks disturbed the dust. Ascanio opened the fridge.

"Empty."

I didn't have a good feeling about this.

"Kate?" Derek called.

I stepped outside. The yard looked perfectly ordinary. Green grass, shrubs, and bird feeders. Many, many bird feeders in every shape and size. I could see at least two baited cage traps under the bushes.

Derek stepped closer to me.

"I smell one of Roland's people."

Great. "Which one?"

"I don't know. But this scent was at his base when we went to talk to him. Now it's here."

I went back inside and moved to the first bedroom. Dark stains marked the round doorknob. I reached into my pocket, drew a length of gauze, wrapped it around the handle, and swung it open.

The stench hit me then, like a slap to the face. Bones tumbled toward me, and I jumped back as they rolled onto the filthy carpet.

"Holy crap," Holland said.

If the bedroom had carpet at one point, there was no way to tell what color it was. At least six or seven inches' worth of small animal bones covered the floor. A lot of bird carcasses. A few raccoon skeletons, some cat bones. They probably had a problem with missing pets in this neighborhood. All the bones were clean and smooth. I reached down with my gauze and picked up a small dog's femur. The marrow had been sucked out.

"Picked clean," Ascanio said.

She must've been throwing them in through the window, because there was no way she could've opened the door without all of them falling out.

The bones reeked. Decomposition didn't smell like that and there was nothing here to decompose anyway. No, this was the sharp odor of the spit she deposited as she licked the bones clean. No wonder the bloodhounds didn't follow her. This stench made my hair stand on end.

I glanced at Derek. "Can you follow her trail?"

"Sure. Following isn't a problem," he said.

"Let's do that." I didn't want her running around unsupervised in my land, especially if my father's people were involved, although I had no clue why he was interested in her. This wasn't my father's magic, structured, almost scientific in its precision. This was something old and dark that crept about in the night.

"What is she, Kate?" Ascanio asked, as we left the house.

"I have no idea."

W<small>E CLIMBED DEEP</small> into the Blue River woods. The trees took the brunt of the sun's assault, but still, the heat baked us. Sweat collected in my armpits despite the deodorant. Another half hour in this heat, and nobody would have trouble tracking us. We'd leave a scent trail a mile wide.

The river cut through the forest from north to south, flowing through a narrow valley bordered by hills. It had formed during a flare years ago, streaming from the now massive Bryon Lake. Nearly all storm drainage in the area ended up in the Blue River through the tiny creeks and swales, and when it rained, the river rebelled and roared. Right now it lay calm, beckoning me with its nice cold water as we crossed the narrow wooden bridge, heading north, deeper into the woods.

I wished I could take a dip. Ten minutes and I would be ready to go hunt old ladies again. Sadly, no dipping would be happening.

The path turned west, climbing up a slope.

Derek grimaced again. He would never complain, but the scent had to be driving him nuts. Ascanio was equally stoic. Neither of them had belittled the other's wits, fighting ability, or sexual prowess in the last half hour. If I were less badass, I'd be worried.

We'd been walking for another fifteen minutes when Derek paused. Ascanio came to stand next to him. They stared through the trees where light indicated a clearing. We'd reached the top of a low hill.

"Is she close?"

They both nodded.

"The scent is so . . . wrong," Ascanio said.

I pulled Sarrat out of my sheath. Holland pulled a sword out of the scabbard on his hip. Dark, with a no-nonsense epoxy and leather grip, the blade ran about nineteen inches long and at least an inch and a half wide, with a profile that fell somewhere between a falchion and a Collins machete. Holland held it like he'd gotten it dirty before.

If we got Beau's deputy injured, we could kiss the sheriff's cooperation good-bye.

I moved toward the light, walking nice and slow, careful where I put my feet. The two shapeshifters glided on both sides of me. I could barely hear Holland behind me. It wasn't his first time in the woods either.

The trees parted. A clearing spread before us, unnaturally circular, as if some giant had dropped a huge coin in the middle of the woods and forgotten about it for a decade or two. The grass covered the ground, but no trees had managed to encroach on the clearing. The growth around us was new too, the trees tall but thinner than those half a mile back by the river. Must've been a fire a few years back.

I walked to the edge of the clearing. An old woman stood in the light with her right side to me. She wore a pair of beige pants, a white collared blouse with matching beige polka dots, and a white knitted cardigan. It had to be ninety-five degrees, I was sweating like a pig, and here she was, wrapped in wool.

Holland shouldered his way to the front. "Mrs. Boudreaux? I'm Deputy Holland. I need you to come with me."

No reaction.

"Mrs. Boudreaux!"

She didn't even turn.

I walked toward her, sword in hand. Holland caught up to me, while Ascanio and Derek fanned out to the sides.

"Mrs. Boudreaux?" I asked.

She turned to me. The whites of her eyes had yellowed and the red veins stood out, fat with blood. She stared at me.

Holland smiled at her. "Mrs. Boudreaux, it's me, Robby Holland. I'm Gladys Holland's son. You used to knit together, remember?"

She peered at him, swiveling her neck at an angle, like a puzzled dog.

"We were all very worried when you walked off. You didn't even say where you were going." His voice was slightly chiding. "And it's hot out here. Let's get you off this mountain and into some nice cool shade. What do you say?"

Jene opened her mouth. "Little prick."

Nice.

"There is no cause for strong language," Holland said. "I'm sorry, but I'm going to have to insist you come with me."

The old lady turned to me. "You're her. You're *his* bitch daughter."

*Thanks for the reputation bump, Dad.* "Yes, I am."

She stared at me, her gaze unsettling.

*Try me and see how bitchy I can be.*

"I could serve you," she said. "I'm powerful. I have magic. I can blight things. Look, I made this." She pointed to the clearing. "Ten years and nothing except grass grows. I'm quiet and hard to kill."

Wow.

She was trying to peer at me over Holland's shoulder and her eyes, wide open and unblinking, made her face deranged. A darker yellow, like the color of a rotten citrus, was flooding her irises.

"I can do things for you. Magic things. But I need food. You feed me and I do things for you." She nodded. "Bring me children. The poor ones. Nobody cares about the poor ones."

Next to me Derek tensed. Holland stared at her, open-mouthed.

"How many?" I asked.

"Not many. One or two a month. Children are easier. Soft bones."

"Alpha?" Ascanio's voice held a note of warning.

"Have you eaten many children?" I asked. "I need to know if their parents will cause problems."

"Only two," she said. "Years ago. No problems. I threw the bones in the trash. You own the land. I'm the land's creature, so I will serve you and you'll bring me food and guard me from the bigger creatures. It's a good bargain."

"No," I told her.

Derek pulled off his shoes. On the other side of me Ascanio did the same.

I shook my head. "You're an evil thing that eats children. There is no place for you here."

"You can't pick and choose," she said. "I'm part of the land. I was born here. All my people were born here, many generations. I belong here."

"You should've stuck to birds," I said.

"You can't have the good without the bad," she said. "Some creatures eat grass and some creatures eat the grass eaters. We are all born for a reason. You must have monsters to protect your land, and I will protect it well. If you need something, I will do it. I won't even eat humans, only the ones you bring me."

"No."

"You must have servants to do things for you. I can be one. It's a good bargain. This is your land and I'm your creature."

A part of me, the deep dark part that felt the magic pulse last night, puzzled over it and decided that she wasn't unreasonable. The land spawned this monster and I guarded the land, so she was one of mine, too. They were all mine and I could use her.

There it was. Small decisions. Kate Daniels, Queen of the Monsters.

"You are right. You are mine. If you hadn't harmed any-one, I could have let you find a place of your own away from everyone. But you've eaten human children and you want to do it again. There are rules in my lands and you broke them. I'm not here to make bargains. I'm here to punish."

She stared at me, unblinking. Hatred twisted her face. "You think you can stop him. You can't. All of you will die."

I flicked Sarrat, warming up my wrist. I'd promised Beau I'd let his deputy make the call, and I would keep my word. "Holland, I need that go-ahead."

"I can take you in," Holland said. "She'll kill you, but Milton County will protect you. There is due process."

She was past saving, but I had to give it to him, he did try.

Bulges rolled under Jene's skin, like billiard balls moving through her body.

Ascanio pulled two vicious-looking knives from the sheaths on his belt.

"Holland!" Damn it.

She swayed, an eerie sad smile on her face, reached out, and brushed Holland's face with her fingertips, caressing his skin with gentle tenderness.

"Gladys's son."

"That's right." Holland nodded. "Come with me. Let me take you in . . ."

"When he comes through with his soldiers and fire, I'll follow him."

She took several steps back. "And I'll feed. I'll wait until he kills you, Gladys's son, and then I'll suck your bones dry."

Her whole body jerked and shot upward. Her clothes rup-tured, and a huge body spilled out, growing bigger and big-ger. She fell straight down and gripped the dirt with her hands, her elbows up, as if she were about to do a push-up.

"What the hell . . ." Holland breathed out.

Her legs turned within their sockets with a vomit-inducing crunch, until her knees stuck straight up, like the legs of a spider. Her neck lengthened, thickening, the skin dripping down to form a pouch on her throat. Her white hair fell loose around her giant head, her wrinkled breasts sagged to the forest floor, and a thin strip of gray fur sprouted on her spine. Yellowed claws curved from her fingers and toes. She was the size of a bus.

"Hungry!" she screeched, clicking sharp conical teeth. "I'm hungry!"

Beau could take his instructions and shove them where the sun didn't shine. "Hit her!"

The two shapeshifters charged in from the sides. The thing that was Jene Boudreaux dashed forward with cockroach quickness, straight at me.

I shoved Holland aside and sliced across her face with my sword. A bloody line swelled across her skin, severing her lip. She slapped me. I flew back, landed on the grass, and rolled to my feet in time to see her kick Derek with her right foot. He hurtled through the air and vanished into the brush. She must've knocked him down the slope.

I sprinted to her.

Ascanio sank both of his knives into her side. She howled and rolled sideways, right over him. He went down, pinned under her massive body.

I slashed at her shoulder. *Move off my bouda, you bitch.*

She snapped her teeth at me, trying to bat me aside with her giant clawed hand, and dug in, crushing Ascanio beneath her bulk. I sliced at her hand, carving at it with precise strikes. She screeched in pain.

Lots of nerves in the hand. *Hurts like hell, doesn't it? Get off the boy.*

A dark gray shape burst out of the brush and landed on the creature's back. Derek thrust his claws into her spine. Jene rolled the other way, trying to pin him with her weight. He jumped off and landed on my right. Ascanio darted over to us, free. His body twisted into a nightmarish blend of hyena and human. His hackles rose and he cackled.

Jene rolled to her feet and hands. Her side bled, carved like a side of beef—Ascanio had been busy with his knife.

I flicked the blood off my sword.

Jene glanced at the three of us on her right and the stretch of woods to the left, and dashed toward freedom. Holland thrust himself into her path and swung his sword. She jerked her head up, quick like a snake, dove, and gulped him down whole.

Dear gods, she ate Beau's deputy.

A bulge landed in her throat sac and flailed, kicking. She sprinted through the woods, heading west, blindingly fast, scrambling through the forest like some monstrous pallid lizard.

Holland had seconds to live. We'd never catch up and kill her in time. We had to make her turn toward us. To the right, a slope dropped toward the river. When you fled, you naturally ran downhill.

"Derek, herd her! Make her turn southeast along the river."

Derek's eyes flashed yellow. He raised his head and let out a long wolf howl announcing the hunt. The tiny hairs on the back of my neck stood on end. The werewolf and werehyena shot into the woods.

I dashed down the south slope and almost ran into a narrow tree. Nice going. Maybe I'd break my neck and save everyone the trouble.

To the left of me Derek howled nonstop, Ascanio's eerie laughter a bloodcurdling drumbeat to the wolf song.

I caught myself on a tree and paused, surveying the woods. The river lay to my right. A couple hundred yards behind me, a bridge spanned the deep water. In front of me, an old bike path, overgrown but still visible, snaked through the woods, playing hide-and-seek with the shore. If she came from the west, she'd take it.

A huge oak towered to the left of the path. Perfect.

I pressed my back against the bark. I'd only get one shot at this.

The sounds of snapping wood and brush came from the west.

I held my breath.

Closer.

Closer.

A sapling snapped with a loud crack.

Now. I lunged out from behind the tree just as she passed me and sliced across her gullet.

The skin pouch tore open under Sarrat's merciless edge. Holland tumbled out, covered in slime, and drew a hoarse breath.

I had no time to check if he was in one piece. I reversed the blade and thrust it deep between her ribs. Sarrat slid into her flesh with a satisfying hiss, its blade smoking. I twisted sharply to the right. Blood gushed from the wound around the blade.

The monster screamed, her fury shaking the brush.

I pulled my saber free.

The monster whipped around, the skin on her throat hanging like a punctured balloon, and snapped her teeth, trying to bite me in half. I danced back, behind the tree. She followed, crawling up the side of the oak with sickening quickness, her teeth snapping like a bear trap closing. I back-pedaled through the brush, trying not to trip on the forest floor. If her insides matched a human's, I'd sliced her liver and cut the hepatic vein or artery, likely both. If I ran her around enough, she would bleed out.

Ascanio burst out of the woods, speeding up toward us.

The old lady grabbed at me. I sliced at her fingers. She kept coming, oblivious to pain, her face an ugly mask. She was hurting, but killing me was all that mattered.

Ascanio tore into her side, but she ignored him, her gaze fastened on me. I sliced again and again. A moment too slow and she'd grip me into her clawed fist. Strike, strike, strike. This was too much fun.

Derek landed onto Jene's back and thrust a young tree through her. The old lady thrashed, like a pinned bug. Derek ripped into her from above, while Ascanio tore at her from the side.

I ducked in as she thrashed. Her arm passed over me, clawed fingers stretched, and I sliced the inside of her biceps and moved back. One arm down. One to go. *Patience is a virtue . . .*

With a howl, Holland burst from the brush, charged past me, and buried his blade in her neck. She tried to jerk away but the stake held her fast. He hacked at her neck like she was a tree, his sword rising and falling in swift frenzy. Her head sagged to the side, lolled, hanging for a moment by a thread of skin and muscle, then fell and rolled clear. The body crashed into the brush, blood pouring from the stump.

*Okay. That's one way to do it.*

Holland stared at me, his eyes wild, his body dripping slime and blood.

"You're okay," I told him. "You're cool. Everything is okay."

"I quit."

"You're okay. It's shock."

"No. I'm done." He waved his sword at me. "She swallowed me! I was inside her!"

Ascanio cracked up, showing way too many hyena teeth. I gave him the look of death and he clamped his mouth shut.

"I quit!" Holland threw his sword down.

"Okay," Derek said.

"Look, be reasonable," Ascanio said. "We've all been there. One time there was this hungry wendigo . . ."

"Redundant," Derek said.

Ascanio rolled his eyes. "The point is, weird shit happened. Weird shit happens a lot. It's traumatic. Look, she rolled onto me. You don't even want to know what gross things were pressed against my face."

Holland's face jerked.

"Too soon," Derek said. "The man says he quits, let him quit. Here, I'll carry your sword for you."

"What are you doing?" Ascanio said. "He's clearly in shock. Beau assigned him to babysit us. We are difficult to babysit, so Beau must have a lot of respect for the deputy, which in turn means Deputy Holland is good at his job."

"So?" Derek asked.

The magic wave hit, flooding us. The two shapeshifters paused for a moment, acknowledging it, and kept going.

Ascanio shook his furry head. "His entire identity is probably wrapped up in being a deputy. You can't let one incident destroy his sense of self. He needs to be talked off this cliff."

Holland stared at the werewolf, then at the bouda.

Ascanio's mother, Martina, was one of the Pack's counselors. I had no idea he'd picked up that much from her.

"You're not doing a good job of it," Derek said.

"I'd be doing a lot better if you'd stop helping him take the plunge."

I felt a tendril of magic reaching through the woods, delicate, hesitant, searching for something, probing. The magic brushed me and withdrew with elastic quickness.

*Hello, there. And who would you be?*

"Derek, shut up for a second." Ascanio turned to Holland. "Deputy Holland, weird awful crap happened to us today. Because you endured it, that weird awful crap won't be happening to anyone else. Nobody will get eaten. You swore an oath, you upheld your oath. That was a noble thing."

"I don't care," Holland said.

I studied the woods across the river. *Where are you . . . ?*

"It doesn't matter." Derek picked up the old woman's head by the hair and hoisted it up. It was nearly four feet high from chin to the hairline. "Let's talk about this later. We need to take the head to Beau before it starts to smell."

"Why?" Ascanio said.

"She was part of the community," I said without turning. "We need to show proof that we had no choice but to kill her."

A woman stepped out of the woods on the other side of the river, a gauzy dark purple scarf wrapped around her head, hiding the bottom half of her face. She pulled it off slowly, so it hung from her shoulder. About my size and my age, with dark eyes and dark hair pulled into a high ponytail. She wore black pants, soft black boots, and a black coat trimmed with purple and split in the center to allow for quick movement. A black leather gorget shielded her neck, extending into a chest plate of supple black leather that covered her left breast. The chest plate wouldn't stop a sword thrust. It wasn't meant to. It existed to provide her just enough protection so that if she miscalculated by half an inch when she avoided a cut, the graze of the opponent's blade wouldn't draw blood. A katana hung from her belt.

Black and purple again. At least no human leather this time.

The woman looked directly at me and walked to the bridge.

Ah. I see.

Ascanio opened his mouth.

"Quiet," Derek told him.

I strode through the grass toward the bridge, Sarrat in my hand.

We stepped onto the boards at the same time.

The woman stopped. So did I.

She bowed, keeping her eyes on my face.

"The scent from the old lady's house," Derek said behind me.

The scent he'd smelled in Roland's castle and then again in Jene's backyard. Figured.

"I've come for the head," she said, her voice colored with an accent I couldn't place.

Sienna's words came back to me. *The head is important.*

I pondered for a moment. My father wanted the head. Why? It was completely inert. I felt no magic emanating from it.

"No," Holland said.

I glanced over my shoulder. He drew himself straight. "That head is evidence in an ongoing investigation by Milton County. It belongs to the people of Milton County."

I turned back to the woman. "You heard the deputy."

"My orders are to secure the head," she said.

There would be violence. The air was ripe with it.

"You'll have to go through me," I told her.

"So be it."

"Walk away," I told her. "My father isn't worth your life."

"If you kill me, I'll be slain by Sharrim in battle. If I kill you, I'll be slain by Sharrum in his grief. My entire life culminates here. My passage to the afterlife is assured. I'm at peace."

"How about door number three? Turn around and go live a nice life somewhere else."

"You do me a great honor, Sharrim. Defend yourself."

She opened her mouth. A torrent of magic smashed into me. My ears recognized the fact that there must've been a sound, but I didn't hear it, I felt it. It crashed into me, instantly freezing every muscle in my body. It was as if my very cells turned solid. The world slowed to a crawl. I couldn't move.

She'd used a power word against me.

I saw her lunge at a glacial speed, her katana swinging in a glittering beautiful arc, slow, but impossible to stop. Classic attack, two hands, devastating power, born from strength, speed, and precise movement perfected over countless generations.

The sword was coming toward me and I was standing there like an idiot.

I reached deep inside myself and pulled on my magic. Straining was agony. Summoning the power was like grasping my own veins and pulling them out of my body.

The sword reached the highest point and began its inevitable descent.

I *pulled*. Move or die. There was no third choice.

The sword carved its path through the air.

I forced my lips to open a mere crack. The power word was a whisper, a faint breath that escaped my mouth almost on its own.

*"Dair."* Release.

The magic's hold shattered. I shied back. The point of the katana slashed across my face, right to left, drawing a hair-thin line of pain. She struck again, overhead, left to right, too fast to see. I batted her blade aside. Steel rang. She cut at me a third time and I caught her sword on Sarrat. Our blades locked. She threw her entire weight at me, pushing.

My arms shook from the strain. The blades vibrated. Strong.

She grunted, squeezing more pressure. Very strong.

Not strong enough.

I jerked my arms up, throwing her blade and her arms upward. She brought it down, aiming for another devastating cut, but I sliced across her torso, left to right. Sarrat bit deep, cutting across her stomach and coming free, blood flying from its blade.

She fell to her knees and sank down, curling on the ground. So much skill. So much training wasted. Years of practice and study for three seconds of battle and for what? Because my father told her to fetch the head at any cost. She hadn't questioned it. She obeyed.

*"Was it worth it?"*

She was gulping air in shallow breaths.

I crouched by her.

*"Was your life worth this? Can you see the afterlife? Is it everything my father told you it would be? Or is it darkness and nothing?"*

She was staring at me, her eyes wide with fear.

I should kill her and send her head to my father on a fucking pike. Her presence in my land was an insult.

Drops of blood slid from my wounded face, falling into the gash on her stomach. They landed in the pool of her blood, drops of pure fire falling into cooling water, and then something within her blood answered. Her body clutched onto my blood, receptive and eager. Her magic recognized mine. My father had done something to her. The imprint of his power burned within her. He owned her and he had sealed his ownership with magic. I'd felt something similar before on people who were cursed. She was a slave.

*No. She's in my domain. You don't get to keep this one. This one is now mine.*

I dragged my hand over my wound and let my blood fall into her. Commanding her to be released wouldn't do it. I had to supplant his ownership.

*"Hesaad."* Mine.

Her body shook. My father's seal held. I gritted my teeth, pouring magic into her. It pulled her from the brink of death, but she was still his.

"I swore an oath, Sharrim . . ." she whispered. "He's Sharrum . . ."

*"He isn't here. This is my domain. Here I'm Sharratum. Here I rule. My word is the only word that matters."*

The pressure of my power had ground the seal to almost nothing, but couldn't pierce it. It needed to be broken from within. I needed movement or words, some sort of indication, some specific action I could make her do. If she acknowledged and obeyed, it would shatter the seal like the strike of a dagger.

*"Rise."*

She screamed.

*"Rise."*

Convulsions gripped her. She needed help. She'd lost too much blood.

I put my hand above her chest, the surface of my palm a prism through which I focused on the blood inside her. It felt . . . right. I sensed her heart beating and my blood spreading through her like fire. It pumped and each pulse set the intricate net of her capillaries aglow.

Magic bubbled up from somewhere deep within me and flowed out into her. Her body straightened, pulled by my power.

*"Rise."*

The seal shattered in an explosion of power. She rolled to her feet and stood.

Her voice came out strained, in tortured gasps. *"My life . . . for you, Sharratum."*

She swayed, but stayed upright. Blood soaked the entire front of her coat. I could seal her and she would be completely mine. The groundwork was already there.

No. Curran wouldn't like that.

*"Your life is your own. I don't want it. You're no longer a slave."*

I let go. She collapsed on the bridge.

I turned around. Derek stood completely motionless four feet away from me. I'd been concentrating on her so hard, I hadn't heard him walk over. Behind him Ascanio stared at me, his face shocked even in half-form. Holland gripped his sword, watching me like I was rabid.

Damn it. I did it again. I let the magic drag me under. How the hell did it even happen . . . ?

"Sharrim," the woman on the ground whispered. "Let me serve you, Sharrim. My life is yours. My will is yours. Kill me."

Oh crap. Crap.

"Everything I am is yours. All I ask is a good death."

"Why do you keep doing this?" Derek snarled.

"I haven't done anything."

His eyes glowed bright yellow. He bared his teeth, his muzzle wrinkling in an ugly snarl. The fur on his back rose. "Do you think it's fucking easy for Julie? She never forgets that you can override her will with one word. She feels you. Always! Every fucking second of every day."

Julie knew. She *knew.*

"She already loves you as much as she can. I would die fighting for you." He stabbed his clawed hand at Ascanio. "He would die for you. Isn't it fucking enough, Kate? How much love and devotion do you need that you keep making slaves?"

It felt like he had stabbed me.

"I didn't make her into a slave."

"She's bleeding out and all she wants is for you to love her and kill her. What the hell do you call that?"

"I didn't enslave her! My father did. I broke their bond. She's free now."

"I'm so sorry, Sharrim," the woman on the ground whispered. "I didn't mean to make things difficult."

"Will you obey any order she gives?" Derek snarled.

"Yes."

Derek pointed to her. "Don't lie to me, Kate. I'll do almost anything for you, but don't lie to me!"

He didn't believe me. He was right there when it happened and he didn't believe me. Curran wouldn't believe me either. Julie knew she couldn't refuse my orders. Everything I built was collapsing around me.

The magic tore out of me and I screamed into it. The land screamed with me. Water shot up from the river, the trees jerked up as if pulled straight by an invisible hand, and every weed stood perfectly straight. Derek clamped his hands onto the bridge rail. Holland flew back. Ascanio caught him and spun him around, grabbing the rail and shielding the deputy with his back.

I screamed, the frustration boiling out of me until it was finally gone.

Water collapsed back into the river, drenching us with spray.

I had to fix this. I had no idea how and I was suddenly so tired.

I exhaled and turned to Derek. "Have I ever lied to you?"

He didn't answer.

"Have I ever lied to you, Derek?"

"No."

"I'm telling you right now I didn't turn her into a slave. I could've, but I didn't. I don't know what she is. I don't understand why she is acting this way. But we're going to find out. Pick her up. We'll take her to a medmage and when she's better, we can ask her questions."

He stared at me.

"If you won't carry her, then I will," I told him. "But she would be more comfortable with you because you're stronger. Or you can walk away. That will be fine, too."

Derek scooped the woman off the bridge. Ascanio picked up the old woman's head.

We started down the path back to civilization.

I'd fucked up. I didn't cross the line but I came close enough to see the abyss at the bottom. Explaining this to

Curran would be really difficult. Derek was right there and he didn't believe me.

"What's your name?" I asked the woman.

"Adora."

"We're going to take you to the emergency room, where a medmage will work on you. Please don't tell the medmage anything about my father or me. If he asks how you got this wound, tell him to ask me."

"Yes, Sharrim."

Derek's eyes shone.

"Also, please don't call me Sharrim. Call me Kate."

"Yes, Kate."

I needed to figure out exactly what she was before I saw Curran, because I didn't understand it myself and I didn't want there to be any misunderstandings. I knew what I did and what I didn't do. If I made it into a "believe me because I am me and you know me" argument, he would give me the benefit of the doubt, but I didn't want that. I wanted to prove to him with absolute certainty that I hadn't enslaved this woman. I hadn't crossed the line. I'd ridden an elephant up to it and run back and forth along its edge while a mariachi band played in the background, but I hadn't crossed it.

"What kind of language was that?" Holland asked.

"What?"

"When you were talking to her on the bridge, asking questions, what kind of language was it?"

What was he on about? I spoke English.

"I'm going to have to write a report," Holland said.

I looked at Derek. "Did I speak another language?"

"Yes." He didn't look at me.

"What did it sound like?"

"It hurt," Ascanio said.

"But do you remember any actual words?"

"*Estene kari la amt-am.* That was the last thing you said," Derek said.

*You're no longer a slave.* Oh fuck. I understood it. I've been speaking it. All this time I thought my magic was saturating my words. Fuck.

"Put 'language of power' into your report," I said.

"Okay," Holland told me.

The Milton ER was our first stop. We left Adora there. I paid for the first twenty-four hours of treatment and told Adora to stay there until I came and got her. The medmage spelled the cut on my face closed and told me to not expect miracles in regard to whether it would scar.

We walked into Beau's office headfirst. It barely fit through the double door. The sheriff of Milton County looked at the head, looked at us, assessed the sorry state of his deputy, reached into his desk, and extracted a feather.

"This was found where the horses were. The two brothers identified it as belonging to the winged devil."

I took the feather. It was long and glossy, a pure black that seemed to swallow the light, except for the very tip where a thin orange-red flared as if someone had dipped the feather into liquid fire. Only one being had feathers like that—Thanatos, the angel of death, with black wings and a flaming sword.

As soon as I got to a working phone, I'd need to call Teddy Jo.

"You need to tell Curran," Derek told me as we walked back to our cars.

"Stay out of my relationship."

"I don't want you to turn into someone else," he said quietly.

"I won't." Back in the woods when he was screaming in my face, I'd wanted to crush every bone in his body. I'd stomped on that urge before it went anywhere, but it was there. There were few things that terrified me. That did.

I HAD TO do a dozen things. I needed to call Teddy Jo. I needed to speak to Sienna. I needed to look through my notes on my father to see if I could find any reference to what Adora might be. Instead I dropped Ascanio off near his mother's house, dropped Derek off at Cutting Edge, and turned around. I drove through the city as the sun slowly rolled toward the horizon. By the time I got to the Keep, the heat of the day had begun to ease. Evening was coming.

I walked into the Keep, identified myself to the sentries, and one of the guards walked me to the medward. New rules. Jim had decided I shouldn't be walking around the Keep unescorted. It didn't even bother me. I'd gone numb.

They'd put Andrea in a corner room, the one with large windows. I walked in. She was eating fried chicken and Raphael was holding Baby B.

Andrea saw my face and stopped eating.

"I've come to hold the baby," I told her.

She nodded to Raphael. He got up and gave his daughter to me. I took Baby B. She stirred a little in her sleep and snuggled against me.

"The other room has the rocking chair in it," Andrea said, pointing through the open double door. "There's a nice window there."

I went into the other room and sat in the rocking chair by the window, Baby B in my arms.

"Is everything okay?" Raphael asked quietly in the other room.

"Things are kind of fucked up right now," Andrea said. "I'll tell you later."

I rocked Baby B. It was just me, the baby, and the slowly dying evening.

I wasn't sure how much time had passed.

Someone walked in. I listened to the steps. Julie.

"Hi," she said behind my back.

"Hi."

She came over and sat on the floor by me.

"What's up?" I asked.

"Derek talked to me." Julie sighed and hugged her knees. "Derek is a dummy. Why is it that guys can't keep a secret?"

"It was a pretty big secret."

"Well, it wasn't his to tell."

"When did you find out?" I asked.

"Roland told me when you went to the Black Sea."

"Is that how long you've been talking to him?"

She nodded.

"He's poison."

"I know."

I looked at her. "Why, Julie? Is it power? Is it knowledge?"

"It's because I love you," she said in a small voice.

"What?"

"You're twenty-eight," she said. "Voron left Roland's service almost thirty years ago. The last up-to-date information you have on him is thirty years old. When Voron died thirteen years ago, you lost even that. Roland has done a lot in thirty years."

"I don't need you to spy on Roland for me. It's too dangerous. You're sixteen years old. He is over five thousand years old, possibly older. You can't trust anything he says. You can't even trust anything you see there. He's manipulating you and grooming you."

"Yes," she said. "He is. He would be manipulating me and grooming me anyway. He wasn't going to leave me alone, Kate, so at first I wanted to learn as much as I could to shut him out. Then . . ."

"Then?"

"You're right. I'm sixteen years old. He doesn't remember what it's like to be sixteen. He doesn't understand it. To him everyone is a child. His own childhood was long and happy. He was a pampered prince. But I starved on the street. I learned how to read people and manipulate adults when I was ten." She bit her lip. "I kind of thought he would be more subtle about it. Maybe if I didn't have you and Curran, or if he had gotten me really young like he did Hugh . . ."

"You keep thinking that you've got this, but you don't, Julie."

"He manages what he shows me," Julie said. "But I'm not you, so he doesn't manage quite as much. You're his daughter, his precious jewel. He's so proud of you. I'm an expendable tool. He wants to sharpen me, use me, and then throw me away when I've served my purpose, just like he threw away Hugh. He's less careful with what he lets me see."

"All the more reason not to interact with him."

"You could order me not to do it," she said.

"I won't. It's your life, Julie. You're a person. As much as it makes me freak out, you have to be free to make your decisions, even the wrong ones. But I think it's dangerous and stupid, and I will tell you so."

"In great detail. With a scary look on your face." Julie sighed.

"Yes. But in the end, they are your decisions. You're not a baby."

"Sometimes you treat me like one."

"I'll treat you like a baby when you're fifty. Get used to it." I looked at Baby B. "I didn't do it to own you. I did it to save your life. I had no choice."

"I know. You knew I would hate it, but you did it anyway, because you love me." Julie swallowed. "So did I. I talked to Roland even though I knew you would hate it. It's your fault. You were my role model."

"Great."

"I didn't mean it that way. That was a joke." Julie looked down at her feet. "He's teaching me. I think he means for me to be the next Hugh."

"Hugh is one of the most lethal fighters I know. You're nowhere near that. Your magic isn't combat magic."

"It is now," she said.

My heart turned over in my chest. "Power words?"

She nodded. "Also incantations. Makes the power words a lot easier."

"You always wanted combat magic." It bothered her that she didn't have any. At first, we put her into a private middle school. The kids there had combat magic and she didn't. It made things harder on her. She didn't fit in and she kept running away.

"I did," Julie said. "Now I have it."

That was how he got her. There were four main incentives that moved people to do things: power, wealth, knowledge, and emotion. He offered her power and knowledge, two out of four. She belonged to me, so he couldn't take her outright, but he could poison her. He could push and shape her until he made her into another Hugh.

I wanted to believe that she wasn't his creature. I wanted so much to believe that she had kept her independence, but the fear sat inside me like a brick.

This was what Curran must've felt like when I assured him I would fight the magic changing me. Ugh.

"The girl is sahanu," Julie said.

"Mmm?"

"Adora. She's sahanu."

Sahanu meant "to unsheathe a blade" in ancient Akkadian. Specifically, to draw a dagger.

"And the other two on the wall?"

"Sahanu also. I was going to tell you, but Roland came out and then you were angry."

"Are they elite troops of some sort?"

"He made them to fight Erra," Julie said. "He showed them to me before. I think that when he felt your aunt waking up, he became concerned that he wouldn't be able to control her, so he created the Order of Sahanu. He got the idea from a documentary on assassins."

I must've moved because Baby B stirred and started whimpering. I rocked her, making shooshing noises.

"He bought a bunch of children and put them into a fort," Julie whispered. "Somewhere in the Midwest. And brought in really good teachers. He turned the whole thing into a religion."

"Shhh . . . Shush . . . He would never allow himself to be an object of worship." When you let people worship you, their faith had power over you. My father would never tolerate anything imposing on his will.

"He isn't. They worship the blood."

Baby B opened her mouth and cried with all of the despair her little heart could muster. I got up and took her to Andrea.

"I see how it is." She squinted at me. "While she's quiet,

everyone wants to hold her, but when she cries, give her back to her parents."

"Yeah." I winked at her.

Andrea gave me a long look and cuddled Baby B to her. Julie and I left the room. We walked through the Keep in silence. The walls did have ears here. In the courtyard, only my car looked out of place. Peanut was nowhere to be seen.

"How did you get here?" I asked her.

"Derek dropped me off."

I opened the car and she climbed into the passenger seat.

"For the sahanu, there is only one way to receive the ultimate reward in the afterlife. They must die in service to your blood. If one of the blood kills them or if they manage to kill one of the blood on the orders of another, they get to the extra-special level of heaven. If they fail, they are condemned to a frozen hell. It's sick and twisted."

And I had no idea if she was telling me the truth or only what my father wanted me to hear. I'd have to verify this. If this was true, then it explained Adora's panic at being set free. And now she was my dirty secret. I had no idea how to break it to Curran.

"Are you mad at me?" Julie asked, her voice small.

"No." I was plenty mad at myself. "I'm worried."

"I can take care of myself," she said.

"He will hurt you. That's what he does."

She smiled, her face in profile with the backdrop of the evening sky behind it. She looked so young right then, but her smile was bitter.

"When I talk to him, I never forget what he did to Hugh."

Ouch.

"Promise me you will never do that to me."

*"I will never exile you. I will never prevent you from leaving."* I sank enough magic into those words to make a dozen wards.

She hugged her knees.

"You're my daughter, Julie. But you have to promise me that if you see me treat people the way my father does, you will leave."

"Don't say that."

"Promise me, Julie."

"Okay. I will leave. But you're not going to do that, right?"

"Right." I would fight to my last breath to remain me. I didn't know if I could win, but I'd be damned if I gave up.

*Hold on, Father. We will have a conversation regarding my kid and everything else. I promise you that.*


WHEN WE GOT home, Curran wasn't there. Walking into my kitchen was like putting on my favorite T-shirt. By the time I made myself and Julie a sandwich with bread, cheese, and leftover roasted meat and brewed a cup of tea, I felt almost normal. There was still time to make some phone calls.

I called Teddy Jo first.

"Yes?"

"Hello, winged devil. Are the Pegasuses rideable?"

"Kate?" He sounded startled.

"Yes."

"Good evening to you, too."

"Good evening, Teddy Jo. How's life, how's the family? Are the Pegasuses rideable?"

"First, pegasi. It's not the original Pegasus. To answer your question, yes, they are rideable. For the right person."

Right person, okay. I picked up a legal pad. This was going to cost me.

"You there?"

"Sure." Hey there, I'm Kate, I came to do my twelve labors. Where do I sign up? I was really beginning to doubt the whole oracle thing. "How do I become the right person?"

A long silence.

"Teddy Jo? Are you okay?"

"Some things you just don't do," he said. There was an odd finality about his voice that told me he wasn't talking about flying horses.

"Are you in trouble?" I asked.

Silence.

"Level with me. Are you in trouble?"

"Yes," he said.

"How bad?"

"Bad."

"How do you get out of trouble?"

Silence.

"It's been a long day, but I don't mind driving to your place if you would rather talk in person." Translation: my patience is short and I will drive over to wherever you are and shake you until you tell me.

"I'm supposed to arrange a meeting between you and someone else. I was sitting here thinking about it when you called."

"Is it the kind of meeting I don't walk away from?"

"I don't know."

"What do they have on you?"

"They have something of mine. Something that I have to have to remain me." I could hear it in his voice. Whatever they took had him scared, and Teddy Jo didn't scare easily.

"So what you're telling me is, I've been invited to an interesting meeting and you weren't going to tell me. Not cool, Theodore. Not cool."

"Kate . . ."

I needed to get to Mishmar as soon as I could. But judging by Teddy Jo's voice, he needed help and he needed it now. He was doing a good job of hiding the desperation, but it was there. I had a feeling all of this was somehow connected.

"We've been friends, what, four years now? Five? I expected better of you. Where are we going and when?"

"I'll pick you up tomorrow at your house." His voice regained some of its normal grumpiness. "Nine o'clock. Wear boots and bring your sword."

"I always bring my sword."

Julie brought in a stack of mail and put a white envelope in front of me.

"Good. I'll be bringing a harness."

"A harness for what?"

"For whom. For you. It's easier to carry you that way."

I sighed. "Are we flying?"

"I'm flying. If you're lucky, I won't drop you."

"If you drop me, I'll be very put out."

"I'll keep that in mind."

I hung up and opened the envelope. Inside on a crisp piece of paper embossed with roses, an outrageously curvy cursive said:

*With great pleasure*
*We invite you to the union of*

## Kate Daniels

*and*

## Curran Lennart

"What is this?"

"It's a wedding invitation," Julie said.

"I didn't order any."

Julie grinned at me. "Roman."

Ugh. That's right. I waved the envelope at her. "It has flowers on it."

"Did you want gore, swords, and severed heads?" she asked.

Smartass.

Speaking of severed heads . . . I picked up the phone and dialed Sienna's number. She picked up immediately.

"What's the significance of the head?"

"I have no idea."

"But you knew it was important."

"The head is an anchor. When you look into the future,

some things are out of focus, but some vital events are more clear. Think of it as coming to a crossroads. If you've met the conditions, you take the right fork; if you fail, you take the wrong one."

"Okay." That made sense.

"The head was one such point. I saw you turning the head over to some sort of law enforcement. My guess is that Roland's people saw it, too. They knew it was an anchor, and so Roland probably took steps to make sure it didn't happen. Did you have to fight?"

"Yes."

"And you won?"

"Yes."

"Then congratulations."

Congratulations were premature. There were questions about it that bugged me. For one, if my father wanted the head so much, why did he only send one sahanu to get it?

"So these anchors, they're like checkpoints I have to clear?"

"Yes, in a sense."

"What's the next one?"

"I don't know. I'll call you when I do."

"Thank you."

"It's not too late to turn back," Sienna said. "This is a dangerous path for you. I don't like where it ends."

"Are we still on track?"

"In a manner of speaking."

"Then we'll keep going. Thank you for your help."

I hung up.

"So the head wasn't even important?" Julie asked.

"Apparently not."

My phone rang. I picked it up.

"You have something that belongs to me."

Control. Zen. Screaming in ancient languages would not be zen. "You don't say. You enslaved that poor girl. You're despicable, Father."

"You're a disobedient foolish child. I gave her security and serenity of purpose."

"So you admit you sent her into my territory?"

"I admit to nothing."

"Come on, Father. This is unbecoming. I don't understand why you only sent one. Really, you think so little of me?"

"I sent one because I felt one was sufficient. She wasn't meant to kill you, Blossom."

Ah. She was only meant to disrupt my attempts to keep him from killing everyone else I cared about.

"Return Saiman to me."

"No. Also, this is utterly ridiculous. Why do I have to choose between the meat and vegetarian option?"

"What?"

"You are the princess of Shinar. Your line stretches back beyond known history. You shouldn't have to make your guests choose a single option. Your wedding should be a feast."

I pried the wedding card open. Inside, a smaller RSVP card said, *Please indicate if you prefer a vegetarian course.*

"If he can't pay for a suitable meal for his own wedding, I will provide the kind of feast that will make the tables break. I will make sure that your guests will have a banquet they will never forget. Greater than any your eldest guest can remember and more magnificent than the youngest will ever experience again."

So help me, I would murder Roman. I'd hack him to pieces with an axe and then hack those pieces into smaller pieces. He'd sent my father an invitation to my wedding.

"Father, you are sending mixed signals. You dispatched a woman to murder me today and now you're upset about my wedding reception?"

"It's not my fault you decided to marry a pauper. Besides, you enjoy a challenge."

"I can't talk to you anymore. I had a rough day and I'm going to bed."

"Kate—"

"Stay away from my kid."

"Perhaps you should ask the child what she wants."

"I did ask her. She's right here and now I'll have to

explain to her that Grandpa is evil and enslaves people. Good night."

I hung up and looked at Julie.

She recoiled. "He isn't my grandpa!"

"Don't worry, I'm sure it's more disconcerting to him than it is to you."

I drained the rest of my tea and went to bed.

Eɪɢʜᴛ ʜᴏᴜʀs ᴏꜰ sleep felt like pure heaven. I woke up and lay on the bed for a long time, happy to not move. Curran sprawled next to me. He'd come home after I went to bed. I must've been more rattled than I thought, because when he walked into the bedroom, I woke up, grabbed Sarrat, and made it two whole steps toward him before I realized what was happening, which earned me a round of applause and calls for an encore. Then he saw the scar and acted as if half of my face had been hacked off. He almost dragged me to the Guild's medmage, but I threatened to stab him and I must've been vigorous enough to reassure him I was in good health. Of all the people I could've decided to marry, I had to choose him.

Afterward he took a shower and fell into bed next to me and we passed out in a happy exhausted tangle. Now I didn't want to get up.

Teddy Jo would be here soon. Ugh.

I rolled out of bed. A hand fastened on my ankle and pulled me back in. I landed next to him. Gray eyes laughed at me.

"How's my face?"

"The scar's looking better."

"It's a scratch." It's good he didn't see it before the med-mage spent half an hour on it. According to Ascanio, he would've been able to see into my face.

"So, Julie's home," he said.

"She is."

"Have you come to an agreement on Roland?"

"No. The only way to stop her from talking to him is to order it, and she called my bluff. I won't do it."

"She knows?"

"He told her," I ground out. "She's known for months."

The look on Curran's face was priceless. All cold concentrated fury. If he could've gotten his hands on my father in that second, Roland would regret ever learning Julie existed. I kissed him. I loved him for that.

"According to her, she's gathering information on Roland for us," I said. "There's nothing I can do. I have to trust that she's learned enough in the time we had her and that she's independent enough to fight off his influence."

"We need to do something about your father. Soon."

"Yes. He called the house upset about the reception dinner."

"I know. He called the Guild as well."

"Really?"

Curran nodded. "He and I had a conversation. I told him that it was a bit late to play father of the year, but if he behaved himself, we would make sure to save him a seat at the wedding."

I laughed.

The doorbell rang. I glanced at the clock. Eight. Too early for Teddy Jo.

"I got it!" Julie yelled. Quick thumps announced her running down the stairs. "Kate! Kate, it's for you! Kate!"

The urgency in her voice jerked me right out of bed. I grabbed Sarrat and dashed out of the bedroom onto the landing. People filed into our lobby, carrying bolts of white fabric. A short Asian woman in a black dress looked up at me and arched her eyebrows.

I realized I was standing on the landing in a tiny T-shirt and underwear, holding a sword.

"Who are you?"

"I'm Fiona Katsura."

Clan Nimble. "Why are you in my house?"

"I'm here to fit your wedding dress."

"I didn't—"

"Of course, you didn't. You didn't mean any disrespect." Fiona put her hands on her hips. "Our family has been designing wedding dresses for three generations. We don't just sew, we create art. Designers come all the way from as far as Los Angeles and London for a chance to look at our work. Customers take out loans to purchase one of our gowns. Your dress has been on our project desk for months, back when you were still the Consort. Many sketches have been made and rejected. Countless hours of thought and consideration went into planning. Four appointments have been made, the last only three weeks ago, appointments you have failed to keep, no doubt because of your busy schedule. So when a strange man calls the Keep, and asks if we have your measurements and notes on your dress, and inquires if we would be willing to part with whatever we had already made so he could have his *tailor*"— she said the word so sharply, I checked myself to see if I'd been cut—"finish it in time for the wedding, we all knew that there must've been some horrible misunderstanding."

I would strangle Roman. There was no way around it.

"Well, ex-Consort, if you can't come to our studio, we have brought the studio to you."

"I'm sorry. I really am but I don't have time to—"

Fiona narrowed her eyes. "Jun?"

A young Japanese man stopped by her. "Sister?"

"Bring the ex-Consort to me."

"Curran!" I backed away from the railing. "Curran, help!"

Laughter exploded in the bedroom. Bastard.

I STOOD IN the middle of the floor, trying not to move while three of Fiona's people, two young women and a man in his midtwenties who looked a lot like her and Jun, sewed me into a practice gown. Jun, Fiona's brother and enforcer, positioned himself in front of me. The real wedding dress would apparently come later and, according to them, I'd have to do at least two more fittings. I could barely contain my joy.

"Please stop grinding your teeth," Fiona said. "It's very distracting."

"This one or this one?" Jun held up two squares of lace.

They tried to make me pick one out of twenty different samples. I told them I didn't care, so they resorted to the process of elimination.

"Left." The one on the right clearly had been stolen from some grandma's coffee table. "Teddy Jo will be here any minute."

"When he's here, you can go," Fiona told me.

A needle poked my thigh.

"Sorry, ex-Consort," one of the seamstresses said.

I looked at Julie snickering in the corner. "Where is Curran?"

"Curran can't be here," Fiona said. "It's bad luck for the groom to see the wedding dress before the wedding."

"Who made that rule?"

"It's tradition," Fiona said.

"I don't care about tradition."

"Tradition is everything," Fiona said.

"Julie, where is he?"

"He went out to check on the horses."

"Really? He hates horses."

Julie's eyes sparkled. "He said it was very important for him to check that they were still there. And that he was also there and not here when you snapped."

When I got out of this dress, I'd give him a piece of my mind.

"She keeps flexing." The seamstress on the left said.

"How much difference is it making?" Fiona said.

"About an inch overall. She's very muscular," the man said.

"Stop talking about me like I'm not even here."

The seamstress on the left pulled on the fabric. "If you want me to take up this slack and she flexes during the wedding, we'll have a problem."

"She's a human," Fiona said. "I don't care how muscular she is, she isn't going to rip it like the Incredible Hulk."

"She won't rip it, but it will skew this seam right here."

Fiona frowned and tapped her pencil on her lips. "Let it go?"

The seamstress let go of the fabric and all five stared at my waist. *Keep looking, it will do a trick.*

Someone knocked. I turned.

"Do not move!" Fiona snapped.

Jun opened the door and Barabas stepped inside. He took in the scene and gave me a brilliant smile.

"Ah!" Fiona said. "Perfect. Unbiased opinion." She marched over to me and pulled the fabric tight. "No slack?" She let go. "Or slack?"

"No slack," Barabas said. "It gives her an almost hourglass figure. Kate, which way do you like it?"

"I don't care."

"The ex-Consort has been most uncooperative," Jun said.

"I can't imagine why." Barabas grinned wider. "She's usually the embodiment of patience and cooperation."

Christopher stumbled into the house, walking backward, his eyes wide.

Something was wrong. "Christopher?"

He turned to me, his face shocked, the corners of his mouth slack with terror. "Thanatos."

"What?" Barabas asked.

"Thanatos is coming." Christopher's voice shook. "The reaper of souls is coming to take one of you to the afterlife."

Oh boy. "No, that's Teddy Jo. He's a friend."

"Chris." Barabas moved in front of the door. "Remember how we spoke about visual cues? Look at my face. I'm not upset. Look at Kate. She isn't upset."

"It's okay, Christopher," I said. "Teddy Jo and I have a business appointment this morning. He's actually a nice guy. He's coming to pick me up."

Panic slapped his face. "No! Don't you get it? He is coming for someone's soul!"

And now the book burning made total sense. He clearly had a Greek underworld fixation.

"Deep breath," Barabas said. "Calm . . ."

"He'll take no one." Christopher's voice dropped deeper. "I won't allow it."

"Calm . . ." Barabas repeated.

Christopher jerked his hands up and shoved Barabas aside. The weremongoose flew across the floor and smashed into the wall to the left of me.

Oh shit.

Christopher's body expanded, ripping through his clothes. He opened his mouth and his canines grew, curving down like vampire fangs. Red smoke spiraled out of his back. "Stay inside!"

He ran out the door.

"What the fuck?" Barabas charged after him. I grabbed the hem of my gown and ran after them.

I burst onto the lawn. Barabas spun around, searching the street.

No Christopher.

Nobody outside except Teddy Jo flying in from the west on his dark wings.

"Stop!" I yelled, waving my arms. "Stop!"

Teddy Jo waved back at me.

The gown tangled around my legs and I nearly tripped. I grabbed the hem and ripped the skirt all the way to my waist.

"What the hell was that?" Barabas snarled.

"I don't know."

"Where is he?" Barabas spun around.

"I don't know."

Julie dashed onto the lawn.

A piercing scream rolled through the air. Fear grabbed me into a tight fist, an instinctual deep terror rising from somewhere within, from the place where the primal fears of fire, darkness, and predators lived. Barabas let out an odd high-pitched chatter that no human mouth should have been able to make.

A winged shape swooped down from above, propelled into an eagle dive by enormous blood-red wings. Somehow Teddy Jo saw it and careened to the left, banking hard. The creature that used to be Christopher spread its wings, trying to slow, and landed on the lawn. He was muscled like an antique statue. He opened his mouth, his fangs glistening. Madness churned in his ruby irises.

"What the hell!" Teddy Jo screamed.

I rushed at Christopher. Barabas beat me by half a second, but before he reached him, Christopher beat his wings and shot into the sky. The weremongoose's arms closed over empty air.

Christopher flew up and smashed into Teddy Jo. The angel of death threw his arms up trying to deflect the blow, but the impact of Christopher's body knocked him sideways. If he used his flaming sword, Christopher was a goner.

The two winged shapes spun in the air, ripping at each other, black wings and blood-red wings slapping against each other again and again.

Another scream. Terror gripped me, crushing my ability to think. It couldn't be . . . Crap. Crap, crap, crap.

Teddy Jo fell from the sky.

I jumped one way, Barabas jumped the other, and Teddy Jo crashed between us like a rock. He rolled to his feet, huge wings sweeping the ground. Blood spattered his face and chest. Above us Christopher flew up, getting ready for another dive.

"That's an avatar!" Teddy Jo snarled at me. "Damn it, Kate!"

"I didn't know! Where is your sword?"

"I don't have it! I can't fight him without the sword."

Of all the times to not bring the flaming sword.

"Get inside before he hurts himself!" Barabas pointed at the door.

"Himself?" Teddy Jo turned purple in the face.

Christopher plummeted from the sky and landed in front of the doorway, blocking the entrance with his wings.

The car. It was our only option.

"Stay behind me." I put myself between Teddy Jo and Christopher and began moving sideways toward the Jeep. The back row of seats was down. If he folded his wings, he'd fit.

"Chris." Barabas approached Christopher, his arms raised, open palms up. "Hey. It's me. Calm down. It's okay."

Christopher pulled his wings to him, covering himself completely. The wings snapped open and he took off into the air. The wind blast knocked Barabas off his feet.

"Run!" I pushed Teddy Jo toward the Jeep.

He sprinted across the lawn. Christopher swooped over him. Teddy Jo landed by the Jeep, pressing against it. I covered him, trying to block Christopher's access. Julie crouched next to me. Teddy Jo pushed us aside and dashed around the car, wedging himself into the narrow space between the two vehicles. Christopher dived at him, but the gap was too narrow. He flew up, circling. I saw his mouth open and clamped my hands over my ears.

Christopher shrieked and the world drowned in fear. My thoughts scattered . . .

*So afraid . . .*

*Have to run.*

. . .

I heard myself screaming.

Barabas was screaming next to me, abject terror turning his face into a bloodless mask. Julie was on the ground, curled into a ball.

Curran leapt over the seven-foot fence and ran to me.

"Help!" I yelled.

He looked up, his eyes following Christopher back and forth as he circled us in the air. Curran's muscles tensed. He gathered himself, jumped up as if shot out of a cannon, knocked Christopher out of the air, and landed on top of him on the ground.

Christopher tried to rise. Curran's body twisted into

warrior shape, packing on muscle and pounds. He strained, keeping Christopher down.

I threw myself on him, adding my weight to Curran's. Barabas landed on the other side, clamping Christopher's left arm. Julie grabbed Christopher's leg.

"Christopher," Barabas called. "We're all safe. You don't have to hurt anyone. Nobody's in danger . . ."

Christopher snarled, baring his fangs, and stood up, heaving all of us up with him.

"Curran!" I yelled.

"I've got him." Curran's body thickened again. He was almost completely lion now. Hundreds of pounds of weight, but Christopher was still standing.

"Chris!" Barabas called.

Christopher screamed. Every nightmare I'd ever had came together and punched me in the face.

. . .

I had to stay. I had to hold him down. I had to or he would kill Teddy Jo.

I had to protect Teddy Jo.

Tears wet my cheeks.

Behind me Maggie shot out of the house, barking at the top of her lungs, and bit Curran's ankle.

"Julie," he growled.

She let go of Christopher, grabbed the little dog, and carried Maggie back into the house. Every muscle in my body shook under the strain of keeping Christopher down.

A rider on a black horse galloped up and dismounted.

"I've got this," Roman called out. "I've got this!"

He reached between us and stuffed a clump of dark fabric into Christopher's mouth.

Christopher flailed. My legs left the ground and I swung free above the grass.

Roman's staff opened its eyes. He thrust it into the ground. Magic shifted around us.

*"Syra mat zemlya, ne dershi ty ego!"*

Christopher sank into the ground up to his hips. Curran grabbed his right arm, while Barabas wrapped himself around his left.

"That ought to do it," Roman said. "Greeks and their wings. Flying here, flying there, screaming their heads off, scaring the horse."

The fashion division of Clan Nimble applauded from the doorway. Nice of them to help.

"Christopher," Barabas called. "Christopher!"

Christopher ignored him.

Sometimes an educated guess is the best you've got. "Deimos?"

Christopher's face snapped toward me.

"Deimos?" Barabas asked, his voice hitting a high note.

"Son of Ares, the Greek god of war, and Aphrodite, the goddess of love."

"A god?" Barabas asked. "What is he a god of?"

"Terror."

Christopher stared at me. If looks could kill, I'd be down on the ground breathing my last breath.

"How?" Curran asked me.

Gods couldn't manifest except during a flare. "I have no idea. Deimos must've been inside Christopher and he saw Teddy Jo, recognized him as Thanatos, and lost his mind."

The Johns Hopkins psychiatrist did say Christopher would need an incentive to want to heal. This was not what I had in mind.

Teddy Jo pushed the two Jeeps apart, marched out, and punched Roman in the jaw.

Okay. The world had really gone insane.

The volhv stumbled back a couple of steps. "What the hell was that for?"

"You know what for."

"I didn't take it."

"No, but *he* did."

"I wasn't involved in any of that. It's your own fault. If you hadn't chased after naked women at night, you wouldn't be in this mess."

"I thought she was in danger," Teddy Jo ground out.

"Sure, you did. Keep telling yourself that."

Teddy Jo took another step forward.

Roman's dark eyebrows furrowed. "Watch it, birdie, before I break those wings off. I already got one of you. I have no problem adding another."

Nice to know that in a crisis his Russian accent evaporated. I stepped between them. "What's going on?"

Teddy Jo waved his arms. "What's going on is I was flying here to meet with you and you sicced the son of Ares on me. I'm a demigod. That's a full-out avatar. How is he not disappearing?"

"Nobody knew he was an avatar. You triggered his transformation. It's not my fault you left your sword at home."

"I didn't leave it, damn it all to Tartarus!"

"Baby," Curran called, his voice saturated with controlled exertion. "Take Teddy Jo and go. Christopher isn't going to calm down until you leave."

I didn't want to leave. I wanted to stay and figure out what was going on with Christopher. But he was right. Christopher wouldn't calm down until Teddy Jo was out of sight and striking range.

I ran inside, pulled off the dress, threw it at Fiona, and ran upstairs. Two minutes later I was back, wearing my normal clothes, Sarrat on my back.

Teddy Jo held out a leather swing on chains. "Sit."

"You said a harness. That is not a harness. That's a playground swing."

"What if she falls?" Roman asked.

Teddy Jo's eyes bulged a little. He was at the end of his patience. "If she falls, I'll catch her."

"That's it." Roman thrust the staff at me. "Hold him. I'm coming with. I'll be needed for negotiations anyway."

Teddy Jo rolled his eyes.

"I'm not taking chances with this wedding. She's going to walk down the aisle, and I'm marrying her and Curran."

Teddy Jo looked at me. "You're having him officiate at your wedding? Do you know what he does?"

"Could you please have this discussion somewhere else?" Barabas asked.

Roman stretched his arms and popped his neck, as if about to take a swim. "Take care of my horse, please." He planted his feet, took a deep breath, and exhaled. "I hate this part."

Bones crunched. Roman threw himself on the ground. Black feathers exploded and lay flat, and a raven the size of a human stared at me with brown eyes.

Holy crap.

I hugged Curran, who was still holding Christopher-Deimos in an arm lock. "Love you, I'll be back soon. Don't let him drink any blood."

"Get into the swing," Teddy Jo said.

Christopher strained, screaming into his gag. I wedged myself between Barabas and Curran and hugged him. "I'll be back. Don't worry."

He continued to struggle against Curran's hold. He had Christopher's face and Christopher's hair, but aside from that nothing else remained. Christopher was gentle. The creature that fought so hard Curran's muscles bulged keeping it down was anything but gentle. I really hoped I hadn't watched the person I knew as Christopher die in the transformation.

Julie dashed out of the house. "Sienna called."

Damn it all. "What did she say?"

"Beware the dragon."

Well, wasn't that a cherry on top of my morning.

FLYING WAS OVERRATED. Heights were very overrated. Flying with wings was probably less overrated when said wings belonged to you, but when you were dangling in a swing that bopped up and down every time the angel of death carrying you beat his wings, you reached a new level of appreciation for walking. Walking was amazing and awesome, and I really wanted to do it again as soon as possible.

"Kate," Teddy Jo called out. "How are you going to ride a pegasi? You're terrified of heights."

"I'm not. I just don't like them."

"You really, really don't like them."

*Thank you, Captain Obvious.* I stared straight ahead. Looking down made every hair on my body stand on end. I had to do it. There was no other choice.

Unfortunately looking straight ahead was boring, so I kept coming back to trying to process the whole Christopher thing and failing. If he were Deimos's avatar, he shouldn't have been able to exist. I couldn't quite get around that.

"Do you want to tell me what happened to your sword now?" I shifted my grip on the chain. If I squeezed any harder, my hands would cramp up, and I needed my hands to hold my sword.

"I was flying home," Teddy Jo said. "It was dark. I saw a naked woman stumbling along the road below me. I landed to see if she was okay. She told me a monster was in the woods. I pulled out my sword and then I woke up in the mud, in the middle of the forest. A voice told me to bring you to the same spot within three days so a bargain could be struck."

"What kind of voice?"

"Female. Very beautiful."

"And what does this have to do with your punching Roman?"

"His god took it."

"You think Chernobog took your sword?"

"I don't think. I know. Look down."

We'd been flying north toward the Chattahoochee National Forest and then over it. I locked my teeth and looked down.

A black stain spread below us. Massive trees, so dense you couldn't see through their crowns, stood shoulder to shoulder, their leaves such a dark green they looked black. A narrow road snaked its way around the black woods.

"Did you talk to Roman about it?"

"Yeah. He says he doesn't know why that happened."

"If Chernobog wanted to talk to me, why didn't he use Roman?"

"Nobody knows that either."

"Why does he want to talk to me?"

"You keep asking these questions. I gave you all of the information I have."

"Anything you can tell me about the woman?"

"She had blue hair."

Ahead of us the enormous raven that was Roman swooped down.

"Hold on," Teddy Jo said.

"I thought I'd throw my arms up like on a roller coaster."

"Your funeral."

"Better not be. I die, you might never get your sword back."

We dived. Wind whistled past my ears. The ground rushed at us.

Below us, the raven twisted back into a human.

The ground hurtled toward me at an alarming speed.

*We are all going to die . . .*

Six feet above the grass I decided to take my chances. I jumped out of the swing—the ground punched my feet—and rolled upright.

Roman clapped.

"What the hell?" Teddy Jo asked, landing. "I would've set you down."

Legs unbroken, arms unbroken, and best of all, solid ground under my feet.

"I'm okay."

Roman laughed.

"Don't laugh."

"Can't help it." The smile slid off his face. "It might be the last time. Nothing good will come from your entering this forest. This isn't a place where normal people are welcome."

"I should be right at home, then."

"I'm serious, Kate. Here the old powers rule. Elemental powers. It's not too late to turn back."

"It's always too late," I told him.

"Do you remember how to talk to the gods?"

"Don't ask for anything, promise nothing, and accept no gifts."

Roman sighed. "We shall go, then." He headed into the woods. We followed, picking our way through the underbrush along a narrow trail.

"Why didn't Chernobog tell you that he wanted to talk to me?" I asked. "It would've made things a lot simpler."

"He did," Roman said. "Sometimes he wants things and I talk him out of it. I thought we had agreed to let you be. You have enough on your plate."

"Your god went around you," Teddy Jo said.

"He did. I tried to tell him it's a bad idea, I tried to tell Kate it's a bad idea, and nobody listens to me. And so here we are." He waved at the darkness in the woods.

"You didn't try very hard to talk her out of it," Teddy Jo said.

"I respect her," Roman said. "She knows what she's doing. If she says she wants to talk to my god, then so be it. Besides, if Chernobog wants to talk to you, he'll find a way."

Speaking of respect . . . "I have a bone to pick with you."

"Oh?"

"Did you send my father a wedding invitation?"

"Of course I did."

"Did you clear it with me?"

Roman bent an eyebrow at me. "You weren't available."

Around us black woods crowded the path: black trunks, black leaves, black roots. You'd never know it was noon and a few dozen feet above us, the world was bright and full of sunshine. Here darkness ruled. There was something primal about it. Something primitive and old. Things with narrow glowing eyes stared at us from the black brush. This forest gave me the creeps.

"My father called me, all offended on my behalf that the wedding dinner isn't sufficiently feastlike."

"Umm," Roman said.

"Curran is also now offended because my father referred to him as a pauper."

"Umm," Roman offered.

"And then you called over to the Keep and offended the dress designers, so they hunted me down this morning and invaded my house."

"You do need a dress."

"You're not a wedding planner, you're a menace. Stop planning my wedding."

"I'll stop when you start."

"There is nothing to plan."

Roman turned to Teddy Jo on the trail next to him. "Do you see what I have to deal with?"

"What does this wedding look like in your head?" Teddy Jo asked me. "Is it like the family gets there and then this Russian shows up and marries you?"

"Pretty much."

"No," Teddy Jo said.

"It's my wedding. It's for me."

"No, your wedding night is for you. The wedding is for everyone else."

"I told her," Roman said. "Weddings require preparation. It's a significant, hopefully once-in-a-lifetime event where you swear to love and cherish another person, not casually but through thick and thin. It's a promise that is meant to be kept forever. Honestly, Kate, do you want to get married? It's a serious question."

I sighed. "I want to get married. And maybe I would like to be there to pick the flowers and choose the dress and select the menu. But war is coming. My future is on fire and I have to put it out if I hope to have any future left . . ."

They weren't in front of me anymore.

I clamped my mouth shut. The two men had disappeared. I stood alone. Ahead of me the trail nearly vanished too, all but melted into a bog about fifty feet wide. On both sides, black water slicked blacker mud. Massive black trees bordered the bog, their branches braiding high above me like the fingers of two hands interlaced into a single fist.

Apparently, Chernobog wanted privacy for this conversation. Calling for either Roman or Teddy Jo would do no good. This was his forest and he made this happen. I could stand here, at the edge of the bog, or I could move forward and get on with it.

I stepped into the mud. It squelched under my weight with a wet sucking noise. Step, another step, a few more . . .

Something watched me from the depths of the woods. My skin felt too tight from the pressure of its gaze.

When alone in a dark forest waiting for an audience with an evil god, the most prudent course of action is to be quiet and wait. "Prudent" wasn't one of my favorite words.

"Hello? I've come to borrow a cup of sugar. Anybody? Perhaps there is an old woman with a house made of candy who could help me?"

"Marrying for love isn't wise."

The voice came from somewhere to the left. Melodious, but not soft, definitely female and charged with a promise of hidden power. Something told me that hearing her scream would end very badly for me.

I stopped and pivoted toward the voice.

"Marry for safety. Marry for power. But only fools marry for love."

When a strange voice talks to you in the black woods, only idiots answer.

I was that idiot. "Thank you, counselor. How much do I owe you for this session?"

Mud squelched. Small twigs broke with dry snaps. Something moved behind the trees, on the very edge of my vision. Something dark and very large.

"Love fades. Love is beauty, youth, and good health. Love is sharing a moment in time. Bodies fatten, sag, and wrinkle."

And she kept going with her spiel. That's the trouble with ancient gods. No sense of humor.

A long sinuous body slithered behind the trees, enormous, taller than me, wide like a dump truck. It didn't end; more and more of it kept coming, sliding through the bog. The voice was on the left, the slithering darkness on the right.

"Youth passes you by, and before you know it, the two

of you are walking two different roads. Then comes pain, disappointment, and often betrayal."

"Fascinating," I said. "Is there a point to this, or did you go through the trouble of stealing Thanatos's sword to discuss my impending marriage?"

Brush rustled. The massive creature slid behind me, circling the rim of the bog. Peachy. Just peachy.

I turned to follow its movement. A large bird sat on a thick tree branch above me and to the left. Her long feathers draped down into a silky plumage that shifted between indigo, blue, and black. Her head was human with a shockingly beautiful face framed by a mane of blue hair. A gold crown sat on her head. Her chest was human too, with perfectly formed breasts.

Sirin.

I stood perfectly still.

Of all the mythological birds in the Slavic legends, Sirin was the most dangerous. Like Veles, the god who was her father, she was born from magic and the very essence of nature and life, the arterial blood of existence, unbridled, uncontrollable, and as unpredictable as the weather. Sirin, *burevestnik*, the storm bringer. And seeing her always meant one thing: many people would die.

She looked at me with big blue eyes.

"Hello, *burevestnik*," I said. "Will there be a natural disaster or a battle in my future?"

She laughed, raising her wings, and peeked at me through the gap. "A battle. A bloody battle."

The dark thing behind her slithered forward. A huge black beak came into the light, followed by a reptilian face the size of a car, its obsidian scales gleaming slightly. Two tentacles streamed from above its beak, like the mustache of its Chinese counterpart.

Aspid. One of Chernobog's dragons. His tail was still lost in the woods somewhere behind me. He had to be hundreds of feet long. All of my skill with the sword wouldn't be able to stop it. This was the old magic. The type of magic that existed when my father was young.

Aspid stared at me with big golden eyes, his head rising. Massive paws with claws as big as me sank into the black mud of the bog. I saw the beginnings of folded wings draped over his shoulders, the array of emerald, sapphire, and diamond scales on their surface catching what little light there was.

Sirin smiled, fluttering her wings. Veles must've lent his bird-daughter to Chernobog. They were related by marriage.

"Why did you come?" Sirin asked.

Honesty was usually the best policy. "Because my friend was in trouble."

"You're still human enough to have friends," Sirin said. "Perhaps we will bargain with you after all."

"What do I have to do to get the flaming sword back and walk out of these woods with Thanatos and Roman unharmed?"

"Roman has nothing to fear here," Sirin said.

I kept my mouth shut. I had already asked my question. The less I spoke, the better it was for my health.

"Will you bargain with us, Daughter of Nimrod?" Sirin asked.

Bargain with the God of Destruction and Absolute Evil or the giant dragon eats you. No pressure. "I'll hear you out."

The darkness binding the trees parted. Magic swelled, like a cold black wave about to drown me. Roman emerged from the bog and moved toward me. The staff in his hand turned into a huge black sword. His eyes glowed with white, so bright his irises were invisible in the whiteness. A dark crown rested on his brow; its tall spikes, shaped like razor-sharp blades, stretched a foot above Roman's head.

The volhv stopped before me.

Whatever made Roman himself was no longer there. The creature that stood in front of me wasn't Roman. It wasn't even human.

Chernobog didn't manifest. He possessed and his priest was his willing vessel.

Someone had to speak first. Clearly, he wasn't going to.

"Why am I here?"

Aspid slithered forward and coiled around me.

"You will fight a battle," Roman-Chernobog said in a voice that was at once deep and sibilant, the kind of voice that should've belonged to Aspid, who was twisting his enormous body around me. The magic in that voice chilled me to the bone. "Let the slaughter be in my name and I will return the sword and the Greek to you."

Careful. That way lay dragons. Literally. "What benefit would you derive from this?"

"Power."

Okay. "Could you be more specific?"

Aspid's coils drew tighter, bumping my back. I pushed at the massive scales with my hand. "Stop. I'm trying to speak to your father. I'm not going to agree to anything until I understand the nature of the bargain."

"People worship lighter gods because of the gifts they hope to receive," Sirin said from her perch. "They worship darker gods because of fear. For that fear to stay alive there must be punishment when respect is lacking. But one cannot punish when one's followers are few. There is an imbalance."

Now it made sense. Roman had complained before that he wasn't invited to any namings, births, or weddings, but the volhvs of Belobog and other lighter gods were. Gods like Chernobog and Veles were getting the shorter end of the stick. That created an imbalance, one that Chernobog felt pressure to correct.

In ancient times Chernobog wasn't so much worshipped as appeased, because if the ancient Slavs forgot the appeasement, he would remind them. Atlanta was a hub and it drew people from all over the South, but even so, the population of Slavic pagans was too small for any effective punishment. If he decimated them, it would take even longer for the balance of power to be restored. He'd be shooting himself in the foot.

But if the battle was dedicated to him, each death would boost his power. That was a hell of a thing to promise.

"Do you understand, human?" Sirin asked.

"Yes. I'm thinking. Do the souls of the dead killed in Chernobog's name belong to him?"

"I lay no claim to the souls," Roman-Chernobog said.

"How would this dedication take place?"

"My volhv will consecrate the field to me."

I looked at Sirin. "What is Veles's role in this?"

"Veles lays no claim to the field or lives lost on it. For now."

I faced Roman-Chernobog. "If we consecrate the field to you, every death upon it becomes a human sacrifice."

Sirin snapped her wings. Aspid opened his beak, his golden eyes staring at me. Apparently, the fact that I wasn't a complete idiot was really surprising.

There was no way out. If I declined the bargain, neither I nor Teddy Jo would get out of this swamp. If I died, my father would take the city and crush it.

If I took the bargain, I'd be making a business arrangement with the God of Evil. No good ever came from making deals like that. No good ever came from making deals with gods, period. Especially when what he was asking for wasn't mine to grant.

What should I do? How do I make the best of this mess? I wished I could've asked Roman for advice, but I highly doubted Chernobog would let me do that and even if he did, there was a pretty obvious conflict of interest.

"What if there is no battle?"

"There will be a battle," Sirin said. "First, you will fight for your lover. If you win, you will fight for your heir. You will not survive. One of these battles will end you."

"Maybe I'll patch things up with my father."

"You will not," Sirin said. "Beware, Daughter of Nimrod. I have seen your death and it is a horror you cannot imagine."

Awesome.

"Decide," Roman-Chernobog said.

I would need ammunition against my father. The Witch Oracle had foreseen the battle, Sirin had foreseen the battle, so the battle would be happening. Curran would die. Atlanta would burn.

Consecrating the ground to Chernobog and feeding him the power of all those deaths . . . There was no darker darkness than this dragon winding around me. This would have far-reaching consequences. There hadn't been a large-scale human sacrifice in the world for years. I would be opening a door that so many good people had fought to keep closed. I would be giving Chernobog a foothold in Atlanta.

But I'd be an idiot to turn down his offer. I wouldn't even make it out of the swamp. It was my responsibility to defend the people in my land. It was my burden. I had to do whatever I could to make them safe. My father was an immediate danger. Chernobog was a distant, vague future threat. I didn't need anyone's permission. I could do it.

"Decide," Roman-Chernobog repeated.

I raised my head and looked the god in the eye. "No."

Aspid hissed.

"You're asking me for something not in my power to give. I guard the land. I do not own it and I do not own its people. They pray to their own gods."

"Then you die," Roman-Chernobog said.

"If you kill me, my father will take over the city and all the lands around it. He doesn't suffer any competition to his power. The witches and volhvs are afraid of him and oppose him. He knows this. Right now, your worshippers live in the land I guard. I don't make any demands on them. They worship whoever they choose. Once my father comes through, that will be over. Most of those who honor you will die in that battle. Those who survive will be punished and enslaved for opposing my father. If you kill me, nobody in Atlanta will be left to say your name." I looked at Sirin. "Tell him."

The look on her face said she already had.

"You asked me here to bargain. Let me bargain with you."

Silence fell. This was the part where I would get eaten. I'd make it as expensive for them as I could.

"What do you offer?" the god said.

"If you agree to help us crush my father's forces, I will invoke your name before the troops gathered in front of me. I will tell those who fight with me that you will be present, so they can witness your power for themselves. I'll make sure that they know your name so they may choose to pray to you. If your power is as great as the power your volhv has shown, that battle will bring you many converts. I will not make this bargain with any other god. No matter how much aid Belobog or Perun offers me, I will reject it. I will not go to their volhvs for help and I won't seek their counsel. You will be the only Slavic god on the field that day. You will be honored, feared, and remembered. Years from now, they will tell legends about this day and your name will be spoken."

Silence.

The god's eyes shone brighter. "Done."

Darkness swirled around Roman and withdrew back into the forest. He blinked, as if waking up, his massive sword again a simple staff, and his head bare.

Aspid hissed and slithered to Roman, the serpent dragon's huge head level with him. If he opened his mouth, he could swallow the volhv in one gulp.

Roman shook his head, clearing it.

The dragon opened his mouth, his teeth like long curved sabers. Oh crap.

"Roman!" I started toward them and sank into the mud.

Aspid's long serpentine tongue flicked out and wound around the volhv. I sped up, splashing through the bog. There was no way I could make it through all this muck in time.

Roman blinked again and smacked Aspid's nose with his hand. "What did I say about kisses? No kisses unless invited."

Aspid's tongue contracted. He pulled Roman into his mouth.

I sprinted.

"Yes, I love you, too," Roman said from inside the forest of teeth. "I need to go now. Come on."

The dragon opened his mouth and put Roman back into the mud. The massive serpent looked at me, hissed, and slid into the forest, his obsidian body going and going . . . It would be comical if it weren't so damn scary. I glanced behind me. Sirin was gone.

"Happens every time," Roman said. "He misses his father. I'm a substitute until he sees Chernobog in the next flare."

"You have a weird life."

"Look who's talking." He shrugged. "It's not that I'm that evil, really. I'm just beloved by evil things."

A sword wrapped in black canvas rose from within the bog hilt up, like some strange flower. I gripped the hilt. It was cool to the touch. Huh. The last time I'd used it, I'd had to get special gloves and wrap the hilt in three layers of cloth. I pulled the sword free. Some people pulled swords out of stones and went on to rule Britannia. I pulled a sword out of the mud and tried not to think about what I had done.

"This way." Roman started through the woods. "Well, that was fun."

"I did the best I could," I told him.

"Not questioning that." He dragged his hand over his face. "My uncle will have to be told. Professional courtesy. This is going to really upset the power apple cart. That's why the Dark God didn't use me."

"Why?"

"Because if I had known what he wanted, I would've talked him out of it. You have no idea the shit I've stopped."

"He wanted the whole battlefield dedicated to him."

Roman grimaced. "I know."

"At least this way, once he is on the battlefield, he won't be claiming human sacrifices."

"It won't be him," Roman said. "It will be me on the battlefield channeling his power." He grinned. "I will be a battle volhv. This will be my first time. I'm excited."

"I didn't mean to rope you into this."

"I didn't mean to bring you into a scary swamp. Things happen."

"How often are Sirin's predictions wrong, Roman?"

"Do you want the true answer or the one you can live with?"

"That often, huh?"

He nodded.

The trees parted. Teddy Jo stood in the middle of the road, looking confused. The sun was to our right. We'd lost a few hours somehow.

He saw us and shook his head. "I've tried going through the woods twice. I keep ending up on this road."

"I believe this is yours." I pulled the fabric off the sword. The blade burst into flame. I tossed it at Teddy Jo.

He caught the blade. His whole body realigned itself, standing straighter, taller, his shoulders wider, the color of his skin brighter. Teddy Jo a second ago was a pale shadow of the one standing in front of me now. I never realized how much the sword meant. And he'd let me borrow it once to pull a prank on Curran.

"What did you trade?" he asked.

"Nothing important."

He glanced at Roman.

"I'll tell you later," the volhv said.

"Nothing important," I repeated. "Let's get home. Tell me about the pegasi, Teddy Jo."

He held out the swing and I wedged my butt into it. Now we had to go home and sort out what had happened to Christopher. If he was even Christopher anymore. At least we'd gotten the dragon out of the way. Thank the Universe for small favors.

ROMAN HAD DECLARED that turning into a crow for the second time in one day was above his pay grade. He whistled, made some kissy noises with his lips, and a black horse trotted out of the woods. He mounted bareback and headed to the house.

I climbed back into the swing. Flying really was overrated, but it was fast, and beggars couldn't be choosers.

According to Teddy Jo, the pegasi couldn't be tamed, but they could be enticed.

"They're curious and they like adventure," he said, as we flew southwest. "You're going to walk up to the herd and offer them a gift of some sort. Carrots, sugar, whatever. If you're interesting enough, one of them might come over and decide to go adventuring with you."

"And if none decide to adventure?"

"Then there's nothing we can do."

Oh boy.

"Why do you need a pegasi, Kate?"

"I need to get to Mishmar."

"What is Mishmar?"

"My father's magic prison in the Midwest."

Teddy Jo chewed on that. "Why?"

"I'd rather not say. But I need to get there as soon as possible."

"Well, they are damn fast. Faster than me flying. I took one to Miami the other week. Made it in six hours. You need one as soon as possible, I take it?"

"Yes." It had been three days since I found out about Saiman's kidnapping, which left us with twelve days until my wedding. In Sienna's original vision, I had married Curran and our wedding led to the battle. But with the way I was altering the future, I had a feeling the battle would happen before that.

"Then we'll do this tonight. I'll pick you up around eleven. Can you be packed and ready?"

"Yes. Can I ask you to drop me off at Milton's ER? I need to check on a patient there."

"You sure you want to be dropped off at Milton? That's a long trek back and you have no horse. I can wait."

"Why are you being so nice all of a sudden?"

"Well, since you got my sword back, I figure I can be cordial for a day or two. It will wear off."

"Yes, it would be awesome if you waited for me."

"Will do," he said.

Milton Hospital occupied a squat solid building that looked less like a hospital and more like a bunker with narrow windows guarded by grates, thick walls, and spikes on the roof. Most hospitals now looked that way. Things that fed on humans were drawn to the scent of blood, and hospitals were full of bleeding people.

"Depressing places, hospitals," Teddy Jo said, landing in the parking lot behind some large trucks. He shrugged his shoulders and his wings vanished. "Visiting a friend?"

"Something like that."

"I'll come in with you. I could use a nice chair."

I left Teddy Jo in the waiting area. An older nurse, rail thin, with pale blond hair twisted into a bun, walked me to Adora's room. The sahanu sat on the bed, flipping through a newspaper. Her color was good. Considering that her intestines had been spilling out twenty-four hours ago, it was a great improvement.

She saw me and tried to get up.

"No, no, stay where you are," I told her.

"Yes, Kate." She bowed her head.

The nurse gave me an odd look. I sighed.

The nurse turned to Adora. "If you need anything, I'll be down the hall."

Translation—*yell for help and I'll come running.* I couldn't really blame her. I smelled like a swamp and the sword wasn't exactly helping my trustworthy image.

I pulled up a wooden chair and sat in it.

"How are you feeling?"

"Much better. I will be useful soon."

I tried to think like Martina. Ascanio's mother was one of the Pack's counselors and she'd helped me before. Sadly, I had neither her skills nor her experience.

"Is it important to be useful?"

"Yes."

"Why?"

"All things must have a purpose. My purpose is to serve one of your blood."

"But you're not a thing, Adora. You're a person."

"People must be useful, too."

Well, she had me there. This wasn't going well. "Tell me about yourself."

"I'm fast and strong. I'm proficient with bladed weapons but prefer Japanese-style swords. I possess three power words but can use only one at a time. Among my generation, I'm ranked fourth."

"Why fourth?"

She hesitated. "I'm very fast, but I have a limited magic reserve compared to two others and a limited kill ratio compared to three others. Also I kill better at short range."

"How many sahanu were in your age group?"

"Originally, twenty-two."

She wasn't surprised by the word. Julie's information seemed to be accurate.

"What do you mean by 'originally'?"

She hesitated. "Some people died. Some people were taken from the fort before completing their studies, because they were needed elsewhere."

"How many completed the course of study with you?"

"Nine."

"I saw a large dark-skinned woman who wears chain mail and carries a hammer."

"Carolina. She's ranked eighth."

She didn't seem worried.

"There was also a man with a patched trench coat."

"Razer." She paused. "Ranked first."

"Tell me about them."

"Carolina is powerful but not as fast as me. Her magic produces a telekinetic push that's devastating at a range of up to five meters. A quicker fighter or a ranged opponent can take her out. She's best in a team of two or more, where someone can watch her back."

"And Razer?"

"Razer is faster, stronger, and more precise than me. His magic is more powerful than mine. He kills his opponents and sometimes he eats their flesh."

"Is Razer fae?"

She nodded.

That's what I thought. There had been reports of children born to seemingly normal parents with facial features and abilities consistent with those of the fae as described in legends. Mostly in urban areas up north, ones with a large concentration of Irish immigrants, such as Boston and Weymouth. By the last census, six percent of Atlanta's population had claimed Irish ancestry. I knew this because the Pack had detailed maps of the city and at one point I was asked to help tag them by the mythology of their culture. In the post-Shift world, where you were from mattered because the myths and legends of your homeland followed you.

Nobody knew exactly what the fae were capable of. Some called them elves, some called them fairies, the fair folk, or Tuatha Dé Danann, but everyone agreed that they were bad news.

"What are his powers?"

"I don't know," she said. "I only fought against him twice. He didn't use magic to win."

That meant he won on speed, strength, and skill and she had more than a normal human's dose of all three. Razer would be fun.

"Are there any other fae among the sahanu?"

"Yes."

"Among the nine?"

"Irene is fae," Adora said. "I think."

"What are her powers?"

"I don't know." Her mouth quivered. She didn't want to disappoint me and she must've been worried about my disapproval. She was under enough stress already from everything I had put her through. I had to move on.

"Thank you. When you feel better, I'd like you to write down everything that you think is relevant or useful about the other sahanu of your generation. Is there an age category older than yours?"

"No." She shook her head. "We are the first generation. There are younger generations."

Ugh. "How old are you, Adora?"

"Twenty-four."

Only four years younger than me, but there was an almost childlike simplicity about her. Her world was clearly defined: making me happy and serving me was good, being useless to me was bad. She was giving me all of the information I wanted without any hesitation. Two days ago she would've likely died to keep that information secret from me, but now, with her allegiance shifted, Adora kept no secrets, like a young child who instinctively recognized an adult as an authority figure and was eager to prove she was smart and resourceful. Most people were at least somewhat jaded by their midtwenties, but for her there were no shades of gray. It wasn't the naiveté of someone who believes the world is a nice place; it was an innocence, bolstered by the childlike belief that she was doing the right thing, because a person of power and authority assured her she was.

I needed to put a crack into that worldview. There had to be something in her psyche that rebelled against the view of my father as perfection wrapped in golden light.

"How long have you served my father?"

"Since I was seven."

"Is that when you were brought to the place where the sahanu are trained?"

"Yes."

"Did you have a family before you were brought there?" If there was any human emotion in her, I should get a spark now.

"Yes. Some children were orphans, but I wasn't. My mother and father were very well compensated. I was chosen because of my magic."

My father, never missing a falling star. "Did you miss your family?"

She hesitated. I held my breath.

"Yes. But now the sahanu are my family."

And yet she gave me information that would help me kill them without any hesitation.

"Were you angry that your parents sold you? Did you feel abandoned? Did you think it was unfair?"

She opened her mouth and closed it.

"My father isn't here. Your instructors aren't here. It's only me and you. Did you think it was unfair?"

"Yes," she said quietly. "I cried. And I missed my mom, my dad, and my sister."

"Do you think other children might have missed their parents, too?"

"Yes." The strain was showing on her face. Too much. I had to change the subject.

"Have you ever killed for my father?"

"Yes." She exhaled. We were back on familiar territory.

"Who did you kill?"

"During training I killed several martial artists and weapon masters."

"Why did you kill them?"

"For practice."

"Were they forced to fight?"

"No, they were paid to kill us."

That was a familiar tactic, one my father learned from Voron. "What about after your training was complete?"

"I killed the Followers of Guram. They had taken one of Sharrum's people and killed her, and he was displeased."

I'd run across the Followers of Guram before. They were a nasty sect and they liked skinning people with tattoos, which they considered a mortal sin, to curry favor with whatever god Guram prayed to. Guram was a prophet of sorts and the rumor was that once you heard his sermon, you would become a devotee. Law enforcement stomped them out, but they were like a hydra. You crush one head and another pops up in a different city. Although I hadn't heard about them for a few years.

"How many of the followers did you kill?"

She smiled a small smile. "All of them."

Wow. "How long did it take you?"

"Two years."

"What about Guram himself?"

"I killed him, too."

"How did you feel about killing all those people?"

"Sharrum wanted them dead."

I finally realized why she disturbed me so much. She was what Voron had wanted me to be. A killer without any remorse, without any doubt or questions. Point and watch the blood spray.

My father had done that to her. Like he told me, he'd given her serenity of purpose. And she was serene. The only time she became agitated was when I tried to send her away. My father was the closest thing to a god she knew. When your god orders you to kill and accepts full responsibility for it, it frees you from guilt, shame, and doubt.

This had to stop. My father had to be stopped.

"Adora, what do you want to do?"

"I want to serve you."

"And if I said you couldn't, what would you do?"

"I would kill myself."

No doubt in her big brown eyes. Nothing except complete devotion.

"You wouldn't go back to my father?"

"I would be killed. I wouldn't be useful any longer. But if I had no choice, I would return to Sharrum."

I had to walk her back to civilization if it was the last thing I did.

"Why don't you like me, Sharrim?" she asked in a small voice. "I'm not the highest rated, but I've trained the hardest. I'm diligent."

"I don't dislike you, Adora. I don't want to use you because people shouldn't be used. People should follow their own paths in life."

"But I want to serve you. That's the only way I can get into heaven."

When we stood over Jene's body, Ascanio had said that Deputy Holland's identity was wrapped up in being in law enforcement. But Holland didn't grow up being a law enforcement officer. He likely had friends outside the sheriff's office, family members, people he went to high school with. A whole net of people to catch him if he stumbled. Adora had no one. She grew up as sahanu. That was the only thing she knew. She'd lost her family and devoted her whole life to being the best assassin she could be because my father assured her she would get to heaven.

I would have to shatter that belief. I would have to explain to her that everything she had done, all the training she worked so hard on, all the lives she took were in the name of a lie. It would be like taking a lifelong devout Christian and showing them irrefutable proof that God didn't exist. Her whole world would collapse. I spared her life and now I would have to dismantle everything she'd held as truth for the last seventeen years. It wasn't just cruel. It would be devastating. It would crush her. It would've been kinder to kill her.

I looked at her and my insides churned. I hadn't spared her because I was impressed with her skills or because I thought she was worth saving. I hadn't saved her because I saw myself in her. I'd saved her because I wanted to send a big loud "Fuck You" to my father. Him sending her into my territory offended me. It made me angry in a way I hadn't been angry for a very long time.

Deep down, if I listened to the voice inside me, I wanted to march into his castle, crush him, and take every scrap of land he owned. It wouldn't be enough to win. I wanted to humiliate him and take his land. To hoard it like a dragon.

What the hell was happening to me?

"Are you well, Kate?" Adora asked.

I was a piece of shit. She was a person, an actual real human being, and I had decided to play God with her life. When I had a chance to turn her into a slave, I stopped because I recognized that Curran wouldn't like it. I should've stopped because it was the wrong thing to do. Because I didn't make slaves.

"Kate?"

How could I have gone so far? How do I fix this? If I went any further down this road, Adora would be the first of many.

"Kate? Are you sick?"

No. I had to find whatever it was that made me *me* and hold on to it. And I owed it to Adora to tell her the complete truth as gently as I could. I would need help. I would have to go very slowly. Baby steps.

"Adora, what is it you like to do? When you're not working for my father, I mean. When you have free time."

"I don't know," she said.

"What is your favorite food?"

"Candy."

Okay. Candy I could do. "I'm going to travel for a couple of days. I'd like you to stay here and recuperate, so the doctors can continue to treat your wounds. My Herald will come and check on you. Let her know if you need anything. However, if you don't want to stay here and want to leave, you don't need my permission. You are not a prisoner. If my father's agents contact you, you don't have to go back with them, but you can if you want to. It's your choice. Okay?"

"Okay."

I'd almost made it to the door when she called, "Kate?"

"Yes?"

"You will come back for me?"

"Yes." *If I don't die.*

"And then I will be useful, yes?"

"Yes." I would go straight to hell. When I died, a hole would open under my feet and I would shoot right down there.

I walked to the waiting area and stopped by the cashier. "I'd like to pay for the next week."

She gave me a number. I pulled out my wallet, took out a check—I'd learned to always keep a couple in there, folded in half—and wrote it out. I added fifty bucks to the check and pointed to the little gift shop and bakery behind me. "Also, I would like a small bag of each kind of candy you have brought to her."

"If her doctor says it's okay."

"Let her have the candy." Knowing how thorough my father was with his tools, Adora would likely heal fast.

*I'm about to destroy your world, here is some candy. Ugh.*

Teddy Jo stood up and we walked outside. "Who is she?"

"Were you listening in?"

"It's only a few feet down the hallway and I have sharp hearing."

"She's what happens when my father wants a weapon who never questions him. She also might be the biggest mistake I've ever made." I climbed into the swing.

"I'm sure it's not that bad," he said.

It was bad. Sooner or later I would have to explain it to Curran, too. We didn't keep secrets from each other. We talked. Given a chance, I would explain what Adora was and convince him she wasn't a slave. Curran loved me more than anyone I'd ever known. He would hear me out. That wasn't what stopped me. If I let him see Adora, he would ask me why I didn't kill her. I couldn't lie to him. I would have to tell him everything, about my father, about wanting to take his land, about watching Adora bleed and puzzling over sealing her into service as if she were an object to be owned.

I didn't want him to know how far into the dark I went. It scared me when I thought about it.

I did it. I owned it. Like it or not, I would have to deal with it after I came back from Mishmar. If I came back.

"I'll need to stop by a smithy," I murmured, and realized I'd said it out loud. "Sorry, was talking to myself."

"They have medicine for that."

"Thank you, Doctor."

"You're welcome. Why do you need to stop by a smithy?"

"To buy powdered iron."

I SAT ON the back porch outside, waiting for Teddy Jo. The sky was black and deep. A spray of glittering stars shone from above. The night breathed.

I'd stopped by the Guild and talked to Curran. He'd put a team together for Saiman's rescue. The Pack shared what they had learned scouting and Curran did manage to find a merc with the ability to communicate long distance. They called her a mouse witch and I found her sitting in Barabas's office, with two bats hanging off her clothes, a squirrel on her shoulder, and a tiny owl in her hands. Tonight the owl and the bats would fly to the castle and attempt to find Saiman. If they did, she would be able to talk to him through them.

I told Curran about my meeting with Chernobog. He told me about Christopher. The moment the magic wave ended, his wings disappeared and he stopped struggling. They pulled him out of the ground. He picked up Maggie and went back to his house. Barabas tried to talk to him, but Christopher curled up in his hammock, hugged his dog, and refused to communicate. Barabas stayed home to watch over him.

I'd hugged Curran and kissed him good-bye. He kept asking me nonsense questions. He didn't want me to go. I didn't want to go either, but eventually I had to leave to gather my things.

I stopped by the smithy and bought a pound of powdered iron. Legends existed for a reason.

At home I called Jim and asked him to have the remains ready tonight, in three hours or so. He said he would.

I made a call to Martina and explained about Adora. I didn't sugarcoat it. She said she would talk to her and she wanted me to come and have dinner with her as soon as I could. I promised I would. Then I talked to Julie about it. She would check on Adora while I was gone.

I'd packed some clothes, jerky, nuts, and bread to last me a couple of days into a backpack. I took two canteens and a roll of toilet paper. Considering the excursions Voron used to send me on, my supplies made me feel downright pampered. There was nothing left to do but wait.

Teddy Jo was taking his time.

The noise of the back gate opening made me turn. Christopher walked out from behind the house and came to sit next to me.

"Hey," I said.

"Hi." He smiled. It was the same shy smile I was used to seeing on his face. Like shaking hands with an old friend. But his eyes no longer had that faraway dreamy look, as if he were seeing things that nobody else could see.

"Where is Barabas?"

"He fell asleep," Christopher said. "We had a long day."

"You're up late." Small talk with the god of terror.

"I'm coming with you."

"Why?"

"Because I've been useless for too long."

Oh boy. Not the useless thing again. "Christopher, Teddy Jo will be taking me."

"I won't fight with him again."

"Your wings disappeared with the magic. The tech is still up. I don't think he can carry us both."

Red smoke spiraled out of his shoulders and the massive wings snapped open.

Right.

"Everyone was tired out from fighting me," he said. "All of them wanted to be reassured that I wouldn't snap again."

"So you pretended to lose your powers when the magic wave ended?"

"It was the considerate thing to do. I've been so privileged to have people worry for me that I've forgotten what it's like to have people afraid of me."

"We weren't afraid. We were worried."

"The part of me that is Deimos knows fear, intimately. Barabas was afraid. He was so afraid that his fear shone like a beacon."

"Barabas will adjust. I don't think he was afraid of you, Christopher. I think he was afraid for you. I was, too. I didn't want to lose you."

Christopher nodded.

"Is everything okay between you and Barabas?"

He looked into the distance. "Things are complicated at the moment. Before, I wasn't in my right mind. Now he doesn't know who I am."

*Who are you, Christopher?* "What about you? How do you feel about it?"

"I love him."

I wished I knew what to say.

"There is something in your backpack," he said. "It keeps tugging on me."

I reached into my bag and pulled out a small mason jar with a tiny yellow spark in it. "Hold this for a second."

"What's this?"

"It's a flare moth." I dug some more in my bag. "When you release it, it flies up and the higher it flies, the brighter it is. Here. Is this it?" I fished out a simple yellow apple and offered it to him.

He took it gingerly from my hand and held it up. "The apple of immortality. Where did you get this?"

"Funny story. Teddy Jo dropped them off one night out of the blue. He said he didn't know what to do with them and he was pretty sure I could handle them given my family history. I made them into a pie I was going to feed to Curran on our big date. I'd lost a bet to him and promised to serve him dinner naked."

Christopher smiled.

"He stood me up. It wasn't his fault, but I didn't know it at the time and I was really pissed off, so I trashed the food and I buried the pie."

"Buried?"

"It seemed like a good idea at the time. I had enough apples left to make Curran another pie later. Anyway, a few months after that I came back to my house near Savannah and found a brand-new apple tree. I talked to Teddy Jo about it and we decided that the apples were way too dangerous to leave unattended, so we dug out the tree and he replanted it by his cabin. He brings me apples every time some grow. He says the tree wants him to do it."

"Have you eaten them?"

I nodded. "So far no immortality. But they do make a killer jam if you add some lemon peel. I thought the pegasi would appreciate them."

He gave the apple back to me and laughed quietly.

I held out my hand. "Kate Daniels, daughter of Nimrod the Builder of Towers, Guardian of Atlanta."

He looked at my hand and then took it with his long slender fingers. "Christopher Steed, twenty-second Legatus of the Golden Legion, god of terror."

We shook.

"Legatus of the Golden Legion." I whistled. If a Master of the Dead was especially gifted, he was selected to join the Golden Legion, the elite of the elite among my father's navigators. The Legatus led them, the same way Hugh used to lead my father's soldiers. The Legatus answered directly to my father.

"I climbed to power," Christopher said. "It wasn't given to me; I excelled and took it. I have . . . regrets."

We all have regrets. "Let me tell you about my friend. His name is Christopher. He thinks he could fly if only he remembered how. Turns out he can. He's kind and gentle.

He tries to help even when things are difficult and he's terrified. He once went into Mishmar to rescue me. He takes care of his little dog and he tries to cook for Barabas, because we all know that Barabas is awful in the kitchen."

"He isn't . . . Yes, he is."

"That's the only Christopher I know. I never met the Legatus of the Golden Legion. No desire to meet him." I looked at him. "It doesn't matter what you were. It matters what you are now."

"You forgot one title in your introduction," he said.

"Oh?"

"Kate Daniels, daughter of Nimrod the Builder of Towers, Guardian of Atlanta. Savior of Christopher."

"Don't," I told him.

"I would've died in that cage."

"My father shattered your mind and tortured you. I tried to correct his wrong."

"Nimrod didn't shatter my mind. I shattered it myself." Christopher looked up at the night sky and a shadow of something vicious crossed his face. "I was the most powerful Legatus on record. One night your father invited me to dinner and made me a proposal: he had developed a way to implant a deity into a human host. The process had some limitations. The deity had to be well known enough to have a distinct presence, but not self-aware enough to interfere with the human host's ego. It had to have almost no followers, so the host's will would not be affected. The human had to have a vast reserve of natural magic, enough to sustain and feed the deity's powers. He compared it to standing in the middle of a storm and absorbing all of its fury into yourself. Such a person, he said, would surpass both the Legatus and the Preceptor of his Iron Dogs. He would truly be his second-in-command. He was very persuasive."

"Did you say yes?"

"I said no."

"You said no to my father?"

"I did. I told him that a storm could power you or tear you apart and I didn't want to be ripped to pieces."

That took some serious balls.

"He said he understood. I told him that d'Ambray would make a better candidate. We all worshipped your father, but he had Hugh the longest, since Hugh was a child. He would do anything Nimrod asked of him."

And what a wonderful reward Hugh got for his devotion.

"He said the process wouldn't work on Hugh. His healing power was too strong and would reject the alien magic. We mused about it. We finished the dinner. I don't remember getting up but when I woke up, we were in Mishmar and he had already started. I remember pain. Excruciating pain. It didn't stop for an eternity. I decided then that if I lived, Nimrod would never benefit from what he had done to me, so when I absorbed Deimos, I turned all of my power inward. There is only so much terror a human psyche can handle."

The willpower required to do that to yourself had to be staggering.

"I don't know what to say. 'Sorry' doesn't seem adequate. My father really hates hearing 'no.'"

"He doesn't hear it often." Ruby light rolled over his irises.

"Did he try to put you back together?"

"Yes. But he failed. The damage was too massive and I wanted to stay broken. After months of treatment and torture he sent me with Hugh to the Caucasus as a last-ditch effort. He didn't want me in Greece—too many native powers and too risky—but the Black Sea coast was close enough for Deimos to feel the pull of the land. He hoped that proximity to Greece would draw me out, so he told Hugh to put me in a cage, so I could see the sky and feel the wind, and starve me. But I was too far gone. I would've died in that cage, and then you took me out, and you and Barabas took care of me ever since."

The memory of him in the cage triggered an instant rage. No human being should've been treated like that, starved, dying of thirst, sitting in his own waste.

"What will you do now?" I asked.

He smiled, baring vampire fangs. "When you fight your father, I will soar above you. I want to be the last thing he sees before he dies."

So far I had the god of evil and the god of terror on my side. My good-guy image was taking a serious beating. Maybe I should recruit some unicorns or kittens with rainbow powers to even us out.

Teddy Jo walked out onto the porch. "Here you . . . Damn it."

Christopher gave him a small wave.

"Can't feel him with the tech up?" I asked.

Teddy Jo ignored me. "What do you want?"

"I'd like to come," Christopher said. "In case something goes wrong. I won't be any trouble."

Teddy Jo opened his mouth.

"Don't be mean," I said.

"Mean? Me? To him?"

"Yes."

Teddy Jo's face turned dark. He sat in the chair next to me. "Answer me this, how do you exist?"

"Forced theosis," Christopher said.

"How?" Teddy Jo asked.

"Ask her father. I remember only pain. It probably began as implantation, a forced possession, but how exactly he went about it is beyond my recollection."

"Did you . . . ?" Teddy Jo let it trail off.

"Absorb the essence of Deimos? Yes."

Teddy Jo shook his head. "It's not apotheosis. Apotheosis implies reaching the state of rapture and divinity through faith. It's not an appearance avatar."

"No," I said. "That would imply the deliberate voluntary descent of a deity to be reborn in a human body, and from what I understand there was nothing voluntary about the process. Deimos wasn't reincarnated."

"There is no word for it," Christopher said.

Teddy Jo rocked forward, his hands in a single fist against his mouth. "That's because it goes against the primary principle of all religion—the acknowledgment of forces beyond our control possessing superhuman agency."

"With the exception of Buddhism," Christopher said.

"Yes. The key here is 'superhuman.' A deity may consume a human or another deity, but a human can never consume a deity, because that implies human power is greater than divine."

Just another night in Atlanta. Sitting on my porch between a Greek god who was really a human and an angel of death who was having an existential crisis.

"This shouldn't be. You can't be Deimos."

"But I am," Christopher said.

"I know."

"It's the Shift," I said. "The power balance between a neglected deity such as Deimos and a very powerful human is skewed toward the human, especially if there are no worshippers."

"It would have to be a really powerful human," Teddy Jo said.

"I was," Christopher said. "I suppose I should say I am."

"Do you retain any of your prior navigator powers?" I asked.

"No."

We sat together on the porch, watching the universe strip herself bare above us.

"Theophage," I said.

"What?" Teddy Jo said.

"You wanted a word for Christopher. Theophage."

"The eater of gods?" Christopher smiled.

"That word is for the sacramental eating of God, in the form of grains and meat," Teddy Jo said.

"Well, now it's for literal eating."

"We should get going," Teddy Jo said.

"So, can I come?" Christopher asked.

"Where? Where do you want to go?" Teddy Jo asked.

"To Mishmar. I could carry her. She wouldn't need a winged horse."

"No. Even if you could carry her that far, you couldn't get there fast enough."

"He's right," I added. "The plan is to escape Mishmar before my father arrives, but it's possible he will catch me there. For whatever reason, he is reluctant to kill me, but he won't hesitate to fight you. If you saw him, what would you do?"

"I would kill him," Christopher stated in a matter-of-fact way.

Well, he would definitely try.

"So that's right out," Teddy Jo said. "You understand why? You come with her to Mishmar, neither of you might get out alive. She's safer on her own."

Christopher nodded. "Well, can I come with you to see the horses? I promise to be good and not scare them."

"Sure, why not." Teddy Jo waved his arms. "The entirety of Hades can come. We'll have a party."

Christopher stepped off the porch into the backyard, spread his wings, and shot upward. The wind nearly blew me off my feet.

"Thank you," I told Teddy Jo.

"He gives me the creeps," Teddy Jo growled.

"You're the nicest angel of death I know."

"Yeah, yeah. Get in the damn swing."

THE FOREST STRETCHED in front of me, a gloomy motionless sea of branches sheathed in leaves. The waters of the Blue River streamed past, quiet and soothing, the light of the old moon setting the small flecks of quartz at the bottom of the riverbed aglow. Thin, watery fog crept in from between the trees, sliding over the water and curling around the few large boulders thrusting from the river like monks kneeling in prayer.

I sat quietly, waiting, a saddle and a blanket to go under it next to me. Teddy Jo had dropped me off and retreated into the woods, adding, "Don't treat them as regular horses. Treat them as equals." Whatever that meant.

Christopher glided above me, somewhere too high to see. Watching him in the sky had made me forget about being suspended hundreds of feet in the air with a whole lot of nothing between me and the very hard ground. Christopher had remembered how to fly. He would climb up, bank, and dive, speeding toward the ground in a hair-raising rush, only to somehow slide upward, out of the curve, and soar. Teddy Jo had rumbled, "You'd think he'd act like he had wings before," then caught himself, and left Christopher to the wind and speed.

Now all was quiet.

Even if I did manage to bond with a pegasi, I'd have to ride on its back as it flew. My stomach tried to shrink to the size of a walnut at the thought. If it bucked me off, I would be a Kate pancake. Life had tried to kill me in all sorts of ways lately, but falling off of a flying horse was a new and unwelcome development.

I had to get a horse. Not only did my idiotic plan depend on it, but Curran's did, too. He would walk his mercs into my father's castle, and he was counting on me to provide a distraction to get them out. Sienna foresaw a flying horse. So far she hadn't been wrong.

A shape moved to the left, in the woods. I turned. Another. Then another. A single horse emerged from the gloom; first, a refined head, then a muscled chest, then thin elegant legs. A stallion, a light golden palomino, his coat shimmering with a metallic sheen as if every silky hair were coated in white gold. Two massive feathered wings lay draped on his back.

Not a Greek pony. Not any local breed either. He looked like an Akhal-Teke, the ancient Turkmenistan horses born in the desert.

I took the apple out and held it in my hand.

The stallion regarded me with blue eyes, shook his mane, and started toward me.

I held my breath.

He clopped his way past me to the river and began to drink, presenting me with a front and center view of his butt. More horses came: perlino, white, golden buckskin, bay . . . They all headed to the river, drank, flicked their ears, and pretended not to see me.

I was out of luck. I sat there and watched them drink, holding the stupid apple in my hand. Should I go up to them making cooing noises? Teddy Jo said not to move and to let them come to me. Well, they weren't coming.

What else could I get? What could I do to get there fast enough? A car wouldn't do it. I had saved an ifrit hound from ghoulism a few weeks ago. Maybe he could carry me away from Mishmar long enough for me to escape my father. No, that was a dumb idea. He wouldn't be fast enough. My dad would catch us and then we'd both be killed.

A single horse peeled away from the herd. Dark brown and so glossy she didn't look real, she stood about fifteen hands high. Her crest and croup darkened to near black, while her stomach was a rich chestnut. On the flanks, barely visible under the dark wings, the chestnut broke the dark brown in dapples. She looked at me. I looked at her. She walked three steps forward and swiped the apple from my palm.

"Hi," I said.

The horse crunched the apple. That was probably as good a response as I was going to get.

I reached out and petted her neck. The mare nudged me with her nose.

"I don't have more magic apples. But I do have some carrots and sugar cubes." I reached into my backpack and held out a sugar cube. "Let me put a saddle on you and I'll give you one."

And I was talking to the magic winged horse as if she were a human being. That's it. I had officially gone crazy.

I reached for the blanket. Her wings snapped open. The left wing took me right below the neck. It was like being hit with a two-by-four. I fell and scrambled to my feet in case she decided to stomp me.

The horse neighed and showed me her teeth.

"Are you laughing?"

She neighed again. Behind me the herd neighed back. Great. Now the horses were making fun of me.

I held out a sugar cube. She reached over and grabbed it off my hand. Crunching ensued.

I extracted the second sugar cube and held up the blanket. "Alright, Twinkle Pie or whatever your name is. I put the blanket on, you get more sugar. Your choice."

SWOOPING DOWN TO the Keep's main tower sounded like an awesome idea when I originally decided to do it. For one, it would let me avoid being seen, and Jim could meet me up there with my aunt's bones, avoiding most of the Keep's population. At least that's how I explained it to Teddy Jo when I asked him to go ahead of me and tell Jim to meet me there.

In theory it all sounded good. In practice, the top of the Keep's tower made for a very small and very difficult target. Especially from up here.

After the first fifteen minutes of flight I decided that I could stop clutching at Sugar every time she beat her wings, which signaled to her that it was time for aerial acrobatics. She threw herself into it with gusto, neighing with delight every time I screamed. I managed not to throw up, she managed not to kill me, and by the end of the thirty-minute test flight we had reached an understanding. I realized that she didn't plan to murder me and she realized that I meant every word when I promised to drop the bag with sugar to the ground if she didn't stop doing barrel rolls. Christopher watched it all from a safe distance. I heard him laughing a few times. I'd never live it down.

However, landing on the Keep's tower presented a whole new challenge. We passed over the mile-wide stretch of clear ground around the Keep and circled the tower. Below me, Jim, Dali, Doolittle, and Teddy Jo were talking. I couldn't see Jim's face from all the way up here, but I recognized his pose well enough. It was his "what the hell is this bullshit?" pose.

Dali looked up, saw me, and waved, jumping up and down.

"Take it easy," I said. "Let's land right here . . . Oh God!"

Sugar spread her wings and dropped into a swan dive. Wind whistled past my face.

"Sugar." I put some steel into my voice. We were going to crash. We'd smash against the stone and there would be nothing left of us but a wet spot. "Sugar!"

Teddy Jo threw himself flat. Jim leapt at Dali, knocking her down to the floor. I caught a flash of Doolittle's face as we whizzed by, Sugar's wings clearing his head by about four inches. He was laughing.

"You're a mean horse!"

Sugar neighed, beat her wings, and turned around.

"Control your horse!" Jim snarled.

"*You* control your horse." Oh wow, now that was a clever comeback. He'd surely drop to his knees and bow before my intellectual brilliance.

Sugar touched down on the stone.

"A pegasi!" Dali pushed her glasses back on her face and reached out to Sugar.

Jim grabbed her and yanked her back. "What's wrong with you?"

She pushed out of his arms and gently patted Sugar. The pegasi lowered her head.

"See? She can sense my magic." Dali rubbed the mare's neck. "You are so beautiful."

"I don't want to dismount," I told them. "I don't know if she'll let me back on."

Teddy Jo picked up two big sacks sitting next to Doolittle, slowly approached us, and handed them to me. I hooked them up to my saddle.

"Blood is in the left, bones are in the right," Doolittle said. "The bones are vacuum packed. The blood has been chilled and is split into three different thermoses."

"Thank you," I told him.

Dali raised her arms. I bent down and hugged her.

"You can do it," the white weretiger said. "You will kick ass."

If only I had her confidence.

"Do you have your food and water?" Teddy Jo asked.

"Yes." He'd already asked me that this morning.

"And your compass?"

"Yes."

"And you brought the ski mask?"

"Yes. It's not cold, though, even up above."

"It's not for the cold. The pegasi like to chase birds. Birds don't like to be chased."

"Okay." Whatever that meant.

Jim picked up Doolittle, wheelchair and all, and raised him up. I hugged the Pack's medmage.

"Good luck," he told me.

"Thank you." I would need every drop.

"Remember, try to bond with the pegasi." Teddy Jo said. "Treat her as a friend, not a horse."

"I would try to be friends with her but she's too busy being a smartass."

"Now you know how the rest of us feel," Jim said. "Who the hell is that?"

I glanced in the direction he was pointing, where a man rode the air currents on blood-red wings. "That's Christopher."

"Who?" Jim looked like he was about to have a heart attack.

"Christopher. He remembered how to fly."

Dali laughed.

Jim stared at me. I had to go before he suffered an apoplexy and the rest of the Pack, with Dali at the head, came after me. "Bye!"

Sugar galloped off the edge of the tower and then we were flying again, the remains of my aunt secure in my saddlebags.

≡ CHAPTER ≡

# 10

BIRDS WERE ASSHOLES. I pulled the ski mask off the nice warm spot in the ruins of a high-rise, where I had laid it out to dry after washing it in a nearby stream, and packed it back into my backpack. Sugar enjoyed flying back and forth through the bird flocks, and they retaliated by diving at me and doing their best to claw and peck the skin off my face and scalp. It took some serious scrubbing against a convenient rock in the stream to get the bird poop off the wool before the mask could go back on my head for the trip back. I'd have to thank Teddy Jo if I made it home. I should've brought one of those antique motorcycle helmets.

When my father had cobbled Mishmar together out of the remnants of Omaha, he'd moved high-rises one at a time, fusing them into a monstrous building. The one I waited in now must've failed to make the cut, because Dad had left it lying on its side atop a low hill fully two miles from Mishmar. From my vantage point, I could see the prison, towering like some citadel of legend over the plain, massive, wrapped in a ring of walls.

The magic was down, but I could feel it, still. Somewhere

deep within its walls my grandmother's bones waited. Her bones and her wraith. Or was it wrath? Probably wrath.

My grandmother longed for the banks of the rivers, where the sun shone and vivid flowers bloomed, shifting softly in the breeze. Instead my father had stuffed her into a concrete tomb and used the magic she emanated to power up Mishmar. She hated it.

Sugar clopped over and nudged me with her nose. I patted her and offered her a carrot.

The winged horse neighed.

"Too much sugar is bad for your teeth."

She took the carrot, but her snort made it plain she wasn't grateful. She was probably bored.

Curran and I had agreed on a simple plan: I would wait until the magic hit and go in just after sunset. If I tried to break in while technology was on the upswing, my father might not feel it or he might decide to stay where he was, since without magic he had no way of getting here fast enough.

Sugar and I had landed at the ruined skyscraper twenty-four hours ago, but the first night tech held the whole time. It was the second night now, and the big red ball of the sun was merrily rolling toward the horizon, so unless the magic decided to reassert itself in the next hour or so, I would be spending another night curled up next to the winged horse. Right now, that didn't seem like a terrible thing. Being away from Atlanta cleared my head. It felt liberating.

At least I had stopped worrying about Sugar flying off and leaving me to fend for myself. She seemed to find me amusing and stuck around. I'd learned to sneak off before taking a bathroom break, however, because she decided that pawing at me with a hoof after I found a secluded spot to pee was the funniest thing ever.

The one good thing about the wait was that it gave me time to think of what I would say. Even if it worked . . . I wasn't even sure my grandmother could understand me. If I failed, there was no Plan B.

"No Plan B, Sugar," I told her. "If I screw this up, Curran dies. The city burns. All my friends will be dead."

Sugar flicked her ears at me.

"It's occurred to me that this would all be much easier if I were evil. I would have serenity of purpose and none of these pesky problems."

Sugar didn't seem impressed.

The light turned red as the sun rolled toward the horizon. The world's pulse skipped a beat. Magic flooded in.

"Yes." I grinned and grabbed the blanket. "Onward, my noble steed. To our inevitable doom and gory death."

Thirty seconds later we took to the air. The tower of Mishmar grew closer, the different textures of its parts flowing into each other as if melted together. Red brick became gray granite transforming into slabs of natural stone, then into gray brick. The amount of magic necessary to pull this off boggled the mind.

Winged shapes rose from the crevices at the top of the tower and bounced up and down on the air currents.

"You're going to drop me off in the courtyard," I told her. "On the bridge. We'll have to do it quickly. Don't go and play with those flying things. They aren't birds. They have long beaks studded with sharp teeth and their wings are leather. They're not nice and cuddly like that flock of geese that tried to take my head off when you flew through it. They will hurt you if you get too close, and I don't want that to happen. I like you."

Sugar snorted.

"If I manage to make it out, I'll release the moth I showed you before. Don't come looking for me unless you see it, and if I'm not back in a day or two, I'm dead and you need to go back to the herd."

Was any of this getting through to her or was I talking to myself? I hoped she understood me, because if she didn't, I'd have a really awkward family reunion when my dad arrived with lightning and furious thunder or whatever other theatrics he would bring to bear.

The wall loomed before us. We cleared it and Sugar swooped down, flying low. Mishmar was a deep pit surrounded by a wall, with the tower rising from the center. A stone bridge stretched from the gates to the tower. Sugar landed straight into a gallop, carrying me toward the enormous door, the hoofbeats of her steps scattering echoes through the vast empty courtyard. She stopped, and I jumped off her back and pulled the saddlebags free.

"Go."

Above us the monster birds shrieked.

"Go!"

She reared, pawing the air, then ran back along the bridge and took flight. I turned toward the massive door. The last time I saw it, we were running out of it, after Curran, Andrea, and the rest came to rescue me. Never thought I would be going through it again.

The memory of me dying slowly of exposure in lukewarm water shot through me. *Thanks, brain. Just what I needed.*

A new bar secured the door, a thick strip of steel controlled by a wheel with eight handles protruding from it. Things moved inside the tower, crawling through the walls, their half-atrophied brains feeling like painful pinpricks of red light in mine. Vampires. Loose and driven near mad by bloodlust. They killed the weak that Roland imprisoned in Mishmar, wore down the strong, and without prey, they fed on each other.

My knees shook. I didn't want to go in. I would do almost anything not to go in.

"Lovely place," I said to hear my own voice. The stone echoes made it sound puny.

Curran was counting on me. I was counting on me. I didn't have time for post-traumatic stress.

I could feel the memory of water on my skin, leeching my will to live. I could hear Ghastek's labored breathing next to me. I could almost see him nodding, his mouth too close to the water as he hung suspended from the metal grate that prevented us from climbing out.

*Come on, weakling. Open the fucking door. How hard can it be?*

I could turn around and leave. Walk away, keep walking, and never come back.

*Open. The. Door.*

The wheel looked impossibly large now and I knew somewhere deep in the core of my being that if I touched it, horrible things would happen.

*Open the door.*

Curran would've begun moving his people in by now. He was en route. If I didn't open the door, my father wouldn't leave for Mishmar.

I grabbed the wheel and spun it. Metal squeaked and clanged, invisible gears turned, and the bar slid aside.

I exhaled and pulled the door open.

Darkness.

I stood in the doorway, letting my eyes adjust. A dark stone foyer, cavernous, its roof supported by two rows of columns. Probably used to belong to some hotel or bank. There had to be an exit that would lead deeper into Mishmar, because we had crossed this lobby the last time I was here, but I couldn't see it.

I moved to the side, away from the sunset light, and waited with my back against the wall.

The vampires stayed away. They had to have heard the bar slide aside and the creak of the gate. They should've come running, but instead their minds hovered above me and to the sides. That meant only one thing. Something lived in this foyer, something so dangerous that the awareness of it penetrated even the bloodthirsty, crazed minds of the bloodsuckers.

I waited, breathing quiet and slow. There was a trick to staying invisible: stop thinking. I cleared my head and simply waited, one with the darkness and the cold wall of stone touching my back.

Moments ticked by. I watched the foot-wide line of daylight cross the stones of the floor as the sunshine slipped through the gap between the two halves of the door. The chamber was roughly rectangular, the columns running along the two longer sides. Most of them had survived, but at least three had fallen, breaking into pieces. The walls weren't perfectly smooth. A shelflike decorative molding ran along the perimeter of the lobby at about twenty feet high. Above it, at even intervals, large reliefs interrupted the stone, depicting modern buildings and people. The floor was polished marble, now dusted with dirt and grime, but still slick. I would have to be careful running.

I stayed completely still.

The attack came from above, fast and silent. I felt it a fraction of a second before the javelin hit, and I dodged right. The short spear clattered on the floor. I jumped back—two shurikens whistled through the space where I was a moment ago—and leapt left behind a column. The column was four feet across and left me two choices: left or right. Not much of a cover.

Open lobby to my left, sliced in half by the narrow light streaming through the gap in the door, a wall to my right. Down wasn't an option; up wasn't either. The vampires squirming above me were too far. Concentrating on drawing them close would split my attention too much.

A shuriken clattered against the column from the left. Judging by the angle, the attacker had to be either twenty feet tall or above ground.

Shurikens were nuisance weapons, meant to distract and panic. Even if dipped in poison, they rarely killed. The attacker was trying to herd me toward the wall.

I lunged right, but instead of running to the wall, I dashed around the column and sprinted into the open space in the center of the chamber.

Shurikens hurtled at me from the darkness, from the spot in front of me and slightly to the left, coming from above. I dodged the first one, drew Sarrat in a single fast move, and knocked the second aside.

The darkness waited. So did I.

*Done? Let's see what else you've got.*

The beam of light coming through the door painted the floor behind me, not really illuminating the gloom, but diluting it enough to see movement. The angle of the shurikens pointed to a spot on the wall near the column. If someone had jumped up and perched on the molding, it would be about right. The twilight was too thick to see clearly, and the wall didn't look any different.

All was quiet. Nothing moved in the direction from which the shurikens came.

I breathed in even deep breaths, Sarrat raised. If the attacker used magic, I couldn't sense it.

*Come closer. You know you want to. Come see me. Say hello. I'm friendly.*

The texture of the wall by the column changed in a single sharp moment. Something was there, then disappeared.

I spun on pure instinct, swinging. Sarrat connected with the blade of a long knife aimed at my ribs, batting it aside, left to right. For half a second, the attacker was wide open, a tall figure in a gray cloak, his right arm thrown to his left by the force of my blow. I lunged into the opening and grabbed the cloak, yanking him toward me.

The fabric came free with no resistance, light and silk-thin under my fingers. The attacker vanished.

Movement, right side.

I jumped back. The knife sliced the air two inches from my throat. The attacker lunged, slashing at my neck with insane speed. "He" had breasts. A woman. I thrust Sarrat's blade up, blocking the dagger. She reversed the strike, and stabbed at my ribs. I danced out of the way.

Stab. Dodge.

Stab. Dodge. She had crazy reach.

Stab. Dodge. Her blade fanned my face.

I let it slice way too close for comfort, stepped in, and hammered a punch to her right ear.

She stumbled and somersaulted backward, putting a full thirty feet between us and landing in a half crouch.

She wore a skintight black catsuit. Black wrist guards and shin guards shielded her limbs, made of durable synthetic fabric, probably with steel or plastic inserts, hard enough to stop a blade and prevent a cut. Some band-like pattern over her torso. Soft black boots, almost slipper-like, a sole with some fabric to hold it to the foot. Swirls of gray camo decorated her skin. The cloak had hidden her hair, but now it was out in the open, so pale blond it was nearly white and pulled back into a short high ponytail. Thin long arms, thin long legs, long neck—room for a good cut if I could get close enough. Long legs were normally an asset for a woman, but not for her. Their length and shape put them past the point of attractive and straight into creepy. There was something deeply disturbing about her silhouette. Inhuman, almost alien. Adora had said there was one other fae among the sahanu. I'd bet my arm that she was standing in front of me, holding a foot-long Teflon-gray tactical knife.

"Sloppy, Irene." I turned toward her and flicked imaginary blood from my sword. "Do better."

She smiled, showing a mouth full of human-sized but sharp teeth, each pure white and pointed, like someone had studded her gums with thirty-two narrow canines.

I had a handful of iron powder in both pockets.

Not much exposed skin. If I used the powder, it would have to be on her face. Right now she didn't know I had it and once the element of surprise was lost, thrown powder was easy enough to avoid. I had to use it when I had a sure shot.

"Today," I told her. "I have things to do."

She tossed her knife into her left hand and pulled out a short tactical sword. Same dark finish, same profile, almost a steak knife but with a sixteen-inch blade. There went my reach advantage.

Irene charged. I dodged the sword thrust and raised Sarrat to parry, but not fast enough. The knife caught my left biceps. The cut burned.

She jumped back, grinned, and raised the knife to her mouth. Her tongue licked the blood.

I pushed.

She screeched as the blood in her mouth turned into needles and pierced her tongue.

"Dumbass," I told her.

She lunged at me, swinging, her blades flashes of movement. I dodged, blocking and waiting for an opening. Left, right, left—her blades rang, meeting Sarrat. Cut, cut, cut—she nicked my right forearm—right, left—searing pain, she cut my left shoulder again—cut, cut . . .

I had trouble keeping up. She was too damn fast. A person with arms that length had no business being that fast. I was blocking at the peak of my speed. A few more moments and I'd get tired enough to slow down.

Cut, cut . . .

Now. For half a second she was in front of me, left arm with the knife extended, right rising up for another slash. I sliced at her left wrist, stepped back, and got my left arm under her right, trapping it. I jerked her forward onto my blade. *You're dead.*

She wasn't there. One second I had her locked in and the next she vanished.

A teleporter.

The knife sliced across my back. I whipped around and barked a power word. *"Aarh!"* Stop.

The power word clamped her. Magic shot from her in a short concentrated burst, shattering my hold. She stabbed at my stomach and made it an inch in. I spun out of the way and kicked her.

She fell, then rolled to her feet, but I was already there, slicing. Sarrat's blade kissed the skin of her long neck, drawing a drop of scarlet. Her eyes darted to the right. She vanished.

Short-range teleporter, line of sight. I spun right and sprinted, darting back and forth, turning myself into a moving target. She'd have to chase if she wanted a shot.

Irene popped into existence in front of me and charged. I blocked her sword with mine. We clashed in the middle of the floor, metal screeching. I muscled her back. She vanished. Damn it.

I jogged right, zigzagging, moving in a rough circle. My stomach hurt. My left arm burned. I was breathing too fast.

She popped up on my right. I dropped to one knee, her long blade whistling over my head, and stabbed to the side. Sarrat nicked her thigh. She leapt back and vanished.

I kept moving, breathing a little faster than I had to,

walking a little slower. I let the point of Sarrat droop a hair too low.

*Come on in. I'm nice and tired.*

A hint of movement sliding soundlessly in the gloom to my left. *Hello, Irene.* I spun to my right and dramatically sliced the empty air. *That's right, I'm scared and chasing ghosts. Enjoy the show.*

I spun back, then front, the sword raised, and kept moving. I really was getting tired. This had to be it.

She trailed me, quiet, patient, a strange creature, shaped like a human but so far from it.

I stopped and took a deep breath, as if to steady my breathing.

She vanished.

The thrust came from the left. I spun away the moment I saw her disappear and she came into my spin, her teeth bared, eyes wide open, expecting easy prey.

I hurled a handful of iron in her face.

Irene screamed. I lunged and buried Sarrat in her stomach, sliding the blade between the reinforced plates of her suit. She screeched higher, her voice sharp. I twisted, ripping her insides, and threw the remaining powder into her gaping mouth. The scream ended, cut off by a choking gurgle.

Translucent wings snapped out of Irene's back. She leapt up, the wings beating in frenzy, sped all the way to the ceiling, then plummeted down, hitting the floor with a wet thud. Not enough power to truly fly, but she must've been a hell of a jumper.

Dark blood wet my blade, brown, almost rust-colored, as if the normal bright red of human blood was tinted with green.

Irene lay in a crumpled heap on the floor.

I wanted to lie down, too. Instead I caught my breath and walked over to her. Rust-colored liquid poured from her mouth. She squirmed in a puddle of her own blood.

I raised my blade and finished it.

.   .   .

Everything hurt.

My left arm hurt. My right arm hurt. My stomach hurt. I'd stopped to slap some bandages on the cuts. I could control the vampires of Mishmar, but if enough of them got together, enticed by my blood, they would be difficult to deal with and I was tired.

Nobody bothered me as I walked down the long hallway. If any other monsters skulked in the darkness, they must've decided I'd be too expensive to kill.

The last time, when we fought our way out of Mishmar, getting from my grandmother's tomb to the door took almost an hour, or it had felt like an hour. We fought the vampires, we moved slowly because I was at the end of my strength, and we had gotten lost at least twice. Now it took barely fifteen minutes.

In front of me the walls parted into an enormous cavern-like chamber, its ceiling lost in darkness, its floor shrouded in fog a hundred feet below. A narrow spire rose from the bottom of the chamber, fused together from concrete, stone, and brickwork. An identical but inverted spire reached down from the ceiling. They met in the middle, two hands clasping a rectangular stone box thirty-five feet high. A metal breezeway encircled it and a narrow metal bridge led to the breezeway from the stone ledge where I stood. Inside the room a magic storm howled, a power so ancient, so mad, that it made me shiver.

"Hello, Grandmother," I whispered, and took the first step onto the bridge. It seemed longer than I remembered. I reached the breezeway and circled the room, my steps too loud on the metal, until I reached the doorway. It glowed with a pale purple light. I took a deep breath and walked inside.

A rectangular room lay in front of me. At the far wall a simple stone altar rose from a raised platform. Five stone steps led to it from the right. Between the altar and me lay my grandmother's body. Long sharp blades, opaque and white, grew from the massive, nine-foot-tall skeleton, some branching, some isolated, some in clusters. One of these blades was now on my back, attached to a hilt.

In life my grandmother was Semiramis, the Great Queen, the Shield of Assyria. In death, her body was no longer a human thing; instead, it had become a magic coral, neither fully bone nor metal, stretching upward and outward, blooming like a lethal chrysanthemum. It burned with the cold fire of magic.

I could still turn back. There was still a chance.

No, I'd come too far to stop now.

I approached the bones. The magic brushed against me light as a feather, and the potency it carried gripped my heart into a fist and squeezed all the blood out of it. The world turned black.

*Breathe . . . breathe . . . breathe . . .*

The magic let go. She recognized me.

I knelt, opened the bag, and gently laid the bones of my aunt by her mother's side.

A wail tore through the chamber. Magic slammed into me, throwing me across the room. I smashed into the wall, every bone in my body rattling.

Ow.

I blinked and saw the gossamer shape of my grandmother. She wore a thin red robe with glittering gold threads running down the length of it. A waterfall of black hair fell in soft curls down her back. She knelt by the bones, her face with its bronze skin and bottomless brown eyes twisted by grief.

I rolled to my feet and stumbled back to the bags. She let me approach. I knelt by her, took out a thermos filled with Erra's blood, and poured it over the bones. They glowed weakly with pale red. I opened the second thermos and emptied it. The bones glowed brighter and dimmed.

Third thermos. A weak glow and then nothing.

It didn't work. I came all this way, did all those things, and it didn't work?

The tempest that was my grandmother stared at me, expecting something. I kept my gaze down. Looking into her eyes was like staring into an abyss. It would swallow you whole.

I had no more blood. Everything that the Pack had collected lay right there in front of me, like a fire laid out to burn. It needed an accelerant . . .

I pulled my sleeve back, peeled off the medical tape on my forearm, and squeezed some of my blood out. Why not? Everything else our family did was connected to blood. I let the hot red drops slide off my fingers onto the bones.

Nothing.

*Work, damn you. Work!*

My grandmother wailed. The magic slapped me and I rolled back across the chamber. My head swam.

I needed this to work. My son would die unless I did this.

I rolled to my hands and knees and crawled back to the body.

How could it not work? I was so sure . . . She was such a stubborn bitch, it should've worked.

The bones lay inert. My blood made no difference. I looked up at my grandmother. The awful gaze of Semiramis drained my soul.

"Help me."

She kept looking at me. She had all this magic. The two of us were bathed in it and I knew that if she could have, she would've helped me.

I sat on the floor next to my aunt's remains. It was over. I was done. I'd tried my best and failed.

I'd failed Curran. I'd failed my unborn son. I'd failed the Pack, the Witch Oracle, the city, everyone in it. She was my last hope. Only two options were left now: become my father's tool like Erra did before me, or die fighting.

I would go back to Atlanta and I would fight. I would fight till my last breath, but I had already failed.

I looked at the specter of my grandmother, bent as if to cradle what was left of her daughter's body. How terrible must it have been for her? At some point my grandmother must've been young and Erra must've been a toddler. I could almost picture them walking together through the gardens my father was trying to resurrect. Idyllic and peaceful, just a young woman and her daughter in a place full of water and bright fishes and beautiful water flowers, before the war.

Before my aunt turned into a monster. Before she watched all of her children grow up and die, killed by the curse of power and magic that was our blood. I had seen my son through the curtain of time. I didn't even know him and already I mourned him.

How in the world did it end like this, in an empty stone shell? This couldn't be what either of them had hoped for. They must've wanted love and family. They must've wanted happiness. Instead my grandmother died after seeing her daughter become a living plague, and my aunt was never happy. She destroyed and killed in impotent fury, and a part of her must've realized that she was trapped by her past and her blood, and so she raged harder and harder, but she could never break free. Even in this age, she awoke and hated being herself so much, she looked for a way to die again.

Tears wet my cheeks. I pulled Sarrat out of its sheath, hugged it the way I used to do with Slayer when I was a child, and cried. I cried for my grandmother, shackled in this concrete tomb so far from home. I cried for my aunt, because I finally understood her. I cried for myself, because I hated feeling helpless and I was so fucking tired of not being able to breathe, and now all my anger was leaking out of my eyes in tears. I cried and cried, my tears falling into the blood. I had nothing left.

Nobody would see it. Nobody would care. I could cry all I wanted and nobody could call me on it.

Finally, I had run out of energy. I wiped my eyes. Time to pick myself up and move on.

My aunt's bones glowed with ruby light.

I froze on my knees.

The loose bones of Erra's body shifted, twisting into a round pile. Blades burst from it, stretching straight up and curving, pressed together into a bulb. The red glow flashed and turned bright. The bone blades curved and opened like the petals of a flower.

My aunt stood within the glow, clad in her blood armor. Sadness shadowed her translucent face, her dark hair falling down to her waist.

Oh dear God. It worked.

Her eyes snapped open. The Eater of Cities saw me. "You!"

She charged me and tore right through me. It was like being passed through a fine sieve made of pain and cold. She whipped around, her face shocked. The red fire around her shot out and gripped my body. My feet left the ground. I flew backward and smashed into the stone wall of the chamber. My head swam. Someone set fire to my lungs. The invisible magic hand ground me into the stone. My bones groaned under the pressure.

"You!" Erra snarled. "I should've killed you. I will now."

Red circles swam before my eyes. There wasn't enough air. I was going to die.

"I wanted to die. You couldn't even do that right. You've raised me with your wailing. How dare you mourn me? Now I'll take you with me."

The tempest behind Erra shifted.

Her eyes widened. "Mother?"

The magic pressure vanished. I crashed to the floor, desperately sucking in air. My lungs burned and refused to expand.

The magic storm coalesced into Semiramis, standing before Erra's translucent form. My aunt stood still, her mouth open, her expression soft.

"Ama," Erra whispered. "Oh gods, Ama."

The magic of Semiramis embraced her. Erra hugged her back, their power mixing. The walls around us trembled from the pressure.

Tears wet my aunt's eyes. She looked past her mother at the bare walls. "Gods, what has he done to you . . ." she whispered. "What did he do . . ."

I finally rolled over onto my back and managed to take a breath. Everything felt bruised. Someone had turned my diaphragm into barbed wire when I wasn't looking.

Erra loomed over me. "Talk."

Great. I had to say the most important thing first, before she squeezed the life out of me.

"He'll kill my son."

"You have a son?"

"No, but I will."

Her magic jerked me upright. If she bounced me off the wall again, I swore I would set her damn bones on fire.

"How certain are you?"

"It's been foretold by several oracles. I have seen it in a vision. There's a battle. He runs my baby through with a spear and hoists it up like a standard."

She'd had sons. She'd loved them, even though they were violent and mad. She had to understand.

"And so you brought me here, into this tomb, and called me back into existence with your tears, weeping by my corpse like some weakling?"

That was my aunt for you.

"To do what?" Erra stalked in front of me, back and forth. "To kill my brother?"

I didn't answer. It didn't seem safe.

"Where is he now?"

"He built a castle on the edge of Atlanta, near my territory."

"Your territory?" Erra barked a short laugh.

"I claimed Atlanta."

She stopped and looked at me. "Claimed it how?"

"He tried to make it his, and I stopped him and made it mine."

"How? Describe it, you imbecile."

*Screw you.* "He made a giant magic spear and tried to stab me with it. I blocked it, then I levitated, and released a big pulse of magic." I waved my arms. "Poof."

"Poof?" Erra turned to my grandmother. "Ama, are you listening to this?"

Semiramis smiled.

"So you are Sharratum now? A queen?"

"I'm not a queen." I had to keep reminding myself.

"And he let you do this?"

"He didn't have a choice."

"What are the terms? There must've been terms."

"He promised me peace for a hundred years and then he built a castle on the edge of my territory. He's taunting me, kidnapping my people, meddling, wanting to control every aspect of my life, getting offended over my wedding reception, sending assassins to . . ."

Erra raised her hand.

I shut up.

"How long?"

"How long what?"

"How long has this been going on?"

"About six months."

"He's been sitting by your territory for six months and hasn't moved against you?"

"Yes."

"You're lying."

"Why the hell would I lie?"

My aunt pondered and flicked her hand. An invisible magic hammer crashed into me. This time I curled before hitting the wall. Bonus points.

"You say you claimed this city. Prove it."

I rolled to my feet.

"*My land. My city,*" Erra mocked. "Little baby princess. Pretender. Weakling."

"Stop mocking me or you'll regret it."

The magic swept me off my feet. I rolled across the chamber. "You own nothing. You possess nothing."

I got up to my feet.

"Liar." She was getting ready for round three. I felt the magic shift. "Imposter. You bring shame to our name."

**"Enough!"** I let my own power tear out of me and smash into my aunt's. **"I've fought and bled for that city. It's mine and I have nothing to prove to you. You and my father brought enough shame to the family name. People cringe when they hear it. If you hit me one more time, I'll throw your bones in the deepest sewer I can find."**

Erra's eyes narrowed. "I'll take your land and rule it as it was meant to be ruled."

**"No! It's mine!"**

"There it is," Erra said. "Do you even know what this thing is that's rearing its ugly head? Of course, you don't."

I opened my mouth.

"Quiet. I'm thinking."

This was the stupidest idea I'd ever had.

Erra sighed. "It's called the Shar. It's an ancient word that came to us from an old language. A word of Adam. It means the right to rule. The urge to obtain and hold land was bred into our family. Do you know why dynasties fall?"

"Because they eventually produce an incompetent heir."

"Yes. The Shar is the insurance that the strongest of our line is always in power. Once you have a taste of it, either it will devour you or you will triumph over it."

"Is my father . . ."

"Consumed by the Shar? He was for a time, but he learned to control it long ago. It is a force within him, it does drive some of his behavior, but there were times he walked away from the land he claimed and stayed away for years. Im is a prince of Shinar. He received proper instruction in the use of his gift as soon as he was able to understand words. But you have very little defense against it. For one, you're too young. You claimed too soon and too much. Second, you have no training. A child should be allowed to claim a small piece of land to become accustomed to the pressure. And third, the Shar is at its peak when two members of our family hold adjacent land. It is its very purpose: to force us against each other until a winner emerges victorious. This is why I chose to make no claim. I had no desire to rule."

"And my father . . ."

"Your father is cruel. He's torturing you. Sooner or later the Shar will drive you to move against him. All he has to do is wait, and he has all the time in the world."

"But why go to the trouble? If he wanted war, why not break the treaty? Nothing stops him."

"He's given you his word," Erra said. "The word of Sharrum is binding. It's the bedrock of his kingdom. The real question is why go through the charade of the agreement in the first place. It makes no sense . . ." She paused. Her eyes shone. "Why should I help you?"

"You are my aunt."

"And?"

"Look around you," I told her.

"What about it?"

"It's the tomb of our family."

My aunt turned slowly, taking in the bare walls.

"My father, your brother, brought your mother here, because he was afraid she would rise and challenge him. He locked her in this stone box so he could control her. Do you know where we are? We're in the heart of Mishmar."

Her face jerked. She'd recognized the name.

"He's using my grandmother's power to fuel it. She suffers. He knows this and does nothing. To him we're tools to be used."

The line of her mouth hardened. I'd hit a nerve.

"Why did you want to die?"

Derision twisted her face.

"Tell me, City Eater. Why did you want to die?"

"Because this wasn't my world," she snarled. "There is nothing for me here."

"It's not his world either. If he isn't stopped, he'll be the last of our line, because I'll fight to my death to protect the man I love and my future child. He'll destroy me, and after I'm gone, he'll murder my baby. Even if he takes the child and lets him grow, sooner or later he'll kill him, because my father can't stand to share even an iota of power. Ask yourself why none of your children survived. Why none of his? It's because he is a creature who eats his young. Our family has no future. He has devoured it."

Her face was completely flat.

"Sooner or later all of us will end up here, and he won't stop until he chokes the life out of the rest of the land. He'll turn this world into a copy of the old one, until it too collapses under his weight, and the cycle will begin anew. Ten thousand years from now, when you've been awakened for the third time, and another girl stands in my place asking for your help, will you ask her why?"

I couldn't tell if any of it sank in.

"Look at it." I raised my hands, indicating the stone box we stood in. "Just look at it."

Magic flared. The image of my grandmother vanished and an inferno of pale purple light blazed in her place, bleeding magic. Erra's translucent form melted into it. I raised my hand to shield my eyes. Magic raged around me, boiling and twisting.

Silence stretched.

"Good speech," Erra said from somewhere within the inferno.

"It's not—"

"What else do you have?"

What else? I grappled with the question, trying to think of something—anything—to convince her.

"He's rebuilding the Water Gardens."

"What about it?"

"He told me you used to love them. You used to play there together. That you had a happy childhood."

"And?"

"Take my memories. I know you can do it, because my grandmother has done it. Look into my head. See the child-hood my father has given me."

The light splayed out and licked me, seizing me into a tight, hard fist. Pain seared my mind, pulling me apart, as if my soul were fabric and it was unraveling thread by thread. I let it hurt me and melted into it, giving up every-thing, all my memories, all my fears, and all of my dreams.


THE SUN WAS warm on my face. Such a hot welcoming sun. A shallow pond lay before me, only ankle deep, a jewel cradled in the green hands of proud cypresses. Small fishes darted through the clear water, golden and white sparks against the turquoise bottom. In the middle of it a pavilion of pink stone rose with a domed roof, no walls, only four arches. A delicate mosaic of colored tiles lined the ceiling, showing the sun, the planets, and the stars, as if a Persian carpet of incredible beauty had been stretched across it. A dark-haired woman sat on the steps of the pavilion, her feet in the water, her blood-red dress floating on the surface of the pond. She beckoned.

I stepped into the pond and walked to her. The turquoise stones felt smooth under my feet. My white dress floated, swirling in the water.

The woman patted a step next to her. She was so beautiful, my aunt.

I sat. She reached for my hair. It was long again, the way I liked to have it. She ran her hands through the brown strands, pulled out a tortoiseshell comb, and gently brushed it.

I saw our reflection in the water. The girl in the white dress had my face but she seemed so young and pretty. Soft, like she had never opened another human being with her blade and let their blood flow on the sands of the pits. Someone had brushed gold on my eyelids. Someone had lined my eyes with black. Someone had put a delicate gold chain around my neck with a red stone full of fire.

Was it really me?

My aunt put a white flower into my hair. "This is what you were meant to be," she said. "The princess of Shinar. Not a mongrel without family. Not some man's attack dog. Not the mindless weapon I saw in your memories. You didn't know about it, your father kept it from you, but it is yours.

"Is this what it looked like? The Water Gardens?"

"Yes."

I could stay here forever. It was so peaceful here.

"This was my favorite place. I wanted to bring my daughters here the way my mother brought me," my aunt said, her dark eyes soft like velvet. "The war destroyed everything you see and I never had any daughters. He rebuilt the gardens, but they weren't the same. It was never the same. All gone now. The splendor of Shinar is dust. We are all that remains."

"I don't want it to disappear."

"It must," she said. "It lives only in my heart. Now it will live in yours."

I turned to look at her. The pavilion was gone. I sat in a room. Gauzy red curtains blocked my view, and in the gap beyond them I saw a trellised balcony. A sticky dark puddle slowly spread on the floor, inching toward my feet. I had seen too many puddles exactly like this. The smell hit me, hot and metallic. An awful crunching sound came from somewhere beyond the veils of red gauze.

"What is this?"

"You wanted to share," my aunt said. "You showed me yours. I'll show you mine."

I drew the curtain aside. The sound got louder, a sickening, chewing, slurping sound.

I pulled the last curtain aside. A bed strewn with a child's toys and colorful pillows. A thing glared at me from the floor. Hairless, gray, awful, with huge owl eyes and bloodstained teeth. It clutched a child's headless corpse in its front limbs. It stared at me and chewed.

"This is the way your uncle died," my aunt said. "Also two of your aunts."

I lunged forward. The thing shrieked, dragging the child's body with it. I chased it. I had to kill it.

"They came from the sea," Erra said. "You won't find their names chiseled into any stone. We obliterated them and their memory. We erased them from existence. They had attacked the kingdoms like a plague, bringing their magic and their creations like that thing you're trying too hard to kill."

If only I could catch it, I would crack its skull like a walnut.

"We were betrayed by our neighbors. We had left to broker an alliance. When we returned, the palace of Shinar was silent. We found only half-eaten corpses."

The thing darted toward my aunt. She looked at it and its bones broke, the big dome of its skull caving in on itself as if stomped.

"*Look outside,*" she said.

I stepped onto the balcony. A vast plain unrolled before me. An army charged at me. Shaggy, huge armored mammoths; strange beasts, their hindquarters striped, their heads too large for their bodies, their jaws filled with oversized hyena teeth; creatures for which I had no name; and people in armor. I glanced behind me. The dark room was gone. My aunt strode onto the field in front of her troops. She wore blood armor. Her loose hair streamed in the wind. Behind her the emerald standards snapped, pulled taut. She began to run, at first slowly, then picking up speed. The troops behind her broke into a charge. To the right, a man in blood armor on a white horse raised a spear and shouted. His horse reared and I saw his face, impossibly handsome and alight with magic. Father . . .

My aunt charged across the field, magic twisting around her.

The first line of the enemy was almost to her.

Erra opened her mouth. Power tore from her, an unstoppable blast that sent the armored mammoths flying.

At the other end of the field, my father raised his hands. The earth split, swallowing the enemy.

The two armies collided. A sword landed next to me. I grabbed it.

"This is also you," Erra said next to me. "This is the wrath of Shinar. They who thought they would murder us, take our cities, and eat our children, they met our anger and it consumed them. It consumed us too, but not before we obliterated their very memory from history. We wiped them off the face of the planet. It is as if they never were."

Around me the battle raged. My father spun in the center of a magical maelstrom. Behind him the earth shuddered and broke loose. A creature of metal and magic, a beautiful golden lion a hundred feet high, burst onto the field. My aunt twisted and sliced the head off an invader. It went flying.

"This is what you are asking me to betray," Erra said into my ear.

*I closed my eyes and imagined the weight and warmth of a child in my arms. When I opened them, my son looked back at me with Curran's gray eyes. The battle was gone. We sat in the pavilion again.*

*I held my son out to Erra. "This is what I'm asking you to save."*

*She took the child from me and looked at his face.*

*"I just want him to live a happy life," I told her. "The war is terrible. It will never end, as long as my father is allowed to be free. He can't stop. Maybe a part of him wants to, but even if it does, he doesn't know how. Someone has to end it."*

*A woman appeared behind us, regal, tall, her wrists heavy with golden bracelets, her flowing dress a deep emerald green. Black kohl lined her eyes, her eyelids and lips dusted with gold. Semiramis reached down, took my son from Erra's hands, and smiled at him.*

THE GARDENS FADED. The grip of the magic released me, its pain an echo in my bones. The arcane inferno died down. Semiramis withdrew, revealing Erra.

"He created an order of assassins to kill me," she whispered. She had seen sahanu in my memories. There was something almost vulnerable in her face.

My grandmother reached for her, wrapping her ghostly arms about her daughter. Magic swirled around them.

"I know," Erra whispered. "I understand."

She turned to me, all tenderness vanishing from her face like a mask jerked aside.

"You will do two things for me. Once this is over, I will choose the burial place for myself and my mother. You will move us there."

"Done." I would've done it anyway.

"And you will abandon the city."

"What?"

"You will agree to never rule the land you've claimed."

I opened my mouth. Everything inside me rebelled at the idea. It was my city, my land, my people, mine . . .

No. It was not mine. I took it, but it was never mine.

I raised my hand.

It was so hard. I wanted to charge across the room and beat her head against the stone until I saw the color of her brain for even bringing it up.

This wasn't me. I wouldn't become my father.

I could lie.

I crushed the thought.

"I promise that the day my father is dead or contained, I will walk away from the land I claimed."

It hurt to say it.

"Not good enough," Erra said. "I don't want you to walk away. I want you to swear to never rule it. You're a queen like your grandmother and her mother before her. Swear to me in the true language."

I opened my mouth. Nothing came out.

"What's the matter, little squirrel? Want to kill me for daring?"

Yes. Oh yes. So much.

I needed to reach deep down and find the strength to do it.

"Your land or your lover and your son. Choose."

It wasn't even a choice.

"**I swear . . .**" Each word was impossibly heavy. The room around us shook. Little chunks of mortar fell from the ceiling. "**. . . to never . . .**" It felt like all the ligaments in my throat would tear. The tomb shuddered. "**. . . rule the land I claimed.**"

It hurt so much.

"**The word of Sharratum is binding,**" Erra said. "**So witnessed.**"

The room stopped shaking.

A cool rush swept through me. Suddenly the air felt lighter.

"The Shar is a persistent bitch," my aunt said. "Giving up the land you claimed is the first step. Watching it being taken by another is the second. Letting them live is the third. If you survive, we will do this over and over, until you reach your equilibrium or it drives you mad."

"Thank you." Universe help me, I meant it.

My aunt waved her hand. "Why did he let you live?"

"According to him, it's because I'm his treasured daughter, his Blossom, the precious one, the one he loves above all others."

I heard my own words and cracked up. Erra guffawed. Once I started, I couldn't stop. The laughter came and came, pouring out, until I had tears in my eyes. We stood there and laughed and laughed.

"Oh, that's good." Erra sat on the steps. "That's good."

I couldn't remember the last time I'd laughed so hard. My stomach hurt. I must've needed it.

"Why do you think he let you live?"

"I have no idea."

"There must be something."

"I don't know. He tried to kill me before. He said that he loved my mother and promised her that he would give her a child like no other, but then foresaw that I would become like Kali, the destroyer of worlds, and so he tried to kill me but failed. He glossed over that part."

Erra pondered it. "If Im tried to kill you, you would be dead. He must've reconsidered. But why?"

"I don't know. Also he inscribed the language of power on me in the womb."

"And you didn't start with that? Let's hope your lion has some brains, otherwise your child will be a dimwit."

Semiramis moved.

"Yes, I know, Ama. Your grandmother says that in this day and age, you could do worse. Show the inscription to me."

"I can't. It only shows up in certain moments. When I claimed the city, for example. He can make it appear by touching me, but I can't."

"Do you know what it says?"

"No."

She rose and touched me. Her hand went through mine. She waved her hand back and forth through my arms. I'd tell her that it felt like being passed through an icy cheese grater, but she would only do it more.

Erra swore. "Being dead has its problems. Although it does give you a certain clarity. I felt my mother when I awoke. I asked him about it and he told me he had left her by the banks of the Tigris. I told him then that if he lied to me, he would regret it."

"He will regret many things by the time I'm done."

"Find a way to record the words and show them to me," Erra said. "We must learn why you're still alive."

"Okay. I will."

I turned to the doorway.

"Where are you going?" Erra demanded

"I'm escaping," I said. "He'll probably arrive in the next few minutes."

Behind Erra the purple blaze of Semiramis flared.

"Yes," Erra said, pronouncing each word very clearly as if talking to someone very stupid or hard of hearing. "That's why you have to take me with you. Because you're an idiot and you need help and I'm the bigger idiot for promising it to you."

I stared at the mass of her bones. "How?"

She turned away from me. "It's time."

Magic raged through the chamber, a furious tempest, filled with grief. The walls shook. I curled into a ball, trying to hide, but it was everywhere.

"I won't be long," Erra whispered, melting into the magic, her voice carrying through the room. "I'm coming back, Mother. And then I'll take you out of this awful place."

My grandmother wept.

I clamped my hands over my ears, shut my eyes, and tried to keep calm.

The room shook and shuddered. My body bounced off the floor.

Suddenly it was quiet. I opened my eyes. A dagger had sprouted from the center of my aunt's bones, a wickedly curved double-edged blade with a bone hilt. A thin line of blood-red script crossed the plate substance of the blade. My aunt's name.

I reached out and took it. It came free with a light snap. The bone flower fell apart into dust.

She'd molded her bones and blood into a dagger and sunk her soul into it. I could never let my father see this knife.

"Hurry up," Erra's voice snapped. "I can feel him coming."

I yanked my spare knife out and slid the dagger into the sheath. It didn't fit exactly, but it would have to do.

"Thank you, Grandmother." I bowed my head and took off.

At some point the fact that I was carrying my aunt the City Eater in my knife sheath would likely hit me and then I would have a nice nervous breakdown. But right now, we had to get out of here.

Outside, red lightning split the dark sky. Wind tore at my clothes and hair. I yanked the canister with the moth out and shattered it on the stone. The tiny insect floated up, growing brighter and brighter, a green spark against the darkness.

*Come on, Sugar. Come and get me.*

The gates of Mishmar's wall flew open. A sphere of fire and light rolled onto the bridge and broke apart, revealing my father. His face was dark. A blood spear formed in his hand.

**"YOU DISOBEYED ME AGAIN, MY DAUGHTER."**

I'd never seen him this pissed off. Not even when I fought with him at his castle. I pulled Sarrat out of its sheath.

Behind us, Mishmar trembled and bellowed like a tornado. I turned around. The tower shuddered. The strange birds took to the sky, their guttural cries swallowed by the noise. Car-sized chunks of concrete and stone broke loose and tumbled down.

**"SHARRIM!"** My father's voice rippled with magic. If the bridge had been metal, it would've melted in fear.

"It's not my fault!" I yelled back.

**"STUBBORN, IGNORANT, IMPERTINENT CHILD! I TOLD YOU NOT TO COME HERE. I WILL KEEP YOU HERE UNTIL YOU LEARN TO OBEY ME!"**

Oh crap.

Thunder punched my ears. A massive crack formed in the tower's wall. The purple inferno of my grandmother's magic splashed and coiled within it.

I turned back to my father and saw the familiar winged shape behind him diving toward me.

"Can't talk now. Grandma wants to see you."

My father snarled, pointing his spear at me. A chunk of Mishmar the size of a small house rolled off the top and plunged down. The entire tower rocked. The purple magic spilled out, its fury mind-numbing. The prison rumbled, threatening to collapse.

My father swore, each curse word charged with magic, and planted his spear on the bridge. Golden light burst from it, battering against the purple.

I charged past him.

Sugar landed and ran toward me across the bridge. I sprinted to her. She turned, stopping for a heartbeat, and I jumped and landed on her back.

Behind us the gold and purple magic tore at each other.

The pegasi took off, huge wings beating. I pulled all of my magic out of myself, trying to shield us.

The two spheres of light exploded.

"Higher, Sugar. Higher!"

The pegasi's powerful muscles rolled under me. She beat her wings, climbing higher and higher. Below us the glow of magic splayed out, as if a second sunrise burned down below. The edge of the explosion expanded toward us. I held my breath. The glow fell a few yards short.

"Did he kill Grandmother?" I whispered.

"Don't be ridiculous," Erra's voice said in my ear. "She is already dead. Besides, your grandmother was the Shield of Assyria. Even if he committed every drop of his power to it, he couldn't stomp her out of existence. She's buying us time. He's got a busy night ahead of him."

"North," I told Sugar. "Fly north." He wouldn't look for us in that direction.

The pegasi turned and fled north, as fast as her wings would carry her.

"And for your information," Erra said, "I wasn't always the City Eater. That's the name our enemies gave me and you won't use it."

Oy. "What were you called before you were the City Eater?"

"The Rose of Tigris. Now shut up and make this horse go faster."

≡ CHAPTER ≡
# 11

ERRA WAS RIGHT. The Shar was real. I felt the familiar pull when I crossed into my territory. I hadn't realized how much it was wearing me down, until I had to slide it back on, like a tired plow horse who was being put back into her horse collar.

All of me hurt. My back was probably bruised from being thrown around. My stomach wound ached. I wanted to get home and sleep.

Sugar unloaded me in front of my house. I hugged her and gave her another sugar cube. "Thank you."

Sugar neighed, bumped my face with her head, and took off into the night.

I didn't make it more than two steps into the house before Curran appeared out of the living room and hugged me to him. He didn't say anything. He just pulled me over, wrapped his arms around me, and squeezed until my bones groaned.

He smelled of blood. I probably smelled worse. My whole body hurt and being hugged felt like being run over by a car. And there was no place I wanted to be more than right here.

"Hey," I said.

"Hey," he said.

"I . . ." *I resurrected my aunt who tried to kill you so hard, you were in a coma for eleven days.* ". . . I'm glad to be home."

"I'm glad you're home, too."

"How did it go?"

"The degenerate is at the Guild," Curran said. "Regenerating."

"Did any of your people . . ."

"No," he said. "King's got broken legs and Samantha was burned, but we got out alive."

He rescued Saiman and got them out alive. I exhaled.

"How was it?"

"It was okay," Curran said.

"We did okay," Derek said from the living room, almost at the same time.

Curran opened his arms, but I held on to his hand. Not yet. I still wasn't one hundred percent sure he'd made it back in one piece. I still needed proof for a little while longer.

In the living room Derek sprawled on the floor on a blanket, his eyes closed, his body human, corded with hard muscle, and covered only with a strategically placed towel. Julie knelt by him, long tweezers in her hand.

"What's going on?"

"Quills," she said. "Very thin quills. There was a magic plant and he decided it would be a good idea to give it a hug. Because he is smart that way."

So they had taken Julie with them. Considering where I'd gone and what I did while there, I didn't have room to talk.

Derek didn't bother opening his eyes. "I wasn't giving it a hug. I was shielding Ella."

"Mm-hm." Julie plucked a thin needle from his stomach. "You shielded her really well. Because it's not like we didn't have Carlos with us."

Carlos was a firebug. The plant must've gotten torched.

"We'll need to work on mixed-unit tactics," Curran said.

He looked tired. It must've been hell. "So what did you do in Mishmar?"

Umm. Ehh. In my head I had somehow expected Erra to stay in Mishmar.

"I saw my father," I said. Start small.

"How was that?" Curran asked.

"He's a little upset with me."

"Aha."

"I broke Mishmar a little bit."

The three of them looked at me.

"But it was mostly my grandmother who did it."

"How much is a little bit?" Derek asked.

"There might be a crack. About maybe seven feet at the widest point."

Derek laughed.

"And what else?" Curran asked.

Perceptive bastard.

"And this." I pulled out the dagger and showed it to him.

"You made a magic knife?" he asked.

"Yes. In a manner of speaking."

"But you still have to get close enough to stab Roland with it," Derek said.

"That's not how it works." *Help me, somebody.*

Curran was looking right at me. "Kate?"

"It's more of an advising kind of knife."

"You should come clean," he said. "Whatever it is, it's done and we can handle it."

My aunt tore into existence in the center of the room. "Hello, half-breed."

Curran exploded into a leap. Unfortunately, Derek also exploded at exactly the same time but from the opposite direction. They collided in Erra's translucent body with a loud thud. Derek fell back and Curran stumbled a few steps.

Erra pointed at Curran with her thumb. "You want to marry this? Is there a shortage of men?"

Curran leapt forward and swiped at her head. His hand passed through my aunt's face. Derek jumped to his feet and circled Erra, his eyes glowing.

"I fear for my grandnephew," Erra said. "He will be an idiot."

The phone rang. "I'll get it." It was probably for me anyway and I desperately needed to escape.

I ran to the kitchen to pick up the phone.

"The baby," Sienna's voice said into the phone. She sounded strained.

"What?"

"The baby is the next anchor. I see you holding a small baby in the Keep. It's not yours. Hurry!"

The hair on the back of my neck stood up. Baby B.

"Roland's going after Baby B!" I yelled, and dialed the Keep's security number, one step away from Jim.

"Yes?" an unfamiliar male voice said.

"I need Jim."

"Who is this?"

Curran plucked the phone from me. "Put Jim on now."

The line clicked and Jim's voice said, "Yes?"

"Is Andrea still in the medical ward?"

"Yes."

"Roland is targeting Baby B," Curran said, his voice even and measured. "We're coming to you now."

"Got it." Jim's voice sounded almost nonchalant.

I ran out the door. Behind me Curran appeared, keys in hand. Julie followed, Derek behind her in Pack sweatpants, pulling on a white T-shirt.

We piled into the car and Curran took off like the street behind us was on fire.

Crap. I'd left Erra behind. Too late now.

The city slid by outside the window. The speedometer said we were tearing down the half-ruined roads at nearly sixty miles per hour. Any faster and we'd flip the car. It felt like crawling.

"Why?" Julie asked from the backseat. "What could Baby B do to him?"

"Nothing," I said. "She's an anchor."

"What anchor?"

I forced myself to speak in complete sentences. "Sienna

says that the future is fluid. She sees flashes of it, pivotal moments during which the future can change. She calls them anchors. Me turning the old lady's head over to the police was an anchor. So was Chernobog's dragon. Either Roland or his oracles can also see into the future. They see the anchors and try to change them to enforce their version of the future."

"What happens if we don't get there in time?" Julie asked.

"We'll get there," Curran said, his gaze focused on the road. "By now Jim has the Keep on lockdown. No outsider is getting close to that baby."

"It's not the outsiders I'm worried about," I told him. Roland's people had managed to subvert the wolf alpha before, the leader of the most numerous clan within the Pack. There was no telling who else he had in his clutches. If something happened to Baby B . . .

"What happens if we fail to secure an anchor?" Derek asked.

"Atlanta burns, a bunch of people die, Roland kills Curran and our son."

Crap. Crap. Would it have killed me to think before I opened my mouth? Maybe he wasn't listening closely.

"Our son?" Curran said, his voice very calm. His face slid into his Beast Lord mask. "Erra's grandnephew."

I was so stupid. "Yes."

"Are you pregnant?"

"Not yet. I will be soon."

"How does our son die?"

"Roland runs him through with a spear."

"How long have you known?"

"That he dies? Since I went to see the witches."

"That we will have a son."

"The djinn showed him to me."

He was doing almost seventy now. We were going to wreck.

"Kate," he said. I knew that tone of voice. That was his line-in-the-sand voice. "What happened to Erra? Did you resurrect your aunt?"

"Not exactly. She isn't technically alive."

He glanced at me, his eyes drowning in liquid gold. He wasn't interested in "technically." His voice came out deep, almost demonic. "Why?"

"Because I desperately need help. Things are happening to me that I can't explain and don't understand. I know that my father will attack and very soon. When he does, I have to defend us and I can't. I have the power but I don't know how to use it, and in using it, I'm affecting the lives of every creature and plant in my lands. I'm afraid that I'll make a mistake and kill everyone in Atlanta. I have to get guidance. She's the only one with the knowledge I need."

"She tried to kill us," Curran ground out.

"I know. But she's a princess of Shinar. The one thing she values above all else is family. Yes, she would've killed me if she was alive and I challenged her, but now things are different. I showed Grandmother to her. It made her furious. I showed her all of my memories and our son. She's going to help us."

"You can't trust her," Curran said.

"Yes, I can. She isn't doing it for you or for me. She's doing it for the survival of her bloodline. What my father is doing is an aberration. The members of our family weren't meant to live forever. We were meant to have families and children. As long as my father lives, no other member of our bloodline will survive. Not even her. She knows about the sahanu."

"What are the sahanu?" Curran asked.

I was hitting it out of the park today with keeping secrets. "He was afraid of her and so he created a religious sect designed to kill her. Now I am their next target. I fought one of them in Mishmar, a female. She was hard to kill."

"Is that why you're bruised and smell like blood?" Derek asked from the backseat.

"Yes. And some of it was Erra. She took some convincing."

"But is she going to help us?" Julie asked.

"She already has," I said.

Curran stared straight ahead. His hands gripped the wheel.

"You're going to bend it," I told him.

He hit me with an alpha stare and kept driving.

"Are you okay?" I asked. *Are we okay, Curran?*

"He's got no room to talk," Julie said.

"Quiet," Derek told her.

"Is there anything else you want to tell me?" Curran asked.

"No." Now wasn't the best time to bring up Adora. "Is there anything you want to tell me?"

"One of the rooms in the castle had a creature in it," Curran said.

"What kind of creature?"

"A large cat," Curran said. "It glowed."

"What happened to the large glowing cat?" Why did I have a feeling I wouldn't like the answer?

"I killed it," Curran said.

"Aha." First, I broke Mishmar, then Curran stole Saiman back and killed my father's glowing cat. Maybe Roland's head would explode.

"It was a saber-toothed tiger," Julie said. "It glowed silver."

Silver meant divine magic. There was no telling what that saber-toothed tiger was or where my dad had gotten him.

"Snitch," Derek said.

She waved him off. "He killed it and then he ate it."

I looked at Curran. "You killed an animal god and then you ate him?"

"Maybe," Curran said.

"What do you mean maybe?"

"I doubt it was a god."

"It glowed silver," Julie said. "It was definitely worshipped."

Oh boy.

Curran swerved to avoid a speed bump formed by tree roots raising the asphalt. "I could worship a lamp. That doesn't make it a god."

"Why did you eat it?" I asked in a small voice.

"It felt right at the time."

"He devoured it," Julie said. "Completely. With bones."

If it was some sort of divine animal and he ate it, there was no telling what the flesh or the magic would do to him. There would be consequences. There were always consequences.

"Do you feel any side effects?"

"Not any I want to talk about with them in the car."

Oh boy.

We passed the burned-out shell of the Infinity Building, the last known skyscraper built before the Shift. Halfway there.

*Hold on, Baby B. We are coming.*

WE TURNED ONTO the narrow side road leading to the Keep. Curran stepped on it. The car accelerated. Wolves appeared from the brush, running parallel to the vehicle. The woods ended and we shot onto a mile-long stretch of open ground between the trees and the tower of the Keep. The heavy metal gates stood shut.

Curran braked hard. The vehicle skidded and stopped two feet from the gray wall. I got the hell out of the car. The wolves sniffed me, a wall of fur and teeth separating me from the gates. The lead wolf raised her head and howled.

The gates opened enough for us to pass through, and the four of us marched inside. Robert, one of the alphas of Clan Rat and the Pack's chief of security, stepped out of the main entrance, waiting for us.

"Anything?" Curran asked.

Robert shook his head. "Not a whisper. No sign of attack, no unusual movement, nothing."

We hurried through the Keep's hallways to the medical ward, passing through pair after pair of sentries.

"The magic is down," Robert said. "If an attack comes, it will be via an agent. There are exactly six outsiders in the Keep right now: two teamsters who delivered a shipment and the four of you."

Ouch.

"What was in the shipment?" Curran asked.

"Paper," Robert said. "My people inspected and cleared it."

The shapeshifters guarded the medward door. If Sienna hadn't called me to warn me, I wouldn't be in the Keep, I wouldn't be holding Baby B, and no attack would come. The future was a self-fulfilling prophecy.

"Baby B is being targeted because my father saw the future with me holding her," I said.

"Why is the baby important?" Robert asked.

"It's an anchor. It's something that has to happen for the right version of the future to happen," I said.

"What's the right version?"

"The one where we don't all die," Curran said.

Robert's eyes narrowed. "I take it Roland prefers a different version."

"If I walk into that room and attempt to hold Baby B, I will provoke an attack."

"If you don't walk into that room, the city will burn," Curran said.

"I take full responsibility," Robert said, and nodded at the guards. The woman on the left swung the door open.

Andrea sat on the bed in the middle of the room, fully dressed, holding Baby B. Raphael stood behind her. Jim and Dali stood to the left, and the two renders, Pearce and Jezebel, to the right. Mahon loomed by the left window, behind Jim and Dali. Desandra stood by the other window, behind Pearce and Jezebel. Doolittle sat in his wheelchair in the corner, out of the way, with Nasrin by him. Everyone looked grim.

The doors shut behind us. Sixteen people, including me. I trusted every single person in this room. I would fight to defend every single person in this room.

There were too many of us here. Jim always erred on the side of caution.

"To end the threat, Kate must hold the baby," Robert said. "Holding the baby will provoke the attack. But not holding the baby will have catastrophic consequences for the future of the Pack."

Andrea's face was hard and her eyes harder.

"If the attack comes," Robert continued, "if at all possible, we need to take the attacker alive. There are important questions that need to be answered."

Raphael's eyes shone with a deranged ruby light. Robert was crazy if he thought he was taking anyone alive.

"Do we have your permission, alphas of the bouda clan?" Robert asked.

Pearce and Jezebel took a step forward at the same time.

"Yes," Andrea said, looking at me like I was a striking cobra. "You have our permission."

Twenty feet separated me from Baby B. I took a step toward Andrea.

The room tensed. Everyone was looking at someone else. Muscles bunched on Pearce's frame. Mahon had somehow grown larger.

Another step.

*Someone do something, damn it. If you're going to attack, do it now.*

Another.

"Cough-cough!" Desandra said.

Everyone spun toward her. Pearce launched himself into a leap, midway in the air recognized that he'd been had, and twisted, landing clumsily on the floor by Desandra. Jezebel exhaled and spun away from the wolf alpha, her face slack with suddenly released pressure. Behind me Derek swore.

"It was getting too tense." The alpha of the wolves shrugged.

I'd strangle her after this. I didn't care if Jim objected.

"Would it kill you to not be an asshole for thirty seconds?" Andrea growled.

Desandra winked at her. "I don't know, I've never tried."

Jezebel ripped a knife out of a sheath and lunged at Baby B in Andrea's arms. I shot forward, but it was too far. I saw the knife slice through the air. The distance it had to travel was so short and the space between me and her was so long . . .

Dali jumped in front of the knife, just as Andrea rolled back, pulling Baby B out of reach.

The knife slid into Dali's chest.

Raphael sliced Jezebel's throat. The impact of the strike spun her.

Dali made a small gurgling noise. Blood poured from her mouth. The blade had hit her heart. The angle of the knife was textbook perfect.

Jim's face snapped into a jaguar's muzzle, the transformation so fast it was instant. Before Jezebel finished turning, he grabbed her throat, thrust his clawed hand under her rib cage, and disemboweled her.

I was still running.

Curran jumped past me, a seven-foot-tall nightmare, and thrust himself between Jim and Raphael. His left hand locked on Jim's shoulder, his right on Raphael's throat. The muscles on his back bulged.

Jezebel crashed on the floor by Curran's feet. The two shapeshifters struggled in his grasp. He held them. He shouldn't have been able to hold both of them. Curran was shockingly strong, but this was off the charts even for him.

Robert jumped onto Jezebel, straddling her, trying to shield her with his own body. "Alive. We need her alive!"

Raphael sliced at Curran's arm.

Jim brought his legs up and kicked Curran in the ribs, ripping himself free. Curran's body shuddered from the impact, but he remained on his feet. He didn't go down.

Jim bounced off the wall, eyes glowing. I jumped between him and Curran, Sarrat in my hand.

Dali made a quiet gasping noise and fell. Jim caught Dali's small body. She was breathing fast in shallow gasps. Black blood poured from her mouth—the Lyc-V saturating her body dying off by the millions. The blade must have been coated with silver shavings.

"Doolittle!" Jim spun toward the medmage.

The magic was down. No medmage healing.

"Hold her," the medmage barked. "Nasrin, scalpel."

Raphael finally broke free of Curran. His eyes had gone completely mad. He shot forward and Mahon clamped him into a bear hug from behind.

Baby B wailed.

How the hell could it be Jezebel? Was it a polymorph in Jezebel's shape?

Robert got off Jezebel, kneeling by her. Julie dropped by the bouda's body into the puddle of her blood.

"Who else?" Robert demanded. "Who else belongs to Roland?"

"Why?" Tears streamed down Julie's face. "Why?"

Jezebel opened her mouth, each breath a loud wet struggle. She was looking straight at me. She struggled to say something.

The room was full of noise—Raphael snarling, Baby B wailing, Jim growling.

"Quiet!" Curran roared.

In the silence, Jezebel's voice sounded too loud. "Sharrim . . ."

She stretched an arm toward me, sliding in her own blood, trying to crawl toward me.

Oh God.

"Bless me . . . so serve you . . . in the afterlife . . . Bless me . . ."

"No," I told her.

"Bless me . . ." Her body shuddered.

"I bless you." Julie pulled Jezebel to her, cradling her head. "Her blood is my blood. You can serve me."

Jezebel reached out with her bloody hand and patted Julie's cheek. Her fingers slid, leaving red smudges on Julie's pale skin. Her chest rattled. Jezebel gasped and died.

Julie screamed, her voice raw with grief.

In the corner Dali went into convulsions.

Andrea marched over and thrust Baby B at me. "Hold her!"

I took the baby. Andrea let me hold her for exactly three seconds and grabbed her back.

Jim turned to us, his face still jaguar. "Get out."


EVERYTHING WAS FUCKED UP.

We walked down the hallway toward the stairs. Derek had taken Julie's hand, pulled her up to her feet, and was now walking next to her, holding her hand in his. She stared straight ahead, her teeth clenched. Tears streamed down her face, but she walked without a single sob. Derek walked, his face stoic, his eyes scanning the hallway in front of us for potential threats. Curran strode next to me, still in warrior form.

Pearce followed us. As we passed the sentries, they followed us, too. Shapeshifters had enhanced hearing. Everyone on the floor had heard the Beast Lord snarl.

It had been the real Jezebel. Had to be. The shapeshifters would've smelled a polymorph. When did my father get to Jezebel? Was it after he got to Julie? Was it before I took the city? We would never know. All I had was a fistful of questions, a dead woman I thought was a friend, and another friend dying from silver poisoning.

Why the hell did Dali jump in front of that knife? Scratch that, I knew why. Andrea would've never allowed her baby to be harmed. I knew that, Jim knew that, but Dali, kind, smart Dali who rarely fought, didn't. She saw the knife and the baby and reacted. And now she was struggling for her life.

My father was ripping my life apart friend by friend. The temptation to march down to his half-finished castle and attack was overwhelming. And that was what he expected me to do. I had to use whatever will I had left to not do it, not until I knew for sure that I had a way to neutralize him.

The anger buoyed me. I could barely contain it and if I thought too much about my father, I'd see red and go blind. I had to think of something else. Anything else.

The stairs ended. We walked into the courtyard. The morning sunshine seemed too bright. It hurt my eyes.

"Out of my way," a deep voice ordered. I glanced over my shoulder. Mahon headed straight for us.

Curran handed the keys over to Derek. "Take her to the car."

"We'll kill him," Mahon said.

"We will," Curran said.

"You're vulnerable and exposed out there in the city. You're welcome to move your people, all your people, shapeshifter and not, into the Clan Heavy house. If not, let me send people down there to reinforce you. I'm not talking guards on every corner, but some muscle. In case."

Curran considered it. "Thank you. We could use the help."

"Take care of the little one," Mahon told me. "Jim will come around."

The Bear clamped his hand on Curran's shoulder, squeezed, turned, and went back inside.

We reached the car. I went to the driver's side—in warrior form, Curran was too big to fit behind the wheel.

"All this is because of me."

"No, all of this is because of Roland," Curran said. "You didn't kidnap Saiman. You didn't attack a baby. All you did and all any of us wanted to do is live our fucking lives in peace."

I loved him so much. "Thank you, but that's not what I meant. I meant that every anchor so far was connected to me. If I hadn't known about the prophecy, I wouldn't have come to the Keep."

"Yes. That's why you and I are joined at the hip from now on."

I arched an eyebrow at him.

"I mean it." He flashed his teeth at me. "I did what you asked. I got Saiman out for you. You did . . . what you had to do. From now on we go together."

"Okay."

I got into the car and drove down the road. The moment we rolled out of the Pack courtyard, Julie broke. Derek wrapped his arm around her. She cried and cried, heartbroken. Julie almost never cried anymore.

If Dali died . . . I didn't even want to think about it. If I had a choice, I would hit my father now, hard and fast, with all of our strength. Instead I had to sit on my hands, because right now we couldn't win. Not until my aunt helped me figure out how to defeat him.

"I didn't know," Julie sobbed. "She took care of me for two years and I didn't know."

"Nobody knew," Curran told her.

"He threw her away. Just like that. For nothing."

I almost said *I tried to tell you before* and bit it back before it came out. Not the right time.

"Why her? Why? She was so nice."

"Because she was close to you," Derek said.

Julie buried her face in her hands and cried.

"I'm so sorry," I told her. "I'm so sorry, sweetie. I'll make him pay. I promise you."

"It won't bring her back," she whimpered.

My heart was cracking and it hurt. *You bastard. You fucking bastard.* "I know. I'm so sorry."

Trees rolled by. For several minutes we didn't talk. I drove and looked straight ahead.

"Where are we going?" Derek asked.

"We're going to the Guild," I said. We were going to work.

"Why?" he asked.

"Because I need Saiman to read what my father wrote on my skin while I was in the womb. The sooner Erra can tell me what it is, the sooner we can kill him."

The car fell silent.

"Well," Curran said. "At least the pervert has a purpose."

THE GUILD OCCUPIED the remains of an old hotel on the edge of Buckhead. When Curran, Barabas, and I took it over, the tower was in ruins, partially because a rogue giant had ripped off its roof trying to eat the delicious people hiding inside. The Guild had a new roof now. A new front parking lot and a new back lot too, the latter fenced in by a solid wall and converted into a training yard. Barabas was trying to push through a permit with the city that would allow us to put an even bigger wall around the building. Any time Curran got a base, he wanted to wall it in. For defensive purposes. He'd tried to wall in our street too, and it took all of us together to talk him out of it.

The Guild was looking good. We were still two hundred thousand in the hole, but we were slowly beginning to recoup that investment.

I parked in the lot. We got out and headed for the building. The inside of the Guild had gotten a face-lift as well. The mess hall was back and the food was actually good this time, which made sense because nothing offended shapeshifters more than subpar dining options. Barabas had insisted on bringing back the koi. Originally a stream had run through the hotel floor culminating in a large pond. Barabas didn't want the stream, but he did somehow find the money for the pond. He said it was therapeutic and got two of the Pack's counselors to back him up. Now a large pond sat next to the dining area, complete with a bridge across it. Five big koi, three gold and two white, slowly glided in the shallow water. The mercenaries kept feeding the fish and I had a feeling the koi would get morbidly obese before too long.

About twenty mercs ate, swapped war stories, and checked their gear on the main floor, waiting for a job or relaxing after one before going home. A dozen voices said hello as we walked in. A second after we stepped through the door, I realized Curran was still in all of his warrior form splendor.

"Woo!"

"Cover up!"

"Rough morning, Curran?"

Curran grinned, showing his big teeth.

"Hey, Daniels, you better put him in check. There are children present," Juke called.

"Where?" Collins asked.

"She means you, dickhead," Santiago said.

"Come over here and say that to my face."

"I would, but you too ugly."

Tension seeped out of me with every step. This I knew. This was familiar. This was my world.

Barabas waved at us from behind the glass. The previous administrator of the Guild considered himself to be white-collar and fully embraced a personal office, expensive suits, and secretaries. The first thing Barabas did was gut his fourth-floor office and sell off the pricey furniture. Then he took over the smallest conference room downstairs, separated from the main floor by glass. He sat there now, wearing jeans and a long-sleeve T-shirt, his desk filled with papers. His door was usually open. Mercs wandered in and out with questions. Usually Christopher hung out in the office as well, or somewhere on the Guild floor, reading a book at the table by the koi, or talking to the Clerk, depending on how he was feeling. Maggie was curled up in her little plush bed in Barabas's office, but I saw no signs of Christopher.

If I were a winged god of terror, where would I be?

I glanced up. High above, on the massive support beams right under the newly installed skylight, a man sat, his right leg bent, his left dangling down, a book in his hand. He had no wings, but his hair was a familiar white. For months Barabas took care of Christopher. Now Christopher guarded Barabas.

"How's our honored guest doing?" Curran called, loud enough for everyone to hear.

"Doing great," Keana, a thin, dark-skinned merc in her thirties, called out. "We got his money in an hour ago."

"How much did we net?" Curran asked.

"The Guild took in two million, nine hundred fifty-eight thousand, six hundred thirty-three dollars and sixty cents," Barabas called from his office.

"Yeah!" Curran pumped his fist.

The Guild erupted in cheers. I cheered, too. He was making them feel like all of them had won, forging them into a unified force, and they had no idea he was doing it.

"Why is the number so weird?" I murmured.

"We charged him his weight in gold," Curran said. "Would've gotten more, but Roland bled him out and starved him, and he needs a lot of food or his body starts to cannibalize itself."

"Where do you have him stashed?" I asked.

"Third floor, the old archive room," Curran said. "I talked to Barabas this morning. Saiman isn't eating or drinking. They had to put him on an IV."

Saiman burned through nutrients the way fire burned through dry hay.

I nodded at Julie. "Come with me."

As we climbed the staircase, I asked quietly, "Feel up to it?"

She looked at me. If she'd given me that look and I didn't know her, I'd consider backing off.

"If it helps kill Roland, yes."

"Good. When I talk to him, remind me to ask him for his help, but don't tell him what I want exactly."

PRE-GIANT, THE OLD archive room had no windows. Post-giant, it had acquired a large window shielded by thick bars in case another monster came rampaging. Saiman lay next to that window, on a bed, bathed in the sunshine streaming through the clear glass. He was pale and bone-thin, a skeleton wrapped in loose skin and hooked up to an IV bag. Normally he maintained a neutral shape, that of a man of undeterminable age, bald, with unremarkable features, neither handsome nor ugly. The creature that lay on the bed now was a foot and a half taller than any human had a right to be. Light blue-green hair framed his face. His eyes were the pale blue of thick ice dusted with new snow. Whatever my father had done to him was so traumatic that Saiman had collapsed into his natural shape.

He was gazing out the window, an odd expression on his face. Looking at him made me want to bring him food and spoon it into him until the normal, caustic Saiman resurfaced. Someone had done exactly that. Chicken soup and freshly baked bread waited on a tray by the bed. Both were untouched.

Calhoun, a short merc with a shock of wild blond hair, got up from his perch by the door. "Tell me you came to relieve me. I'm starving."

"Knock yourself out," I told him. "I'll sit with him."

Calhoun took off down the stairs. I pulled up a chair and sat by Saiman's bed. He ignored me. Julie took the other chair in the corner.

The sun shone on us, warming up the white sheets. Small specks of dust floated in the light.

"There was a window," Saiman said. "The cell was dark,

but there was a window. Too narrow for me to crawl out of and barred, but I could see a small piece of the sky."

"Hope is a bitch," I told him. "It keeps you alive when all you want is to die."

Saiman turned his head and looked at me, his eyes full of winter. "He was draining my blood. As fast as I could make it. When he took it, my body reacted and cannibalized reserves to make up for the shortage."

"What did he do with it?"

"I don't know."

"There was another creature in the castle with divine blood," I said. "An animal. A saber-toothed tiger."

"I heard it roar once," Saiman said.

"Why would he need divine blood?"

"I don't know." He sighed. It rolled through his entire body. "They broke my legs. Every day before the sun would rise, they came in and shattered my bones with a hammer."

Saiman had always been terrified of death and physical pain.

"Why?"

"With that much pain, I couldn't slow down my regeneration. My body healed itself and there was nothing I could do about it." He shuddered.

"It's over," I told him. "You're safe."

"Do you know why I accumulated wealth?"

"Because you thought it would shield you. But there are things in this world that are immune to money."

He looked away from me. "I knew nobody was coming."

His voice told me everything. He sat in that cell with his broken legs, looked at the sky, and wanted desperately to be rescued, but he knew nobody would care enough to rescue him.

"We were coming."

"Why did you save me?" he asked.

"I didn't."

A trace of the old Saiman's impatience touched his face. "Curran did it, but only because you asked him to. The money I paid the Guild is a formality. A pittance. I would've given

Curran everything I have, but I know him. I remember our history. All the gold in the world wouldn't convince him to lift a finger for my sake. He did it for you. Why did you ask him?"

"Do you want the real answer or the one you're comfortable with?"

"I'll take the truth."

"Because you are someone I know, Saiman. You're someone who helped me. Always for a price, but still you helped. You're a selfish prick, narcissistic, egocentric, obsessed with your own importance, but you're still someone I know. I couldn't leave you with my father."

He looked away from me again.

"If it helps, I can tell you that if I left you there, it would give my father the license to kidnap my citizens at will, and whatever he was doing with you likely made him stronger, which is bad for us, since the Oracle is predicting he will burn the city in a few weeks. Would that be easier?"

He didn't answer.

"Rest," I told him. "Eat and rest. You need to heal. And one more thing."

I got up, slid the window up, and pulled the thick metal rods securing the grate up, releasing it. I strained, lifted the grate, and slid it aside. Wind blew into the room, stirring the sheets and papers on the desk.

"You're not a prisoner. You can leave when you're ready." I nodded at Julie. "Come on."

"But you didn't ask him," she said.

*Thank you, Julie.*

"I know. He's in no shape to do it. Come."

"In no shape to do what?" Saiman called.

"Rest," I told him, and left the room.

Julie hurried after me. We walked down the staircase together.

"Why didn't you ask him?" she asked.

"Because he's sitting in that bed, drowning in his trauma and refusing to eat. Now he knows I want something and it will drive him crazy, until he finally eats, gets dressed, and comes to find me to see what was so important."

Right now I would trade places with Saiman in a heart-beat. He could run around and do all of this bullshit, while I lay in a nice soft bed.

The magic hit, rolling over us. The electric lights in the lobby died and the blue feylanterns slowly ignited, growing brighter.

"Kate!" the Clerk called from his counter. "A call for you."

Maybe it was the Keep to tell us if Dali was alive.

I ran down the last few steps and picked up the phone.

"Hello, Sharrim," a female voice said. "Please hold for your father."

"Tell him to go fuck himself."

I hung up and turned away.

Behind me magic splashed.

**"HELLO, DAUGHTER."**

HE DIDN'T.

I turned around. A wall of light bisected the Guild, show-ing my father, his hands behind his back. Yes, he did. Oh he did. Now was really the wrong time to screw with me.

My magic shot out of me. All of the anger I'd been trying to keep under the lid boiled out.

**"Which part of 'go fuck yourself' did you not under-stand?"**

His power was an inferno. **"I AM YOUR FATHER. I AM SHARRUM. YOU WILL SHOW ME RESPECT!"**

**"Respect? You sent an assassin into my land to mur-der a baby! What respect? You're a child killer."**

**"IT WAS YOUR FAULT. YOU PRECIPITATED THIS THROUGH YOUR STUBBORNNESS."**

God, I wanted to punch him in the face. **"You are de-spicable. I'm ashamed to be your daughter. I should walk the street apologizing to everyone I meet for the fact that you still exist."**

**"I MADE YOU. WITHOUT ME YOU WOULDN'T EXIST. I CAN SNUFF OUT YOUR LIFE WITH A**

**FLICK OF MY FINGERS AND MAKE A DOZEN JUST LIKE YOU."**

"Do it." I spread my arms. "Come on. I'm waiting."

Rage shivered in the corners of his mouth. I'd really pissed him off this time. *Good. Have a taste of your own medicine.*

**"DO NOT TEMPT ME."**

"Why is it you haven't killed me, Father? You murdered all of the others. My brothers and sisters. What's the holdup?"

**"I TOLERATE YOU FOR THE SAKE OF YOUR MOTHER'S MEMORY, BUT MY PATIENCE IS AT ITS END."**

Aha. "So is mine. You took my child's caretaker and you forced her to betray everything she stood for. Julie watched her die. I hate you."

**"YOU BROKE INTO MY HOUSE. YOU UPSET YOUR GRANDMOTHER. YOU DAMAGED MY PRISON, AND YOU STOLE MY CAPTIVES. RETURN WHAT IS MINE."**

Captives. He didn't know Curran had consumed the saber-tooth.

"I did no such thing. I didn't go to your house. Your captive—a citizen of my land, whom you kidnapped and kept prisoner—hired mercenaries to rescue him and they did. I'll send you the contract, so your lawyers can explain it to you. Your security is lousy, Father. I would look into that if I were you."

**"I AM SHARRUM OF SHINAR. MY LINE GOES BACK A HUNDRED GENERATIONS. I WILL NOT BE DISRESPECTED!"**

"Nor will I!" My magic raged. The Guild around me shook. "I'm a princess of Shinar, granddaughter of Semiramis, niece of the City Eater, daughter of the Builder of Towers. My line is longer than yours by one!"

Shock registered on his face for a moment before melting back into fury. *That's right. You made me, now deal with it.*

"You will respect my boundaries, Father. You squatted on the edge of my land and you keep trying to provoke me. I haven't broken my word. I've upheld our peace."

"BY TAKING WHAT IS MINE LIKE A THIEF? YOU SHAME ME, DAUGHTER."

The press of his magic was almost too much to bear, but I was too angry to back down.

"I wasn't there. I was in Mishmar, talking to my grandmother. Ask her, if you don't believe me."

His magic punched me. "RETURN THE DEMIGOD TO ME!"

I pulled my magic to me and punched back. The floor under my feet bounced. "No."

The magic was so tight around me, it responded every time I took a breath.

"YOU'RE A POOR EXCUSE FOR A DAUGHTER."

His magic clashed with mine. It felt like the air around us was breaking apart.

"Kate!" Curran snapped.

I glanced around me. The mercs cowered by the walls, but I didn't care. I couldn't give a crap if the entire roof caved in and crushed them all. I would not back down. Not this time.

I raised my chin. "You've killed your own family, Father. Even now, you're trying to reach through time with your hand and strangle its future. You are the reason no descendants of our blood survived. You reap what you sow. I'm exactly what you deserve."

He stared at me, his gaze boring through me. His face stretched and Roland laughed. "YOU ARE, INDEED, MY DAUGHTER."

The light contracted, sucked into its own center, and vanished.

I turned around. The Clerk stared at me, wild-eyed. His nose was bleeding. On my right, shell-shocked mercs blinked. The closest to me bled from the nose and ears. I glanced up. Saiman stood on the third-floor balcony, his face bloodless. Above him Christopher gripped the balance beam, staring at the spot where my father had been, his ruby wings opened wide, his face twisted by fury.

Juke wiped the blood from under her nose and looked at it.

I'd done it again. Damn it. I'd let the magic drag me away from who I was.

"What the hell was all that about?" Juke asked. "All I heard was a weird hissing language with some 'fucks' in it."

The tension hung in the air. I had to say something to break it. "This is nothing. You should see the fit he threw when I told him I wasn't coming to visit for Christmas."

Barabas laughed.

The mercs looked at him, then back at me.

"Family," Curran said, putting his arm around me. "Can't live with them, can't kill them. You ready to go home, baby?"

"Sure," I said.

Outside I stopped. "I did it again."

"I know," he said.

"I'm trying."

"I know."

I had to try harder. "He really wants Saiman for some reason."

"Did he mention the tiger?"

"He thinks we stole it. You still feeling okay?"

"Yes."

I glanced at him. "Why did you eat the tiger?"

He shrugged. "I don't know. It was a compulsion. I saw him and I had to make him not be."

"You worry me," I told him.

He pointed back at the Guild with his thumb. "Pot, kettle."

Some pair we made. There was nothing left to do but go home. I could use a quiet afternoon and a big early dinner before we figured out our next move.


"CAN I TALK to you?" Julie asked me as we pulled into the driveway in front of our home.

"Yes." I knew that tone of voice. Something bad always followed that tone of voice. Something like "I crashed the car" or "I accidentally set the school on fire." I couldn't take more bad news today.

Curran and Derek went inside. I leaned on the trunk of the car. "What is it?"

She stepped close to me and whispered. "Adora is staying in George and Eduardo's spare bedroom."

"What?"

Julie went to the Jeep she or Derek usually took to Cutting Edge, pulled her backpack out, and ran back to me, digging in it.

"He sent some people after her a few hours after you left. I had to move her. The hospital wouldn't let her stay. Here, they took pictures for insurance purposes and I got the extras."

She thrust a stack of Polaroids at me. The first one showed a wall covered with blood. A big spurt of bright red blood, then the characteristic wave pattern as the victim stumbled along the wall. Arterial spray. Another Polaroid, more blood. I flipped through them. Blood on the floor, blood on the walls, headless body, another body crumpled up, a third corpse sagging in the corner, more blood, bloody sheets, and finally Adora, kneeling in the blood and sitting back on her heels, her sword in front of her, a big angelic smile on her face.

Why me?

"She said Roland's people tried to bring her back and she told them she didn't want to go."

Well, at least she made a choice instead of blindly obeying. "So you took her to George's house?"

"I didn't know where else to put her. If I put her into one of the other houses, Curran would smell her. George has people working on her roof, so there are new smells all the time."

"My old apartment?"

She opened her mouth. "Oh. I didn't think of that."

"Did you at least tell George who she was?"

"Yes. George was okay with it. She told Adora that if there was any trouble, she would sit on her."

Coming from an enormous Kodiak, that was no small threat.

"She also wrote down all the sahanu information you wanted." Julie dug in her bag. "It has some blood spatter on it but you can still read some of it . . . Kate?"

I hugged her. "We'll deal with it tomorrow. Tonight we all need to rest. And we need to take time to remember Jezebel, because there might not be much time tomorrow."

"Okay," she said.

We went inside.

My aunt tore through me like a hurricane. "You left me behind."

"Yes, I did."

"You will not do that again."

"Yes, I will, if I find it necessary. Bringing you to the Pack would've resulted in us being torn to pieces."

Erra squinted at me. "What happened?"

"For two years a shapeshifter woman took care of Julie and acted as my bodyguard. I trusted her with my life and the life of my adopted child. Tonight he made her try to murder my best friend's baby. She failed but she injured the Beast Lord's mate."

Erra peered at Julie. "You told me this one was dead."

"I didn't want you to kill her," I said.

Erra peered at Julie. "You gave her our blood?"

"It's a long story."

"You like horses, child, don't you?"

Julie looked at me.

"Go ahead and answer," I told her.

"Yes."

"And wolves. You have an affinity for wolves and wolf-like dogs. They make sense to you."

"Yes."

"What color is my niece's magic?"

"It's difficult to describe."

Erra glanced at me. "You have a child of the Koorgahn. And a throwback to a pure-blood, too. Look at that hair."

Koorgahn? She probably meant kurgan. The only kurgans I knew about were the burial mounds peppering the old Russian steppes, Asia, and southern Siberia. The kurgans served as burial mounds for the ancient race of Scythians, and the earliest ones dated sometime around the ninth century BC . . . They were blond. The ancient Greeks described them as red-haired or fair-haired with blue or gray eyes, and the mummies the archaeologists pulled out of the ancient grave sites matched that phenotype.

"Who are you, child?" Erra asked.

"I'm her Herald," Julie said.

"At least you have a Herald. You've done something right. I need to speak to my niece alone. We'll talk more later."

Julie looked at me. I nodded and she went deeper into the house.

"My father has been talking to her," I said.

"Of course he has. He always wanted one, but they were a proud people. He couldn't buy a child of royal blood and he couldn't broker the marriage of one of his offspring to theirs. First, they knew his reputation, and second, they were afraid to lose the Sight. It was believed that a mixing of two powerful bloodlines could produce a child unable to see magic, and they wouldn't expose one of their own to that risk. When it was clear that magic would vanish from the world, her people killed themselves by the hundreds because they were going magic-blind."

My aunt, the downer.

"Binding a child of the Koorgahn. A dangerous game you're playing, squirrel."

"I was trying to save her. She was dying of loupism."

"Yes, they are susceptible. Wolves, horses, and birds of prey, those are her things. That's how they came to battle, riding their horses, guarded by their birds of prey and their wolves. Your great-grandfather fought a bloody war for thirty years just to keep the people of Koorgahn out of our valley as they were sweeping west. How ironic that you would find one in this age and in this place, yet have no idea how to use her."

"I don't want to use her. She is my kid."

Erra sighed. "We'll talk about this and what happened today later. Now I will go and see if your 'kid' knows the extent of her powers."

"Good luck with that. I can't even get her to clean her room."

I turned and went upstairs. I locked the bedroom door and walked into the bathroom. Curran was already in the shower.

I stripped my clothes off and went in there with him.

He stared at my body. I looked like a gang of street thugs with steel-toed boots had worked me over. I stepped under the water and hugged him.

He hugged me back.


SOMETHING TOUCHED MY EAR. I shrugged off sleep long enough to open my eyes and saw Curran holding the phone. For me. Ugh.

"Yes?" I said into the phone.

"What do you need?" Saiman asked.

Well, he didn't last long. "Let me make you a list . . ."

"Do spare me the smartass comments. What do you need me to do?"

"A way to kill or contain my father. Failing that, I need a record of what he wrote on my skin."

"Your office in two hours."

He hung up. I opened my eyes and looked at Curran. "What time is it?"

"Six o'clock."

"You let me sleep for four hours straight?" I'd stay up all night.

"Sixteen," he said. "It's six in the morning. You needed it."

After the shower I'd crashed. The thing with my aunt had taken a lot out of me, and the thing with Andrea's baby didn't help either. Sooner or later, you had to pay the piper. I dimly recalled waking up at some point, because I had dreamed Dali died and Jim wouldn't let me go to her funeral, but exhaustion had soon dragged me back under.

"Did you have dinner last night?"

"Yes. The kids and I went to George and Eduardo's," he said. "Mahon's bear guards arrived with honey muffins and roasted deer and we all ate ourselves into a coma."

"That's nice." I hugged my pillow. "Will you wake me up in an hour?"

He picked me up and stood me upright on my feet. I punched him in the neck. Not very hard and not very fast. I missed.

"The medmage is here."

"I don't need a medmage." I yawned.

He picked me up, carried me into the bathroom, and set me in front of the mirror. I had acquired a lovely reddish-purple color. Both of my shoulders had turned raspberry red. The edges of my wounds were puffy. Irene must've had something nasty on her blades, or maybe Mishmar wasn't the most sterile environment to get cut in. My left hip, my knees—and probably my back, judging by the lake of pain that pulled in my trapezius muscles—were a deep blue, too.

"My impersonation of a peacock is proceeding as planned."

"Not funny." Curran's expression could've stopped a raging bear in his tracks.

I had tried to seduce him after the shower but he wasn't having any of it. He packed me into the bed, and I was making some sort of smartass quip about his new powers post-saber-tooth-devouring, and then there was nothing. Here's hoping I didn't fall asleep in mid-sentence.

Yep, I probably did.

In fact, I could totally sleep more. I could lie down on this nice cold floor and nap. I yawned again.

"Curran, where are you going?"

"To make breakfast."

Sleep evaporated. My eyes snapped open. If I didn't get

254 * ILONA ANDREWS

downstairs in the next ten minutes, he'd smoke out the kitchen again with bacon.

I made it down in time to save the bacon from a terrible fate. Curran had brought in Nellie Kerning, one of the med-mages the Guild frequently hired. She had set up camp at our dining room table. She was short, plump, and in her early fifties. She also took no prisoners, which was why Curran must've called her in the first place.

"Strip."

I pulled off most of my clothes, leaving on my sports bra and underwear. A woman had to have limits. Nellie examined me.

I caught Curran giving me an interested look. Was he actually . . . Yep, he was checking me out. *Yeah, where were you last night, buddy?* I would've stayed awake . . . Well, no. Probably not.

"Did you play tag with a rock troll?" Nellie asked.

"No." My aunt played tennis with me against the walls. But explaining that would cramp my style.

Where was my aunt?

Nellie sighed. "Why does everyone have to be a hard case? Is it in your job description?"

"Yes. Also I know a were–honey badger you would really like."

"Mm-hm. Let's see if we can salvage this mess."

She was fifteen minutes into the chant when Andrea and Raphael walked through the door, followed by Robert.

"Would it kill you to knock?" I asked.

"Would it kill you to lock your door?" Andrea marched over to me and handed Baby B over. "Here, hold my kid."

Oh boy. I took Baby B. She looked at me and yawned.

Raphael very carefully avoided looking at undressed me and went into the kitchen.

"First, Dali survived, so you can stop freaking out," Andrea said. "And don't get any ideas about things being awk-ward between us because of what happened. Things are not awkward."

"Things are awkward," Robert said. "Your father ordered

a hit on the heir of Clan Bouda, and his assassin injured the Consort."

"Done," Nellie said. "I'll bill you."

I waited until she left, gave the baby back to Andrea, and pulled on my T-shirt and my shorts.

"Is she recovering okay?" I asked.

"I'm forbidden to answer any questions," Robert said.

"What do you mean, forbidden?" Curran asked. The tone of his voice wasn't friendly.

Robert stood a little straighter.

"He means Jim flipped the fuck out." Raphael stole a piece of bacon off the plate. "You and everyone who separated with you are on the Do Not Talk To list. He can't forbid you to visit the Keep because it's against the law, but your access will be severely restricted. And he gagged anyone employed in an official capacity, like Robert here. But unlike Robert, I don't hold an administrative position outside my clan, so I don't care what the fuck he thinks."

Andrea grinned at him. Somebody had earned a whole bunch of awesome husband points.

"He's thinking with his gut instead of his brain," Raphael said. "Nobody realized Jezebel was a double agent, so in his mind, if she was one, anybody could be one. His gut reaction is to shut down the flow of information, fortify, and . . ."

"Retaliate," Curran said, his face grim.

"He can't retaliate," I said.

"I can't answer questions," Robert said. "But I can listen to advice. He didn't forbid me to listen."

"Is there proof that Jezebel acted on Roland's orders?" Curran asked.

Robert didn't answer.

"Probably not," Andrea said. "If there is, that information hasn't been shared with us."

"In the absence of proof," Curran said, "to outsiders this looks like one member of the Pack attacked another. It's a Pack matter."

"If Jim retaliated in force against my father, it would

mean a declaration of war," I said. "He and the Pack are within the land I protect. Roland wants war, but he doesn't want to break the treaty. He will seize any opportunity. Jim's actions will be viewed as an unprovoked attack."

"It doesn't matter," Curran said, watching Robert. "He's made up his mind."

"What would you do if your mate was stabbed in the heart with a silver blade?" Robert asked.

"I would wait until I was absolutely sure that I could destroy my enemy," Curran said. "I wouldn't throw my people away. He can't kill Roland, Robert. He doesn't have the resources. All he can do is kill some of Roland's people and a lot of his own. Roland's forces are disposable. Our people, the Pack, are not."

"The future is a self-fulfilling prophecy."

They looked at me.

"We worked so hard not to provoke him and it doesn't matter in the end," I said. "The battle will happen. We can't stop it."

Curran looked at Robert. "Tell him that after he goes through with it, Roland will retaliate in force. Tell Jim he knows where we live. We'll be here."

"Tell him that he is endangering every person in the city limits," I said.

"Hypothetically speaking," Robert said, "if the attack happens, and Roland retaliates, what will you do about it?"

"She is a princess of Shinar." My aunt burst into existence in the middle of the kitchen. "It is by the grace of her mercy you are still breathing."

Robert stumbled back. Raphael's hands went to his knives. Andrea bared her teeth, cradling Baby B. You could hear a pin drop.

"I have family in town for the wedding," I said into the silence. "My aunt, Eahrratim, the Rose of Tigris."

Curran covered his face with his hand.

"Your pathetic castle is in her domain," Erra said. "She can level it with a thought. If your Beast Lord picks a fight with my brother, how will you survive without her to shield you?"

"We'll fight," Robert said, his body tense, ready to leap and tear.

"And when fire rains from the sky and the earth opens to swallow you, who will you fight then? How much damage will your claws do to a flood? Tell that to your king, half-breed."

My aunt vanished.

Andrea pivoted to me, her mouth open, and shook her finger at the spot where Erra had stood.

"Long story," I told her.

"Tell Jim that after he has his fun, we'll be here," Curran said to Robert. "Tell him that help is here. All he needs to do is ask."

# 13

THERE WERE CARS in the parking lot of Cutting Edge.

"We're agreed?" I asked.

"Fine," my aunt said into my ear.

"Please do not manifest. Please."

"I'm not hard of hearing."

"It scares people," Curran said. "And we want to keep the element of surprise. If Roland finds out that you're here, helping Kate, we'll lose it."

"He won't find out unless your people talk," Erra said. "He can't feel me unless I want him to. That's one of the privileges of being dead—and if the two of you don't shut up, I will let you experience it for yourselves."

I bumped my forehead against the dashboard.

"I'll park," Curran said.

I checked that her dagger was securely in the sheath, exited the car, and walked through the door into the office. All of our desks had been moved aside and put by the wall. Ascanio sat on my desk. He'd called me from Cutting Edge before I left the house asking me if he should let Saiman in. I told him to do it.

A large young woman with a mane of dark curly hair pulled back from her face sat on a chair. She turned when I walked in. Her lips were blue and the traditional *ta moko* covered her chin. Maori. It didn't look smooth either. Someone had used a uni chisel instead of modern tattoo needles.

In the center of the now-empty office, a small raised platform stood. Several full-length mirrors waited stacked against the far wall. Saiman turned as I walked in. I had expected him to be back in his neutral shape. He wasn't. He was six feet tall, gaunt, and frail, leaning on a cane, and the black bodysuit he wore showed off every rib. His face was still that of a frost giant. He'd humanized it enough for people not to stare at him on the streets and that was it. His sunken cheeks made the cheekbones in his face even more prominent. Eyes made of winter ice looked at me from under shaggy eyebrows. Two small night tables and a large wooden chest stood on the floor by him.

"Have you eaten?" I asked.

"Yes. I need you to strip and stand on the platform."

Everybody wanted to take my clothes off today. I pulled off my boots and began to strip.

Curran decided this was a good time to walk in. He looked at me, looked at Saiman, and parked himself by the wall with his arms crossed.

I stripped to my underwear and a sports bra and climbed onto the platform.

"Zoe, if you please."

The Maori woman picked up a large drawing pad and walked over.

"This is Zoe. She is able to see an image for an instant and perfectly reproduce it. Given the impact seeing the writing had on me, we have to take certain precautions."

Saiman nodded and Zoe went to stand behind me.

Saiman waved at Ascanio. The bouda jumped off the table and came over.

"Take a mirror and set it so Zoe can see her reflection."

Ascanio picked up one of the mirrors and set it in front of me.

"A little more to the left," Zoe said.

He moved the mirror and kicked the stand with his foot, opening it. I saw my reflection in the mirror. The bruises were fading.

"And the mirror is supposed to help?"

"Yes. The writing loses potency with reflection."

"How do you know this?"

"Because when I looked directly at you in the Mercenary Guild as you were absorbing a power word, my head wanted to explode. When I looked away and accidentally caught your reflection in the glass, it hurt significantly less."

Saiman took one of the night tables, walked to the right front corner of the platform, and walked exactly six steps diagonally. "Do you remember David Miller?"

"Yes." David Miller was a magical idiot savant. Nobody ever managed to teach him how to use his enormous reserve of magic, but after he died it was discovered that the objects he had handled gained strange powers. His descendants had sold them off to different buyers, deliberately trying to scatter them, but Saiman collected all of them over the years. He'd used Miller's bowling ball to produce a vision of my aunt when we were trying to identify her as she rampaged through Atlanta.

Saiman took one step to the right and placed the night table. He came back, picked up the second night table, walked back to the first night table exactly the same way, turned, and walked to the left for eight steps.

"Wouldn't it be easier to measure?" Curran asked.

"Measuring doesn't work," Saiman said.

"Why?" Curran asked.

"Nobody knows. Counting the steps is a part of the ritual."

Saiman opened the wooden trunk and took out a pink vase with three fake pink roses in it. He walked directly to the first night table and set the vase on it. A lava lamp with pink and blue wax was the next to come out of the trunk. He set it on the second table. The third item was a bright pink fake fur rug. Saiman carefully placed it in front of the platform and turned to me.

"You're standing on a stage Dave Miller built for his daughter when she was a child." Saiman reached into the trunk and pulled out a pink tulle tutu.

"No."

"Yes."

"It won't fit."

"Elastic waistband," Saiman said. "It will fit."

Curran's grin was pure evil.

"Don't you dare," I told him.

"It's too bad the magic is up," he said. "I'd take pictures."

"Shut up."

"Have no fear, Alpha," Ascanio said. "We'll tell no one."

*Kill me, somebody.*

Saiman held out the tulle skirt to me.

"Maybe it will work without it."

"Don't be ridiculous."

"If I put this on, it will be ridiculous."

Saiman waved the pink tutu in front of me. Fine. I snatched it out of his hands and pulled it on over my hips.

Ascanio collapsed into a moaning heap of laughter.

"Now what?"

"Move around onstage. It would help if you danced."

Curran was dying. That was the only rational explanation for the noises coming from his direction.

"You're doing this on purpose," I told Saiman.

"Yes. The purpose being to read the writing on your skin without killing the people who are looking at it. Which reminds me. Ascanio, once she is done dancing, do not look directly at her. It will be very bad for your health and I have no desire to deal with upset Pack parents."

"Yes," I said. "You should both avert your eyes."

"I believe your fiancé will be fine," Saiman said, walking over to the table with the vase. "Dance, Kate."

I stomped around onstage. Saiman was looking at the lava lamp.

"Not enough."

"How do you know?"

"The lamp would glow. We need more. You have to

commit and put in the effort, like the child that was originally dancing on the stage. Try to be graceful this time.
You're a swordsman. Surely you can scrounge up some elegance."

Screw it. "Throw me my socks."

Curran balled my socks together and tossed them at me.
I pulled them on, raised my hands, and slipped into the clas-
sical fourth position. I took a deep breath, fixed my gaze on
the narrow window directly in front of me, and launched into
a double pirouette to pick up momentum. One, two, fouette
turn, another, another, another, pirouette, pirouette, what the
hell, let's go for eight, fouette, fouette, seven, eight, pirouette,
fourth position, arms open.

Botched that last pirouette a bit. It had been a while.

Saiman and Curran stared at me.

"Do you need a shovel to help you pick up your jaws off
the floor?"

Saiman woke up, grabbed the roses from the vase, and
threw them at me. A spotlight drenched me, out of nowhere.
Behind me Zoe screamed. The spotlight vanished.

I turned around. The Maori woman collapsed in a heap,
her hands over her eyes. Saiman hurried over to Zoe, leaning on his cane.

"Ballet?" Curran asked.

"There are so many things about me you don't know."

Voron was Russian. He tortured me with ballet for three
years, until I turned ten years old.

"Is it safe to look?" Ascanio asked.

"Yes."

"We need more mirrors," Saiman called out. "The impact
of the words is too strong. The mirror-to-mirror reflection
should dull it."

It took seven mirrors. After Zoe successfully managed
to reproduce the first drawing, Saiman brought it to me. It
was the language of power, alright, but I couldn't read it. I
got a few isolated words, but most of it didn't look like the
words I already knew.

We kept going and by the end of the hour my head hurt

from spinning and my legs hurt from jumping. Ballet wasn't for the untrained and it had been a long time since I'd had to do it. I was amazed I still remembered how. Voron had said it would help with strength and balance. I mostly hated it.

"I have to take a break," I told Saiman.

"We're only halfway done."

As if on cue, someone knocked.

"See? Serendipity."

"You mean coincidence."

Ascanio opened the door and Roman walked in. He saw me onstage and blinked. "Ehh . . ."

"Don't," I warned him.

He raised his hands. "I do not judge."

Curran tossed me my clothes. I slipped the shirt over my head, pulled on my jeans, and took off the stupid tutu.

A black woman with a head full of bright poppy-red curls followed Roman, pulling behind her a small metal cart full of plates. Roman picked up one of the plates and a spoon, carved a small piece of the cake on it, and held the spoon out to me.

"What is this?"

"Cake."

"Why do I need cake right this second?"

"This is Mary Louise Garcia," Roman said. "She is the head baker for Clan Heavy's Honey Buns bakery."

Mary smiled at me and waved her fingers.

"Mary very kindly agreed to bring over samples so you could select a wedding cake."

"I did." Mary nodded.

"Mary turns into a grizzly. A very large grizzly."

"I know who Mary is," I told him. "I met her before, at Andrea's wedding."

"If you don't pick a wedding cake, Mary will sit on you and stuff all this cake into your mouth until you make a selection."

"Mary and what army?"

Mary smiled at me. "I won't need an army."

"Can he select the cake?" I pointed at Curran. "This wedding involves two of us."

"He already did," Mary said. "These are the choices he narrowed down."

I turned to Curran. "You narrowed it down to sixteen choices?"

"They were all very delicious," he said.

"Were there any choices you didn't like?"

"Yes," he said. "I scrapped coconut and lime."

"After you are done with the cake, we'll discuss flower selection and colors," Roman said.

I would strangle him. "Roman, I have to dance until Zoe can record the rest of the mystical writing on my skin, and then I have to train to work my magic. So no. Not doing it."

Roman heaved a sigh and looked at Mary. "Do you see what I have to put up with?"

"Roman, if I don't do this, Atlanta will be destroyed."

"Atlanta is always getting destroyed," Mary said. "Eat some cake. It will make you feel better."

"Before I forget," Roman said. "Sienna said to tell you to beware . . ." He reached into his pocket and pulled out a piece of paper. "*Crocuta crocuta spelaea.* Apparently it's going to try to murder you. Don't you want to eat some delicious cake before you die a horrible death?"

I sat on the stage and covered my face with my hands.

Curran's hand rested on my shoulder. "Are you okay, baby?"

"No. Give me a minute."

"That's understandable," Roman said. "Take your time."

"What did you say it was that was going to murder me?"

"*Crocuta crocuta spelaea.*"

"Crocuta" usually referred to a hyena, but I couldn't remember any hyena with "spelaea" attached to it.

"Cave hyena," Ascanio said. "Also known as Ice Age spotted hyena."

All of us looked at him.

He rolled his eyes. "I'm a member of Clan Bouda. I know our family tree."

"How big?" Curran asked.

"Pretty big," Ascanio said. "It mostly preyed on wild

horses. They estimate about two hundred twenty-five pounds or so on average."

Of course. Why wouldn't my future have a vicious pre-historic hyena in it?

I exhaled and looked at Roman. "What do I have to do to get you to leave me alone?"

"You have to make all the wedding decisions," Roman said. "You have to select the cake, the colors for the cere-mony, the flowers for your bouquet, and you have to stand for a second dress fitting tomorrow at eight o'clock. You also have to approve the guest list and the seating chart."

I looked at Curran.

"I can take the chart," he offered.

"Thank you." I looked at Roman. "I do all this and you stop bugging me?"

"Yes."

"It's a deal."

"Excellent." He rubbed his hands, looking every inch an evil pagan priest. "I love it when everything comes together."

THE RECORDING OF the writing on my body was done. The cake would have alternating tiers; the first would be choc-olate cake with a white chocolate mousse filling and white chocolate buttercream, and the second would be white choc-olate with raspberry mousse and white chocolate frosting. They told me I could have whatever I wanted, and if it was the last cake I would ever eat, I wanted it to be as chocolate as it could get.

The colors were green, pink, and lavender, because when I closed my eyes and thought of a happy place, I saw the Water Gardens with lotuses blooming in the water. I told Roman that I wanted wildflowers for my bouquet. He duti-fully wrote it down.

"Thank you," I told Saiman, as he packed away Dave Miller's things.

"We're even," he said.

"We are."

He nodded and left.

Roman left too, taking Mary Louise with him. I dismissed Ascanio for the day after we put the desks back where they belonged and then waited for him to be out of earshot.

"He's gone," Curran told me.

I laid the drawings out on the floor.

My aunt appeared before me and looked at the pages.

She frowned. "This is the high dialect. The language of kings. Why would he . . . Switch these two around for me."

I moved the two sheets she pointed at.

My aunt peered at the drawings. We waited.

"Moron." Erra rolled her head back and laughed. "Oh, that sentimental fool! This is what happens when a man is thinking with his dick."

Curran and I looked at each other.

"It's a poem. A beautiful, exquisite love poem to your mother and you, written in the old tongue, in the high dialect, and fit for a king. The scholars of Shinar would weep from sheer joy and the poets would murder themselves out of jealousy. He tells your mother she is his life, his sun, his stars, the life-bringing light of his universe. I'd translate for you but your language is too clunky. He goes on about all the sacrifices he would make for her and how much he adores his beloved and how you are the ultimate expression of their love."

"He still killed her," I said.

"Yes, he did. Lovesick or not, he's still your father." She shook her head. "He inscribed all this on you while you were in the womb. The skill required to accomplish this without injuring the child and with such perfection . . . Your father truly was the jewel of our age. He is a horror, but still a jewel. Here is the important part."

My aunt pointed down at the piece of paper.

"*And all the princes of the land would kiss the earth beneath her feet*—that would be you—*and should she fall, I will fall with her, for we are as one, and the despair would dry the spring of life within me*. Do you understand? You are bound together. He can't kill you. If he does, he will die with you."

My brain screeched to a halt. There was no way.

Curran laughed.

The two of us looked at him.

"It's not funny," I told him.

"It's hilarious."

"Will you cut it out?" I sat down in my chair, trying to process things. My brain was having real difficulties digesting this.

Curran's grin was vicious. "I've been wondering why the hell he invested all that time into Hugh and then threw him away. Hugh almost killed you. Your dad was sitting in his Swan Palace feeling himself inch toward death's door as you died of exposure, and he got so scared, he got rid of Hugh so it wouldn't happen again. It was a knee-jerk reaction."

"This can't be right. I almost died more times than I can remember."

"No, you've been hurt more times than you can remember," Curran said. "Mishmar was the closest you've come to a physical death. Nasrin didn't think you would make it. She told me to make my peace."

"I almost bled to death in a cage when the rakshasas grabbed me."

"No. You passed out, but Doolittle said there was a solid chance of recovery from the start. Mishmar was the worst."

"Is that what you do?" Erra asked. "You keep track of the times she almost dies?"

"Yes."

"Wouldn't it be easier to find yourself some shapeshifter heifer and have a litter of kittens, rather than deal with all this?"

I thought we were over this.

"Well, if I'm banging a heifer, technically the kids would have an equal chance of being calves and kittens," Curran said. "So it might be a litter or a small herd."

"If Curran and I have a litter of kittens, will you babysit?"

Erra stared at me like I had slapped her.

"They will be very cute kittens," Curran said.

I smiled at the City Eater. "Meow, meow."

"You won't have any kittens if my brother is allowed to roam free," Erra snarled. "You came to me, remember that."

"If I kill myself, will he die?"

"You're not killing yourself," Curran said.

"You can't tell me what to do."

He leaned toward me, his eyes full of gold. His voice was a snarl. "This is me telling you: you are not killing yourself."

"Shut up, both of you." Erra frowned. "If this were done in the old age, yes, he would die. In this age, I don't know. The magic is weaker and his will to live is very strong. If you were killed while he's outside his land, he would have a harder time dealing with it."

"So it's not a guarantee?" I asked

"No."

"But it would hurt him?"

"Yes."

"I know he tried to kill me in the womb but failed. He says he changed his mind. He probably changed his mind because he started to feel the side effects of trying to snuff me out."

"If he dies, will she die?" Curran looked at Erra.

"Yes. Probably. Her magic has the potential to be as strong as his, but she's untrained. It depends on where he is and where she is and if the magic is up. He's stronger on the land he claimed, and she's stronger in her territory. Her chances of survival are higher here."

"So we can't kill him?" Curran asked.

"Not if you want her to live."

Curran swore.

I looked at Erra. "How then? How do I stop him?"

"One thing at a time," Erra said. "First, we fight the battle, then we win the war."

THE GUILD CALLED, and Curran popped over there "for a few minutes." Erra retreated back into her blade. She wouldn't admit it, but manifesting tired her out. She'd make a short appearance and vanish.

I sat alone in Cutting Edge. Nobody called with emergencies or dire predictions. I left the front door open and a nice breeze blew through it, ruffling the papers on Julie's desk. Derek's desk was always spartan, Ascanio's was a collection of carefully color-coded folders, but Julie's workspace was a mess of stickies, loose notebook pages, and pieces of paper with odd scribblings on them, sometimes in English, sometimes in Greek, or Mandarin, or Latin. A weirdly shaped white rock pinned down a stack of notecards; a smooth polished pebble the color of pure sapphire—it might have been the real thing for all I knew—lay next to a chunk of green glass, hopefully not from the Glass Menagerie; a little blue flower bloomed in a small clay pot next to a dagger . . .

I needed to go home and practice to control my land. Erra had some exercises I needed to do. But I wanted to sit here for another minute.

I had never wanted any of the war, power, land . . . I just wanted this, a small business where I chose which jobs I took and helped people. This office was my Water Gardens. I made a piss-poor princess of Shinar, but I was an excellent Kate of Atlanta.

Every time I had to use my power, I ran the risk of falling into a hole I couldn't climb out of. Sometimes I teetered on the edge. Sometimes I fell in, caught myself on the cliff, and pulled myself back up at the last possible moment. It was getting harder and harder to stay up there. I didn't know what exactly lay at the end of that fall, but I had my suspicions. Power, for one, but power wasn't the real draw. I had power now and I would learn how to use it with my aunt's instruction. No, what pulled me was certainty.

Once I fell, there would be no doubt. I would do what I needed to do without checking every tiny step against some imaginary set of rules. It wouldn't matter who disapproved of me. I wouldn't have to convince and cajole people. I wouldn't have to bargain for them to please, please make some small, tiny effort to ensure their own survival. I could simply do. I hated waiting. I hated all the political bullshit.

Don't upset the Pack, don't upset the witches, don't upset the Order or the mages or the humans. It was like being thrown into a fighting pit with my hands tied together. I could still fight, but it was so much harder.

If I fell, Curran would leave me. Julie, too. I'd made her promise she would. Derek . . .

Voron used to tell me over and over that friendships and relationships weakened you. They made you vulnerable. They gave other people the ability to control you. He was right. I had ended up in this mess because I ran around trying to keep everyone safe, and now, as I hovered over the abyss, their love tethered me to the edge but their very existence pushed me in. I needed more power to keep them safe. I needed autonomy to make decisions.

In the end it wasn't up to them what I became. It was up to me. Even if everyone I cared about got up and left to never come back, I stood for something. Some things were right and some things were wrong, not because Curran or Julie or Derek approved or disapproved, but because I did. I had a set of rules. I followed them. They made me *me*. I had to remember that.

And I had to own up to Curran about Adora. *Hey, honey, here is a girl I saved against her will. Good news, I'm not her slave master. Bad news, she thinks my blood is divine and if she doesn't serve me with her every breath, she won't get into heaven. I have to shatter her world if she is ever to have a life. And by the way, I did all this, because I wanted to stick it to my father. Because sometimes, when the magic grips me just right, people become toys to me. Aren't you proud of me?* That would be a hellish conversation. With everything else I'd pulled recently . . . I didn't know where that conversation would end.

The wind blew a piece of notebook paper off Julie's desk. I walked over, picked it up, gathered a loose stack of papers, and tapped it on the desk to get it all even.

"It's the lot of the parents to fix the messes their children make," my father said.

I turned around. He stood by the door, wrapped in a plain

brown cloak that reminded me of a monk's habit. The hood was drawn over his head. He held a walking stick in his hand.

"You look like a traveling wizard from some old book," I told him.

"Do I?"

"Mm-hm. Or an incognito god."

"Odin the Wanderer," he said. "But I'd need a wide-brimmed hat and a raven."

"And only one eye."

"I've tried that look before," he said. "It isn't flattering."

We'd been talking for a whole minute and he wasn't screaming at me about resurrecting his sister. Maybe he really couldn't feel Erra.

"Why are you here, Father?"

"I thought we'd talk."

I sighed, went to the back, and got two bottles of beer from the fridge. He followed me to where a rope hung from the ceiling, attached to the attic's pull-down ladder. I handed him the beer. "Here, hold my beer."

"Famous last words," he said.

I pulled the rope. The attic ladder dropped down. I took one of the beers from him and climbed up the steps. He followed me. We crossed the finished attic, where we kept our supplies, to a heavy steel door. I unlocked the two bars securing it and stepped out onto the side balcony. It was only three feet wide and five feet long, big enough to comfortably put two chairs. From this point we could see the city, the hustle and bustle of the street below, the traffic on Ponce de Leon, and beyond it, the burned-out husks of skyscrapers, falling apart a little more with each magic wave.

I took one chair; he took the other.

"Nice," he said, and drank the beer.

"I like it. I like to watch the city." I'd had the balcony and the attic ladder installed two months ago. When Jim found out, he had called me. He worried it was a security risk. Jim wouldn't worry about anything related to me anymore. When a ten-year-old friendship shattered, the edges cut you.

My father drank his beer.

"What was Shinar like?"

He put his beer on the wooden railing and held out his hand. I touched it. A golden light rolled over the city below. I had expected crude, simple buildings the color of sand and clay. Instead beautiful white towers rose before me, drenched in greenery. Textured walkways led up terraces supporting a riot of flowers and trees. Sparkling ponds and creeks interrupted open spaces. In the distance a massive building, a pyramid or temple, rose, the first tier white, the second blue, the third green, topped with a shining gold sun symbol. People of every color and age strode through the streets. Women in colorful flowing dresses, in plain tunics, in military garb, carrying weapons and leading children by the hand. Older kids running, waving canvas bags at each other. Men in leather and metal armor, in robes like the one my father wore, in finery and a couple nude in bright swirls of red and blue body paint, some clean-shaven, some with a few days of scruff.

"No beards?" I said. Sumerian civilization was the oldest on record, and men on the few artifacts that survived always had full, curly beards.

"It came into fashion much later," he said.

"It's not what I expected."

"It was called the jewel of Eden for a reason. I remember the night it fell. That tower with the red roof was the first. I ran out in the street and tried to hold it up and couldn't. The magic simply wasn't there. One by one, the buildings collapsed in front of me. Thousands died."

The first Shift, when the technology wave had flooded the planet.

"Do you blame yourself?" I asked.

"No. None of us had any idea that such a thing was possible. There were no theories, no warnings, no prophecies. Nothing except for the random reports of magical devices malfunctioning or underperforming. Had we known, I'm not sure we would've done anything different. We were driven by the same things that drive people today: make our land better, our lives safer, our society more prosperous."

The vision died and my Atlanta returned.

"I can rebuild it," he said.

"I know. But should you?"

He looked at me. I took my hand away and pointed at the mouth of the street. "Several years ago, a man walked out over there and demanded everyone repent in the name of his god. People ignored him, so he unleashed a meteor shower. The whole street was in ruins. Looking at it now, you would never know. People are adjusting."

"The car repair shop, those squat, ugly shops? That one repairs pots and sharpens knives. What does that other one do?"

"They make shoes."

"So a tinker and a shoemaker."

"People need pots and shoes, Father."

"It's hideous," he said. "There is no beauty to it. It's rudimentary and ugly. There is elegance in simplicity, but we can both agree a man with a thousand eyes couldn't find elegance here at high noon."

My father, master of witty prehistoric sayings. "Yes."

"I can teach them beauty."

"They have to learn it themselves." I pulled out my spare knife. "Tactical Bowie. Hand forged. The blade is 5160 carbon steel marquenched—cooled in a molten salt bath—to strengthen the blade before being tempered. Ten-and-three-quarter-inch blade, black oxide finish. Long, slim, very fast."

I pinched the spine of the blade with my fingers at the hilt. "Distal taper. The blade thins from hilt to tip. About six and a half millimeters here." I moved my fingers to the tip. "About three and a half at the tip. Makes the blade lively and responsive. Pick up a sword or a knife without a taper and it will feel clunky in comparison."

I touched the spine at the point where the blade curved down. "Clip point. Looks like a normal blade with the back clipped a bit. This clip curve is sharpened. If I'm pulling out this knife, I'm fighting in close quarters. This blade profile allows for greater precision when thrusting. It's a wicked slicer, but it's an even better stabber. This knife is one single piece of steel. The guard, the hilt, and the blade, all one piece. Simple paratrooper cord for the grip. You wanted elegance in simplicity. Here it is, Father."

I passed the knife to him.

He held it up and studied it.

"There are countless generations between a simple flint blade and this knife. There is metallurgy, years of experimentation to get the right kind of steel, not too brittle, not too soft. More years to properly temper it. Chemistry. Craftsmanship. Secrets of forging the blade, passed from parents to children, read in books, practiced. Men died for the geometry of this knife. Their deaths helped to refine it into the perfect weapon. This knife represents a wealth of knowledge. But you want to take a big step and simply circumvent the learning process. If you gave this knife to a Cro-Magnon, he would appreciate it. But he wouldn't know why it worked so well. He couldn't reproduce it. Even if you taught him how, he would make lesser imitations of it. All that wealth of knowledge would never be acquired."

"I can make a better knife," he said.

I sighed. "The knife is good enough, Father. It suits my needs. Even if you tried, your blade wouldn't be perfect."

"And why is that?"

"Because you don't stab people on a daily basis." Right. Nice going. The next time I came to his castle, he would be stabbing people to learn the perfect knife design.

"You use a car, Kate. Do you know how it was made?"

"No, but I know people who do. We're talking about the collective knowledge of the people. The knowledge that is a root from which other knowledge grows." I drank my beer. "I bet if you made a better knife, you would confiscate all knives and replace them with yours, because they were better."

"They would be."

"But everyone would have the same knife. There would be no need for progress."

"So you would rather condemn these same people to generations of trying to learn something I already know."

I sighed. "Do you want to be the fount of all knowledge?"

"I want these people to experience beauty and prosperity. I want them to have it now. Not tomorrow, not in the future, but now, because their lives are short."

"If you remove adversity, you remove ingenuity and creativity with it. There is no need to strive to make something beautiful or better if it already is."

"Life is full of infinite secrets," he said. "There is always something needing ingenuity."

"Don't you want them to have pride? An old man remembers his first knife, compares it to the one his grandson made, and is proud to see how far we've come."

"You are naive, Blossom. Let me build a house on this street. Go out and ask the first fifty people you meet if they would choose to live in the house they have now or the beautiful dwelling I built. Every single one of them will give you the same answer."

"There is no getting through to you," I said.

"You are a challenging child. You ask difficult questions."

"I think I'm a very easy child."

"How so?" He sipped his beer.

"You never had to bail me out of jail, chase my boyfriend out of my bedroom, or try to console me because I missed my period and cried hysterically, worried that I might be pregnant. Cops were never called to the house because I had a giant party. I've never stolen your car . . ."

He laughed. "You almost destroyed a prison that took me ten years to build. And you upset your grandmother."

"You sent an assassin to kill a baby," I said. "A baby. My best friend's daughter."

"If it helps, I wavered before issuing the order."

He wavered. Ugh.

"Please tell me that there was something in you that rebelled against taking a baby's life."

"No. I wavered because I knew you wouldn't like it. It would displease you and you would think I was cruel, so I hesitated."

"You are cruel."

"Yes, but it doesn't mean I want you to think I am."

I shook my head.

"You once told me we were monsters. We are." Roland smiled at me. "Things are so difficult for you because you're denying your nature."

"No, please not another parental lecture on the virtues of evil."

"Evil and Good are in the eye of the beholder," he said. "That which benefits the majority in the long run isn't evil."

"It is if it comes from the suffering of others."

"People suffer, Blossom. It's the definition of our existence."

Talking to him was like walking in circles. He bent every argument backward.

"You cost me a ten-year friendship."

"Ten years. A blink."

"A third of my life."

"Ah." He leaned back. "I keep forgetting. You're so young, Blossom. I ask myself why you were born into this broken age. Why couldn't you have been born thousands of years ago? You could've reached such heights."

"Nope. I wouldn't have."

"Why not?"

"You would've killed me."

He laughed quietly. "Maybe."

"Let's be honest, Dad. You've killed everyone else. You would kill me as well, except something is preventing you from doing it. I will figure it out."

"If you died, I would mourn you like I mourned my firstborn," he said. "That death nearly broke me."

"It's so hard to talk to you, because you are the axis on which your universe revolves."

"Aren't we all?"

He quirked an eyebrow at me. It was like I stared in the mirror. Crap. I'd been doing that ever since I could remember and here it was. *Thanks, DNA.*

"You more than others."

We finished our beers and sat quietly side by side, watching the city.

"Do you intend to go through with this foolish marriage?"

"Yes. You'll be relieved to know there will be a proper feast."

"Blossom, come back with me."

I turned and looked at him. Pain twisted his face.

"Come back with me," he said. "Leave this behind. Come home with me. Whatever your price, I'll pay it. We're running out of time, but it doesn't have to be this way. Come home. We have so much to talk about."

All I had to do was get up and walk away with him. He couldn't kill my son if there was no son. It would be so much easier. All this pressure would disappear. I could bargain for Curran's life and the city and take my aunt's place. Become a fully realized monster.

I swallowed a sudden lump in my throat. "I can't."

Sadness filled his eyes. "You can't save everyone, Blossom."

"This isn't about saving them. It's about saving me. If I go with you, I'd have to walk away from everything I stand for. I don't want to be a monster. I don't want to murder people or raze cities. I don't want anyone to cringe when they hear my name. I want to have a life."

He winced.

I reached out and took his hand. "Father, what you are doing is wrong. What you have done for these past years, what you will do after you have restored Shinar, is wrong. You bring pain and suffering. You want to resurrect the old kingdom, but the world has moved on. Shinar doesn't belong here. It is lost. It will never be again. And if you somehow forced this world to obey your will, it would fall the way the old world of magic fell. Stay in the city, Father. Live a normal life for a little while. Come to my wedding, figure out what it is to be a grandfather. Enjoy the small things in life. Live, Father. Live for a little while without ruling anyone."

"You would forgive me all my past transgressions if I stayed?" he asked.

"Yes. You are my father."

If it meant that the city would survive, I would. I would take the look on Andrea's face as she held Baby B, Julie's tears, Jim's flat stare, the knife in Dali's chest, and everything I went through, and I would put it away so they could all go on living.

He patted my hand gently. "I cannot. It is against my nature. Decades ago when I had awoken, maybe. But now it's too late. I am walking this path."

"I'm right. Deep down inside, you know I'm right. This is a onetime offer. I won't let you murder the man I love. I sure as hell won't let you murder my son. You have no idea to what depths I'll go to stop you. I won't let you impose your will on those people you see on the street."

"People must be led."

"People must be free."

He shook his head and sighed. "What am I going to do with you, Blossom?"

"Think about it, Father."

"We are going to war, my daughter. I love you very much, my Blossom."

"I love you too, Father."

We sat together and looked at the city until finally he rose, drew his cloak over his head, and left, melting into the traffic.

Erra appeared next to me, her form so thin it was a mere shadow.

"Good-bye, brother," she whispered.

## ═ CHAPTER ═
# 14

I STOOD IN our backyard as the sun set and tugged on the invisible ocean of magic around me.

"Take and hold," my aunt said.

The magic flexed, obeying my will. All through the land I claimed, the magic stopped, hardening, as if the pliable soft water had solidified into impenetrable ice. It was like working a muscle. Her magic battered my "ice" wall and retreated.

We'd been at this for four hours.

"Release. Take and hold. Release. You're doing better, but you need to think less. The magic of the land is a shield. You're raising it. It should be instinctive, or you won't react in time."

Take and hold. Release.

Take and hold. Release.

"Commit!" my aunt snarled. Magic walloped me upside the head. My vision swam.

"Ow."

"What are you afraid of?"

"That I'll take too much."

"Too much what?"

"Too much magic. Once I fought a djinn and used a power word against him . . ."

Erra rolled her eyes to the sky. "Mother, give me strength. Why would you do an idiotic thing like that?"

"Because I didn't know that we have djinn blood." That was when I learned that a long time ago one of my ancestors was an ifrit, and the presence of her blood in our bloodline made djinn immune to our power words. Which raised the question of what would happen if I ever used a power word against my father. It probably wouldn't work. Hugh and Adora seemed to have no problem using power words against me and their brains didn't blow up, but their blood wasn't exactly as potent as my father's.

Erra's nostrils fluttered. Come to think of it, she breathed. I could see her chest rising and falling. She had no reason to breathe; she was dead. Maybe it was force of habit.

My head rang. "Ow."

"Concentrate! What happened with the djinn?"

"My brain tried to explode. I was dying, not physically, but mentally. The magic was down and there was very little they could do for me. So I lay in bed, feeling myself die, and I reached out and took some magic to keep myself alive. It hurt the land."

Suddenly my aunt's face was half an inch from mine. "Listen to me very carefully. Do not do that again. If you keep doing this, it will make you *akillu*, the devourer, an abomination. You are a queen. Your responsibility is to defend the land, not to feed on it."

"I wasn't planning on a repeat performance."

"Good, because I'll kill you myself if you do that again. It is a sacred rule. Even at my worst, I never resorted to that. When your father's beloved towers fell, he did not feed on the land to hold them up."

"Got it," I growled.

"I don't blame you," she said. "I blame Im. One doesn't simply hand a child a piece of land and let her stumble around in the dark with it. Has he taught you anything?"

"He's offered, but only if I pledged to obey him."

"I don't understand that. He loves nothing more than to teach. He taught all of his children, even the ones he disliked. Even those who had neither brains nor power to do any real damage to themselves or others. You're intelligent, disciplined, and you have power. You're one of the strongest of his children I've seen. Why?"

"I thought about that," I said. "I think it's because I don't matter."

She stared at me. "Explain."

"It's not important for me to know anything about ruling the land. In his mind, I'm your replacement."

She recoiled.

"He sees me as a sword, not a ruler. No matter what he says, I will never get the keys to his kingdom. I'm meant to kill for him and lead his armies at best, and die at worst. I don't know if it's because I'm too old or too stubborn, but there it is. If I blight the land accidentally, all the better. It would make me desperate enough to beg him for his wisdom and he can move me into the place he has chosen for me. If all else fails, from his point of view, I would make a decent vessel for bringing his grandson into this world. I know the prophecy says he will kill my son, but given a chance, I think he would take him. He likes new and shiny things, and my son will be shiny."

Erra stared at me. If I didn't know better, I'd think she was shocked.

"You are not a hireling," she said finally. "You are a child of royal blood. His blood. My blood. It is your right to know these things. It is his duty as your parent to pass them on to you."

I spread my arms.

She squeezed her eyes shut and put her hands over her face. "You, our mother . . . It's like I don't know him anymore. There's nothing left of the golden child he was. Is it because I slept while he stayed awake for another thousand years, or was I just that blind during my life?"

"He isn't wrong," I said. "I do make a better killer than a ruler."

Magic exploded on my chest. I landed on my ass.

"Never put yourself down," Erra snarled. "You are *my* niece. If he won't teach you, I will! I may have never claimed a kingdom, but not because I don't know how to do it or what to do once the claim is made. Get up. You have to practice."

I rolled to my feet. "It wants to change me."

"What does?"

"The land. The Shar. When I use the magic, I feel urges."

Erra's eyes narrowed. "Desire for more power?"

"No, desire to not be accountable for anything. I stop caring about things that are important, like family, friends . . ."

"Listen to me carefully. The Shar pushes you to acquire land and defend it. It fuels your feud with your father. It does not do anything else. What you're experiencing is a different thing entirely. When you sense the land, what does it feel like to you?"

"An ocean."

"Right now, you are a barren rock within this ocean. A part of you feels the great power that lies there and wants to become one with it. There is so much magic there and you are only human. But because you are human, you impose limitations on yourself, things you won't do no matter what. These limitations are good. They keep your ego intact. Without them you would melt into the waters."

"What would happen then?"

"You would become everything you fear. A tyrant, a demon, eventually a god. Hang whatever label you wish upon it. You must find a way to draw the ocean into yourself without losing who you are. You absorb it, not the other way around. That is fundamentally harder than letting yourself become one with it."

I stared at her.

"You're not fighting the land!" she barked, exasperated. "You're fighting yourself. The combined magical power of the land is far greater than you are, but it has no will of its own. Interacting with it is terrifying, because your instincts are warning you about the enormous power difference between you and it. Your fear is pushing you to subjugate it, and fear is telling you that once you impose your will on the land, it will be a slave and no longer a danger. But this is the one thing you cannot do. It will feel like a victory, but in reality it will be the end of who you are. You must find a balance, a place within your land's power. Doing that is a lot harder, and so a part of you rebels against all of the work you must do to get there. Yes, it will feel as if some outside force is pushing on you. I've known people who even heard its voice and talked to it. Some of them went mad, child. Trust me, it's you. You have to overcome yourself. If the land had a will of its own and was wrestling with you, it would be so much easier. You would just crush it and move on. But you are fighting yourself."

"How do I win?"

"That's for you to figure out. One or the other part of you will get the upper hand. It's not important now. Your father is preparing for battle. You must prepare to defend your land and all within it. What we're practicing now is fundamentally different from what you've done before to keep yourself alive. You're taking nothing. You're shaping the magic the way a vessel maker shapes clay and then releasing it. This harms nothing. Feel the magic. Commit. Let yourself sink fully into it, but do not let it pull your essence apart."

I let the ocean of magic wash over me.

"Deeper," my aunt demanded. "I won't let you harm anyone."

I opened myself and let it swallow me whole.

"Finally," Erra said. "Take and hold. Release. Again. Again. Again . . ."

I LAY ON my back in the grass and watched the stars get brighter. I was so tired.

Curran loomed over me. I didn't hear him approach. His gray eyes were dark.

"What?" I sat up.

"I told Derek to meet me here at nine. It's ten now."

Derek was punctual. If he said he would here at nine, he would be here. You could set your clock by him. Alarm pinched me. "Maybe he got held up?"

"He called, said he and Julie were going to run a short errand, and then they would come straight here. That was two hours ago. Julie was supposed to meet with Roman about bridesmaid dresses. He's been sitting in our living room for half an hour."

Something had happened.

I rolled to my feet. "I'll get the car."

Fifteen minutes later we drove out into the night, with the black volhv in the backseat.

"Did they say where they were going?" I asked.

"Near Gryphon Street."

My old apartment was on Karen Road, off Gryphon Street. Crap.

"Thick magic tonight," Roman said from the backseat.

I felt it, too. It was flooding me with power. Streets sped by.

"Any idea what they would be doing on Gryphon?" Curran asked.

Probably moving an assassin who thought I was her key to heaven into my apartment. "Some."

"Feel like sharing?"

"No."

"Kate, I'm getting sick of this. I was cool with Mishmar, I dealt with you bringing the ghost of your aunt into our house, but I'm done with all the secrecy. You know what's going on and now the kids are in danger."

"I'll tell you afterward. It's complicated to explain and you'll be pissed off."

"I'm already pissed off," he snarled.

Not yet. When he was truly angry, he would turn ice cold.

"Look, it's my fault, and now Julie has taken it upon herself to fix my mess. But right now let's find the kids, and I promise you, you can roar as much as you want after."

His eyes were completely gold. The steering wheel groaned slightly under the pressure of his fingers.

He would leave me. I knew it with absolute certainty. When he found out everything, he would leave. This was one straw too many.

"She's right," Roman said from the backseat. "Rescue first."

"Stay out of this," Curran and I said at the same time.

Roman raised his hands.

Curran took a turn. We shot out onto the street leading to the Berkins overpass, a massive stone bridge spanning a field of rubble where several office towers had collapsed and part of the city had sunk.

To the right side, Julie knelt on the bridge. Around her a faint red glow shimmered in a circle. She'd set a blood ward. Within the defensive spell, Derek paced back and forth. Adora knelt by Julie, her head bowed.

Behind the circle a dozen people waited. Two stood out, at the back of the group, a man and a woman, twins in their early twenties, both redheaded, both wearing the black and purple of the sahanu. Five hyenas sat by the female twin's feet, secured by long chains.

"The twins are my father's assassins," I said.

The female twin reached down and took the collar off the first hyena.

"My lord is so good to me." Roman grinned.

"What?"

"It's a bridge." He rubbed his hands together. "I love bridges!"

Arrows hit the car. Magic whined and our windshield shattered.

Curran threw the wheel to the right and braked. The car skidded to a stop, the driver's side facing the bridge. He grabbed the door. Metal groaned. The door came free. Curran heaved it in front of him like a shield. His body tore. Bones grew, powerful muscle wound about them, and fur sheathed the new body. His jaws lengthened, the bones of his skull crunching and moving to make new leonine jaws. Fangs the size of my fingers burst from his gums. Sharp claws tipped the fingers of his monstrous hands. The change took less than a second, and then the nightmare that was Curran in warrior form snarled and leapt onto the bridge.

"Scatter!" the male twin ordered. "He's ours."

My father's soldiers dashed out of Curran's way, clearing the path to the twins.

I jumped out of the car and ducked behind the hood as chunks of sharp ice the size of my fist peppered the vehicle. Mages. Crap.

"Roman!" I yelled.

"I've got it."

Roman straightened, ignoring the ice, and slammed the butt of his staff on the bridge steps, his eyes glowing. The staff's wooden top flowed, turning into a monstrous bird head. The wooden beak gaped open and the staff screamed. Darkness shot out from under his feet, spiraling around him and breaking into a thousand crows. The murder surged around the bridge, like a horizontal tornado, blocking the ice.

I sprinted across the bridge toward the kids.

In the circle Derek was shaking Julie, but her eyes were still closed. He should've been able to exit the ward, but she must've set it closed both ways. They were trapped in it.

Power words were out of the question. Wasting one on individual fighters wasn't worth the risk. The only two words that would affect every single one of the fighters would be *ahissa*, *flee*, or *osanda*, *kneel*, but both of these would hit Julie's ward and Curran. I didn't know how her blood ward would react to power words. Besides I didn't want them to kneel or flee. I wanted to murder every one of them.

Curran reached the twin sahanu. The male twin grinned. His mouth gaped, wider and wider. Fangs sprouted from his gums. His clothes tore, and an enormous werehyena landed on the bridge. He wasn't a bouda. He was too large, almost as large as Curran, and his fur was thick and striped with short smudges of dark brown.

*Crocuta crocuta spelaea*. Crap. Sienna was never wrong.

I was almost to Julie and Derek.

The female twin cackled and the pack of hyenas at her

feet cackled back. The female sahanu jerked the last collar open and dropped the tangle of chains.

"See us, Sharrim!" the female sahanu shrieked. Her skin tore. Fur spilled out. The hyenas at her feet barked and cackled. "Know us! Bless us with your blood when we bathe in it!"

My father couldn't be allowed to educate any more assassins. That creepy pseudo-religious bullshit they were spouting had to end.

The female sahanu snarled. The hyena pack tore across the bridge toward me.

Curran and the male werehyena collided. The werehyena struck at his neck. Curran avoided the blow and clawed at the male werehyena's chest. The female raked her claws across his gray back. He snarled. They had no idea what Curran was capable of when he was seriously pissed off. They were about to find out.

An arrow clattered by my feet. The archers had woken up and realized they had a shot at me.

The first hyena lunged at me. I dodged the massive jaws and opened the side of its neck with my blade. The beast charged me and I kicked it. The hyena stumbled.

In half a second the whole pack would be on me.

I thrust my hand into the ward and detonated it. It shattered, like a pane of translucent red glass, the pieces falling down and melting into nothing.

Julie's eyes snapped open. She cried out as the magic backlash hit her.

The leading hyena bit my thigh, sinking her teeth into me. Like being clamped by a bear trap. I stabbed straight down, severing the beast's spine.

The second hyena leapt at me. A werewolf collided with her in midair, knocking her to the side. The hyena crashed down, its neck broken.

Out of the corner of my eye, I saw a woman lunging at me from the left, swinging an axe. She fell, cut down by a lightning-fast katana strike.

"Sharrim!" Adora smiled at me.

Derek howled. The two remaining hyenas turned toward him.

Eleven targets between me and Curran. I dipped my hand into the blood running down my thigh and forced it into shape. A blood dagger formed in my left hand. I started forward.

Across the bridge the two monstrosities tore into Curran. Bones crunched. The female werehyena's left arm hung limp. A chunk of the male werehyena's right side was missing, the wound red and raw. Blood drenched Curran's fur. I couldn't tell who was winning, but I knew who would be left standing. He would kill them both. If I got there in time, he would leave some for me.

Two women flanked me, each with a sword. Saber on my left, Katana on my right. To the left a man with a large mace rushed Adora.

Saber and Katana split, circling me. If I turned toward one, my back would be to the other.

Saber brandished her sword. It was an older-style blade, larger and heavier than modern variants.

Katana watched me like a hawk, her body in *seigan kamae*: right foot forward with most of the weight on the leading leg; sword directly in front, held with a slight bend to the elbows; the kissaki, the point of the katana, aimed at my eyes. A harmonious balance of both attack and defense.

Saber would fence. Katana would rely on a single strike at the right moment. One accurate cut. Such was the way of the samurai. Their best strategy would be for Saber to engage, with Katana waiting for an opening.

I didn't have time for them to decide when to attack me. I turned ever so slightly toward Katana, shifting my weight to my right leg.

The saber fighter thrust with dizzying speed. Katana struck, a beautiful diagonal blow. A moment stretched into eternity. I shied back, blocking the katana and letting the saber slide a hair from my stomach, drove my blood dagger into Saber's throat, jerked it out, pushed Katana back, and thrust the blood blade into her stomach.

Time snapped back to its normal speed, an elastic band let loose. The two women fell. I knelt, driving the two blades into their bodies, and kept walking. Nine.

The crows vanished. At the other end of the bridge a female mage slumped over, exhausted. I glanced back. Roman leaned on his staff, breathing like he'd run a marathon.

A man lunged at me. I sidestepped his strike and turned, ramming my elbow into his chest. He stumbled back and I sliced his neck open. Eight.

A woman, two swords, fast. I blocked one slash, let the other graze me, and kicked her in the head. She fell and I sank Sarrat between her ribs, ripping up her lungs and heart. Seven.

Curran roared. The male werehyena clamped his side. The female tore at his arm, locked around her throat. The sound of bones crunching—his ribs broke under the pressure of hyena teeth.

A man, a mace, a head rolling on the bridge. Adora. Six.

A woman, lance, too slow. I opened her stomach from side to side and stabbed her when she wouldn't stay down. Five.

An arrow sliced into my left shoulder. Pain. Nothing major. The bowman notched another and fell as Derek shattered his skull. Four.

Curran roared. Blood ran down his face—one of them had gotten him right over the muzzle. The two hyenas circled him, slow. Fighting him tired you out.

Curran limped, favoring his left leg. I knew that move. It was called "come and get it." He'd caught me with it three times, twice with a limp and once with a supposedly injured shoulder. He was inviting a direct attack.

The hyenas closed in, sensing a sure kill.

"For you, Sharrim!" Adora dropped her sword and sprinted forward.

"No!"

I ran after her.

She swiped the tangle of chains that had been used to hold the hyenas, looped one chain around her wrists, and leapt, swinging it out. The chain caught the female were-hyena's neck. The female twin stumbled back. Adora landed on the short wall of the bridge, her back to the eighty-foot drop.

A power word punched the werehyena. Her eyes rolled back in her head. Adora smiled at me and jumped over the edge, taking the female werehyena with her.

Oh God.

The chain tangle slid. I dropped Sarrat and grabbed it. The chain jerked, nearly ripping my arms out of the sockets. Below me Adora dangled over an eighty-foot drop, her right wrist still caught in the chain's loop. The werehyena's body lay broken below.

"Traitor!" an inhuman voice howled behind me

"Let me die!" Adora tried to rip the chain off her wrist. "Sharrim, let me serve in death. Please!"

Fire sliced my back. Someone had tried to slash through my spine. I molded the blood gushing from the cut, forming it into a narrow strip of blood armor, shielding my vertebrae.

If I dropped the chain, there would be no questions. I could tell Curran whatever I wanted. Derek wouldn't talk about Adora, and neither would Julie. Curran wouldn't leave me. I wouldn't have to hide Adora, I wouldn't have to be responsible for her, and I wouldn't have to break her world and tell her I didn't have the keys to heaven.

*Drop her*, the magic insisted. *Drop her. It's the smart thing to do. The right thing to do.*

The pressure ground against me, as if my soul had split in two. One part wanted power, the other knew what was right, both of them wanted Curran, and I was torn in the middle.

*Drop her and everything will be okay. It's what she wants.*

*Drop her.*

*DROP HER.*

. . .

No.

Something snapped inside me, like pieces sliding into

place. I gripped that voice inside of me and choked it into silence. "Do not let go!" I barked. "That's an order."

"Let me go." She was weeping. "I'll go to heaven. I'll serve you forever in the afterlife."

"I'm not a god. There is no fucking afterlife heaven where you can serve me. My father made it up. Adora, don't let go."

A furry arm gripped the chain below mine and flexed. The enormous weight vanished. Curran pulled the chain up, hand over hand, his face all lion, his eyes burning.

Around us, bodies littered the bridge, the male werehyena's head lying by his body, his neck a shredded stump where Curran's teeth had torn flesh and cracked bone. Derek's sides and legs were drenched in blood. Julie lay slumped in a heap, exhausted. Roman's face was bloodless.

Curran pulled a weeping Adora onto the bridge and pulled the chain off her.

She covered her face with her hands. "I'm sorry, Sharrim. I'm so sorry."

I saw it in his eyes. This was one straw too many.

"Get the kids into the car," he said.

"I can . . ."

The expression on his face stopped me cold.

"Get into the car."

I packed Adora into the Jeep. Curran picked up Julie and carried her in.

"Are you okay?" I asked.

"I'm tired," she whispered. "So tired."

Roman picked himself up and got into the car. Derek limped his way to the Jeep. Curran held the front passenger door open for him. The werewolf crawled into the vehicle. Curran shut the door.

"Go home."

"Curran . . ."

"Go home," he repeated, his face iced over.

I started the engine, backed the Jeep up, and turned it around. In the rearview mirror the bridge behind me was empty.

"Is he coming back?" Julie whispered.

"Of course he's coming back," I told her. I had no doubt about it. Curran wouldn't leave me, especially not without talking to me first. "He just needs to cool down."

"I'm sorry," Adora whispered.

"It's okay," I told Adora. "It's okay. You didn't do anything wrong. It's not your fault."

It was mine.

I TOOK EVERYONE home. That was all I could do.

The kids had been moving Adora to my old apartment when they were jumped. Derek wanted to fight, but Julie had made a double blood ward to keep him in. Making one took a wallop of power. Making two wiped her out, but her wards had held out against everything Roland's people were able to throw at them. The werehyena sahanu had run their mouths. Julie was the intended target. They had tracked her to our neighborhood but saw too many of Mahon's bears. I would have to thank him. So rather than go in, they left a scout and caught up with her, Adora, and Derek on the bridge.

I had taken Saiman back and ripped Adora away from my father. He retaliated by trying to take Julie away from me. There was no going back after this.

Erra wanted a full report. I told her Julie would explain. I didn't feel like talking.

Derek's injuries were minor. He bled a lot, but healed quickly. Mine weren't much either. I'd called Nellie and promised her the sun and the sky if she came to patch everyone up. She did. She also issued Adora and me a sedative. I didn't take mine.

Nellie left. I'd called in some cavalry and now I sat on the porch, waiting.

Four people emerged from the night and came onto the porch. I'd called the bears Mahon assigned to guard our street. Raoul, short but so broad-shouldered that he looked almost square, stopped by me. "No worries. We'll sit on them for the night."

"Thanks. If anything nasty comes up, the wards around the house will hold it off."

"If anything nasty comes up, we'll break it." Lilian patted my hand.

"Thanks, guys."

I went to the stables and got my giant donkey. Cuddles must've sensed that now wasn't the time for her "special" behavior, so she gave me no trouble. I saddled her and left.

Around me, the city lay steeped in magic. I breathed the night in and tasted the magic on my tongue. We were oddly at peace, the magic and I.

The lights of the feylanterns blinked in the distant windows, enchanted blue sparks fighting against the darkness. I kept riding. I didn't know where I was going, but I didn't want to stay in our house. It was our house together. Every memory and everything in it was something we'd made together. It felt like I'd ruined it.

I needed time by myself to think and sort this out. I couldn't do it at our house, in our bedroom or on our porch. I needed space. Curran would be back. He would stand by me no matter what, and I would stand by him. I didn't want to be me right this second. If I could've crawled out of my skin, I would've.

I let Cuddles meander her way through the streets until I raised my head and saw we were in front of my old apartment building. I stared at it. When I worked for the Order I would be coming back exactly like this, except riding Marigold. I'd have to punch my aunt for killing my mule. Too bad she wouldn't feel it. I must've unconsciously given Cuddles some cues. Where to turn, which way to go . . .

Just as well. I put Cuddles into the apartment's stables, went upstairs, and unlocked the door. I hadn't had a chance to set any wards after Curran had it remodeled post-my-aunt-wrecking-it, but at least we had put a new door on it. I didn't have the best luck with doors.

I went inside, pushed the door shut, and sat at my kitchen table.

This used to be Greg's apartment, and then it was mine.

There were memories here too, but a lot of them were mine alone.

I sat at the kitchen table and tried not to think. I felt too bruised inside. Numb.

This is where it all started. When I came to Atlanta to investigate Greg's death and eventually ended up in this apartment. Life was so much easier back then, when I was a simple merc. Even working for the Order wasn't too bad. The job wasn't always straightforward, but I helped people more than I hurt them.

Fuck it.

I got up and went into the living room. It was a one-bedroom apartment and even after Greg's death, the bedroom belonged to him and his memories. It was his space. When I lived here, I always slept on the couch in the living room, which was why Curran had put a bed here. And of course, it was almost four feet high, and you needed a ladder to crawl onto it.

I would give almost anything for him to be on that bed right now making fun of me.

I opened the windows, unlocked the bars, and let the night in. Why the hell not. It wasn't like anyone would come to bother me anyway. I took off the leather harness with Sarrat in it and put it on the night table. I pulled off my boots and sat on the bed. I kept thinking my father would wreck my life, but no, turned out it was all me.

A hand gripped the windowsill.

Now I was seeing things.

Curran vaulted into the room, human and dressed. He came over and sat next to me.

"Stopped by the house?"

"I tailed you to make sure you got there in one piece. Talked to the kids after you left. Thought you would be at Cutting Edge, but you weren't. This was the next place. Would've gone to the Savannah house after that."

"Trained detective."

"That's right."

We sat side by side. Outside the window the stars winked at us.

"I leave to clear my head and you run away from the house," he said.

"I didn't run away." Yep, I totally did.

We sat quietly for a few more moments.

"I wanted to tell you about Adora."

"I understand why you might want to hold things back. We both deal with fucked-up shit and we try to shield each other. I don't like it, but I get it, because I've done it before and I can't swear I won't do it again. But I don't understand why you hid *her*. Derek and Julie tried to explain it to me, but neither of them made sense. Did you think I wouldn't listen to you? I've always been cool. I might not like things that you did, but I always listen, Kate. What made you think I would lose it?"

I sighed. "I hid her, because I would have to explain why I didn't kill her."

"Why didn't you?"

"Because her existence made me so mad, my hands shook. I wasn't mad because what was done to her was wrong. I was mad because my father dared to send her into my territory to take what was mine. I wanted to hurt him. If I'd had a knife and could've reached him in that moment, I would've sliced all the flesh off his bones. You have no idea how much I wanted to do it. I took her away from my father, because I wanted to send a big 'Fuck You' his way. Her life at that point didn't matter to me. I didn't care that she was a person. She was a thing. She was my father's toy and I took her away so I could taunt him with her. I almost made her into a slave. I only stopped because some switch flipped in my brain and I realized you wouldn't like it. Enslaving her goes against everything I stand for. That's not me. That's not who I am. I should've stopped because of that. I didn't want to explain it to you. I didn't want you to know this about me."

I didn't look at him. There. It was all out.

"Why didn't you let her go on the bridge? Would've ended all the questions."

I sighed. "Because it would be wrong. Everything that happened to her was wrong. It's wrong to buy children, it's wrong to stick them into a fortress and make them into killers, it's wrong to promise them that they will get into paradise if they obey you, it's wrong to order them to kill people, it's wrong to bind them with your blood, which you told them is holy, and it's wrong to break that binding because you're engaged in a pissing contest with your father. She's a person. She is me, Curran, or at least what Voron wanted me to be. My father didn't come up with this idea out of the blue. He watched Voron teach Hugh and he simply improved on the concept and mass-produced it."

He waited.

"She wanted to throw away her life for me, but I don't deserve her life or her loyalty. The moment I chose to take her away from my father and let her live, I became responsible for her. You saw her. The only time she was allowed into the world was when there was a target and a handler. She deserves to have a life and to be free. If she understood things as they actually are, she wouldn't sacrifice herself for me. She'd spit in my face. I want to give her a chance. I owe her a chance. Even if you'd told me at that moment that you would leave me if I let her live, I would've saved her. It was the right thing to do. My thing. I couldn't drop her, Curran. I couldn't."

"Of course you couldn't."

"It's complicated."

He shook his head. "No, it's pretty simple, actually. You didn't drop her, because that's not who you are, Kate. Because you will fight for her freedom and her life. Yes, it is a mess and it's yours to fix. Running away from all of this and pouting by yourself in your old apartment isn't the best way to deal with it."

Pouting? I looked at him. "Why are you here? Weren't you walking away the last time I saw you?"

"I walked away because I needed to clear my head and figure out what the hell was going on. And because I was so angry, I couldn't see straight. I killed that asshole and I still wanted to keep killing. The rage wouldn't stop. Then I cooled off, I talked to Adora and the kids, and realized that tonight was the first time I had seen the real you in days. You found another misfit with no place to go and were ready to protect her with everything you had."

"I didn't . . ."

"Yeah, you did. You're like a crazy cat lady, but you collect killers instead of fluffy cats."

"I don't collect killers."

"Yes, you do, and those who aren't killers turn into killers by the time you're done. You made Julie into a maniac. That child has more knives on her than a squad of the PAD. Christopher was the only stray who couldn't fight, and now it turns out he's a god of terror. Why am I not surprised?"

"I don't need to listen to this." I had enough guilt as it was.

He gave an exaggerated sigh. "What am I going to do with you? You're a walking catastrophe."

"Get the hell out of my apartment!"

"Why? So you can sit here in your solitude and mope some more?"

"I wasn't moping."

He grinned at me. "Poor sad Kate, all alone with her sadness . . ."

"Curran, stop while you're ahead, or I swear, I'll kick you until you fly right out of this window."

He pounced on me. I tried to punch him, but it was like trying to wrestle a bear. He gathered me up and pulled me to him.

"Go away!"

"I love you," he said.

I stopped struggling.

"Where the hell would I go without you, Kate? No matter where I went, you would be there in my head. I would miss you every moment of my life."

"I would miss you, too."

He squeezed me to him, his gray eyes laughing. "I brought you something."

He pulled out a folded piece of lined paper and held it in front of me.

*New Plan*

*1. Get Awesome Cosmic Powers.*
*2. Nuke my dad.*
*3. Retire from the land-claiming business.*

Below in his handwriting, he'd added several lines.

*4. Get married and start a family.*
*5. Have children. Hopefully not screw them up too
    badly.*
*6. Live a life we're proud of.*

He squeezed me to him.

There was nothing about the Guild there. Nothing about power or wealth. It was just him and me.

"Am I enough?" I asked.

"Always," he said. "Come on, baby. Let's go home. It's late."

"Do we have to go home right now?"

His hold on me shifted. "No, we don't. But there is a bed here and no children, so if we stay here, I can't guarantee your safety."

I looked at him. "How much danger do you think I'm in?"

Little golden sparks flared in his gray eyes. "You have no idea."

"We've been together for two years. I think I have some idea."

He leaned over me and kissed me, his mouth sealing mine. It was more than a kiss. It felt like a promise and I kissed him back, making promises of my own. His hold on me tightened. His hands gripped me. The kiss broke. I opened my eyes and saw his, focused on me and heated from within by something wild.

I flipped onto my knees on the bed and kissed him, again

and again, tasting him, his tongue, his lips, my hands sliding over his hard shoulders, his muscles tensing under my fingers. "I love you," I whispered.

He buried his face in my neck. His tongue painted heat on my skin. He knew where to kiss, the sensitive spot right below my ear. It sent delicious shivers all the way down my spine.

"More . . ."

He kissed me there again. His teeth nipped the skin, the slight ping of pain a shocking burst of pleasure. I gasped. He pulled me to him, possessive, completely sure I would let him. His hand slid up my back, under the T-shirt. I stretched from the sheer pleasure of it. He unhooked my bra, rocked me back, and then he was on top of me, looking at me from three inches away. "Mine."

"Always."

He tugged my T-shirt up. I tried to wriggle out of it and he caught it halfway up my arms, pulling the fabric tight. I couldn't move my arms. His mouth closed on mine. He kissed me, hungry, so hungry. Heat surged through me. I wanted him so much. I needed him to love me. He kept kissing me, his stubble scraping my neck, his hand caressing my breasts, my side, lifting me toward him. His tongue teased my nipple, pulling a moan out of me. The world shrank to him. I wanted him between my legs.

He let me go and I wrapped my arms over him and pushed him to the side. He rolled on his back and I landed on top of him. I pulled my T-shirt off, threw my bra aside, and pulled his shirt off of him. My Curran . . . How did I ever end up with him? The way he looked at me made me want to strip naked and dance just so he would pounce.

"Your move," he said, his voice rough.

I kissed his lips, moved down and kissed that chest, stroking him, sliding my hand lower, over the ridges of his abs, down to the hard length of him in his jeans. He drew a sharp breath. I unzipped him and slid my hand up and down his shaft. He groaned, straining, trying to stay where he was.

Any more and it would be torture for us both.

I hopped off of him and pulled off my jeans. When I was done, he grabbed me, already naked and ready to go. His hand caught my hair. His body caged mine. I wrapped my legs around him. I had no patience left. He pushed my legs off him and slid down. His mouth closed on me, his tongue in the perfect spot. Each lick, each touch coaxed pleasure out of my body. He kept going, faster and faster, insistent, the wet heat growing hotter until the climax burst through me. I cried out and forgot about everything as waves of bliss shook me. He was on top of me, thrusting, long and hard, all of him focused on me, all of him mine alone. We were making love and when the second burst of pleasure came, we shared it.

He was right about the danger. I had no idea.

MY EYES SNAPPED open. A noise came from the street, the very particular noise of claws scraping brick outside my window. Next to me Curran lay still, his eyes open. My head was on his chest, his right arm around me.

A clawed hand grabbed the windowsill and a furry, thin creature landed on it and hunched over, its face a nightmarish blend of human and rodent.

Last time a vampire, this time a wererat. There was no peace to be had in my apartment.

The wererat inclined his head. "Former Beasssssht Lord. Former Consssssshort."

I knew that voice. I'd met him before; he was Robert's favorite surveillance agent.

"Hello, Jardin," Curran said, his voice calm.

"The former Conssshort's father is away from hisssh basssshe. When he returnssh, he will find only asshess."

"Jim burned my father's base?"

Jardin nodded. "You can shee the glow in the eassst."

Oh, Jim. I knew why he did it. Dali was hurt. She was his world. He wanted to retaliate, the Pack expected him to retaliate, because that's what a strong shapeshifter leader would do, and so he retaliated. Curran might have done the same.

"I'm to tell you that war issh coming. Thesshe are dangeroush timesh. Friendsh mussht look out for each other if all are to shhhurvive."

"We heard your message," Curran said.

Jardin nodded and leapt off the windowsill into the night.

"Robert is scared," I said.

Curran nodded, his hand stroking my shoulder. "There were probably heavy losses."

"Jim isn't going to come to us, is he?"

"No."

"We still have to protect the Pack. It's on the land we claimed."

"Can you block his magic?" Curran asked.

"Erra says I can. I won't know for sure until I try."

"Do you trust your aunt?"

I turned over and looked at him. "There are certain moral principles that rule my aunt. They are what her childhood was built on. Honor and love your parents. Guard the land you claim. Have children, teach them, and guide them so the family may live on. My father trampled all of them like a runaway bulldozer. She will make him pay for it. I don't think she'll betray us, but if she does, we'll deal with it."

"But is she making you stronger?"

"She is. But magic alone won't be enough, Curran."

"We'll need an army," he said.

"YOU NEED AN ARMY." My aunt paced back and forth in my kitchen.

It was morning and I was on my first cup of coffee. My head throbbed.

"How can you not have a throne room?" Erra peered at me. "Where do you receive supplicants?"

"Here, or at the office." I walked over to the counter to pour myself another cup of coffee. Curran had left on a morning run through the woods. He said he needed to burn off some energy after last night. All I wanted to do after last night was sleep for twenty-four hours straight. Where the hell he got his energy I didn't know, but I sure would've loved to have some of it.

Julie sat at the table, watching my aunt with a sour expression on her face, and sipped her coffee.

"Is the office that place where you did a ridiculous dance?"

"Yes."

"And you have no other dwelling? No palace, no fortress?"

"No."

"You make me want to stab you."

"I have that effect on many people."

"How is it you're still alive?"

"I'm hard to kill." I drank my coffee.

"Not that hard."

"You couldn't do it."

"I didn't really try."

I looked at her from above the brim of my cup. "You tried. I was there."

Julie grimaced.

"What's wrong with you this morning?"

"She doesn't like my banner."

Why me? Why? I counted to five in my head.

Curran walked through the kitchen door. "What's wrong with the banner?"

"It's blue," Julie said.

"Why is it blue?" my aunt demanded.

"Because it's the color of human magic," Julie said.

"It's the color of every human mage out there," Erra snapped. "It's not fit."

I raised my hands. "I don't care about the banner."

My aunt reached over and smacked me upside the head. Magic exploded against my skull.

"If you do that again, I will drop your knife into a manhole for a few days."

"Don't make empty threats," Erra said. "You won't survive the next few days without me. When you want to threaten someone, you must mean it."

"I mean it."

"You remind me of me." Erra groaned. "You are the punishment for all my transgressions."

I smiled at her.

"Always remember you are a queen," Erra ground out. "Banners are important. They are symbols. When a scared child barely old enough to hold his weapon comes to a field of battle to raise his spear for you, your banner will be the first thing he sees—and the last, as he lies dying, gazing at the sky. Your banner tells him what he is dying for."

"Well, what banner should I have?"

"You are the only living female within our bloodline. You would inherit In-Shinar from me as I inherited it from my mother, while your father would hold Im-Shinar. The oldest female of our blood always holds In-Shinar and flies its green banner. It is your right."

"Nobody knows what Shinar is," Julie said.

"Her father does."

"Will her father recognize the banner?" Curran said.

"Yes," Erra said. "He will."

My father would see the banner of his own family on the other side of the battlefield. It would hammer home the point: he was fighting a civil war.

"Let's split it," I said. "Green for Shinar and blue for Atlanta."

"Green with a blue stripe," my aunt said.

"Fine," Julie grumbled.

"Go across the street," Curran told Julie. "George's cousin owns a textile shop. See what they can do for us. We need large banners. A lot of large banners."

"Finally," Erra said. "Someone who understands. Bring me samples, child. The shade of green must be exact."

Julie got up, sighed to let us know she was suffering, and left the room.

"This still doesn't solve the problem of our not having an army," I said.

"What are Roland's typical tactics?" Curran asked.

Erra sighed. "He will make a fist out of his troops and

punch your Pack fortress with it. Straight-on assault with overwhelming force. Im has been taught tactics and strategy, but he has no interest in it. That's why he relies on others to lead his armies and only assists when he has to."

"He would've fought Grandmother," I thought out loud. "She didn't seem pleased, so it must've taken a lot out of him. The last time I saw him, he seemed tired. Then he'll get home and find a burned-out ruin. That will make him livid. Erra's right. He will want to crush the Pack with one blow."

"We need soldiers," Curran said.

"The Guild won't fight without a lot of money on the table," I said. "We can't afford it."

"Pay them out of your dowry," Erra said.

"I have no dowry."

"Your father will give you a dowry."

"We are preparing to fight him on the battlefield."

"Those two things are completely separate," my aunt said. "No princess of Shinar ever went to her wedding without a dowry."

"Even if we had the money," Curran said, "at this point, the mercs aren't trained to fight as a unit. Give me six months, and we can field them, but right now they would be fodder. We can pick up a few choice fighters from the Guild, but no real numbers to speak of."

"Fine. Who else do we have?" Erra asked.

"The god of terror and the dark volhv," I told her.

"The one from yesterday? The handsome one?"

"Yes." Roman would just love that. He was so disturbed by Erra yesterday, he didn't even crack any one-liners. He just sat quietly with a freaked-out look on his face when she demanded that we explain the fight to her. I would have to wait for the right moment to drop that one on him.

"That's good, but it's not an army. Your half-breed friends will lose this battle if you don't field troops, because your father will bring enough force to crush them."

"We can get the Order to help," I said. "They will defend against Roland."

"How many soldiers?"

"Twelve," Curran said. "They are elite troops. It's not an army."

"Who can you compel into service?" Erra asked.

"I can't compel anyone," I said. "I can ask for help but it would take time and diplomacy."

The witches might help. The College of Mages would take too long. They spent more time deliberating what to get for lunch than most people spent choosing a house.

"We don't have time," Curran said. "Can you strip the People's vampires from them and run them on the field?"

"Yes. They wouldn't do anything except run in a horde, but yes."

"You mean to tell me that Im left his necromancers here? In that gaudy nightmare of a castle?"

"Yes."

Erra rolled her head up and looked straight at the ceiling. "Gods give me patience. How many?"

"Probably a hundred navigators, give or take thirty depending on how accomplished the journeymen are. Around four hundred vampires."

At least that's how many I ballparked the last time I had reviewed them. I made it a habit to pass by the Casino and check on them periodically.

"There is your army."

"They're loyal to my father. They are terrified of him."

"No," Erra said. "They're loyal to the blood and the promises it holds. As soon as your Herald gets here and we get the banners, you will go and take control of your army. You will make them obey."

She was right. We needed the navigators and the undead. We needed them to survive. But Ghastek wouldn't serve me.

"How? I can threaten them, but they would only turn on me in the fight when it matters most."

"Why do people follow your father?" Erra asked.

"Because . . ." Landon Nez, the Legatus of the Golden Legion, flashed before my eyes. What was it he said . . . "Because being in his presence is like being in the presence of a god who loves you. When he smiles, it's like the sun has risen. When he withdraws his affection, it's like winter."

"Exactly. You will go into that white crime of a palace, you will show them that you love them above all others, and you will take your legion. I once took a city with five men and a lame goat. If I can do that, you can convince the necromancers to pledge themselves to you. Do this or die."

I looked at Curran.

"We need troops," he said. "If you don't win their loyalty, they're a wild card. Either they'll leave the city and reinforce Roland, or he'll use them as a knife in your back."

"If you can't lock them in, you'll have to kill them," Erra said.

I looked at her.

"This is war," my aunt said. "If you fail to convert them, you must kill every vampire in that wretched place."

"Any active necromancers would be lobotomized." When a vampire piloted by a navigator died before the navigator severed the connection, the navigator's mind couldn't deal with the death.

"Perfect," Erra said.

"That's not who I am and that's not what I do."

"Then bring them under your banner. You can't dance around hard decisions anymore. Your father won't."

Convert a bunch of Masters of the Dead who think they run the world. Piece of cake.

Adora came down the stairs. She was wearing an old pair of my jeans and a T-shirt. Julie must've given her clothes yesterday.

I turned to Curran. "I want to hit the Order first. Will you come with me?"

"Yes."

I turned to Adora. "I want you to come with me, too."

An hour later Curran, Adora, and I walked into the Order of Merciful Aid. It looked nothing like I remembered. The gray paint was gone. The carpet, too. The hallway was painted light beige; the floor was sealed concrete. Even Maxine's desk had undergone a face-lift—brand-new and flanked by a luxuriously ergonomic office chair. The old prim secretary smiled at me.

"We're here to see the knight-protector."

"Go ahead," she said.

We walked into Nick's office. When Ted Moynohan occupied it, it was a dark cave decorated with all things Texas. Gone were the burgundy drapes, the massive desk of cherry wood and samples of barbed wire on the wall. Now it was a wide, well-lit space, with plants and pale, thin curtains. Nick sat behind a desk of blond wood. He raised his head as we approached.

"Yes?"

"This is Knight-protector Nick Feldman," I told Adora. "He runs the Order's Atlanta chapter. Do you know what the Order is?"

She nodded.

"Nick worked undercover in Hugh d'Ambray's inner circle for two years."

I turned to Nick.

"This is Adora. She is sahanu."

He sat up straighter. The name made an impression.

I had thought the best way was to take baby steps. I was wrong. If I didn't clear things up now, she would keep sacrificing herself for my sake.

I took a deep breath and looked Nick in the eye. "I'd like you to explain to her exactly what my father and I are."

Nick smiled, and there was not a shred of humor in that grin.

Nick talked for almost forty-five minutes. Sometimes I added things to clarify, sometimes Curran did. To say Nick didn't sugarcoat things would be an understatement. In his two years undercover, he had been forced to see things and do things that violated the very core of who he was. He let his hate flow.

Adora sat quietly through it all, her face stoic. Sometimes she looked to me or Curran for confirmation. When he finished, she said, "Thank you." I couldn't tell if any of it made an impact.

Nick fixed me with his stare. "The Pack burned Nimrod's base."

The Order always had good intel. "Yes."

"He isn't going to let it slide."

"No."

"When and where?" Nick asked.

"At the Keep," Curran said. "Direct assault with overwhelming force, as soon as the new magic wave hits. In daylight."

"Blood is best viewed in daylight," Nick said.

I nodded. "He wants the shapeshifters to see their relatives die in gory detail."

"We could use help," Curran said.

"We'll be there," Nick said. "As an independent force."

"Thank you," I told him.

"This doesn't mean I like you," he said.

"I don't need you to like me, Nick. I need you to show up at the battlefield and kill as many of my father's troops as you can."

Nick smiled.

Outside Adora looked at me. "Did that man tell the truth?"

"Yes."

"And your father, Sharrum? He lied?"

"Yes."

"There is no heaven?"

"I don't know if there is a heaven," I said. "But I know that you won't get there by serving my father. There are many different kinds of evil. Some people are evil because they like to cause pain. Some people are evil because they are selfish and care only about themselves. He is the worst kind of evil. He believes he knows how to bring about a better future, and, if he has to, he will pave the road to it with corpses of innocent people. He has no boundaries. There is nothing he won't do to get his way."

"What about you?" Her eyes narrowed.

"I'm trying not to be evil. Sometimes I succeed. Sometimes I don't."

"So you're like him?"

"Yes. When I didn't kill you the first time, it was because I acted exactly like him."

"But you saved me the second time, too?"

"Slavery is wrong, Adora. People should be free to make their own choices. They might be bad choices, but it doesn't matter. I didn't want you to die before you realized that there's a whole life you could live on your own terms. You don't have to take anyone's orders. You are in charge of yourself. I broke my father's hold on you. I'm responsible for you. I'll try to help you as much as I can."

"Because you feel guilty?"

"Because it's the right thing to do," Curran said.

She narrowed her eyes. "How do I know you and that man aren't lying?"

"You don't," I said.

"You have to look at what everyone has to gain," Curran said. "Kate says that Roland is an evil liar. Roland says that his blood is divine and will get you to the happy afterlife. One of them has to be lying. If we suppose that Roland is lying, what benefit does he derive from it?"

Adora frowned. "My loyalty."

Curran nodded. "He gets to use you and your skills. And if you suppose that Kate is lying?"

"She derives no benefit," Adora said. "If I believe her, I won't serve her."

"Yes. She has no incentive to lie. People go through the trouble of lying to get something they want. Kate doesn't want anything from you, but she feels responsible for you. She wants you to have a life that's your own."

She pondered it. "I'll follow you, Kate. I need to follow someone. It's too much change all at once. But I'll think. And I'll find out more, so I can decide who's lying. And if I decide not to follow you anymore, I will leave."

"Fair enough," I said.

"And I won't call you Sharrim anymore, even in my head. You're not my queen."

"That's fine."

"And you will ask me if you want me to do something."

"Will you please come with me to the Casino to impress the Masters of the Dead?"

"Yes," Adora said. "Yes, I will."


WE STOPPED BY the Guild next. Curran went to talk to the mercs and I made a beeline for Barabas's office. Barabas had posted the sign-up sheet for the battle. There were seven names on it already. It was hanging between next week's menu and the petition to add free weights to the training yard. There was a deep and meaningful life lesson about the nature of human existence in there somewhere, but I didn't feel like looking for it.

"How are we going to pay them?" I asked.

"Battle spoils," Barabas said.

I stared at him.

"It's a time-honored tradition." Barabas bared his teeth at me. You could almost see the mongoose under his skin.

"Can I talk to Christopher?" I asked.

"He's his own man."

I lowered my voice. "How are things?"

"Horribly awkward. Also confusing. I used to have to keep track of when he bathed and ate. Now he's patrolling the grounds. We discussed your father last night. Christopher may be the smartest man I've ever spoken to."

"And that's bad how?"

Barabas heaved a sigh. "It's complicated."

"I thought you found intelligence attractive."

"I do. As I said, complicated."

I stepped outside the office and waved at Christopher on the beam.

He dropped down. His wings snapped open at the last moment and he landed gently on the floor.

"Show-off," Barabas muttered.

"I'm going to the Casino," I said. "I'm going to try to convince them to fight on our side."

Christopher frowned. "It will be difficult."

"The alternative is for them to reinforce Roland."

"You could kill them." He studied me.

"Yes, that would be the smart thing to do, but I'm not going to kill them. If I fail, I will let them leave the city."

"Why?"

"Because there is a difference between war and murder. Killing them would be murder."

"Do you want my help?"

"Yes. No pressure. I understand if you say no."

Christopher looked down at his bare feet, worn-out jeans, and white T-shirt.

"I'll need different clothes. A suit."

"We can get that."

"Okay," he said, and started toward the exit.

I leaned into Barabas's office. "Do you want to come help pick out a suit for Christopher?"

"No," Barabas said firmly, tapping a stack of papers against his desk to even it out.

"Why?"

"Because I don't need to see him in a suit."

Curran walked over to me. "Parks came back from the Casino. He says they are refusing customers."

They had been given the order to evacuate. We had to get to them now.


I SAT IN the passenger seat of our car and watched Julie walk toward the Casino. The beautiful white palace all but floated above the parking lot. She strode between the long stretches of rectangular fountains carrying the green and blue standard.

Next to me Curran sat quietly, watching Julie. He reached over and covered my hand with his.

"Nervous, ass kicker?"

"No. I don't want to kill them." I would if I had to. I wished I didn't have to. The technology was up. If I went in there during magic, I could've used it to impress the navigators.

"You can do this. You will walk in there like you own the place and you will kick ass. Don't let them think and don't give them any reason to doubt. Walk in and hit them with everything you've got."

In my head, I kept going through the People's leadership. The lineup had changed over the years. Currently, there were eight Masters of the Dead. First, Ghastek and Rowena.

Orlando Beasley, a trim, short black man with smart eyes and a quiet, cultured voice. Constance Hyde, an older woman with a platinum head of hair who always looked mildly displeased. Ryan Kelly, tall, well-built and well-groomed, every inch a CEO, except for his purple Mohawk. Filipa, a Hispanic woman, about my age, who wore glasses with a red rim and never said anything in my presence. Toakasu Kakau, a dark-eyed woman of Tongan ancestry, in her forties, with a white smile and the kind of no-nonsense gaze that stopped you in your tracks. Dennis Pillman, a tall, thin man with a two-thousand-dollar haircut, whose suits were always a size too large.

Julie walked through the gates into the Casino.

"It's time," my aunt said in my ear.

I stepped out of the car and followed Julie. Curran walked next to me. Adora shadowed me on the right. She'd changed back into her sahanu outfit, but instead of purple she'd now added a green-and-blue scarf. I didn't want to touch that with a ten-foot pole.

Christopher Steed walked on Curran's left. Barabas had no idea what he was missing. The coal-black suit combined with Christopher's nearly white hair made a killer impression. The seamstress in the shop had actually stammered while cutting and sewing the slits for his wings. Time was short, but the suit was a necessity. The Masters of the Dead had to recognize him.

"Feel the land," Erra said in my ear. "Feel it breathe."

It felt odd after last night. Before, the land was an ocean, and I stood within it, distinct and separate, like a rock. Now the ocean and I had melded. I was no longer a rock. I was . . . I didn't know what the hell I was. A tangle of seaweed, a current, something that stretched to the farthest reaches of my land. Still distinct, but no longer separate. And I couldn't touch any of that magic with the technology up. Not even a drop. My aunt had been clear on that.

"This is your land," Erra said. "You protect it. Your blood waters it. You've bonded with it for months. Reach deep inside you and sacrifice for its sake."

The Casino loomed, the vampires within it a constellation of bright red lights in my mind. The two men guarding the entrance saw us coming and stared straight ahead, determined not to notice us. Denial was the better part of valor.

I needed to convince Ghastek and the Masters of the Dead. Once they committed themselves, the rest would follow. I had to get them to see me not as Kate Daniels, but as my father's daughter.

I walked onto the Casino's main floor. Usually the din of slots hung above the floor, but today the casino was completely silent. Journeymen moved back and forth, carrying boxes. Julie stood in the middle of the open space, holding her standard. My standard. The journeymen ignored her.

Rowena emerged from the side entrance and approached me. She was the only woman I knew who could be equally radiant in a gown or a business pantsuit like she wore now.

"Sharrim, we are honored by your presence. You caught us at a busy time, unfortunately."

"Oh?" "Oh" was nice and neutral.

"We've received some orders from headquarters." Rowena stepped closer to me and whispered, her voice urgent, "You should leave, Kate. It's not safe for you here."

"He's pulling them out of the city," Christopher said.

Rowena glanced at him and clamped her hand over her mouth. Her eyes widened. She backed away toward the stairwell and almost walked into Ghastek as he descended the stairs. The remaining six Masters of the Dead followed Ghastek. The gang was all here. They looked like they had left a board meeting.

Ghastek saw us. His gaze fixed on Christopher.

"Nice touch, Kate. But this man is not Christopher Steed," he said, making sure his voice carried. "This is Saiman. This woman isn't sahanu, although she's dressed like one. Clothes are easy to acquire."

Ghastek two, Kate zero.

"Five miles, sixteen hundred and thirty-five yards," Christopher said.

Ghastek winced.

"What is that?" Ryan Kelly asked.

"That's his real range," Christopher said. "This is how far he can send a vampire before risking losing the connection with its mind."

"You're wrong," Filipa said. Apparently she was able to talk.

"No," Christopher said. "That's why I passed you over, Matthew."

Ghastek took a step back. Christopher had used his real name.

"It wasn't politics and it wasn't your petty fight with Kowalski. It was because you lied and shortened your range by two hundred yards on your official evaluations. You didn't want me to know the full extent of your power. I required complete transparency."

Curran smiled next to me.

"Very well," Ghastek said. "You have Steed. This changes nothing."

Ha!

"Should Adora also demonstrate her skills?" I asked, my voice so sweet you could dip a pancake into it. "Would you like to pick a target?"

"No. Now that the theatrics are out of the way, what can we do for you?" Ghastek said.

Here we go. "My father intends to attack the Keep at the beginning of the next magic wave. I intend to defend Atlanta against this invasion. I'd like you to join me."

"You expect us to fight?" Constance asked.

"Yes."

"Against your father?" Ryan Kelly asked. Even his purple Mohawk seemed incredulous.

"Yes."

Toakase shook her head.

Ghastek raised his hand. "No."

"Think about it," Curran said. "It will make sense to you."

Ghastek's eyes narrowed. He was running through possible scenarios in his head, trying to figure out what he'd missed. Maybe we'd get lucky and he would talk himself into it. *Reach deep inside and sacrifice.* I wish I knew what the hell she was talking about, because it would sure help right about now.

Pillman checked his watch. "This is ridiculous. After this morning's phone call, we're under no obligation to humor her any longer. Just throw her and her has-been shapeshifter out."

Erra tore into existence in front of Pillman and backhanded him. The Master of the Dead flew back and fell on his ass.

"Bow, worm!" My aunt's magic raged. "Bow before my niece. You're not fit to lick her boots."

The Masters of the Dead froze, horrified. Rowena's face turned completely white. Next to me Adora unsheathed her katana. Blood-red wings snapped out of Christopher's back.

A sharp calculation was taking place in Ghastek's eyes. Above us vampires sprinted as he pulled them to him. Julie was a full twenty feet from me. This was about to turn bloody.

Now. I had to do it now.

*Show them that you love them above all others.*

I did love this land. I loved the city and the people within it. That's why I fought so hard to protect it. I couldn't ask it to give its magic, but I could give up a little of my own. I reached deep inside me and took the magic the same way I had taken it from the land, except now it came from within my soul.

It hurt.

"There is no need to shout." I stepped toward Pillman, and my aunt moved out of my way. The Master of the Dead stared at me. His pupils widened. I reached for him. My hand almost glowed, as if dusted with gold. "Are you hurt?"

He reached out, hesitant, and touched my hand. I grasped his fingers. "Rise."

"You . . ." Pillman stood up, his face stunned.

"Behold In-Shinar," Julie intoned. "Daughter of the Builder of Towers, niece of the City Eater, Guardian of Atlanta."

Burning my own magic hurt so much. I couldn't let them see the pain.

"Don't be afraid," I told Pillman. "I'm not my father. He

doesn't value you. I do. He is far, unreachable, and distant. But I am here."

He swallowed, his fingers fastened on my hand. I motioned toward the others. Pillman took one hesitant step back. Then another. That seemed to be as far from me as he was willing to go.

"My father doesn't recognize your talents." I looked straight at Ghastek. "I do. I know what you're capable of."

Their faces looked torn between hope and fear, caught in some weird emotion I couldn't pin down. The technology was up and I stood among them, emanating magic. And each second I did cost me more than they would ever know. It was that or the city would fall.

They recognized this magic. Some of them had seen it before, because I saw the excitement and fear in their eyes. They were drawn to it like moths to a flame. It was the magic of my blood, the one that made the vampires possible, except now it was directed at them. They wanted my approval. I sensed it. Beyond them journeymen stood unmoving, shocked.

I finally pinned down their expressions. Awe.

Rowena knelt. Filipa was praying, her voice an urgent whisper.

Ghastek walked toward me and went down on one knee, looking up at me.

"What are you doing?" he whispered.

"Saving all of us from being drowned in our blood and my father's fire," I whispered. "He's going to throw you and your vampires at the Keep. You will be decimated. Your vampires will be gone; your position within Atlanta will be eliminated. If you survive, you will have to start from scratch, Ghastek."

His face told me he didn't want to start from scratch.

"You're outside the inner circle. It will take you years to climb higher. Even if you become his Legatus, your life will be short. He will never care about you, Ghastek. I care. You are my friend. You are the best there is at what you do. This is your chance. Don't do it because of what's happening now. Do it because it makes sense."

"You know my price," Ghastek whispered.

"I know." The irony was that he already had what he was asking for. He was my friend. I already cared about him. I would already do whatever I could to keep him breathing.

"Swear it," Ghastek said.

I smiled at him. My voice rang. "Rise, Legatus of my Legion. Work with me, advise me, be my friend, and you will live forever."

THE AIR OUTSIDE the Casino tasted sweet.

"How did you do that?" Curran asked.

"She burned her own magic," my aunt said. "If she were a normal human, you would've seen her aging."

The look on Curran's face was indescribable.

"Relax, half-breed," Erra said. "She has lifetimes to spare. That wasn't half-bad for your first time. You'll get better with practice."

"I won't."

"Why not?"

"Because I have no plans to conquer. I don't want any more troops. I don't want to do any more persuading."

"You say that now."

I turned toward her. "Look inside me."

Erra's eyes narrowed. "You mean it. You have no ambition."

"No. I don't want to conquer or rule. I want to contain my father."

"This will be interesting," my aunt said.

Behind us the banner of In-Shinar, a field of pure emerald green with a single blue stripe, streamed from the spire above the Casino's walls.

THE PACK ARRIVED in time for dinner. One moment our kitchen was empty and Curran and I were quietly cooking dinner, while Julie tried to make it through some ancient text Erra decided she should read. The next it was filled with shapeshifters. Jim and Dali, Robert, and Andrea and Raphael. Jim's face was flat. His eyes told me that he hadn't come because he wanted to patch things up with me. He'd come because his back was against the wall. Our friendship was truly over.

"Where is the baby?" I asked.

"With about a dozen babysitters in the bouda clan house," Andrea said. "You just want me for my baby."

"Yep, you nailed it."

"Peace offering," Robert said, holding an envelope out to Julie.

"What is it?" she asked.

"Jezebel's confession," Robert said. "We found it in her quarters. Some of it is addressed to you."

She grabbed the envelope and bolted to the living room couch with it. I could still see her. That was the fun of an open floor plan. We were never too far from each other.

"Give me a CliffsNotes version?" I asked.

"Jezebel, Salome, and the woman who was supposedly their mother joined the Pack when Salome was seventeen and Jezebel was fifteen," Robert said. "Clan Bouda failed to verify their background."

"Oh please," Andrea said. "Please make it sound like it is all our fault."

"The clan had very low numbers at the time," Raphael said. "This woman showed up, told my mother a sob story about running away from abuse, and offered herself and two able fighters who were almost adults. My mother took them in."

"He approved it." Andrea pointed to Curran.

Curran shrugged.

"Veronica, Jezebel and Salome's supposed mother, left the Pack about four years after joining," Andrea said. "According to Aunt B's records, she met a man from Montana and went with him. Salome and Jezebel stayed behind."

"Jezebel had written a summary of her life before joining the Pack. Does the word 'sahanu' mean anything to you?" Robert asked.

"Julie, can you get Adora for me?" I asked. Julie got up and left the living room.

I went into the hallway, took a framed photograph off the wall, and brought it into the kitchen. It showed Julie and her friend Maddie, smiling and making cute faces at the camera. Jezebel loomed to the side, watching over them.

Julie returned with Adora. I showed her the photograph. "Do you recognize this woman?"

"Isabel," Adora said. "She and her sister, Leanna, were in the fort with me. They transform into hyenas."

"What happened to them?"

"One day they disappeared. We were told they were needed elsewhere."

"Thank you." I turned to Robert. "Sahanu is an order of assassins created by my father."

"He must've pulled them out of training and inserted them into the Pack," Curran said.

"That appears to be the case," Robert said.

"It says here she did it for me," Julie said, her voice quiet. She took the papers and went upstairs.

"Jezebel's assignment was to get as close as possible to the Beast Lord," Robert said. "When Kate entered the picture, Jezebel saw an opportunity. She and Salome put on a show for Aunt B and afterward Salome suggested that Jezebel should be reassigned. Then her assignment changed. Julie became her priority. She loved Julie very much. She wanted to separate with you but was ordered to remain with the Pack. Eventually, she was ordered to kill Andrea's child. She refused and was told that Julie would suffer if Jezebel failed."

"Where is Salome now?" Curran asked.

"Dead," Jim said. "Anybody who touches Dali is dead. Anybody who helps them is dead."

Dali sighed. "I'm okay. I'm here, I'm alive, and I would appreciate it if everyone butted out and stopped making a giant deal out of this."

It hit me. Jim was an excellent Beast Lord: smart, efficient, and painfully fair. He would be admired and respected, but he would never be loved the way Curran was. Curran had wanted to be loved, needed it because he'd come to the Pack as an orphaned kid. Jim didn't want to be loved by anyone except Dali. He didn't need friends. He didn't want anything else. Only Dali.

"Why are you here?" Curran asked.

"You know why," Jim said. "You've taken the People. Are we at war?"

Oh my God, you moron.

Dali elbowed Jim in the ribs. "What he meant to say was he is sorry that duties of his office and his own paranoid nature caused him to overreact."

Jim looked like someone had hit him on the nose with a rolled-up newspaper. "Yes."

"And he knows that both of you have been his friends, of which he doesn't have many, for years. He is aware that you would never do anything to harm us or the Pack and that you have protected us on several occasions and have been injured as a result several times."

"Yes," Jim said.

Dali looked at him. Clearly, there was more.

Jim turned to me. "I apologize."

"Not a problem," I told him.

Jim faced Curran. "And I would be honored to still be best man at your wedding."

Jim was who he was. This was the best we were going to get, and we wouldn't even have gotten that without Dali.

Curran smiled. It was a bright, infectious smile, the kind that could change the mood of an entire hall of shapeshifters. I had seen it in action before. It signaled that all was forgiven. The tension in Jim's body eased. But I knew Curran better than Jim did. Curran would never forget this.

"Who else would be my best man?" Curran said.

The mood in the room lightened.

Curran leaned back. "You burned Roland's castle. He will retaliate the morning after the next magic wave hits."

"We'll be there to defend you because you are within our borders," I said.

"We're coming either way, Jim," Curran said. "Without Kate's protection, he will shatter the Keep with magic."

Jim looked at me. "Can you stop him?"

"I can stop his actions against the land itself. I can't stop him from physically riding onto the battlefield and sniping people with his magic."

"Roland will bring an overwhelming force," Curran said. "It's a show of strength. And he's angry. He wants to crush you."

"He will breach the walls at the very least," Jim said.

"You should let him," Curran said.

Jim thought about it. "Yes. I should."

Curran got up and got a piece of paper. I reached for the phone.

"Who are you calling?" Jim asked.

"Ghastek and then Roman. If we're going to plan, they should be in on it."


FIVE DAYS LATER I stood on top of the Keep's main tower. The sun rose above the horizon, its first rays banishing the twilight. Clear, crystalline blue sky spread above me. The woods around the Keep stood still. Birds sang. It was so peaceful.

Almost a week had passed since Jim's attack on my father's tower. The first magic wave came and went without any action from my father, but last night magic hit hard and Jim's scouts reported a large force heading our way. This was it.

Somewhere within those woods, Curran and the bulk of our forces hid.

Christopher waited next to me. Behind me the seven Masters of the Dead stood, each with a single vampire parked by their feet like a mutated hairless cat. Jim put renders all around us with Desandra in the lead. We wouldn't be able to enter the main Keep, but he understood what was about to happen. If my father attacked with his magic and if I blocked that attack—which was a pretty big "if" at this point—people had to see it. The Masters of the Dead had to see it.

The Keep below us swarmed with shapeshifters. Jim was front and center, Dali next to him.

Jim had shared intelligence from his scouts. My father couldn't pull the entire Golden Legion together on short notice, but he had put together a force of over two hundred undead, enough to decimate an army five times that size. He'd kept human reserves in Virginia, something none of us knew about, and they had arrived last night. Together with his mages, the Pack scouts estimated that he was fielding almost three thousand combatants.

Jim had called for a complete mobilization. Everyone older than eighteen would fight. Anyone above sixteen could volunteer. He ended up with around six hundred troops. We brought one hundred twenty vampires to the fight. Ghastek had gotten every journeyman with half a hint of talent and put them on the field. He stood next to me now, the skin on his face too tight.

We were outnumbered and outgunned, several times to one.

"Wondering if you shouldn't have rolled the dice?" I asked.

"No. It's too late."

A red light claimed the horizon, glowing like a second sunrise. Wolves fled from the woods and sprinted to the safety of the Keep.

"It begins," my aunt said in my ear.

If I failed, everything was over.

In the distance trees collapsed as if torn aside by an invisible tornado half a mile wide. Smoke billowed, white and thick, and lightning crackled within it. My father was coming.

"Take and hold," Erra's voice whispered.

"Hey, Kate? You're nobody's bitch," Desandra said.

Behind me, one of the navigators drew a tense breath.

The smoke was almost to the boundary. My father's fury loomed, a magic storm devouring all before it.

I felt every drop of life within the land I claimed. It was enough to make you go mad.

The storm rolled across the land, swallowing the distance in hungry gulps. A hundred yards.

Eighty.

Sixty.

A sound like the roar of a distant waterfall rolled through the land.

Forty.

*Take . . .*

Twenty.

Below me in the Keep, the shapeshifters stood frozen.

The trees before the boundary collapsed, snapped like toothpicks, and were sucked into the storm.

*And hold!*

Magic shifted like a mountain that somehow moved. It wasn't an isolated stream or a burst. The entirety of the magic around us changed somehow, and everyone felt it.

My father's storm splashed against an invisible boundary and stopped. Smoke billowed. Lightning struck, licking at the boundary with glowing snake tongues. The storm didn't move.

It pushed.

I held.

The storm melted into nothing.

Ghastek laughed.

I released the magic.

The ground trembled.

*Hold.*

The budding earthquake died.

A ball of fire appeared in the sky. It hurtled toward us, an enraged inferno of red and yellow, threatening to demolish everything in its path.

*Hold.*

The impact shook me. The fireball evaporated in midair.

Ghastek grinned at me. "My queen, you have inspired me greatly. I shall now go and do what the Legatus does."

"Don't strain anything," I told him.

"I won't."

The vampire picked him up, grasped a metal pole on the

side of the tower, and slid down. The other Masters of the Dead followed suit. Pillman lingered.

"Yes?" I asked him.

"I . . ." he faltered.

I let the magic suffuse me. "Are you afraid?"

"No," he said.

"I'm always afraid," I told him. "Before every battle. Use the fear. It will make you sharp."

He nodded, and his vampire took him off the tower.

"You're starting to scare me," Desandra said.

"That's one off the bucket list." I took a deep breath and yelled at the top of my lungs. "Chernobog! Living darkness, father of monsters, I ask for your aid in battle. I invoke your name. Lend us your power. Those who are afraid, let them pray to you and hear their prayers."

Okay. The invocation was done.

"He's coming," Erra said.

In the distance the trees fell. Five huge shaggy forms burst out of the forest, their massive tusks wrapped in metal. Behind them vampires galloped with their odd jerky gait, followed by human troops.

"Are those fucking mammoths?" Desandra asked.

"Yes." Enormous, colossal mammoths, bigger than any reconstructions I had seen. Where the hell did my father get mammoths?

Desandra's eyes lit up. "Kate, get off the tower, so I can get down there. I've never killed a mammoth."

"Christopher?" I asked.

He leaned back. Blood-red wings snapped open from his back.

"Whoa." Desandra backed away.

Christopher picked me up and leapt off the tower. We glided and turned right. I craned my neck. The ground gave under the leading mammoth, and the massive beast collapsed into a hidden trench. A chorus of eerie cackles filled the air. Jim had put boudas into the trenches.

Christopher's eyes turned blood-red.

"Are you okay?" I asked him.

"The battlefield is calling." His voice wasn't his own.

"Can you hold on for a little while longer?"

"I'll try."

We swung toward a large oak. Christopher plunged down and landed, setting me down next to Barabas and Julie. Barabas looked like he'd jumped out of some D&D book featuring thieves and assassins. He wore leather armor and carried a sharp knife. A dark rag covered the bottom part of his face. Above it, his eyes were blood-red with demonic horizontal pupils. Julie stood holding the reins of our horses. She would be riding a roan mare. We all agreed that Peanut was much too beloved to take into battle. I would be riding Hugh's mean Friesian. No horse on this battlefield would stand up to him.

Around me a sea of vampires waited, each bloodsucker crouching, perfectly still like a statue, a stripe of bright green running down their spines.

Christopher closed his wings around him and walked off, pacing, gripping his left forearm with his right hand so hard, his fingers turned the flesh completely white. Barabas walked over to him. I couldn't tell what was being said, but I caught Barabas's voice, soothing, calming . . .

A battle horn roared.

I ran up to the oak and climbed up the rope ladder Jim's people had conveniently left in place for me and clambered to the wooden platform at the top. Next to me a vampire crouched.

"Ghastek?"

"Of course," Ghastek's dry voice said from the vampire mouth. "Did you expect Santa Claus?"

I gave him my hard stare and turned to the field. We were in the woods on the south side. The Keep was a little to the left of me, and my father's advancing forces were to the right. Somewhere to my far right, Curran and his forces waited. I had kissed him this morning and didn't want to let go.

A battle raged less than half a mile from us, across the open ground. Two mammoths made it past the trenches and battered the Keep walls while waves of my father's troops splashed against it. Vampires swarmed up the stones and shapeshifters met them among the parapets. The fortress held.

No sign of my father.

"Erra?" I said softly.

She appeared next to me.

"I cannot tell you how disturbing this is," Ghastek said.

"You're telling me. You know she killed my favorite mule?"

"You killed me," Erra said. "I think we're even."

My father wouldn't commit to the field until he was reasonably certain of a victory. And that wouldn't happen until the Keep's front door was kicked in.

The bodies of shapeshifters fell from the wall. Argh.

"Your lion built it too well," Erra told me.

"Yes, everything is my fault."

"What's going on with Steed?" Ghastek asked.

"He's having difficulty with bloodlust."

"It is really him?"

"Yes."

"Life moves in mysterious ways," Ghastek said.

Blood smeared the gray stones of the Keep, as the mammoths threw themselves against it again and again. The left side of the wall trembled, rocked, like a rotten tooth ready to come out, and collapsed. My father's troops flooded into the gap and broke like a wave on shapeshifter claws and teeth.

*Come on.*

Bodies flew. People screamed.

*Come on, Father. Come to the slaughter.*

Minutes ticked by.

More bodies.

A new line of troops spilled onto the field and in its center a shiny chariot sped, drawn by horned horses.

"Is your father riding a gold chariot?" Ghastek asked.

"He's a product of his times. It's what he grew up with."

"There is nothing wrong with a gold chariot," Erra said. "It's meant to be symbolic."

We watched the line of troops advance, gaining ground

against the isolated clumps of shapeshifters. Slowly Jim's forces retreated to the Keep.

Not yet.

The trenches emptied as boudas scrambled toward the Keep. Jim's forces broke and ran for the safety of the walls, leaving their dead on the battlefield.

Now.

I looked down. "Now, Christopher!"

He shot into the air, spinning as he rose. Barabas waved at me and sprinted through the woods, heading east to where Curran's forces waited.

The trees across from us, on the other side of the battlefield and to the right, turned black. Dark magic gathered there, cold and terrible. The trees rustled and a gigantic black dragon head emerged from the trees. My father raised his hand. Golden light poured from it, shielding the troops directly around him.

Aspid slithered across the field. Roman rode atop his head, feet anchored, his arms opened wide. A black crown rested on his hair. Behind him black smoke stretched like an impossibly long mantle. A wall of black flames, thirty feet tall and twenty feet wide, cut the field in two in the dragon's wake.

I scrambled off the tree. Two vampires stepped forward, spread a sheet of clear plastic on the ground, and knelt on it. I felt the navigators let go and grabbed their minds. The bloodsuckers opened their throats in unison and I crushed their minds as they bled out.

I sliced my arm, let my blood mix with that of the undead, and felt it catch on fire with my power. The red spiraled up my legs, climbing higher, over my thighs, over my waist, forming armor. It felt clunky.

"Awful," Erra said. "You are an embarrassment. Stand still."

My aunt circled me, words of a long-forgotten language falling from her mouth. It felt like forever, but it took only seconds. When I looked down at myself, I wore blood armor. My aunt stopped in front of me and rested her ghostly fingers under my chin.

"Go and free yourself from your father."

"I will," I told her.

I swung onto the Friesian. He pawed the ground, his nostrils flaring. Julie was already on her mare, her eyes wild and scared.

"Raise the banner."

She raised the flag, and the green standard of In-Shinar fluttered above us.

I let the stallion go. He tore out of the woods at a gallop. We burst into the open. The wall of black flames rose to the right of us, and within it monstrous mouths and claws writhed, grabbing any who strayed too close and tearing into their bodies. We had cut my father's forces in half. I was on the Keep side of the flame wall, and Curran and his mercs, the Order, and Jim's reserve were on the other.

More vampires poured from the other side of the woods. Roland's troops still pressed their attack on the Keep, not realizing what was happening.

Above the Keep Christopher dived from between the clouds, his wings opened wide, like a fallen angel. He opened his mouth and screamed.

The mass of troops churned, as hundreds of men and creatures tried to flee in unison, away from the Keep and toward the smoke. Christopher screamed again and again, his shriek gripping my spine with an icy hand even from this distance. The offensive broke apart. People fled. Christopher swooped down, grasped a writhing body, and flew up, burying his fangs in the man's neck.

We tore into the retreating troops. I swung Sarrat, slicing, severing necks and backs. Around me vampires swarmed without a sound, silent, merciless, slaughtering everything in their path.

The field was chaos. Men, beasts, shapeshifters, and animals clashed, screaming, snarling, and ripping at each other. The air smelled like blood. Harpies dived through the sky. One aimed for me and a winged form shot out from the clouds and sliced it in half with a flaming sword. Teddy Jo. I didn't think he'd come.

A vampire headed for me. Not one of ours. I rode it down. The stallion stomped on the undead, and I finished it, crushing its skull with my magic. Across the field, green and bare undead crashed against each other, fighting silent duels.

A massive beast shaped like a leopard but twice that size leapt at me. The impact of its weight took me off the horse. Claws scraped my blood armor. I thrust Sarrat between its ribs, twisted, heaved it off me, and rolled to my feet.

A ring of fighters waited for me.

They charged me and I danced. It was a beautiful dance, of blood and steel and severed life. My breathing evened out. The world was crystal clear, the sounds crisp, the colors vivid. Everything I tried worked. Every strike found its target. Every thrust pierced a body. They cut and slashed, but I didn't wait for them. I kept cutting, losing myself in the simple rhythm.

They'd come here to kill me. They died instead. Corpses piled up at my feet. My aunt was laughing. And then they broke and ran.

I looked up. The wall of black flames was thinning. I could almost see through it.

"Retreat!" I screamed. "Retreat now!"

The green-striped vampires fled from the field toward the Keep. Once the wall went down, my father would be able to reach them. The bloodsuckers would die by the dozens and so would the navigators piloting them.

I turned. The black smoke had dissipated. The entire front of my father's army was gone. Mammoths lay like burial mounds of fur. Bodies, vampire and human, sprawled on the grass.

Most of the remaining army gathered around my father, forming a mass of bodies. I saw Curran roaring, enormous, demonic, tearing into monsters left and right. The mercs followed in his wake.

My father froze in his chariot, his face bloodless. One moment he had a vanguard and now it was all gone. He wasn't looking at me. He was looking to the left. I turned my head and saw the sea of green-and-blue banners the bloodsuckers had left thrust into the dirt as they retreated.

**"Glory to In-Shinar!"**

The hair on the back of my neck rose.

I spun around.

Julie sat on her horse, holding my banner. Her voice rolled, charged with power. **"Glory to In-Shinar!"**

The air screamed as the first blast from Andrea's sorcerous ballistae tore through it. The green missiles shrieked over my head and pounded the front of my father's remaining force. Bodies flew, burning with magic fire. Andrea's ace in the hole.

My father raised his hands. A sphere of light appeared in front of him, shielding the troops. The missiles crashed into it, their magic splashing over the light and falling down, powerless.

My father brought his hands together. The corpse of the mammoth about two hundred yards to the left of me shuddered. Magic built within it, spilling out as thin green smoke. I reached for the magic around me and froze it, but the green smoke thickened. Whatever he was doing couldn't be blocked by the land's defenses. I started toward it, climbing over bodies.

The carcass burst. Three creatures emerged, clad in tattered rags. A foul magic wrapped around them. I had felt many fucked-up things over the years, but this . . . this felt like death. Every instinct I had screamed at me to turn and run the other way.

"Plaguewalkers," my aunt snarled in my ear.

"Shapeshifters are resistant to disease."

"Not this disease."

I ran, scrambling over the bodies.

The plaguewalkers started toward the Keep.

A ballista missile smashed into the middle of the three and exploded. They kept walking. Shit. Magic didn't do anything. They had to be physically cut down.

Shapeshifters burst from the hole in the Keep wall. The first shapeshifter, a lean wolf in warrior form, reached the leading plaguewalker. Ten feet from it, the wolf collapsed, clawing at his face. Another shapeshifter, another fall.

Where the hell was my stupid horse?

The plaguewalkers moved forward. Arrows flew from the Keep and sank into the plaguewalkers, but they kept going. They would keep walking, just like that, until they walked straight into the Keep.

A huge Kodiak bear charged through the shapeshifter ranks. The leading plaguewalker raised his hand.

I heard Curran roar.

Lesions split Mahon's hide. He kept running, too fast, too massive to stop. Pus slid from the wounds, falling to the ground.

I was running as fast as I could.

The bear tore into the plaguewalkers. The massive paw crushed the first one's skull.

All of Mahon's fur was gone now. Pus drenched his sides. The great bear of Atlanta spun and slapped the second plaguewalker's head. The creature's skull cracked, like a broken egg.

The third plaguewalker raised his hands. A stream of foul magic poured from it. The flesh on Mahon's sides rotted away. Bone gaped through the holes. Oh my God.

The bear threw himself onto the last creature and missed, collapsing. I lunged between the plaguewalker and Mahon. The creature stared at me, its eyes glowing green dots on a rotting face.

I sliced. The plaguewalker flitted away, as if made of air.

The blood armor on my hands turned black. Bits of it began to chip away.

I thrust Sarrat into the plaguewalker's chest and withdrew. Foul slime dripped off the blade. The creature seemed no worse for wear. I wasn't doing enough damage.

Curran landed atop the plaguewalker and locked his hands on the creature's shoulders. The plaguewalker shrieked. Curran's hands blistered. He roared and tore the creature in half. The pieces of the plaguewalker's body went flying.

The first corpse was re-forming.

"Curran!" I screamed, pointing with my sword.

He spun around. The first plaguewalker was rising like a zombie from a horror movie.

A white tiger landed next to us. Dali opened her mouth and roared. Magic emanated from her, sliding over me like an icy burst of clear water. The pieces of the plaguewalkers rose up, melting as if the air itself consumed them.

She purified them. Wow.

I dropped to the ground by Mahon. The Bear shrank into a man. The skin on his torso was missing. His hands and face were a mess of boils. Oh God. Oh my God.

Curran, still in warrior form, knelt and cradled the dying man.

Mahon saw him. His lips shook. He struggled to say something.

"Best . . . son. Best . . . could ever have."

"Shut up," Curran told him. "You're not going anywhere."

"Best . . ." Mahon whispered.

Nasrin knelt by Mahon, chanting.

Curran rose. His gaze fixed on my father's chariot.

My father had to die.

"We take the shot!" I yelled at him.

He glared at me, his eyes pure gold.

"I'm on my land. I'm strongest here. We can end this now!"

A pale light slid over his body. He fell on all fours, growing larger. All traces of humanity vanished. Only lion remained, the biggest lion I had ever seen, woven from bone, flesh, and magic. He wasn't human. He wasn't an animal. He was a force, a creature, a thing that was beyond the understanding of nature's human stepchildren.

I grabbed Curran's mane and vaulted onto his back. He didn't even notice. He charged across the battlefield toward the chariot and my father in it. We burst into the melee like a cannonball. He tore and bit. I sliced and cut, and we forced our way through the bodies, through the flesh and blood, closer and closer to my father.

He turned around.

He saw us coming.

Our gazes met.

Curran leapt, sailing above the mass of people. I raised Sarrat. We would end this here.

My father saw the promise of death in my eyes. In that fleeting instant he understood I knew we were bound and I didn't care.

We landed in an empty chariot. My father had vanished.

Curran roared. I clamped my hands over my ears as the chariot beneath me shook.

He leapt off the chariot and raged across the battlefield and I raged with him until there was nobody left to kill.

# EPILOGUE

"WHAT IS IN this flower crown?" Fiona sniffed the air.
"Smells odd, doesn't it?" Andrea said.

"Good things," Evdokia told her.

"She will thank us later." Sienna winked at me.

I stood in a huge tent set up in the Five Hundred Acre wood, while Fiona, Andrea, and Julie put the final touches on my wedding outfit. The night had fallen, the magic was in full swing, and the tent was lit by bright golden globes Roman had found somewhere and set up. The light was warm and cheerful, the tent smelled of honeysuckle, and all my friends were here. For some odd reason I felt completely terrified.

The three witches of the Witch Oracle had come in to bring a flower crown woven of beautiful white flowers that looked like tiny tulips with pointed petals, and never left. Dali had come in for something and never left either. Desandra brought fruit and parked herself in the corner. Adora sat quietly by the entrance. I had a feeling she had decided to guard it. Martina, Ascanio's mother, was munching on some pastries next to her.

The flap of the tent opened and Martha came in, followed by George.

Behind her Mahon's voice roared. "I will have cider if I damn well please."

Martha sighed. "The man is in a wheelchair. He lost half his weight. He's bald like a cue ball and all he wants is his cider."

"Let Dad have his cider," George said. "He earned it."

"He'll be sick tonight, mark my words."

George grinned. "Here, Kate, we brought you a glass of wine. For courage."

Only three days had passed since the battle. I'd offered to postpone the wedding, but Curran insisted.

Martha walked up to me and patted my cheek. "You look beautiful. That boy has no idea how lucky he is."

"I'm sorry. We should've waited."

"No." Something hot and angry flashed in the older woman's eyes. "Don't you dare be sorry. That man may have almost taken my husband from me, but he won't take the joy out of my son's wedding. We celebrate. That's what Mahon wants and this is what I want."

Silence claimed the tent.

"Okay!" George said. "Now that Mom's done being scary, here is your wine."

"Red wine?" Fiona squinted at the glass. "Kate, if you spill the wine on yourself, they'll bury you in this dress."

"Maybe wine isn't a good idea," George said.

It was a great idea. I took the wine and drained the glass.

People giggled. Rowena slipped into the tent and smiled at me.

Julie dabbed my mouth with a napkin. "Now we have to re-lipstick."

"Will all of you stop?" I growled.

"Shut up," Andrea said. "We're not done prettying you up."

"I'm pretty enough as is."

"Yes, yes, you are. You are the prettiest. Now hold still so I can fix your lipstick."

"Try not to pass out," Desandra said. "I almost passed out at my wedding. Of course, it was a really nasty wedding, but still."

"What happens if he shows up?" Julie asked.

The tent went silent.

"He won't," I said. "But if he does, I'll deal with it."

"There." Andrea stepped away. "Perfect."

"Does she have all the things?" George asked. "Something old, something new . . ."

"The dress is new," Fiona said.

"Something blue." Sienna pointed to a single blue flower in my crown.

"Something old." I touched the pendant around my neck. Martha smiled at me.

"Something borrowed?" Andrea looked around.

Rowena unclipped a small amber brooch from her dress and clipped it to me. "Here, you can borrow this."

"Knock, knock," Ascanio said outside the tent. "Is everybody clothed?"

"Yes," Martina told him.

"That's a shame." He stuck his head in. "Oh, hi, Mom."

She rolled her eyes.

"Everybody is ready. Also Curran says if you want to elope, there's still time."

"She doesn't want to elope!" Fiona said. "She wants to showcase this dress."

"Roman says for you to come out and take your seats."

"Okay, okay, we're coming." Desandra got up. "Tell him to keep his black panties on."

Ascanio squinted at me. "You are gorgeous, Alpha."

"Go away," Martina told him.

Everyone filed out of the tent one by one. Only the witches were left.

"The boy is right," my aunt said next to me. "You make a passable bride. Miracle of miracles."

"Thanks."

The three witches stared at Erra by my side. I had taken her to them after the battle. We talked for a while. Plans were made. Curran wouldn't like them, but sometimes the hardest choice was the right one.

"We've talked with our people," Evdokia said.

"What you suggested is possible," Sienna said.

"We'll need a conduit," Maria added.

"Then find one," Erra said. "She is already doing enough."

"It's easier said than done," Evdokia said. "That's an awful lot of power to channel. A mere human won't do."

"Is that a yes or a no?" I asked.

"It's a yes." Evdokia looked like she was about to cry. "Unless we find another way."

"There is no other way," Erra said.

"We could ask the White Warlock," Sienna said.

The two other women turned to her.

"You've lost your mind," Evdokia said.

"Her? You want to ask that abomination?" Maria looked like she'd spit to the side, then thought better of it.

"She has enough power," Sienna said.

"Come on." Evdokia shepherded them out of the tent. "We'll talk about it later."

The tent was empty except for me and my aunt. I looked in the mirror. My hair fell loose. The dress clasped my shoulders with white embroidery that shimmered as if made of silver. The breathtakingly patterned gown curved over my breasts, dipping between them lower than I would've ever dared, and hugged my waist before sliding over my hips and butt. The shimmering white skirt was all diaphanous layers, so thin that they moved even now at the slightest draft. The dress should've been heavy because of the embroidery, but instead it felt and looked so light, as if made of clouds. I looked like a fairy-tale princess.

I turned and walked to the tent flap. Outside a bonfire roared. Between the tent and the flames, tables stood groaning with food and flowers. The rows of chairs were filled with people: the Pack, the Masters of the Dead, Luther and the ifrit hound, the Order, Teddy Jo, Beau and his deputies . . .

Everybody was here. My heart hammered.

At the fire, Roman stood in a black robe etched with silver. Next to him Curran waited. He wore a tuxedo. Jim stood on his right. On the other side, Dali waited. She was my maid of honor.

Curran bent forward and said something to Roman. Roman nodded.

I was getting married. Dear God.

"Is he worth it?" Erra asked.

"Always."

Music started, sweet and haunting. It was my cue to go on.

The magic was so thick tonight. It was all around me. The flower vines draped on the trees glowed weakly with a magical golden light, mirroring the strings of feylanterns strung above the tables. The woods didn't look real.

I would walk to the altar and I would get married. But I had to take that first step.

I swallowed and walked out. Everyone fell quiet. Curran turned. His mouth opened. He stared at me, like he'd never seen me before.

*Just keep walking.*

I reached the altar. A little girl stepped up next to me, holding a ring on a pillow. A little boy stood next to Curran holding an identical pillow with another ring.

My future husband remembered to close his mouth.

Roman was talking. I heard his voice, but I was looking at Curran and he was looking at me.

"Love is a complicated thing," Roman said. "For some it's fleeting and fickle. People fall in love fast and then they fall out of it faster than they can blink. For others, it's a lifelong commitment. It can render you helpless or give you power. It can bring you bliss or misery. But true love, the one that endures through time, love that is pure joy, love that nothing in this world can shatter, that kind of love is rare. The two people standing before me today have it. They fought for it, they endured for it, and they earned it. Tonight we are privileged to celebrate their love with them."

Curran was grinning. I grinned back.

"Repeat after me," Roman said. "I, Curran Lennart . . ."

"I, Curran Lennart," Curran said, "take you, Kate Daniels, to be my friend, my lover, the mother of my children, and my wife. I will be yours in times of plenty and in times of want, in sickness and in health, in joy and in sorrow, in failure and in triumph. I promise to love no other, to cherish and respect you, to care for you and protect you, and stay with you, for all eternity."

I held out my hand and he slipped a ring on my finger.

"Your turn," Roman told me. "I, Kate Daniels . . ."

"I, Kate Daniels, take you, Curran Lennart, to be my friend, my lover, the father of my children, and my husband. I will be yours in times of plenty and in times of want, in sickness and in health, in joy and in sorrow, in failure and in triumph. I promise to love no other, to cherish and respect you, to care for you and protect you, and stay with you, for all eternity."

I took the ring from the pillow and slid it on his finger.

"I now pronounce you husband and wife," Roman said. "May your life be rich in blessings and poor in misfortunes. May you see your children's children grow up and make you proud. May your fights be short, your laughter loud, and your passion hot. May you live long and die happy. You may now kiss each other."

Curran reached for me. I kissed him and the world faded.

We broke apart, turned, and I saw my father standing behind the tables, wrapped in his cloak. He smiled at me and vanished.

Roman waved his arm and a murder of crows shot out of the forest, flew above our heads and up into the sky.

"I don't do doves," Roman said.

Then there was cake and toasts and gifts. We jumped over the Ivan Kupala bonfire. The party got loud, then louder. People laughed. Wine flowed. We danced, and then everyone danced. The Pack danced, the People applauded.

Curran wrapped his hands around me. "Hey."

"Hey."

"Come with me. I have to tell you something."

I followed him behind the tent. "What is it?"

He picked me up and took off into the woods. I laughed and wrapped my arms around him. "What are you doing?"

"I'm kidnapping my wife."

We shot through the woods. "Do you even know where you're going?"

"Yes."

He turned and stopped. We were under a massive tree. To the right the narrow brook gurgled its way through the forest. A blanket waited under the tree next to a cooler.

"You planned this."

"Yes, I did." He knelt on the blanket, still holding me. "You look . . . You look."

I cracked up.

"And whatever the hell that scent is from those flowers is driving me crazy." He took my crown off and looked at me. "Nope. Not the flowers."

I kissed him, tasting him, teasing his tongue, and he kissed me back, eager and tender. The kiss turned possessive, and when I came up for air, I wanted all my clothes off.

"I finally caught you," he said. "You can't get away now. I love you, Kate Lennart."

"I love you too, Curran Lennart," I whispered, and kissed him, enjoying every delicious moment. "For all eternity."


MARRIED LIFE WASN'T much different than single life, I decided, reaching for the stove. It had been two weeks since our wedding. Things were almost back to normal. There were still breakfasts to be made and bacon to be cooked. Atlanta was slowly picking up the pieces.

The Pack had lost sixty-two shapeshifters. Nineteen were younger than twenty. The Jackal alpha became a widower. Desandra lost her beta. Clan Nimble's alpha pair mourned their oldest daughter. Both of Barabas's legs were broken when a magical bull knocked him off his feet and then trampled him. Christopher had a full-on nervous breakdown and almost leveled what remained of the Keep's wall before Doolittle managed to convince him that Barabas wouldn't die. The wall was now being rebuilt.

Two knights of the Order and four mercs didn't come back from the battlefield. My father's chariot had been stripped and dismantled. The golden panels turned out to be real gold, which was completely unsurprising, knowing my father. The surviving mercs claimed it as spoils of war, and the Guild had made a fortune off it. We'd have no shortage of volunteers for the next battle.

A quarter of the Casino's vampires were destroyed. Oddly, Ghastek didn't seem concerned about it. He had this strange smile on his face when I talked to him about it. After I was done, he'd leaned toward me and said, "He fled." I had a feeling that was all he cared about. Just when I thought I had Ghastek all figured out, he threw me a curveball. But he was right. No matter what we did or said, one inescapable fact remained. We had beaten my father. We won the battle. We didn't win the war. The war was still coming. But we had beaten him this time. He lost.

I opened the oven. The smell of cooked bacon hit me. Mayday. I charged across the kitchen into the bathroom and threw up.

Oh no.

I cradled my stomach, reaching with my magic, gently, softly, and felt a tiny spark.

"Kate?" Curran said outside the door. "Are you okay in there?"

"Yeah. I'll be a minute."

I washed my mouth, splashed cold water on my face, and opened the door.

"Is something wrong?" he asked.

"I'm pregnant," I said.

# The Kate Daniels Novels
## by Ilona Andrews

When it comes to the supernatural underworld of Atlanta, it's up to one woman to keep the paranormal elements in check: mercenary Kate Daniels.

Find more books by Ilona Andrews by visiting prh.com/nextread

"Andrews's books are guaranteed good reads."
—Patricia Briggs, #1 *New York Times* bestselling author

"One of the best urban-fantasy series ever written!"
—*RT Book Reviews*

"Andrews delivers only the best."
—Jeaniene Frost, *New York Times* bestselling author

www.ilona-andrews.com
ilona.andrews
ilona_andrews